MALICIOUS DESIRE

LANEY KAYE

CROSSWORLDS PUBLISHING, AUSTRALIA/UNITED STATES

About the Author

Laney Kaye is the pen name of best-selling Australian author, Leonie Kelsall.

She spent her youth in the rural areas of South Australia, and seeks to recreate that lifestyle as an adult—apparently mainly by homing a ridiculous and diverse number of animals.

A professional counsellor with a keen interest in the empowerment of women, she enjoys messing with heads by day and imaginations by night.

https://www.leoniekelsall.com/laney-kaye-s-books

Copyright © Laney Kaye 2019

ASIN: B07RSMG969

ISBN-10: 1099802245

ISBN-13: 978-1099802249

ISBN: 978-0-6486584-0-5

ISBN: 978-0-6486584-9-8

CrossWorlds Publishing

Australia / United States

Cover Design: Black Bird Book Covers

For Taylor
Who Keeps the Faith,
And Believes I'm The Little Engine That Could
~ Acknowledgments ~

This book could not have come into being without the help and support of so many people...so I'll try to list them in the order they came into my (writing) life.
Glen Chamberlain and Malcolm Mackenzie, extraordinary teachers who are doubtless oblivious to the impact they had on my career.
My original critique partners, Sidney T. Blake, Margaret Telsch-Williams, and C. Hope Clark, who drilled me on writing technicalities and offered support and encouragement.
Marty Mayberry, who has taken every step of this convoluted journey with me...I think the definition of insanity may be something we need to discuss!
Sandie Docker, who creates the most articulate sentences and evocative imagery, yet is also capable of swearing like a trooper when I need someone to share my tantrums.
Long term writing buddies, Elena Jagar, who reads every word I write, and Sophie Gonzales and James Ormonde, who not only

provided constructive criticism and feedback on points within this text but have always been in my corner when it counts.

My lovely beta readers, primarily Julie Formston, who has a glass of wine and encouraging words available at all times.

Taylor, my road-trip buddy, plotter extraordinaire, and always my most staunch supporter, who chastises and cheerleads with equal enthusiasm. Love you, baby.

And finally, but most importantly, thank you to those brave women who shared their stories and made this book possible. You have both my gratitude and my admiration.

Trigger Warnings

Please note this book includes multiple trigger warnings, including but not limited to:

Domestic violence
Child abuse
Rape
Forced detention
Depression

CHAPTER 1

Hooked talons embedded in flesh, the eagle yanked at the corpse. Muscle and sinew ripped apart and a rotted leg snapped free.

Kayla gagged, flooring the accelerator to swerve the minibus around the kangaroo's entrails. She had lost tally of the road kill as kilometres of red dirt highway unfurled before the windscreen.

Dust and decay coated the back of her throat. She drained the last of her water bottle and tossed the container into the footwell. Out here, she could literally drink enough to drown, yet still be thirsty. The steering wheel wedged into place with her knees, she stretched both arms above her head. Yawned. Blinked as slowly as she dared. Her eyes watered in the luxury of a few seconds' darkness.

Her students' excitement had shortened the fourteen-hour journey to the campground, but three days of surf, sun, and late nights meant this final leg of their trip home sucked. Maybe not so much for the kids; comatose with candy, their small bodies sprawled across bench seats behind her. At least the '*are we there yet*' chorus had silenced for a while. Kayla peeled her thighs off the seat, one at a time, the skin below the hem of her khaki shorts sticking to hot vinyl, and leaned forward to peer into an empty cup balanced on the console. Three hours and not a bend in the road to dislodge it. She inhaled the nostalgia of a caffeine jolt, then tugged the phone from her pocket. Not that checking made time go any faster, but calculations provided distraction. Safety hid in numbers.

Adult company would have lessened the monotony, but close quarters invited an exchange of confidences. For two years she had avoided the inquisition that came with a placement in a remote area school, and she wasn't about to share a damn thing now. Per regulation, three parents accompanied the excursion—but they did so in the luxury of a private vehicle that would reach home far sooner than the five hours remaining by Kayla's calculations.

Home. A three-roomed cement block, devoid of person-alisation. Just the way she liked it, because nothing to love meant nothing to lose.

Her solitude didn't equate to loneliness. It signified freedom.

A blowfly droned along the side window, competing with the music from the earbuds looped around Kayla's neck. The glass squealed as she dragged it along the grit-filled track, and super-heated air billowed in. 'Go on. *Bug-ger off.*' She grinned at the lame joke. As the fly scurried to the breach, a flicker of movement drew Kayla's attention back to the road. Kilometres distant, the straight line of the horizon met the sky; but far closer a row of exclamation points punctuated the stark contrast of blue on red.

The bus hurtled forward. Kayla hunched over the steering wheel, her knuckles whitening. *What the hell?*

A human chain blocked the dirt highway.

Gooseflesh prickled her sweat-slicked arms, but she rubbed it away. She had nothing to fear, not out here. She had outrun her nightmares by eight years and thousands of kilometres.

Her eyes darted to the rearview mirror. Dust distorted the reflection, creating hills on the arid plains, hot air cavorting above the ghostly dunes. A battered truck wavered like a beacon on the vibrating surface and her shoulders eased. First vehicle she'd seen in hours.

She lifted her foot from the accelerator as the outlines took on form, three men ranged across the road. As the sandy verge consumed the tyres of the slowing bus, her fingers closed around the phone in her lap.

Pointless.

There was no coverage in the middle of the desert. No bloody anything, in the middle of the desert. Stowed under the rear seat, the school's satellite phone may as well have been on top of Uluru. In any case, it was for emergency use only.

The men sauntered toward the bus.

They'd broken down. Happened all the time. Dirt in the fuel, overheated engine, blown radiator. A hundred possibilities.

Kayla's forehead furrowed as her gaze ranged the plains, searching for their vehicle rather than focus on the elephantine sway of the leader's belly, grey flesh brushing his thighs with each step. She leaned toward the partially open window. 'Hey. What's up?' *Damn.* The quaver in her voice revealed weakness, and that was unacceptable. Mother had taught her better than that.

The man huffed to a standstill. 'Get out.'

Blood drained from Kayla's face, surging to her muscles. She gripped the wheel. 'What?'

A dingo pack, the other men circled in. One splayed his hand against the windscreen, tipping a black cowboy hat to the back of his head as he nodded in greeting.

The fat man's menace chilled the midday heat. 'I said, get out.'

Kayla squeezed her knees together, her bowels suddenly loose and churning. 'There's a t-truck right behind me. With the rest of the teachers. And parents—' Damn, she had to get a grip. She could lie better than this.

The truck throbbed noisy reassurance as it pulled alongside, a faded logo identifying it as a supply hauler for one of the remote Aboriginal settlements. There'd be at least a couple of adults aboard—because nobody was stupid enough to travel alone out here.

Kayla sucked in a ragged breath as the driver clambered down. Scarecrow skinny, he didn't look any kind of guardian angel, but at least he was there. Whatever the other men were after, they'd back off now. She scrubbed a hand across her chest, the pulse pounding beneath her palm.

The scarecrow dipped his chin at the group clustered around the bus. 'All under control?'

Cowboy Hat nodded. 'Yeah, Tomas. She's right.'

Kayla's breath ripped at her throat. *Jesus.* He was with them.

Her foot trembled over the accelerator. But two men stood in front of the bus—even she couldn't drive through them. Could she?

Coins spilled as she scrabbled for her wallet in the centre console instead. 'Money?' She cleared her throat, forced control into the words. 'I don't have much. Here. Take it all.'

As she held out the wallet, the window exploded. Shards of glass showered her, the children's screams shredding the barren landscape.

Tomas reversed the handgun he'd slammed into the window and waved it at her. 'Out. Now.'

Blood from a gash across Kayla's cheek splattered her hand as it trembled toward the CB radio.

The third man, barely more than a teenager, wrenched open the bi-fold door, the piston lock hissing like a cornered snake. He hurdled the two steps into the bus. 'Get up.' Snatching at her ponytail, he yanked her over the gearbox.

She scrambled to release the pressure on her scalp.

The kids were already on their feet. Whimpering. Reaching for her. Face glistening with tears, five-year-old Jacob started down the aisle, but Kayla thrust out a hand as she stumbled down the steps. 'No, stay there. Stay in your seats.'

Acne scars vivid against a flush that could be nerves or exuberance, the youth slammed her against the searing metal panels of the bus. His feverish breath raked her face. 'Damn, Tomas, you picked good,' he said fawningly, eager for the older man's approval.

Tomas circled in. 'I did indeed, Les. Looks like we get a bonus while we wait for the money.'

Wait for money? Thick and black as tar, dread oozed through Kayla, turning her knees liquid.

The fat man's blubbery face creased. 'But that'll spoil the goods. They won't pay up.'

'Bullshit,' Tomas spat. '*She's* worth nothing.' He gestured toward the children pressed against the bus windows, tears and snot running down their faces. 'They're our investments, so make sure you look after them. This one, though,' his fingers scraped up Kayla's neck, his voice dropping to a murmur as his narrow face loomed close. 'The way I figure it, she's all ours.'

'What the hell do you want—?'

He hit her. Hard. Open-palmed across her face.

Odd, disconnected words skittered like frightened beetles through the vacuum of Kayla's brain. But only a harsh sob escaped her lips.

Jet eyes watched her unblinkingly. 'I *want* you to not speak until you're invited.'

The fat man recoiled, then spoke quickly 'If you're taking orders, darlin', I want a beer. Bloody desert has got me dry as a nun's nasty.' He patted his belly, calming a restless child within.

'Shut it, Fatty,' Tomas snapped. His focus returned to Kayla. 'I do apologise. But as you can probably surmise, your *appearance* has taken us a little by surprise.' He leaned closer, a black-lacquered fingernail caressing her burning cheek. 'And, while I will, of course, consult with my colleagues, I suspect what we now want is *you*.'

Was she permitted to speak now? Kayla's brusque tone fought to mask her fear. 'Then let me radio in our position. The school can collect the kids—'

Tomas's coffin-shaped nails dug into her forearm, stealing her words. Doubled over with exaggerated mirth, he pointed a shaking finger at her, then swept his arms wide, inviting the other men to share his incredulity. Like a switch had been flipped, his urbane façade disappeared. 'The bitch thinks she's good enough to exchange for these little sperm donations! No, no, sorry, darlin'. The world only gives a shit about kids and three-legged puppies so, unless you're about to whelp, you're purely entertainment value. Now,' his face twisted into a malicious mask. 'Shift that cute ass of yours up those steps and get those kids out here. We've a lot of ground to cover.'

Tomas's next slap stinging her backside, Kayla leapt into the comparative safety of the bus. Her chest tightened as she surveyed the children, their questions muted by fear. She had to get them out of here. Now. Fuck the not-running-the-men-over shit. Could the bus outdistance the decrepit truck?

She swung towards the driver's seat.

Froze.

Tomas leaned against the door, one foot on the step, handgun trained on the nearest child.

Maddie. Turning back to the kids, Kayla slammed her hip into the side of the seat, trying to block Tomas's line of sight—*line of fire*—and crooked a finger. 'Maddie, come here.'

The girl slid from the bench and scrambled toward her. The movement released the other children and they crowded the aisle, sobbing and clutching at Kayla as she murmured soothing lies. 'It's okay, kids. Everything's fine.'

'But Miss P, your face is bleeding.'

'I know, Jacob. It's only a little cut.' Her trembling finger-tips traced the swelling, then pinched her lips closed. Holding in her fear.

This couldn't be real. Shit like this didn't happen in Australia. Maybe she had white line fever. Or perhaps she'd dozed off.

Yet the children clearly shared her nightmare.

She dropped to her haunches, making eye contact with each child 'Okay, kids, listen carefully.' Ryan hung back, and she reached for him. *Shit. Blood all over my hand.* She snatched her hand back, wiping it on her shorts before tugging the boy into the group. 'Eyes on me, kids.' *Not on the guy pointing a gun at you.* 'There's a problem with the bus, so we're going to leave it here and go home a different way.'

Bottom lip pouting, Liam took his twin sister's hand. 'But I like our bus.' The six-year-old harboured a strong sense of ownership toward anything their dad, the local mechanic, worked on, and he delighted in listing the faults of every vehicle in the small town.

Kayla wet her lips, forcing encouragement into her tone. 'I know you do, Liam, but we're going to have a bit of an adventure before we head home. We have to be quick, though. Mum and Dad are waiting for you and Lily.'

Maddie elbowed in front of the older boy. 'Can we go back to the thea?' she lisped. 'I like the thea. Please, Miss P, can we go back there?'

'We will, I promise.' Guilt threatened to steal Kayla's words. Who was she to make promises? 'But not now. Come on, bring your bags. I'm going to get the first aid kit and put a bandaid on this graze. Do you think it's bleeding as much as Ella's foot did yesterday? And that was only a tiny little cut, wasn't it?' Ignoring the muttering malevolence outside the bus, she kept her voice level, swallowing the hysteria that bubbled up from her gut.

The kids dragged their bags into the aisle and Kayla cinched the medical bumbag around her waist. What else could she carry? The sat phone? If she could get to it, hide it in the first aid kit...

The muzzle of the gun beckoned.

No time. Her gaze darted around the bus. Christ, there had to be something here that could help them. Save them.

Nothing.

She forced steel into her spine. *Show no fear.* A child-hood lesson, forged in pain and blood, it would serve her well now.

'Come on, kids. Make sure you have your hats.' She led them from the bus, Maddie's tiny hand worming into hers. Shoulders squared, Kayla assessed the men standing in a loose semi-circle around them. Two of the men looked away. One stared back, his eyes as emotionless as stagnant pools.

Numbers. She had to focus on them. That always worked.

For long seconds, she counted the deafening echo of her heartbeat, then she turned to face Tomas. 'We're ready.'

Another lie, fit to match the rest of her life. She was so far from ready, so unprepared for this. Whatever *this* was. Because she wouldn't permit the word, not even in her mind. That would make it real.

As though the flies wading in the blood oozing down her cheek didn't prove it real enough.

'Huh? Tomas squinted at her. 'Ah. Okay. Get them into the back of the truck. We've a-ways to go on the road first. Greaz, toss them up there.'

A man stretched a hand toward Ella, hair spilling across his face from beneath his cowboy hat.

'Don't touch them,' Kayla snarled, shoving in front of the child.

Greaz's palm grazed Kayla's waist, his fingers sliding under the edge of her shirt. 'Happy to keep the touching for you, darl.'

Liam threaded his arm between her legs, clinging tight to her thigh, and Kayla scooped the boy up, his tears hot on her neck. The desperation in his grip strengthened her resolve; like hell she'd let anyone touch her kids. Still, her legs shook as she turned to the dark maw of the rear of the truck. God, why hadn't she ploughed through the bastards when she had the chance?

Liam's wiry black hair, the tips sun-bleached to white-blond, cushioned her face as she whispered, 'Li, it's going to be okay. I promise.'

She wouldn't go to Hell for lying.

She was already there.

Determination plastered on his face, seven-year-old Ryan moved toward the truck. The eldest, he tried to set an example. The twins, Liam and Lily, were six, the other three little more than babies. Maddie had turned five last week. Dressed in a fairy costume, she'd brought in chocolate cupcakes covered in pink sprinkles. Her first term at school. Her first school excursion.

Maybe her last.

Ryan's leg overhung the backboard of the truck as he clambered aboard, and Kayla snatched at it. *You're as good as dead if you get into a stranger's vehicle.* The school lectures of her childhood were unequivocal. Then, the words had enticed with the potential of escape, but now they were reversed: if she didn't get the kids into the truck the kidnappers would kill her, and the children would be defenceless.

A spiked collar of fear tightened around her throat. *Kidnappers.* She'd allowed the word.

She released Ryan's leg and hefted the other five children into the oven, trying to convince herself that she wasn't imprisoning them, wasn't sealing their fate. Because what choice did she have? Her gaze ranged the vast, empty desert once more. Then, the metal tailgate searing her palms, she scrambled into the truck.

'Miss,' Ella's freckled face loomed pale in the gloom. She hid behind Kayla's shoulder, peeping at the two men hauling themselves aboard. 'That man's picking his nose.'

A sudden beat of insane laughter forced itself up Kayla's throat. 'I guess his mum didn't teach him any better.'

Greaz tipped his hat back, a grin splitting his face. 'Burn, Les.'

The acne-faced youth didn't unplug. 'I reckon some of the boys got a real treat lined up for you, bitch.'

Why the hell hadn't she shut up? It wasn't like she'd not had enough practice. Skewing herself on the narrow bench, Kayla turned as far away as the crowded confines of the trailer would permit.

She refused to allow any emotion.

Too damn scared to be scared.

CHAPTER 2

The children crumpled close to Kayla on the metal bench in the stifling trailer. They dozed, repeatedly jolted awake as the vehicle crossed rough terrain.

Kayla avoided looking at the two men sitting on the ledge opposite, but she couldn't avoid inhaling the sludge of their body odour.

'Taking too fucking long,' Greaz muttered from beneath his cowboy hat. 'Why the hell aren't we there yet?'

Les's eyes slewed toward him. 'Be there when we're fuckin' there. Tomas knows what he's doing.'

'You're so far up his arse. No amount of money's worth this bullshit bloody sauna.'

'Dead set? I'll take your share then.'

'Fuck off.'

Les caught Kayla's eye, and bared neglected teeth at her. She wedged a trembling hand under her thigh. The heat suffocated her brain, but she needed to think, make a plan to get them out of there.

Grinding gears fractured the tedium and the vehicle slowed to a halt.

The doors of the metal coffin screeched open, sunlight haloing a slight figure in the opening. 'Out.' Tomas didn't bother to glance inside. 'Gotta walk now.'

Though the children had roused at the noise, they lay limp. Kayla eased her numb arm from beneath Lily's narrow shoulders and formed a fist to force feeling back into the muscles. Stumbled toward the opening.

One of the men offered his hand to help her from the trailer, and Tomas's cackle split the deserted landscape. 'Get over yourself, Fatty. You don't need brownie points with this one. She's on the house.' He surveyed Kayla, then grimaced. 'You're a mess. Still, I reckon you'll get worse. Get the kids ready.'

Kayla ignored Fatty's hand and jumped from the truck, tucking straggling hair behind her ears. 'They need food and drink first.'

'Water. That's it. On the radiator.' Tomas's gaze searched across sand marked by scrubby grey foliage and low dunes. 'We'll be walking all damn night and probably half of tomorrow too, if you don't hurry those little shits up.' He swivelled back to her, his eyes narrowing. 'I can't have any of them holding us back. You understand?'

Kayla bit at her lip. He was lying. Had to be. He wanted money, so he needed to keep the kids safe. And that would give her time: she'd find a way to get them out of here.

She lifted the children down and shepherded them to the front of the truck. Unhooked the bug-encrusted canvas water bag. 'Here, kids. Cup your hands together. Like this, Maddie.' She formed her own hands around the girl's. 'Do you remember when we learned about the Aborigines, and

Liam and Lily showed us how their Old Fella made containers out of strips of bark? Perhaps we'll go for a walk and search for bark. We could make our own cups.'

Feral camels ravaged the sparse bushes of the desert, stripping every shred of bark and leaf. But she had always been good at lying. A family talent.

Ella snatched at her shirt. 'I don't want to walk. My legs hurt. And I cut my foot on a shell at the beach, remember? I can't walk. Where are my shells?' The girl's tremulous voice took on a whine. 'You said I could take them home. You said we're going home.'

Water dripped from Kayla's hands and disappeared into the sucking sand. 'We are, Ella. But we're taking the long way around. Ryan, you take charge of the water, please.' She moved away from the kids, hoping Tomas would follow. They didn't need to hear anything that came from his foul mouth, but maybe she could glean information from him. 'Why are we walking? We'd get wherever faster in the bus.'

Examining his nail polish, Tomas snorted. 'Reckon I'm idiot enough to leave vehicle tracks for the constabulary to follow? Anyway, your bus wouldn't make it where we're going. I dumped it two hundred clicks back. Lit the sucker up like a bonfire.' His eyes glazed as he stared into the distance. 'Guess the parents will think you got lost and ran off the road. Toasted their kids.' One finger traced the indent in his chin, over and again. 'You know what? Maybe I'll let them grieve a little. What's the saying? Hunger is the best seasoning? Well I reckon gratitude is the best wallet opener. When I tell them the kids weren't barbecued, I'll be a hero. Won't need to demand any ransom.'

If Tomas believed he would be hailed a saviour when

they were found hundreds of kilometres from their intended destination, he was mad.

Good. She could escape from an idiot.

'What would you have done if the parents had been in the bus? Or if I'd been a guy?' His answers might evidence how prepared he was, give her some clue, some plan. Some hope.

'Reckon you need something to gag that runaway mouth of yours.' Tomas jerked at his crotch, but she hoped he was putting on a show for the guys who moved between the trailer and the kids. The teenager, Les, clearly idolised him, though Greaz seemed less enamoured. 'I did my homework. Looked for schools with female staff. Spoilt for choice around here, seems a lot of chicks take posts out bush. Guess you're all looking for Prince Charming with a dirty great station, aren't you?' He smoothed one finger along Kayla's forearm.

She willed herself not to pull away. She had put up with worse caresses. The more he talked, the more she would discover. And the quicker she'd get them out of there.

Tomas pulled a packet of Marlboros from his pocket, offering them to Greaz before lipping one out of the box. 'You ever hear about the Faraday kidnappings, way back in the seventies?' He waved the packet at her. 'Smoke?' She grimaced and he cackled. 'Health hazard, huh? Probably not something you need to be worrying about.' The unlit cigarette danced between his lips. 'See, Eastwood, the guy in charge of those Faraday dudes, he was hell smart. He targeted a single teacher school with only a handful of students. We planned to do the same, bust in and cart you all off.' He squinted, lighting the cigarette, then tossed the lighter to Greaz.

'But she did us a solid, right?' Greaz spoke through a cloud of smoke.

'Sure did. Brought the kids right to us. And putting every detail of the itinerary of your little excursion up on the school website—' Tomas kissed his fingers and blew the salutation toward her. 'Masterpiece. You couldn't have made it easier for us if you'd been in on the deal.'

Kayla twisted a button on her shirt, the thread stretched to breaking point as she stared across the desert, frantically cataloguing every detail as she tried to look disinterested. *Faraday.* That teacher had escaped and saved her students. It could be done. Her hair drifted across her face, the hot breeze constantly reshaping the small hills as God played in his sandbox. She shivered. Because maybe it wasn't God.

With no road in sight, grit swiftly obscured even the faint evidence of the truck's passage. The sun sat low in the west. Though the heat remained oppressive, she knew there would be no slow mellowing to evening, no tropical dusk. With desert abruptness, the glowing orb would drown in the sand, one moment blinding sunlight, the next cold, moon-frozen darkness.

She might escape in the dark. But not with six small children.

Tomas loped off a few paces. Without turning his back, he pissed into the wind. Les giggled as ants scurried from the burning stream.

Apparently dismissed, Kayla spun to follow the kids, who had climbed back into the familiarity of the trailer.

'Where you going?' Les adjusted his collar against his burnt, blistered neck as he strode toward them. As Kayla grabbed a strut on the trailer to haul herself in, rough fingers seized her chin, jerking her head around and snapping her grasp on the bracket. 'Don't you ignore me. Tomas reckons I'm in charge of you for this little walk, you understand?'

In a gutter reflex she'd thought long outgrown, Kayla's tongue chased around her parched mouth, summoning what little moisture hid within. Spat full in his face.

Les's hand dropped to her throat, an ugly flush igniting his acne. 'You fucking filthy bitch—'

His grip tightened, and Kayla scrabbled against his hold. Black spots crowded her vision. Her breath sawed in her throat. Her nails dug into his fingers, trying to peel them free. The blood thundering in her ears almost obliterated the sniggers of the other men.

'Go on, man. Do her.'

'Leave her be, Les.' Tomas's voice cut through their excitement. 'You want her able to walk. You can sort her out later.'

The chokehold released, and the blackness purpled, then receded. Tomas stood a few feet away. He flickered his tongue, the tip surgically split, the two pieces moving independently. A snake's tongue, tasting the wind.

Or a demon's.

Les looked to Tomas for permission, then jabbed his index finger into the centre of Kayla's forehead, forcing her retreat until the tailgate smacked her back. 'You slut, I'm going to fuck you right up for that.'

She braced against the metal, her hand guarding her bruised throat as her breath sawed painfully. Had she learned nothing from her childhood? Anger could be both weapon and defence, the perfect disguise for the emptiness within her. But she had to maintain control of the only emotion she ever allowed. She couldn't afford to antagonise these men.

Not until she had a plan.

Her legs shook so badly she could barely clamber into the trailer.

Lily's whisper echoed. 'I need to go for a wee.'

God, not now. 'Okay, Lily. I'll take you in a moment.'

The girl's frizzy brown hair trembled with urgency. 'But I need to go *now*.'

If she split the kids up, how could she protect them all? Panic surged, but Kayla forced it back down. She couldn't lose it, not over this. She had to stay in control. For all of them. 'Come on, then. You have to be quick.'

As she helped the child out of the truck, Fatty caught her eye and indicated with his chins. 'Bring them round the other side. I'll watch them while you take her.'

With several of the kids snivelling now, she had no choice but to trust him. She nodded curtly. Almost felt grateful toward the fat bastard. 'Boys, you wait right here while I take the girls behind those rocks, okay? Then it's your turn.'

Minutes later, she guided the boys back to where Fatty leaned against the hood as Tomas and Greaz hauled their bags from the trailer. 'Can you watch them for a second more?'

Fatty's jowls wobbled. 'What the hell now?'

'I have to go.' Like a kid, asking permission. Her knuckles ached as she clenched her fists.

'Hurry it up.'

Kayla nodded fake gratitude as she noted his weakness: a glimmer of humanity. She knew how to pick her mark, how to target and manipulate a man. She would cultivate him.

Tomas snorted as he dumped the bags nearby. 'No one's stopping you, teach. Unless you're after someone to hold your—ah—hand? Or if you want me to stand guard over you while you do it, I'm not entirely averse...'

The men brayed and Fatty's gaze slid to the distance.

Damn. She'd lost him. 'Wait here, kids. I'll only be a second.'

Strewn across the flat landscape like a giant's abandoned game of marbles, a tumble of boulders offered scant privacy. She squatted quickly and relieved herself. Fumbled to zip her shorts, her eyes closed, seeking safety behind the lids. But only for a moment.

The children crowded her as she knelt to rummage through their bags, stuffing the two largest carriers with snacks and drinks salvaged from the holiday stash.

'You want that junk, you'll carry it yourself,' Tomas said. 'We're not your fucking donkeys.'

Ella's arm flopped across her shoulders. 'Miss P. I want to go home. I want my mummy.'

'I know, sweetie.' Kayla tugged clothes from a bag and layered them onto the luminous-eyed child's unresisting but unhelpful form. 'We'll go home soon, but we're going for a walk first. Remember?'

Liam sniffled. 'I wanna go home, too. Why are these men mean? I don't like them. I *hate* them. I wanna go home.' The last word stretched on a wail.

Kayla swallowed hard. For the first time in her life, she longed to go home, too. 'Maddie, you hold hands with Liam, because he's a little bit scared, okay? You're big enough to help me because you're five now.' The fingers she splayed for the kids to count trembled, so she bunched them into a fist. *Get a grip.*

The children were so brave, grouped into a solemn cluster—or were they terrified into obedience? She remembered that feeling. Not everything dulled with the passage of years.

She placed Liam's hand in Maddison's sticky grip. How had she not noticed before how little they were? Young. Innocent. She had to keep them safe. Although it wasn't beatings that caused the deepest scars.

No one knew that better than her.

CHAPTER 3

The passage of time marked only by endless steps, a steady fall in temperature, and the howl of dingoes, Kayla carried Maddie, clutched to her chest like a limpet. Ryan she tugged by the hand, encouraging him through the sand. The other four children slept on the shoulders of their kidnappers as they trudged through the night.

As the sun reappeared on the horizon, sweeps of ochre and blue painting the desert, Tomas called a halt. The vast, empty landscape forced Kayla and the children to remain dangerously close to the men sprawled on the ground, the open prison more secure than any barred cell.

Though extra clothes and melted chocolate bars wouldn't ensure survival, Kayla had carried the bags all night, a tiny act of defiance. Now, shoulders rubbed raw by the nylon straps, she dropped the supplies. 'Here, kids. Breakfast time.'

Greaz lurched to his feet and snatched the box of muesli bars before she had it open. 'Hey—' she bit back the protest.

'Smart call, teach.' He tossed the carton to his mates. 'Here, get into this. Better than Tomas's shit.'

Jacob's eyes followed the movement hungrily, though he didn't make a sound. The kids learned quick.

His face pasty, Fatty hunched over the stolen food. 'How much further?' he wheezed.

Tomas chewed and swallowed before replying. 'If you'd helped us haul the shit in here last month, you'd bloody know.'

Though she'd counted steps incessantly during the night, the figures had long since ceased to be anything more than a metronomic ticking in Kayla's brain. She pulled out another box of muesli bars and snapped each slice in half to distribute between the children. No nuts for Liam, and Maddie hated sultanas—ever since Lily told her they were dead flies.

Tomas flicked his tongue into his canteen's mouth, then tilted the flask toward her, raising an eyebrow. She shuddered, and he laughed. 'Your loss. Come on, get those kids moving.'

Hours passed to the dirge of the children's moans and sobs. Sporadic curses from the men. The occasional keening cry from a hawk as it soared above bleached camel bones. The sun hammered the anvil of the earth.

Kayla counted steps again. Every twenty thousand she dropped the bags, applied sunscreen to the kids. Didn't waste any on herself. Blisters bloomed and burst on her exposed skin, the ooze brief bliss.

More hours. Each step came slower than the last until, stumbling into a valley between dunes, Kayla sank to her knees in sand hot enough to scorch her flesh. Head bowed, too exhausted to cry, too tired to fall. She couldn't carry the bags any further. Couldn't carry herself any further.

Yet, though she knew she would fare better alone, surrender was less of an option than it had ever been in her life. Responsibility for the children was both her burden and her privilege. Inch by inch, she forced her head up.

A few metres ahead, Tomas dropped his pack. The other men dumped their human cargo, then slumped to the sand. Tomas hiked a thumb toward a dune. 'Get off your arses. Clear away this shit.'

Shift the dune? Kayla stared: the sun had fried the last few of Tomas's marbles—yet Les and Greaz pulled folding shovels from their packs and scrabbled to comply with his madness. She fumbled the last of the bottled water from her bag. 'Here,' she croaked to Maddie. 'Drink, pass along.' It felt so good not to be moving. A tiny blessing, if she could simply hold onto it for a few minutes, instead of considering what lay ahead.

Les blew his nose between his fingers and flicked the yield to fry on the dirt. 'Here you go, boss.' As always, he seemed overeager to please. He stepped aside as Tomas strode to the face of the dune he had excavated.

Two boulders bordered a vague depression, and metal screeched as Tomas scrabbled between the rocks. Wrestling a sheet of corrugated iron free, he dropped it aside, then bent to pry up another.

Kayla's heart contracted: Tomas wasn't mad. He had something hidden. And that ability to plan, that cunning, made him an even more dangerous adversary.

Except who was she kidding? Hours had passed, she had lost the advantage of night, yet still she had no escape plan.

Tomas unclipped a flashlight from a karabiner on his

belt, then gestured at the cavity he had revealed. 'Right, bring them on in. Get the bags, don't leave anything out here.'

Les smirked at Kayla. 'How about we start your tour with my bedroom?'

'If you've that much energy, you could've dug out the bloody door by yourself,' Fatty muttered.

Kayla peered into the excavation. A small cave gave way to a near-vertical shaft leading into the bowels of the earth.

Further from help.

Ella snatched at the back of her shirt. 'No! I don't want to go in there.'

Kayla turned. Her stomach tightened as she noted Ella's whitened nostrils, her heaving chest. *Shit. Please, not now.* She dug in her pocket. 'It's okay, Ella. Here's your inhaler. Take a puff, then we'll climb down together.'

The girl tugged away. 'I don't want to. It's dark in there.'

'Hurry it up,' Tomas snarled, kicking a cascade of sand over the lip of the tunnel.

'Ella, puffer. Now.' This time, the child complied. 'Good girl. Now we can get out of the sun. It'll be nice and cool inside, you'll see.' The hole offered sanctuary, yet still Kayla hesitated. If they remained outside, a search plane might spot them. Even walking all night, they couldn't have covered a vast distance since dumping the truck.

The dirt-coloured truck.

Probably impossible to see from the air.

Don't think that way.

She licked at her crusted lips. The parents would raise the alarm, and they *would* be found. But she didn't need the phone Tomas had crushed beneath his heel to tell that the hottest part of the day approached, and that presented the most imminent threat.

To the kids, anyway.

Ella sobbed, still trying to pull her back. Kayla knelt. 'Ella, you need to calm down. Do you hear me? Concentrate on your breathing. I promise it will be all right. We need to get out of the sun, then we'll all feel better.'

Thin arms locked around Kayla's neck. 'I want my mummy. I want my mummy *now*.'

How much of a monster was she that, even in this moment, she was envious of a child who could cry for a mother whose arms would offer refuge?

Ella's wailing set off the other children. Only Ryan remained stoic, his eyes glazed with effort. Kayla twisted her mouth into a smile to match her crumpled heart, beckoning him closer. 'Ryan. You're going to be my deputy. Like a policeman, okay? We'll help the little kids down into the shade. Can you do that for me?'

Ryan nodded, though his lip quivered.

Christ, she relied on the help of a seven-year-old.

Blinking her sun-scarred eyes into focus, Kayla cautiously descended the first step. The tunnel stank of sour, unaired soil. But it was cool.

In front of her, Greaz struck a match. Who still used matches? He should flick a Bic. That's what Mother used. Bright neon cigarette lighters had littered every surface of their home, so Mother only needed to stretch an arm to light the next fag.

Kayla shook her head, tossing the errant memory away to skitter into the darkness.

Cowboy hat tilted to the back of his head, Greaz lit kerosene lanterns hooked onto shiny steel spikes on the rough-hewn walls. His hat bobbed out of view, moving along the tunnel.

Count the steps. Count everything.

Eleven, deep, uneven ledges led down, the irregular height marking them as natural formations. The children crowded behind her, trying to escape the men who followed —yet rushing toward the man who led them deeper into the earth. Kayla pressed a palm to her spasming chest. Panic, or lack of oxygen?

The kids jostled and her feet slid, her fingers raking rock. Her backside smacked the earth with enough force to wind her.

'Move it,' Tomas growled behind them.

Legs dangling over the step, she inched forward on her butt. Close to a metre drop this time. Triceps quivering with strain and weariness, she lowered herself. Turned, and lifted each child onto the slope of hard-packed earth, made slippery by rivulets of ancient water seeping through the calcite-encrusted walls. 'Slowly, now.'

The cave roof lowered and the passage narrowed, the horizon encroaching until it loomed centimetres from her face. Claustrophobia cemented her lungs. She couldn't breathe. Couldn't reassure the kids.

She squeezed Ryan's hand, her unshed tears conjuring stars among the shadows of the jagged walls.

The steep descent took only minutes before the tunnel opened into a vast cathedral. Slime-dressed walls curved out and up, the roof ballooning more than eight metres above them.

Kayla's pent-up breath exploded, adding to the children's whimpers. 'Okay, kids, we're almost done. It's nice and cool in here, isn't it?' She couldn't allow the men to recognise her fear, but every syllable she spoke invited terror to betray her. 'The kids need to rest.'

Dirt plumed as Tomas's pack hit the floor. He rubbed his face with cupped hands. 'Thought I told you to keep her quiet, Les? Greaz, you get a fire going here. Fatty, light one down there.' He jerked his chin at a shadowed opening then turned to Kayla. 'This is home until someone feels like bailing you lot out.' A slow leer chased away his exhaustion. 'Some of you, anyway.'

The kids were too young to understand his insinuation. They had to be. Or she had to at least tell herself that.

'That way.' Tomas directed the beam of his torch on Fatty, who squeezed down a narrow tunnel, reversing his trucker cap when the visor brushed the roof.

After more than fifty metres, Fatty led them into a cave the size of a basketball half-court. Almost circular, the only access appeared to be the tunnel from the cathedral.

Thousands of tons of rock above their heads forced Kayla's heartbeat louder. 'Food?'

Tomas hawked phlegm toward a tumble of small boxes. 'There. C'mon, Fatty, got that fire going yet? Just leave it. It stinks like shitty little kids in here already.' He jabbed a finger toward Kayla 'You keep them quiet, you understand? If I hear them, it'll be worse for all of you.'

Fatty furtively pressed a box of matches into her hand, then followed Tomas, leaving the cave lit only by the guttering fire. A mound of thin blankets lay among half-a-dozen cardboard cartons. Water oozed down one wall, a fetid, rotting odour rising from the tiny pool it formed. A plastic bucket, inked with a cartoon of a steaming turd, sat alongside.

Lily's bottom lip thrust out, but now her words were

almost without inflection. 'I don't want to stay here.'

'Only until it's cool enough to go home.' Kayla tried not to imagine accusation into the girl's brown-eyed stare. She was telling them the truth. Sort of. She just needed time to work out how to escape.

That was all she had ever needed. She'd managed it before. She had to be able to do it again, now that it really mattered.

'Come on, everyone snuggle into a blanket and we'll sing rounds. This is proper camping now we've got a fire, isn't it? We should have brought marshmallows.' And a knife. A gun. A satellite phone. 'Who's been camping before? Jacob? You start us with a song, then.'

She realised her mistake instantly: Tomas said to keep the kids quiet. 'We're going to do it differently today. We'll give whisper-singing a try. You have to sing so quietly the person next to you can only just hear the words.'

The new challenge failed to engage the exhausted children, and the desultory singing soon gave way to murmured complaints and tired snuffling. Kayla moved around the group, tucking each child into their blanketed nest. Stroked Ella's sweaty hair from her face, one hand resting on the girl's chest. Normal?

How would she know? The child needed her mother.

The children fell asleep too quickly. Kayla would prefer they stay awake, make demands and distract her from her thoughts.

She pulled her shirt tight against the clammy chill, her teeth working the edge of each permanently ragged fingernail. But, well established by her childhood, guilt worked evil fingers of blame around the shuttered door of her mind. How much of this was her fault? She'd persuaded the parents that camp would be a valuable experience for their kids, yet hadn't the plan really been to satisfy her own inner child, the one who had dreamed of escape? Then, hungry for praise, she'd posted the details of the trip on the school website. She had chosen to pull the bus over, she'd physically placed the kids in the truck. She'd led them underground, where there was no hope of being found.

Yet at least they weren't in danger. They were out of the sun. Had plenty of water. Kayla sucked in a shuddering breath as she tried to convince herself she had made the right decision. Regardless of the amount, the government would pay the ransom and, assuming Tomas didn't pursue his delusion of being hailed a hero, they would be released in a day or two. No need for her to ration the food, then.

But she should definitely organise it. Divide by six, calculate caloric intake. Keep her mind occupied. Unlike emotions and memories, calculations and facts provided safe boundaries.

Sweat drying prickly tight on her blistered skin, Kayla wrapped her arms around her knees, rocking back and forth.

Her teeth chattered.

She couldn't count.

Couldn't pretend not to think. Not to realise. Not to be aware.

Although the children would be ransomed—and she would keep them safe until then—her own lack of value had been made clear.

For so many years.

And if this was how it ended, in this squalid tomb, then life had totally fucked her over.

Right from the very beginning.

CHAPTER 4

Captain Nick West stared sightlessly at the photographs littering his desk. One hand flipped a pen, end over end. Constant movement to protest forced inactivity.

Tossed aside, the pen rattled across the polished wood, and Nick scrubbed at his face with both hands. Groaned. Faced the pictures again. Twenty-three hours since the missing person's report had been filed. Thirty-two hours since the last sighting. Usually nothing this fresh landed in his lap. The Tactical Assault Group conducted domestic counter-terrorism operations and hostage recovery. T.A.G didn't search for broken-down school buses.

The chair creaked as he leaned forward to shuffle a pair of A4 prints. Shifted another so it headed a new row. Ignored the tic in his clenched jaw.

Six kids. Seventeen pictures. Each family had provided multiple photographs, as though quantity evidenced their love. Nothing on the teacher, though. No family stepped forward and the Education Department had yet to send through her file.

The printer in the corner of the small office whirred into life, and he scowled. He'd shoved the mouse, woken the computer and pressed the print command. But he didn't want to view another accusation of his uselessness.

He swirled and swallowed the dregs in his coffee cup. Winced. Three hours hadn't improved the palatability or added the caffeine hit he needed.

He tugged his starched uniform straight, then raked both hands through his regulation-length hair. Pulled on his left earlobe twice, a habit he'd deliberately copied from Dad years ago and had no intention of dropping. Clinging to the most mundane of memories helped ease the pain a little.

The printer vomited out the image and he added it to the spread. Not that he needed it. Coming in early, he'd studied the pictures all day. Committed each child to memory. Tried not to dwell on the knowledge that, with each hour spent in the desert, the likelihood of their safe return became more remote.

Hell, he had to stop thinking like that. Too many life-or-death missions—emphasis firmly on death—had perverted his imagination.

Broken-down bus. That was it.

The kids were pigeon pairs; three girls, three boys. He could identify any of them in a crowded hall, recite verbatim their date of birth, family members, identifying characteristics. Damn, he even had their favourite food down pat.

What he couldn't do was imagine how the parents felt. He had no experience in that area.

And didn't want any.

His fingers drummed the desk. How the hell did a busload of kids vanish? Police had tagged the time the vehicle refuelled. Chips, water, chocolate, and a coffee purchased from an isolated roadhouse. Nine hours remained unaccounted for between then and the time the parents reported the non-arrival of their children. Nine hours at an average of eighty clicks in a diesel bus gave a range of seven hundred kilometres.

His gaze flicked to the map spread across the left wing of the L-shaped desk. The flat terrain favoured an aerial search, but it also meant the bus wasn't limited to the highway. Tracks and trails and windblown paths masquerading as roads riddled the desert like lines on an old man's hand.

His finger traced routes on the textured paper. Somewhere, the teacher had inexplicably taken a detour. Simple as that. Aerial would spot them, retrieval teams would be dispatched. There was nothing here to get his adrenaline pumping, no tour of duty or terrorist threat.

So why the hell did his gut twist so bad every time he scrutinised the photos?

A knock on the doorframe snapped his head up. Lieutenant Steve Colley flipped a hand in salute as he entered. 'Captain West.'

Nick waved down the token gesture. After five tours, he and the army medic were closer than brothers. In private, they ignored protocol. Despite being centered in the barracks, at this moment Nick's office was private.

Colley frowned at the photos. 'What d'you make of this?'

Nick chose to misunderstand. 'Multiple photos, six kids.'

A waft of cologne accompanied the shake of Colley's head. 'I mean, our involvement.'

'Got me beat. Since when is T.A.G put on standby for a Missing Persons? The brass are hiding something. And all

I've got on the teacher is a name. No picture, no departmental file.'

Colley picked out a photo of a dark-haired girl, a little older than his own daughter. His lips flat-lined, hard and thin. 'You reckon there's something suspicious about the teacher?'

'Wouldn't have a clue. Too little information to make a call.'

'We're mushrooms, then?'

'Kept in the dark and fed bullshit. All we know is she drove six kids into the desert and they disappeared.' The chair spun across thin carpet as Nick strode to the window to stare at the parade ground a level below.

Behind him, Colley dropped into the leather chair facing the desk. 'The ordinaries check out? Breakdown? GPS failure?'

'Waiting on aerial.' He turned to the desk, gesturing at the topographical sheets. 'But look at these. She didn't need a GPS. The highway's straight as a sniper's shot.'

'So, you're thinking...?'

The steel barrel of the pen bowed between his fingers. 'That's just it. I've no bloody idea. I'm not thinking.'

Colley snorted. 'You're never not thinking. C'mon. Lay it on me.'

Nick shook his head. 'I want it to be a missing bus, a wrong turn. This is Australia, man.'

Colley nodded. The shit they'd seen didn't mean a thing, not here. They couldn't allow it to. He stretched back, his body a lean plank, hands linked behind his head. 'Long day. Want to hit the pub when we stand down? Schnitzel night.'

Nick returned his gaze to the map. He didn't need a visual on the loneliness in Colley's invitation. 'Thought you smelled like a hooker's bedroom. Not your access weekend, then?'

He'd warned Colley against marriage. Against emotion, really. Women were to be appreciated and enjoyed. Cherished, even. But not loved. Never loved. The women Nick chose were undemanding and uncomplicated, interested only in his physical attributes and prowess. Which was damn perfect, because he sure as hell didn't need to know them on any other level.

Colley, though, had been ruled by passion and Greek tradition. Angela *had* been a nice enough chick, but now all Colley had to show for dropping fifty grand on a wedding was divorce papers and visitation rights.

Nick shook his head. 'Sorry, mate. Got something on.'

Colley cracked his knuckles. 'More like something off. Y'know, there are only so many women in the world. You could look to sharing them around—' He jerked to his feet and stood at attention as a shadow darkened the open doorway.

Nick did likewise, remaining rigid until the entering officer snapped a salute.

'At ease, gentlemen.' Major George Kimber's tone exuded authority. His carefully chosen and distinctly enunciated words iced an argument far more effectively than shouted curses, and Nick had spent twenty years modelling his behaviour on their commanding officer.

Kimber brandished a sheet of paper. 'Intel just in. Aerial sighted a burned-out wreck.'

Nick sagged. Damn. He hated fire. No one screamed like a person being burned alive. Mouth cottony, he forced the word out. 'Rollover?'

Kimber's gingery features creasing, he shook his head.

'No. That's the anomaly. Aerial is certain it's a bus or campervan, so it seems likely to be our target. But it's upright and only partially incinerated.' He scanned the map spread on the desk, then pointed to a coffee mug housing pens.

Nick passed him a ballpoint.

Finger tracing map gridlines, Kimber marked a red X. 'Here.'

Colley's hand hovered protectively over the photo of the dark-haired girl. 'Signs of survivors?'

Lips pursed, Kimber frowned. 'Nothing from the air. Police are a couple of hundred kilometres out, ETA three hours. It's already dark, but they'll report in when they get there.'

Nick tugged at his ear, staring at the photos. 'Doesn't add up. That's flat land. No roads marked, though there'd be trails. Why would they be out there? And a diesel engine doesn't spontaneously combust.'

'Exactly,' Kimber agreed.

Shuffling the photos, Nick tapped the short edge of the sheaf against his desk, staccato explosions puncturing the sudden silence. 'Take it we're not standing down, then?'

Kimber sucked his teeth. 'No. There's nothing to be gained by sitting here all night, though. Be ready to move out in the morning, contingent on the police report. It'll take the ATV's two days to reach the site.'

Nick saluted Kimber's departure. 'Sir.'

He eyed Colley. Though dismissed, neither of them would sleep.

CHAPTER 5

E ach time Mother hits me, the dressing table shakes and the pills Dad says will make her better spew from their container, like candy from a piñata I once saw on Saturday kids' TV. The empty booze bottle rolls back and forth, smacking into my face, and my stomach lurches at the sickly smell. But it's okay, there's nothing to come up.

Mother's arm rises and falls. 'You-slut-I-wish-I'd-never-had-you.'

The burning across my legs blots out her chant. I know how to deal with pain. If I don't think about it, don't tell anyone, it doesn't hurt so bad.

Mother tires quickly, dropping her stick onto the mound of dirty clothes at my feet. 'Get out of my sight.'

I stagger toward my room, refusing to touch the stickiness on the back of my thighs. My steps falter at the bathroom, fingers reaching toward the door handle. I could take Dad's razor again, no one ever notices. One more slice. That way, it would still be my blood, but I'd be in control. And then I could tell myself that Mother didn't hurt me; I chose it for myself.

But she might hear.

Instead, I stumble further along the uncarpeted passage that reeks of cat wee—though we've never had a pet—and sneak into my room, silently closing the door.

Remain standing, so my blood doesn't stain the grimy sheets.

Wait.

Within minutes, Dad's uneven tread creaks the floorboards as he makes his way from the lounge to the main bedroom. Pauses. Then creeps nearer.

I hold my breath, happiness welling inside me.

A grunt as Dad bends, and a forbidden treat appears in the crack beneath my door, the wrapper crinkling noisily in the terrified hush.

I adore the sound of those footsteps.

They're the proof that Dad loves me.

Kayla jerked awake. Dad?

She shook her head clear. *Dad's dead.* She was all alone now—except for the kids. Her gut cramped. Held for ransom, her students should be safe—yet the sound of footsteps stole her conviction.

Tailed by Fatty, Les emerged from the dim tunnel. He sidled around the edge of the cave, then feinted toward the huddle of sleeping children. Laughed as she lurched to defend them. 'What ya gonna do, bitch?' His voice broke. 'Anyway, Tomas says time for you to come earn your keep.'

Dread pounded through her veins in a sickening wave. This was it, then, and there wasn't a damn thing she could do about it. Nothing but close her eyes, as she'd done so many times before.

She obediently followed Les into the gloom of the tunnel. He glanced back. 'That's right. You move when I say, or else...' He jerked his head toward the children.

No! She lunged toward him, her fists clenched. 'Don't you bloody touch them.'

Les swayed back.

He's frightened! Power surged through her, and she stepped closer. She'd been good at controlling men, but dominance had never previously been her tool. Now, she would use whatever she had.

Les's fist caught her on the cheekbone, her skin splitting like over-ripe fruit. Her chin snapped to the right and she crumpled, protecting her head with her arms as his boot sank into her side.

Jesus, she'd misjudged him. Teeth clenched on her bottom lip so she wouldn't wake the children, Kayla absorbed the blows. Practice made her perfect.

For this, at least.

Fatty's feet shifted restlessly near her head. 'You're getting her dirty, and Tomas won't like that.'

Les kicked once more. 'You going to get up, bitch, or you want me to help you?' His hand twisted in her hair, jerking her to a sitting position.

Spitting blood, she struggled to her feet, favouring the side he'd kicked. Swiped at the crimson drool with her forearm. Mother had taught her to always hide the evidence. Besides, if the kids saw, they'd ask more questions for which she had no answers.

She staggered between the two men down the long, dark tunnel.

'Jeez, what'd you do to her?' Greaz whined around his beer can as Les shoved her into the cave.

'Wasn't me,' Les lied quickly.

Knife in hand, Tomas scowled. 'Clean her up.' He turned

back to a massive stalagmite and ran his fingers over initials carved in the calcium crust.

As he poured water from his flask over her head, Les shot furtive glances at Tomas.

'Leave it.' Tomas sheathed his knife and moved toward them. 'Did they hurt you?' His tone concerned, he ran a long-nailed finger up the side of Kayla's jaw.

The panting fear of her breath bounced off his hand and back into her face.

With gentle fingers, Tomas traced the gash on her cheekbone. A frown creased his brow. Then his fingernail jabbed between the puffed edges of raw flesh. Blood trickled down his wrist, and Kayla jerked back as his forked tongue traced the red stream.

Bile shot up her throat, and she dragged her gaze from his hand, forcing her eyes to the rocks behind him. Counting the cracks.

Tomas sighed. 'Boys, boys. It seems we need some rules for this game. From now on, you keep your paws away from her face, right? You know I like pretty.'

Kayla shut her eyes. She knew how to play the game, too. Her rules. Slowing her breaths, she willed herself into the place where no one could touch her, no words could hurt her. With neither expectations nor desires, no one could fail her. Like all the others, these men wanted sex and, despite the years, she hadn't forgotten how to trade her body to get what she needed. But this time, her price would be the children's safety.

'What a shame we don't have any privacy,' Tomas said. 'Guess we'll have to ask these gentlemen to turn their backs.'

He yanked her shirt free of the jeans she'd pulled over

her shorts, the buttons cascading into the fire's coals like coins into a fountain. Paying for her squandered wishes. Cupping her breast through the t-shirt, Tomas pinched her nipple.

Her knee slammed into his groin.

Agony writhed across his face.

Pain exploded behind Kayla's ear, the cave spun in neon spirals, then faded away.

WHERE WAS SHE, and why the hell was she wet?

Tepid water splashed Kayla's face and she spluttered, shaking her head. Moaned as the movement drove a spike through her temple.

'Had enough beauty sleep?' Canteen in hand, Greaz loomed over where she sprawled on the hard floor. 'No, don't bother getting up. You'll do just fine there.' He glanced over his shoulder. 'C'mon, lads. She has to be punished and I've one sweet idea.'

Punishment. She knew all about that. She rolled her head, swollen cheek mashed against the floor. Tomas was barely visible across the smoky expanse of the cave, lounging near a fire. Les and Fatty stood behind Greaz.

She focused on Fatty. 'The kids?'

He glanced warily at his comrades, then jerked his head toward the tunnel. Mouthed 'Asleep.'

Greaz dropped to straddle her, his knees tight against her waist. He yanked off her t-shirt, her head slamming to the ground as he catapulted her bra toward the cave roof. 'Now there's a pretty sight.'

Les guffawed.

Kayla grit her teeth. *Ignore them.* They were only looking. She'd allowed plenty of men to look. Rescue was on the way, she had only to buy the children's safety until it arrived.

Greaz pulled at his moustache. 'Tomas said we have to be patient while we're stuck down here, and I reckon the only way to pass time is to have a bit of a game.' He jerked his chin at Les and Fatty. 'You two, hold her ankles and wrists.'

A long knife, worn on his belt like some wannabe cowboy, whispered from its leather sheath.

'Don't mess her up,' Les said, suddenly anxious.

'Jesus, you fucking scared of Tomas or something?' Greaz grumbled, though he lowered his voice cautiously. The cold tip of the knife dragged across her stomach. 'Going to kiss me, teach?'

Kayla's tongue glued to the roof of her mouth. This wasn't like any game she'd played, trade she'd made, nor punishment Mother meted out.

Greaz dug the knife into her flesh, scoring a shallow line up toward her waist.

Her teeth gouged her lower lip, the taste of blood metallic in her mouth, and the man's drooping moustache lifted. 'Going to kiss me now, teach?'

Nostrils flared, she sucked air into lungs cramped with fear.

Again he sliced through her skin.

She was accustomed to the tug of steel on skin, but it should be followed by release, the clean slice of a blade allowing the pain to ooze down her forearms or thighs. Control of a blade purged the anguish.

But she didn't have control.

Fatty pinned her wrists, but kept his face turned away

from Greaz's work. She bent her fingers until she could touch his hand, get his attention. Maybe he'd put a stop to this.

He blinked, but avoided her gaze. Just like Dad.

Four times Greaz and his knife repeated the question, and four times she refused to answer. She could tolerate so much more pain than he could imagine. Plus, if the game kept them occupied, it was preferable to anything else they had in mind. Maybe, just maybe, if they delayed long enough, rescue would come before she had to trade.

Greaz waved the bloodied knife. 'C'mon Fatty. You be noughts. They're harder to carve. Here's my cross.'

Fatty shook his head, a wave of sour sweat accompanying the movement.

'Jeez, you a fucking fag?'

'I ain't gay.' Fatty pawed her breast in proof. 'It's just I can think of better things to do with a chick.'

Greaz twirled the end of his moustache. 'Yeah, well it's not like I can't think of other shit. But Tomas wants first dibs, and some cow put him out of action for tonight. Mind, if I wanted a fight with my fuck, I'd go hit on my missus.' He glanced across the cave and lowered his voice. 'But maybe we should have some fun while Tomas is busy nursing his dick? A kid would be better behaved than this numb bitch.'

Kayla froze, holding her breath.

Fatty recoiled. 'You're fucking sick, man. We're not hurting the kids. Tomas said we get the money and get out.' He clambered to his feet and waddled toward the fire, Les scurrying after him.

Kayla sucked air back in greedily. The pain was a small price to pay for the knowledge she had gained: Les was scared of Tomas and, although Fatty hadn't saved her, there were lines he wouldn't cross. She'd been right: soft, insecure in his obesity, she could manipulate him.

'Pussy.' Greaz slashed another two crosses into her abdomen.

Kayla grabbed at her burning stomach. Her hands slid in the blood. *Damn*. She shouldn't have flinched, shouldn't have reacted. She'd let Greaz see how much it hurt, and her pain would become his power.

Greaz grinned. 'I win. Go on. Get out of here.' He yanked her up, letting her stagger against the wall as he swaggered away. 'Chuck us a beer, Les. Warm as piss, but better than nothing. Worked me up a thirst.'

Belying his size, Fatty darted across the cave. Seizing Kayla under the armpits, he dragged her a few feet down the dark tunnel and propped her against the jagged wall. Disappeared, then returned with her shirt. The fabric screwed against his gut, he hesitated, his mouth working silently.

Her mother used to do that. After every beating. Like she wanted to say something, but could never find the words.

Fatty frowned, threw the shirt at her, and returned to his comrades.

Kayla crept down the tunnel, hugging the dark like a blanket. The children sprawled around the glowing remnants of the fire in the smaller cave. Six, still six, all there, all okay.

As okay as they could be in the bowels of Hell.

Curled close to his twin sister, Liam raised himself on one arm. 'I want to go home.'

Hand braced against the wall, Kayla stayed away from the fire. 'I know. We will soon, I promise.' If she moved into the light, they'd *see*. But she craved the sparse warmth. As though it could stop her trembling.

'When soon? You said that before.'

If he sounded whiny or angry the question would be easier to tolerate. But the boy's tone held only disappointment. She'd let him down. 'Shh, Liam. I know I did.'

Her forearm a rigid band of protection across her stomach, she ducked her chin, hiding her face behind her hair. She needed to get to the filthy puddle and clean herself up.

'But I want to go now.' Jacob chimed in, clambering to his knees.

'Me too.' The whisper snuck from her mouth. *Oh Christ, me too.*

Jacob's thin moan dissolved into tears. 'Ryan's bossing me around. He can't boss me around. That's bullying. Tell him to stop.' He kicked at the other boy.

Desperation edged Kayla's tone. She needed time. Time to re-centre. Time to find her courage. Time to work out how the hell she was going to save them.

'Go back to sleep, Jacob. Lie here, in front of the girls.' Was it wrong to use him to shield the girls? Dare she assume the boys were in less danger? Tomas had ordered the kids be kept safe, but it was clear Greaz had other ideas.

What if Tomas can't control his men?

THEY'D LEFT HER ALONE. Hours or days; Kayla didn't know. The shallow lacerations networking her stomach had stopped oozing.

Fashioning spoons from the pull tops of the cans, she'd fed the kids from the supplies of beans and stew. Several times. Probably more than they needed, given their inactivity. But in the dark, she had no way of estimating the passage of time—and little else she could do to provide them comfort.

The fire supplied sparse warmth and even less light. Covered in dirt and ash, the children were too quiet. They roused reluctantly when forced, flaring into brief arguments before lethargically drifting back to silence, neither awake nor asleep.

As she poked twigs into the fire, Kayla tried to force her sluggish brain to reason. What were the symptoms of carbon monoxide poisoning? Should she extinguish the fire, consigning them all to inky blackness? Tempting. Amongst the children's imagined terrors of the dark, she could hide from the monsters inhabiting her reality.

The flame flickered. Fresh air must drift through from the larger cave, or from some crack in the rock, some slivered chink to the normality of the outside world. She needed to provide the kids with an illusion of that normality. They knew the truth, but would embrace her lie—because sometimes hiding from reality was the only way to survive.

Her chilled muscles stiff, Kayla clapped her hands. 'Come on kids, up you get. Make a circle. It's a bit too squeezy to play duck-duck-goose in here, but we'll tell stories until recess time.' As Ella crawled into the imagined safety of her lap, Kayla swallowed a gasp of pain. 'Okay, stories.'

Her mind was blank.

Fairy tales hadn't figured largely in her life.

As she recited a couple of stories in a hushed monotone, Kayla scanned the cave, searching for something, anything, that she'd overlooked. Armed with rocks, could the kids overpower the kidnappers? If the older boys stood on either side of the entrance, could they strike from behind with enough force to stun the men? She would deal the fatal blows. Crush the bastards' heads with the heaviest boulder she could lift.

But then what? If, by some miracle, they escaped, the desert would kill them.

No, they had to wait for rescue. It couldn't be long now.

A gritty shuffle forecasting his arrival, Greaz stooped in the low tunnel, chewing the end of his moustache. His gaze played over the children's recumbent bodies, where they had again fallen into a restless sleep. Kayla's muscles tensed, ready to protect whichever child he chose. Greaz formed a pistol with his hand, index finger pointed at her, then hiked the thumb over his shoulder. Swivelled and left.

She let go her breath. Shook Ryan awake, braving the startling blue of his wide-eyed trust. Eyes of an angel in a filthy face, blond tangle of hair a wild halo. 'I have to go and talk with the grownups. Can you stay awake and take care of the fire? When everyone wakes up, practice the tables again. Try and go all the way up to the four times, like we did earlier.' *Or yesterday, or last week, or whenever it was.* 'You'll need to help the littlies.'

Jacob elbowed in, his arm jabbing her stomach. 'I want a job too, Miss P. I'm nearly big as Ryan. It's not fair he gets all the jobs.'

Kayla's hands fluttered to her abdomen. 'You're right, Jacob. I think you could be a really big help. Ryan's my deputy and you can be his deputy. You're Deputy-Deputy, okay? You help Ryan share out the food in this box.' She tapped her foot against the box, avoiding bending.

Jacob placed a possessive hand on the carton, nodding solemnly.

Kayla glanced around the cave. She could tell by their breathing the other four children were awake, but they didn't move. What else needed to be said? She had to hurry, or Greaz would come back. 'Make sure everyone has a drink after you eat, that's really important. Remember we talked about drinking enough? Then you all lie down for a nap, and I'll be back before you wake up.' *Please God, at least make that part true.* She wasn't asking for herself.

No more procrastinating. She had to go. 'Okay, Ryan? You're the teacher now. Ella's spare puffer is in her pocket. Do you remember what to do with it?' *Jesus.* She forced the boy to take responsibility for another child's life. Ruffling his hair, she winced at the gritty, dusty texture between her fingers. The children needed sunshine and fresh air. But history proved that wishing brought nothing. Nothing good, anyway. She needed action, and she needed to focus.

Logistics. Ninety-seven reluctant paces through the narrow tunnel to the larger cave. Far enough to muffle sound? But she'd be quiet, this time, trade fair and square. She had reneged on the unspoken deal she had with the men, and the mistake would cost her now.

The air foul with fumes and fury, a scowl creased Tomas's narrow face. 'Good of you to join us.' On the opposite side of the fire, Fatty hunched his shoulder, turning away. Les leaned against the wall, one foot hooked on a ledge behind him, a cigarette hanging from his lips. Smoke curled from it, adding to the pool clouding the ceiling, where stalactites became mountains thrusting from the blue ocean of an inverted world.

Kayla clasped trembling hands over her stomach. 'The ransom is paid?'

Tomas slung his beer can aside. 'Let me tell you something,' his yellowed eyes burned into her skin and she had a sudden fierce, ridiculous hope that liver disease would instantly consume him. 'Even when the money comes, you're going nowhere.' He jerked his head at Greaz. 'Get her on her back. And hold her good this time.'

Greaz seized her, snuffling against her neck as he shoved her legs out, dropping her to the ground. Les tore at the shirt knotted at her waist and yanked off the t-shirt beneath.

It's only sex. It means nothing. Her mantra. At fourteen, she had discovered sex bought affection, attention, validation. Everything she had been denied. She'd learned to both desire and despise men's pathetic protestations of love.

But Tomas made no such claim. He stood over her, masturbating with short, rhythmic strokes. Then he dropped to straddle her, his knees pinioning her ears.

It's only sex. The thought hard to hold onto, her pulse ramped up, fear suffocating her.

Greaz forced her mouth open, but then snatched his fingers away. 'Jesus, Tomas, I'm not wanking you. Let me get my hand out first.'

The odour of stale armpits and nicotine smothered her. Tomas's tumescent flesh glowed white like a long-dead fish. It should be slimy.

She bit him, and it wasn't.

Tomas rolled away, his howls of anguish echoing around the cave.

Kayla clambered to her knees, retching. *Christ, what have I done?* She had to submit, never fight back.

Mother had taught her that.

Father had died because she failed the lesson.

Crouched over, Tomas mewled, stroking himself as his hysteria abated.

Maggots of fear writhed and multiplied beneath Kayla's skin. Head bowed, she waited. The punishment would come. It always did.

The boot caught her in the kidneys, lifted her from her knees, and sprawled her across the ground. Her ankles and wrists seized by eager hands, rocks cut into her chest.

A serpentine whisper slithered through the expectant hush as Tomas drew the leather belt from his jeans. He flicked the strap into her face, the buckle cracking against her teeth. 'Now you'll get what you deserve.'

Deserve. The word stole the last of her hope.

CHAPTER 6

Nick West's eyes watered and burned, the curvature of the earth obvious across the vast saltbush-studded plain he scanned from the rear of the Unimog. But the hot, dusty ride in the back of the truck rated a damn sight better than sitting at a desk, images searing his brain while he waited for mission approval.

The police investigation of the burned-out bus had revealed no human remains, but tracks indicated the presence of another vehicle, and multiple adult footprints were cast. It had taken four days to locate the second vehicle, a truck hidden beneath tumbleweed and sand. Another two for Intel to pinpoint a possible location for the abductees. In that time, the media received a garbled message, the unidentified sender fluctuating between claims of saving the children and demands for ransom.

Wary of funding a terrorist attempt, the government mobilised T.A.G to attempt a pre-emptive rescue mission— and that assignment rested on Nick's shoulders. Failure could result in the kids' deaths, their images added to his collection of repressed memories.

It was becoming mighty crowded in there.

He jerked his foot up, brought the boot crashing down on the steel-plated floor of the truck.

The sergeant seated on the opposite bench tightened his grip on his rifle barrel, the stock clamped between his feet. 'Jeez, Cap What you do that for?'

'Cramp.' Nick yawned, feigning relaxation.

Steve Colley grinned across the dust-filled interior. 'Knackered, Captain? Not surprised. Thought I glimpsed a blonde energiser bunny's cottontail last night, streaking down the hallway.'

'Stress relief, Lieutenant. You should try it once in a while.'

The sergeant leaned forward, elbows on knees. 'Wait, you mean Cap's limiting himself to one at a time?' His glance invited ribaldry from the other four men. 'What's the story, Cap? Feeling your age?'

'He was sure as hell feeling something,' Colley said.

Nick ignored the heckling. After half-a-dozen deployments, the guys knew to grab a laugh when they could.

Phillips wasn't laughing, though. 'What the fuck, hey?' He shook his head. 'Since when does shit like this go down here?'

'World's changed.' Colley leaned back against one of the struts supporting the canvas cover of the rear of the ATV. 'Any sicko has an endless feed of ideas, thanks to the internet. We may as well be back in the Middle East.'

Nick snorted. 'Remind me how many years of med school you did to come up with that psych eval, doc? Can tell we're not back in the sand pit: I still have my rat pack.' He patted the pack on his hip. More than once, Colley had talked him into sharing his rations with some mangy mutt in the deserts of the Middle East. And more than once he'd handed it to equally hungry kids.

He retrieved a packet of gum from his shirt pocket, folded a stick into his mouth, and tossed the package through the gloom. Phillips caught it one-handed. 'This bastard knocks off a busload of ankle-biters and demands ransom. Classic money grab, upscaled by the numbers involved.'

Colley stood easily in the swaying confines. 'Yeah, that's —' The vehicle lurched to a halt.

On his feet instantly, Nick pulled the canvas door wide. 'End of the line, gents.'

Rifles held across their chests, the men jumped from the truck. Explosions of red dirt clouding their boots, they strode to join a second squad from an identical desert-patterned 4wd truck.

Disembarking the air-conditioned comfort of a Land Rover, Major Kimber waved the thirteen men over, his cultured tone at odds with the inhospitable surrounds. 'At ease. We're thirty-seven kilometres from the area the radio scan indicated. We can't take the vehicles in any closer, the hostiles may have scouts out.' He brushed an imaginary speck from his shirt, then spread a map open on the scorching hood of the Rover. 'Satellite imaging hasn't picked up activity, but in lieu of a better option, it seems this run of subterranean caves offers logical harbour. We're going to have to hoof it in there.'

Colley broke in. 'My gear?'

'You and Corporal Smithson hump your basic meds.'

Basic meds meant a twenty-kilo pack in addition to standard gear and weapons. Accustomed to the weight, Colley nodded, but consternation sharpened his tone. 'Seven civvies, though, sir.'

A gust of hot air lifted the corner of the map, and Kimber slammed it with his palm. 'I'm well aware, Lieutenant. This bore, three kilometres west of the cave, is one of the major factors in Intel's decision to pinpoint the cave run: the perpetrators will need access to water. We extract the group, pull back there. The base team will bring in the 'mogs with your additional med supplies.'

Phillips leaned over the map. 'This is some frickin' huge blank space, huh? The Yanks would have a chopper in here, stat.'

Alongside Nick, the sergeant snorted. 'Lucky we're a damn sight tougher than those pussies, then.'

'I meant for the kids. It's a hellish ride in these trucks. Be different if we'd scored the Rheinmetall units instead of these dinosaurs,' Phillips said.

Major Kimber skewered him from beneath ginger-tinged eyebrows. 'Murumalata represents the closest feasible extraction point. We convey the victims there and the RAAF will get fixed-wing onto their airstrip.'

Convey. Nick screwed his mouth tight. Why the hell did that have to bring up an image of bodies? Children's bodies.

Kimber's pale blue gaze turned to him. 'You'll take squad A, Captain, and approach from the south-east. Lieutenant Sommers, squad B will circle in from the south-west. Watch your proximity. Lance Corporal Smithson and I, as squad C, will set ourselves up on this small ridge.' He jabbed at the map with a freckled forefinger. 'Given the terrain, it has reasonable visibility of incoming traffic. If I give the word, squads A and B pull out—fast. Questions?'

Nick stared at the map. He had a gut feeling they were marching into some kind of fresh hell.

CHAPTER 7

The knocking brings a smile to my lips. Knocking means power.

My lover fumbles for his glasses on the bedside table. He scurries to the window, his naked butt flashing white. Pulls aside the curtain 'How old did you say you are?'

'You know I'm fifteen.' Hell, yeah, he knows. That's half my appeal.

He runs a hand through the salt-and-pepper of his hair. 'Jesus. It's the cops.'

I slouch from his bed, wrapping a towel around me as I wander from the room, ignoring his babble. The control feels good; I'm powerful in the face of his fear. This moment, this feeling, is my payment for allowing him to have my body. For listening to his lies about love.

'Mikayla Petrovic?' The summons follows the sharp rapping on the door.

Odd. The cops usually turn up as a response to calls from concerned citizens aware of their neighbours' unhealthy interests. They never know my name before they pick me up.

I yank open the front door, silently daring the officer to drop his gaze to the too-short hem of my towel. A woman stands behind him, but I ignore her; I only have power over men. 'Yup?'

'Mikayla Petrovic?'

'Yup.'

'Miss Petrovic, I'm sorry to inform you there's been an accident. You'll need to get dressed.'

'An accident?' I feign innocence. Dad hid the alcohol, but as Mother snored I'd placed the bottle on her bedside cabinet, among the confetti of her tablets. Breasts sagging like deflated airbags on either side of her chest, she'd roused to swear at me. And I had felt no remorse. Only hope.

That was days ago. Days I spent earning a roof over my head by being flat on my back.

The policeman stares at the bottom of my towel. Fiddles with the radio clipped to his belt. I slide one knee forward, angling my hip provocatively. Not that I need him, but it's a habit. 'Is she dead?'

The cop is startled into truth. 'Yes. I'm sorry, she is.'

I'm so in control, I manage not to smile.

But he's still speaking. 'I do need you to dress though, Miss Petrovic. Your father's in a critical condition. We've been trying to locate you for a number of hours.'

My knees buckle, my shoulder slams into the door frame.

Not my father.

...KNOCKING.

Kayla frowned, her eyes closed. The police were here to take her home again.

Except that didn't make sense: there was no home to take her to, no going back.

Still the noise continued, sporadic pops. She forced her eyes open, the walls of the small cave contracting and receding as she traced the sound. The crackling of the fire.

A child murmured in the murk, 'Can we go home now?' The words rote, they held no inflection of interest.

'Soon.' Same question, same answer. How many times?

'I want my mummy.'

'I know. Go to sleep. Please, go to sleep.' The hoarse plea scraped the scarred tissue of her throat. Agony ripped and burned through her back. Pressing the heels of her hands into her eyes, she tried to force away the memories of what the men had done. Of the leather belt rising and falling, metal studs biting into her back. Her hands sticky, she yanked them away. Stared at them. So much blood.

Nothing in the first aid kit could deal with this, yet she had to stop the flow. Had to preserve what little strength she had.

As though she could use it to save the kids.

She hobbled to the pool at the rear of the cave. Biting back a moan, she slumped to the ground and scrabbled with the knot she had tied in her buttonless shirt, hoping the fabric tangles could somehow protect her.

The shirt spread on the floor, she scooped clay from the pool and smeared the filth across the fabric. Pulled the shirt back on and crossed the edges over her bruised chest, forcing the cool mud to kiss her tortured flesh.

Don't think about the pain. Thinking makes it real.

Footsteps.

Coming for her again.

How many times had the men forced her down the tunnel, how long had the children been held in this underground hell? So much longer than the two days she had promised them. Perhaps she could calculate it by counting the empty cans, but she didn't dare. That knowledge wouldn't be power. It would be defeat.

Still, her gaze ranged the littered floor. *The cans.* If she fashioned a lid into a blade, could she slit Tomas's throat? Or if she armed the kids, could they fight their way out? Escape the cave, and let the desert take them.

At least that would be clean. Swift.

Except now...now she couldn't even bring herself to move across the cave, bend to pick up one of the lids.

The whispering children fell mute as the men entered. They were young, not stupid; they knew she couldn't fall over and injure herself every time the men forced her from the cave. If she kept lying to the kids, she would lose their respect.

But if she didn't, they would lose the last of their innocence.

She shrank back as Greaz strode into the cave. His hands stuffed in his jean's pockets, the kids were safe for the moment, but still she watched his every move. He scowled at Tomas, who followed him down the narrow passageway. 'So, what now? Why the hell is this taking so long?'

Tomas eyed her students. 'Because they don't know what's good for them.' He pulled a knife from his belt, dropping to his haunches near Jacob. 'Or, more correctly, they don't know what's good for their kids. We can't afford to lose our leverage, but we can, let's see, encourage them to *appreciate* that leverage.'

Kayla thrust to her feet. 'Get the hell away from them!' She'd pegged Greaz as a loose cannon, but Tomas had been adamant about guarding his investment. Something had gone wrong. Lily and Liam reared up, screaming echoes of her anger, but Ryan curled in a foetal position, arms wrapped around his head, crooning a dirge. 'You go near them and I'll fucking kill you!'

Greaz laughed.

Tomas straightened and shook his head sorrowfully. 'You're a slow learner, aren't you? Time for another lesson, then. Someday you're going to realise that if you mouth off at me, you pay the price.'

Another lesson, which would keep the men away from the children. Another lesson, which would bring rescue closer.

Because it had to come soon.

Kayla squatted slowly alongside Ryan, careful not to allow the agony to seep into her tone. 'We're going to play statues, kids. Do you remember how? You have to lie still as you can. I'll leave the room and I might be super quiet, or I might make lots of noise like I was practicing just then. But when I sneak back in, I'll see who's moved.' She had to inject normality into this nightmare—despite the madness of her instructions, muttered in the smoke-filled gloom.

She shook Ryan's shoulder. 'Ryan? Come on, get in your position now. Liam, are you staying there with Lily? Jacob, not next to Ryan. You'll end up poking and fighting, and then you'll both be out of the game. Move over next to Maddy, instead. Everyone in their spot? Remember, when I c-come back I'll guess if anyone m-moved.'

The kids had to be her primary concern, but fear wormed beneath her skin and dread crushed her chest, suffocating the soothing words she needed to find.

She knew what waited for her in the other cave.

'Enough.' Greaz seized her arm, dragging her through

the tunnel after Tomas, then thrust her onto the ground in the larger cave.

She tried to curl into a ball, but the men yanked and cut the ragged remains of her clothing away, the knife slicing indiscriminately through flesh and fabric. Nylon twine, twisted around her ankles and wrists and looped over small boulder-bedposts, held her spread-eagled naked on the floor. Again.

Stalactites hung above her, spears frozen in flight. She closed her eyes, praying they would fall.

Count. Just count. Something. Anything. Heartbeats. Breaths. Seconds of my life passing, leaving, ending.

Thousands of breaths later, the foul odour told her that it was Greaz who crushed her into the stone floor.

Sex. It's only sex. It means nothing.

'Open your eyes, bitch.'

'I've seen shit before.' She blanched as the words escaped without conscious thought. *Never answer back.* The unwritten rules had been beaten into her for fifteen years. Why did she disobey now?

Greaz shifted his gut and sank a meaty fist into her stomach.

Her diaphragm spasming, Kayla kept her eyes closed. The man's urge to maim would feed on her exposed fear.

More knowledge for which to thank her mother.

'Fuckin' smart-mouthed bitch. Untie her.' Greaz levered himself up. Grabbing her left hand, he placed one foot in her armpit, caressing her arm as he straightened it. 'Look at me, slut. Look and see what I'm gonna give you.'

The tension in her arm increased, the tendons stretching, her elbow locking into place with a click.

She kept her eyes closed.

Greaz increased the pressure, her shoulder pinned by his foot. 'I said, look at me.'

Teeth clenched, she refused.

Greaz yanked upward, twisting her arm.

He had no way of knowing her joints were loosened by years of dislocations, that the appointments—a different medical practice each time—had been both terrifying and exhilarating, as she trotted out the rehearsed lie about fictitious gymnastics classes, and Dad rewarded her deceit with ice-cream and his relief.

The joint popped and she screamed, but then deliberately fell limp, her eyes still closed. She knew how to win this game.

'You moron, Greaz. There's no point screwing her when she's out of it.' Tomas said. 'Though I guess we're all pretty much done, right?'

The pain ate into her shoulder and she bit down into her lip, her body rigid with a sudden rush of hope. They were finished with her?

'I'm not,' Les whined.

The glimmer of hope eclipsed by a surge of renewed fear, Kayla fought to hold in the sob of defeat that exploded in her chest.

'Well, no one's stopping you, champ. No rules here.' Tomas's voice faded, but was he moving away, or was her consciousness slipping? She slit her eyes, allowing the tiniest sliver of vision.

Fatty gestured toward her. 'Hurry up, then, Les. I want another go.'

'Jesus,' Les said. 'Like Tomas said, only cowboys fuck dead meat. You got no principles? I'm going for a fag.'

As Les left, Fatty glanced around furtively, fiddling with his fly.

Kayla relaxed her body, limbs splayed and unresisting, though her mind worked frantically. This man had evidenced the tiniest amount of humanity. She knew he felt some remorse, some stirring of compassion. In her previous life, he would have been an easy mark; now she had to convince Fatty that he could be their saviour.

But then he dropped onto her and she couldn't think anymore. Groaning in thick enjoyment, he trailed wet kisses across her gashed cheek as his hips pounded betrayal into her.

Then he lay there, panting.

Eventually, he clambered to his feet, tugging the knife from his belt. His rough thumb tracked the silver tracery of old scars crisscrossing her thighs. 'You like this kind of stuff, don't you? I'll give you a little present, then.'

His blade gouged her leg, dragging through the skin. 'Now you're mine forever.' He kissed the tip of his finger and pressed it to her thigh, stroked her cheek, then waddled toward the steps.

Love and betrayal, just like Dad.

Kayla rolled to her knees, her left arm jelly-fishing uselessly across her chest. She choked back a scream. If she made a sound, the men would return. Instead, she rocked back and forth, trying to ride out the agony.

Experience guided her trembling fingers to the swollen mass of her shoulder. More painful than memory had allowed her to recall, but not dislocated.

Her legs shook with reaction, and she closed her eyes to shut in the nausea clawing up her gullet. Fatty had been her only hope, but his similarity to her mother didn't end with his mouth. He'd used her, abused her, and discarded her.

Kayla slumped against the vandalised stalagmite, her face pressed to the damp, chalky surface. Embraced the darkness.

SHE DIDN'T WANT to be conscious. Hell, she didn't want to be alive. But voices intruded and she clutched the stalagmite, her eyes almost closed. However much time had passed, the stone chill had seeped into her bones. But it left her blessedly numb. Physically, at least.

'Hey, Fatty, got yourself a Barbie?' Les jerked a thumb toward her. 'Like the pose.'

Tomas guffawed. 'Fatty look like a Ken doll to you? Go shut those kids up—carefully. Not long until they buy our tickets to Bali, right?' His glee hinted at insanity far more terrifying than his cruelty, and Kayla shuddered. But he was protecting the kids once again, and that was all that mattered.

He yanked a handful of her hair, but she kept her eyes closed, remained unresponsive as he tugged her head from side to side. 'Wash some of this shit off her. I bloody hate filth.'

Greaz dragged a twenty-litre drum across the cave. 'Speaking of shit, I'm bloody sick of eating crap. I want a steak.'

'You and me both. But soon enough you'll be able to buy yourself a restaurant.'

Greaz chortled. 'Hey, Fatty, that'd have to be a Macca's

for you, wouldn't it? They even got them in Bali?' He upended the drum of water over her, and Kayla gasped.

Tomas's attention snapped back to her. 'Still with us, then?' He looked her over and shook his head. 'Damn, but you're a mess. I'm not touching that. Fatty, get her out of my sight. And I told you to go shut those kids up.'

She shrank back as Fatty draped a shirt over her, then pulled her up and bundled her down the tunnel.

They were getting out. Soon.

CHAPTER 8

Nick halted his unit after six hours hard march through terrain that could have been anywhere in the Middle East. Even with years of hardening, his thighs pulsed from bracing against the shifting sand and grit infiltrated his laced boots to rub his skin raw. It would almost be better if the kids weren't here, hadn't had to *get* here.

He tugged at his ear, forbidding the images his imagination strove to sear on the blistering desert canvas. 'Okay, we're within coo-ee. Eyes off, gents. Don't want reflections giving us away.' Removing his own sunglasses, he unshouldered the shortwave transmitter, then spoke quietly into the receiver. 'Strike distance.'

Kimber's authority travelled clearly across the kilometres. 'Complete a thirty-minute, repeat, three-zero-minute reconnaissance. Maintain radio silence.'

Nick holstered the transmitter as a static crackle indicated Lieutenant Pete Sommer's radio presence. He caressed the stock of the Austeyr assault rifle slung over his shoulder.

'Okay, Sergeant, you're on me. The rest of you take five. We'll go see if we can find anything interesting.'

Flanked by Max, he strode from the group, squinting against the reflected brilliance of coral-coloured sand. 'Five hundred metres out, we crab.'

Swatting at a cloud of bush flies, the sergeant grunted.

Nick grinned beneath the sniper veil wrapped across his face. 'Personal hygiene issue, Sergeant? They're sure as hell not interested in me.'

An insect dive-bombed the wet oasis of the sergeant's mouth. He spat out the corpse and ran a hand across his chin. 'They've probably got better taste.'

'Maybe so.'

Fifteen minutes later, they topped a low crest on their bellies. The dark opening to a cave angled into the side of a dune in the wind-hollowed valley beneath them. The sun silhouetted Lieutenant Somers and Squad B on the far side of the depression.

A piece of open-weave sniper veil draped over the lens, Nick studied the cave mouth through binoculars. A pile of half-buried rubbish lay to one side. Some of the kids had made it this far, then. 'Rookies.'

'Trap,' Max observed with habitual pessimism.

A figure appeared in the opening, and Nick burrowed further into the hot sand. 'Want to put money on that?' A fierce grin spread across his face: now he could do something, instead of staring at photos.

The man settled on a boulder, a shortened rifle balanced across his knee. He dropped something, cursed, and leaned down to retrieve it. Then he rolled a cigarette and struck a match. The distinctive odour of tobacco accompanied the flare, and voices carried clearly across the hot, still air as another figure appeared in the cave mouth.

The man on the boulder spoke without removing the cigarette glued precariously to his lower lip. 'Where's Fatty? With the little shits or the slut?'

'Watchin'.'

'Yeah, I bet he's watching. Turd's too fat to do much else.'

Nick held his breath, head turned to one side like he'd enhance his perfect hearing.

The second man giggled. 'I meant he's watching the kids. Can't work out if the stupid bastard cares, or if he's so slow he's still trying to do the math with the money.'

Sweat trickling down his back, Nick watched for long minutes as the men drained a bottle of rum before retreating into the cave. Then he nodded at Max. They slithered down the hill and crouched into a run to cover the bare ground back to the squad. Creating their own breeze, they moved fast. The lookouts signalled them back into base.

Hunched over the shortwave, he fought the urge to demand Kimber allow them to rush into action. The sun beat against his shoulders with a physical pulse, the heat made worse by immobility. Inaction always made every thing worse.

'Indications are we have three hostiles,' he summarised. Kimber wouldn't utter a word until he possessed all the facts. 'One of the two we had eyes on carried arms. A sawn-off .22.' He fingered his own high-velocity rifle. 'They downed the best part of a bottle of rum.'

'Almost looks too easy.' Sommers' caution rang tinnily over the comms. 'They're either rank amateurs or damn good actors.'

Nick tapped the mic against his chin, replaying the

scene in his mind, checking for anything he'd missed. 'Atmosphere is too relaxed to be contrived. They're anticipating the payout, celebrating early.'

Kimber's tone was clipped. 'How did you arrive at the numbers?'

He could practically hear the major's cogs turning. 'Minimum estimate. They stated a third person was in the cave with the kids, along with someone we took to be the teacher.'

A breeze sang through the sands and the radio emitted a soft, metallic hum. Serene and peaceful, with no indication of the evil happening nearby. He remembered this false security. Remembered letting his guard down as they strode among Afghani friendlies, with dogs sniffing for scraps around the sand-coloured dwellings, veiled women raising a hand in shy greeting, children playing in the street, wide grins splitting their happy faces as they ran up to the patrol, begging for treats.

He remembered the betrayal as a spray of bullets indiscriminately scythed down men and children.

Now, he never relaxed.

Kimber's decision barked across the kilometres. 'There's only one way in for us, and we have to hope that means only one way out for the perps. We can't wait for the transfer. Hijacking the bus in such a remote area, then managing to spirit the kids away like this? Even if they're amateurs, they're organised. Well planned, well executed. They sure as hell aren't going to repatriate the victims and risk being identified.'

Nick scowled at the dunes. Kimber was right but, just once, it'd be nice to discover a little honour left in the world. A series of dull thuds sounded from the radio, and he could imagine the major drumming his fingers against it as he committed his men. The senior officer never made a decision lightly.

Kimber continued. 'That being the case, time is not our friend. We hit them tonight. Go in fast and quiet, but if there's sign of movement, we draw them into the mouth of the cave, and dispose of them there.'

Kimber's plan was sound, as always, but meant hours of inaction, when intuition urged Nick to rush, as though time wasted would cause irrevocable harm.

Colley cut in. 'Dispose?'

There was a beat of silence before Kimber responded 'Orders are to bring them back to stand trial, but take no chances. Use necessary force. I can't risk an approach with the vehicles until I know you've got the victims clear, so radio in once the perps are contained. You rally at the bore, we won't be far behind with the 'mogs. Questions?'

Nick thumbed the radio. No questions: no choice. The attack had to be at the witching hour, the perpetrators made vulnerable by the lowest ebb of their circadian rhythm. 'Squad two, converge on the south-west rise above the cave. Synchronise at 1613 on my mark...three, two, one, mark. Strike at 0300 hundred hours.'

And pray it was soon enough.

CHAPTER 9

Her eyes had only been shut for minutes, she couldn't have slept. The stone ledge rammed hard against Kayla's back, blood smeared wet across her knee.

Fresh blood? She didn't recall where it came from, or what had caused the injury. Hell, what *did* she remember? Had more days passed, days she chose to forget, days she had failed to care for the kids?

Her shoulder throbbed, but it wasn't the raw pain of a new injury. Or perhaps it was, but overshadowed by the agony that encased her body.

Liam watched her, and Kayla creased her face into a semblance of a smile. Like that would make all the difference. 'Liam, fill that cup with water please, and bring it to me.' Her voice a croak, she cleared her throat. Gagged on blood clots. *Have to swallow, or he'll see.*

'Please, Liam, bring it here. I fell over and cut my knee. See the blood? I need some water to wash it.' Her voice failed.

'We were waiting for you.' The six-year-old handed her

the water, his eyes fixed on hers, avoiding her injuries. He knew the truth. But he also knew their pretence was safer. Because if you pretended hard enough, one day your fantasy might become real.

She gulped the water, thick with grit. 'I'm sorry, Li. You know sometimes I have to leave the classroom for a few minutes. It's the same down here, but the dark makes it seem longer.' How much longer? Hours? Days? 'I see Ryan has been taking care of the fire.'

'I helped.' Liam puffed out his chest. 'And I stopped Lily crying.'

'How did you manage that?'

'I told her to stop or else.'

'Or else what?'

Liam drew himself tall. 'Nothing. Just or else.'

She smiled, the first genuine one she could recall in so long. They were getting out. Soon. She remembered that much. Allowed herself to remember that much. 'That–'

Greaz strolled into the cave, swinging a toy baseball bat. 'Tomas wants you back in the boudoir.'

Manoeuvring to her knees, Kayla lurched upright, quick to comply so he wouldn't assault her in front of the children. The horror of their imaginations could be no match for the reality. Her legs wobbled, and she had trouble placing her feet. They drifted and she stumbled, grasping at the wall with her right hand.

Greaz caressed the shiny aluminium shaft of his bat. 'You like baseball?' He thrust his tattooed forearm, hazed by regrowth, in front of her face. 'Babe Ruth. Fucking Legend. And take a look at this.' The tiny charm he pulled from his filthy shirt swung on a silver chain like a hypnotist's pendulum. 'Sweet, huh? Took forever to find it. Footballs, ice skates, unicorns; you name it, the internet had everything else.' He dropped the necklace and whirled the toy bat in a circle, warming up for a game, then prodded her in the back until she stumbled dutifully along the corridor.

Tomas groaned and made of show of clambering from his position alongside the fire, as though *he* ached. 'Miss Petrovic. It appears you're of no further use to me right now.' He looked her up and down, and then chuckled. 'Actually, I suspect you're no use to anyone. But how about we let the lads make that call? In fact, I'll tell you what. You make it through the night with them, and you can stay here with the kids when we clear out.'

Les interrupted in high-pitched concern. 'You going somewhere, Tomas?'

Tomas threw his arm across the youth's shoulders. 'I'll stay for a while to watch Greaz's special. But then I must pop out—I need a decent sat signal to check the offshore transfers have gone through. Nothing for you to worry about.' He turned back to Kayla, lowering his voice in a sinister imitation of intimacy. 'However, *you* should worry. Because me and you,' he moved a manicured finger between his chest and hers, invisibly tying them. 'We're always going to be together.' He tapped her temple. 'I'll always be right here with you.'

A shudder rippled through her. Accustomed to the nightmares that never released her, she shouldn't fear his words; yet premonition shrivelled her gut.

Greaz stalked toward her, tapping the baseball bat against his palm. The stench of nicotine and alcohol roiled her stomach. 'Looks like you have to earn your freedom, then. Once more for the crowd in the back, huh?'

CHAPTER 10

The twelve uniformed men lay on their stomachs among the spinifex and saltbush on the dune. The persistent bush flies gave way to the high-pitched whine of mosquitoes, feeding on exposed skin. A hypnotic glow flickered deep within the cave.

Nick forced out a measured breath. Moth to a flame, he wanted to charge in there. Pull the kids out. He could taste the victory.

Lips barely moving, he kept his voice low. 'Nice of them to leave the night light on for us. Let's go.'

The men slithered down the hill. At the base, Nick signalled his team flat to the ground, then crawled to the opening. Moving slowly, he controlled the hastening urge of adrenaline. Anticipation prickled his hair. Mouth dry, pulse strong.

The possible imminence of his doom enhanced his existence, and he relished each of the sensations, a convicted man enjoying his last meal.

He peered into the cave. And down. Dimly lit, the

sloping passage echoed with emptiness. At his signal, the squad moved to his side.

Though his mind pumped urgency, his hands reinforced his calm, barely audible directions. Control, always in control. 'Pairs. Single file. Two-metre separation. Squad B, eyes left. Mine, eyes right. Sergeant, on point at the entrance. Okay. Let's do it.'

The men slipped through the opening, dropped silently down a series of deep steps, then squeezed sideways along a narrow cleft in the earth.

The tang of kerosene fouled the air. Despite the stench, Nick pulled the sniper scarf from his face, every sense alert as they edged deeper underground. Shoulders contorted to ease through the tunnel, he resisted an urge to rub at his eyes as he emerged into a massive cave. Blue smoke clouded a stalactite-hung ceiling. Two adults lay beside a central fire. A third man's paunch threatened to topple him from the camp chair he overflowed, the seat visibly vibrating with his snores.

Nick signalled two men to the side of each body.

Sliced his hand down in a karate chop signal.

Phillips dropped on one knee into the middle of a body, the air leaving his victim's lungs in a rush. Corporal Weaver stuffed a bandanna into the gaping mouth, yanked back the target's arms, and cinched zip ties around his wrists.

The other pair of soldiers simultaneously performed similar manoeuvres, their captive loosing a yelp of surprise.

Nick kicked the stressed leg of the camp chair. It buckled, the fat man sliding to the floor in a jellied puddle of surprise. Colley gagged him and tugged cable ties tight. Grunted as he levered the carcass upright.

Dazed by sleep and drugged by alcohol, the kidnappers

put up no fight. After days of planning and hours of waiting, the ease of the arrest disappointed Nick, his thirst for action unquenched. But, despite the speed, the takedown wasn't completely silent.

Nick shoved his rifle barrel into his captive's meaty gut and yanked free the gag. 'More of you?' he snarled, nostrils flared with distaste. His finger twitched against the trigger. This bastard kidnapped children.

A stranded fish, the man flapped his mouth soundlessly.

'Are. There. More?' Nick ground out, his voice low. Colley jerked the slug's bound hands up behind him, encouraging the reply.

'N...no.' Urine soaked the captive's pants, disappearing into the chalky dust.

Nick scowled. He loathed weakness. And cowardice. And bullies. Fuck, really, there was a lot of shit that ate at him. He poked with his rifle. 'The kids. Where?'

The man blubbered, jowls trembling as he tried to ingratiate himself. 'The other cave. I'll show you. They're all okay. I helped them, I fed them, I looked after—'

Nick thrust the gag back in the captive's mouth and wiped his hand against his fatigues. 'Haul them out.'

As his squad hustled the kidnappers toward the cave entrance, Nick pointed two fingers at Colley and Sommers, then hiked a thumb at his own chest. 'On me.'

Rifles poised for combat, the soldiers followed him to a smaller tunnel.

Nick halted. Something raised his hackles, and he sniffed at the air. The fat bastard confirmed they had their targets, yet a pungent, too familiar smell—fear? Smoke? Maybe death? —tied lead to his feet.

He ignored the crush of dread and claustrophobia and forced himself on.

A dead fire, grey coals, and stray embers. And around the ashes—children's bodies.

Collages of death flashed before Nick's eyes. Too many corpses. Too many children. Too much history. *Shove it down inside. Lock the box.*

Scan the cave for threats.

Breathe.

Colley pushed past and rolled the nearest child onto her back. With a ragged gust of relief, he nodded. 'This one's good.'

The girl murmured but didn't wake.

One. Nick swallowed the lump in his throat. Even under the filth, he could identify the child. Maddison.

Five to go.

Colley stretched his hand to the next child.

Something flickered, darker on darkness, in his peripheral vision. 'Hold it right there.' He shouldered his rifle. Sighted along the barrel. Night-vision scope was useless in the close confines. 'Identify.'

Colley crouched protectively over the child.

A voice rasped from the shivering shadows. 'Leave them alone, you bastards! Don't you dare touch them.'

Female. He kept his rifle trained on the slowly emerging form.

Colley rocked back onto his heels, his words echoing in the subterranean prison. 'Miss Petrovic? We're with the Australian Defence Force. Tactical Assault Group. We're here to take you home.'

CHAPTER 11

Kayla glanced frantically from the soldier on his knees alongside Maddie, to the colossus in the mouth of the tunnel, his rifle aimed at her stomach. A third man stood near the putrid latrine, swivelling from the hip to constantly search the cave.

There should be money, an exchange. Not soldiers and guns. Not more men.

A torch flashed toward her and she shrank back, lifting her hand to shade her eyes. Slowly. Everything slow. 'But the ransom—it's tomorrow.' She'd calculated the hours, minutes and seconds that she needed to survive, to protect the kids.

The tall soldier lowered his rifle. 'No payoff. It's over.'

She lurched forward and tugged Lily and Liam, intertwined as usual, to their feet. 'Then get the kids out of here.' Tomas could slither back at any moment.

Huge in her small world, the giant's voice threatened to shake the rocks from the walls. 'On it.' He turned toward the man now hunched over Jacob. 'Give them a once over, Lieutenant. Let us know if we're good to go.'

The soldier with the Red Cross armband nodded. 'Sure Cap, give me five.' He patted Jacob's shoulder and stood. Kayla shrank back into the gloom as he faced her. 'Any problems you're aware of, Miss Petrov—' The death flare of an ember lit the room. 'Shit, what happened to your face?' He moved with surprising speed, the rocky wall preventing her retreat as he reached toward her split cheek.

She slapped at his hand. 'Nothing. One of the girls has asthma. Her puffer's almost empty.'

Distracted, the medic looked back toward the children. 'Ella Spencer, right? I have her spare inhalers. Which one is she?'

'Ella, sit up.' Trained by fear, the children lay awake but immobile, waiting for orders.

Ella sat and the rest of the kids scrambled to clutch at Kayla, all grimy faces and huge, untrusting eyes.

Jacob tugged at her filthy shirt. 'We going home now, Miss?'

Dare she tell them that they were safe? They should be, yet every fibre of Kayla's being screamed awareness of the men.

The medic checked Ella's respiration but flashed a grin at Jacob. 'Sure, mate. Reckon you can show us the way out of here?'

Half-hidden behind Kayla's hip, Jacob stared up at him suspiciously. Liam muscled in. 'Jacob's only little. I'm bigger. I'll show you.'

'No, I'm big 'nuff!' Relinquishing his hold on her shirt, Jacob pushed forward, ready to do battle. Kayla snatched at his shoulder, held him back.

The medic nodded. 'Well, seems we're going to need a bit of help. Jacob, is it?' The little boy nodded solemnly. 'Jacob, see the big dude over there? Yeah? Well, he's my boss. Captain West. How about you show him the way out? And my new mate here—' He paused till Liam gave his name. 'Liam can show me. It's pretty dark and our groups might get separated. This way, you guys are in charge of making sure we all get out safe. Okay?'

'But there are bad men...'

The captain spoke up from across the cave, loud enough for all the kids to take note. 'The bad guys are all gone. You won't see them anymore.'

She should be doing that. Taking control, calming the kids. Getting them the hell out of here. Pain surged and snatched at Kayla's words. 'Okay, kids, let's go.'

Her jeans cinched tight by bruised flesh, she ushered the children through the steep tunnel. Scrabbled on her knees and one hand to drag herself up each high step. Aware, every second, of the men around her. A lifetime of men she'd used, and who'd used her. Men she couldn't escape. And now, new men to avoid.

Fresh air seared her lungs as they emerged from the cave. Torch beams sliced the darkness, a terrifyingly vast world unfolding around her. Her head felt thick, stuffed with cotton wool. *Good.* She would lock on to that feeling, ignore the craving for the familiar support of cold stone, the fetid safety of her cave.

The captain flicked the cover from his watch, dim luminosity haloing him. 'We'll make the dam easy before dawn. Move out.'

Another soldier loomed in the night shadows, a blanket-swathed child in his arms. 'Here, this one's asking for you.'

She shook her head, stepping back. Refusing the burden. The responsibility.

The medic called across the gloom. 'Wait up. I need to check you out, get some antiseptic on your face.'

'No!' Kayla snatched the bundled child, using her as a shield. She couldn't stand to have the medic near, to allow him to touch her. She wore the shirt Fatty had thrown her, not her own blood-stained rags, but still she couldn't risk discovery. Mother said there would be punishment if anyone found out about her injuries.

She couldn't take any more punishment.

'It's fine. I slipped going down the steps. Just get the kids out of here. Get them home.'

Maddie's voice muffled against her chest. 'I want Mummy.' She reeked of smoke, soil, and shit.

Kayla had brought the child to this hell. Now she would carry her to freedom.

THREADED BETWEEN CRYSTAL STARS, the contrail of an airliner foamed the frosted sky. Kayla stared at it as she plodded, envying the safety of the passengers in a metal box hurtling through the air, eight thousand metres above the ground.

It seemed they walked forever. Maddie on her hip, Kayla hid her face in the child's hair to avoid the torchlight as the medic made constant rounds, checking on the children the soldiers carried. 'Are they okay?' she asked him each time he passed, terrified his answer would change. Could they truly have escaped their hell without injury?

No. Not escaped. Been rescued.

Escape would infer she had finally done something right.

'They seem fine.' Sounded like a smile in the medic's reply, but she didn't risk looking at him to find out. 'Disoriented, but not dehydrated. Confused and tired, but not injured.'

Her hand tucked between the buttons of her borrowed shirt to support her injured arm, Kayla eyed the Red Cross insignia on his sleeve. He would carry a sling, drugs. But she couldn't ask. She needed to get the kids to safety, then somehow disappear before her filthy secrets were discovered.

The captain's voice startled her. 'Okay, this is it. Dismount, kids. Let's set up camp.'

The soldiers quickly built a fire and the children crowded it, gorging on the novelty of rat-packs the men handed around. Kayla stood back from the flickering light. She needed to act normal. Not arouse suspicion. 'Okay, toilet. Who needs to go first? No, Liam, *needs,* not *wants.*' Her heart beat faster. Without Fatty to watch over them, was it safe? Everything seemed dangerous, unfamiliar.

She accepted a torch from one of the soldiers, careful not to make contact with his eyes or his hands. Led Ella into the darkness. If she kept moving, perhaps the pain wouldn't catch her—and neither would the medic, who kept demanding to check her over.

But she couldn't keep moving, because the kids were exhausted. Wrapped in thermal blankets they fell asleep, as though they'd not slept for days. Low discussion bounced between the men on the far side of the fire. Kayla kept an eye on the medic, barely visible in the twilight. He had no right to touch her, he could go to hell. A tiny part of her sparked at the power of refusing him. So many men who'd not listened, this one had to be different. She had to make him be different, she had to reclaim the control she'd lost.

Except she had lost it so very long ago, years before, when the policeman knocked on the door. When she'd realised that her dream of being free of her mother had killed her father.

When she became an accidental murderer.

A child whimpered softly. Kayla lurched to her knees, then bit back a moan, the pain halting her. But she couldn't allow that. The children were out of the cave, yet still it wasn't enough; *she* wasn't enough. Mother had re-emerged from the ashes of the car crash, haunting her with the taunts of years past. *Weak. Useless.* Kayla had to prove her wrong.

She had to get the children home.

On broken hands and torn knees, she crawled to Ella. Curled into a nest of blankets, the girl wept in her sleep, her face creased and wet. Kayla pulled her close, tucking her into the slight protection of the crook of her shoulder.

Around them, the nocturnal desert was noisy, the whirr of cicadas broken by the hoot of an owl and the terrified squeak of its prey. The distinctive odour of wild pig rustled through the spinifex. The noises grew into a resonating chorus, expanding and echoing in her head. The numbness in her body dissipated, fingers of pain playing xylophone on her spine. The night air iced her hot skin.

Hand cupped over her face, she controlled her breathing, fighting the panic that clawed at her chest. She had promised the kids that escaping the cave would fix everything, that the world would return to normal. They mustn't see she was...broken.

She forced herself to her feet. Her flesh prickled with goosebumps, even as sweat exploded from her pores. *So hot.*

She needed water. And she needed to clean herself up before it was light enough for the men to see anything not hidden beneath her voluminous shirt.

The captain glanced up, and she froze like a rabbit in a spotlight. He didn't move toward her. The mineral-rich smell of artesian water wafted on the warming air. She followed the smell, stumbling to the bank of the waterhole fifty metres away. The moon floated at the bottom of the hollow, and she staggered down the slope. Scuffed the sneakers from her heels and slid her feet through mud slimy with bird droppings. Waded into the dam.

The chill seeped up her thighs, the water boiling against her tormented flesh. She fumbled single-handed with her shirt. *Fatty's. Give it back.*

No. *Those* men weren't here. The soldier had told her that. More than once. But then, where were they?

She shook her head, unable to force the thoughts into a logical sequence. The promise of the sweet, cool water grew louder every second, drawing her deeper. *Water washes away sin.* The buttons refused her stiff fingers. Pain seared through her shoulder as she dragged the shirt over her head. Her knees buckled. The inky oblivion of the lagoon rushed toward her.

The last of the air from her lungs bubbled past her face.

She'd wash away her history and drown her future.

CHAPTER 12

Nick halted on the high rim of the waterhole, a canteen in each hand. He squatted on his haunches, waiting for the teacher to finish bathing. Her presence had stilled the cacophony of chirrups and squeals near the pool, but beyond the camp, the sporadic barks of wild dingoes punctured the night.

The teacher gasped as the water climbed her legs, and he grinned; the chill of still water in the desert was always a shock to the unwary. But her anguished moan as she tugged off her shirt jerked him to his feet. Then she slid beneath the dark surface.

Silence.

He plunged down the slope, an avalanche of dirt and rock and uprooted spinifex racing him to the base. Six strides brought him to the floating body, her hair fanned on unseen currents like a slow-spreading oil slick. He scooped her up and struggled to the bank through the sucking slime.

Cresting the rise, he almost collided with Colley.

The medic's face puckered, he placed two fingers on the side of the teacher's neck. 'Unconscious. What happened?'

Nick lifted one shoulder, deliberately slowing his breaths. Control. 'Went for a swim without water wings, I guess. Water's bloody cold. Though—' Incomprehension tightened his grasp. 'She feels hot.'

Shifting his burden, he brought his hand into the dim light. 'Holy—' Ruby droplets sparkled reflections of the fire as they fell to the thirsty sand.

'Yours?' Colley barked.

'No.'

'Shit. Wait.' The medic dashed back to the campfire, grabbed his pack, then raced back. Tossed a Mylar blanket across the sand near a rocky outcrop. 'Set her down. Keep her out of the dirt.'

'Out of the dirt? Did you see where they were living?' As Nick complied with the medic's directions, awkwardly lowering the woman so she lay on her side, Colley's torch flickered over her t-shirt. Wet and dark.

'Not water.' Colley peeled up the hem. 'And stuck. Take the light.' Producing shears from webbing strapped across his chest, he grasped the hem of the shirt and slid his open scissors up the fabric. Then from the neckline down one short sleeve. Still, the fabric stayed in place. He eased the woman over onto her chest. Then he eyed Nick grimly. 'Hold her, mate.'

Nick nodded, resting his palms on the woman's shoulders.

Grasping the raw edges of the shirt, Colley tugged the material apart like he ripped off sticking plaster. 'Oh fuck. Jesus Christ, look at this.'

The medic rarely swore. Nick glanced once, then looked

away as Colley worked the fabric free with scissors. 'What the hell? Didn't you check on her?'

'She refused treatment. Said it was only her face, though she was favouring her right arm. But I didn't figure on this. Fuck, not this.' Colley tossed the shredded material aside. 'Okay, that's about all of it.'

Nick forced himself to look again, breathing shallowly through clenched teeth to avoid inhaling the foulness of the bloodied mass before him.

Colley sat back on his heels. 'I can't give her Penthrox while she's slipping in and out of consciousness. Grab your trauma kit, we need to get the bleeding under control. Bastards. God knows what else they did to her.' He glanced at the wet denim of her legs but quickly refocused on her back. 'One thing at a time.'

Without giving it a name, they both knew what the men had done to her. They'd seen it before. But not here, and not like this.

Nick blocked the images Colley's words conjured. He had long ago learned the danger of associating a face, an actual person, with pain. He stripped off his damp shirt and tossed it over a rock, then retrieved the package of Quick Clot sponges from his kit.

Face-down on the blanket, the unconscious woman moaned and writhed beneath the medic's touch. The sun still hours away, sweat betrayed Nick, beading his forehead and trickling down his neck. His hand hovered unwillingly above the girl's flayed back.

Colley frowned. 'Clean her up, so I can get antiseptic on. Look. Here. And here.' He indicated the angry yellow stripes of pus exposed as he wiped away blood, which instantly welled again. 'This is shit. Real fucking bad shit.'

Forty minutes later, Colley pulled off his gloves, rubbing his palms against his pants. 'I'm out of haemo gauze. I need the damn supplies Kim's carrying.' He pointed at Nick's shirt on the rocky outcrop. 'Is that dry? Chuck it here. And grab me the other med kits.'

Nick seized the opportunity to escape. 'I'll hit the short-wave. Get an ETA on the 'mog.' He scrubbed his hands against his eyes, trying to rub away the new nightmare image that crowded his others.

THE CHILL RADIATING through the thin blanket and into the bunched muscles of Nick's thighs, rocks dug into his lower back and he shifted restlessly. Compared to the agony of the unconscious woman curled alongside him, he had nothing to bitch about.

As Colley used up the remainder of their med supplies, the woman had flickered in and out of consciousness. The medic tried to calm her, but she had pushed him away, sobbing incoherent protestations. Eventually, Colley left her where she settled, huddled small against the rocky outcrop, the side of her face mashed to the granite like she drew comfort from the stone. Rigging an IV, he'd instructed Nick to keep watch while he made rounds of the kids.

Now a low moan dragged the woman awake. Her voice rough, like her throat was sandpapered, she came out of her corner fighting before she had even focused. 'Get away from me.'

She couldn't want that any more than he did. 'Sure. But you have to keep still.'

Pain shot across her face in the dim light, but she spat fury like a feral cat. 'Why the hell should I do what *you* say?'

Nick raised his hands in mock surrender, then pointed to the IV bag balanced on his pack, a clear line snaking into her arm. 'Only a suggestion. But you're getting my shirt all bloody, and I'm pretty sure that's a disciplinary offense in some obscure rule book.'

Her breath hitched, face going paler than should be possible.

Damn, he shouldn't have mentioned her injuries. It wasn't like he hadn't encountered this before. Victims of war, women were trophies for the victor, consolation for the defeated.

But there was no war here. And her back...Jesus, her back.

He grabbed his mug from the sand and pressed it into her hand. 'Drink.'

She lifted the cup a couple of centimetres, then her hand dropped nervelessly to her knee. Coffee slopped onto her damp jeans.

Where the hell had Colley got to? 'Here.' He held the mug to the girl's lips. The metal rim rang under her chattering teeth. As he leaned forward to screw the cup back into the sand—screw it right through to bloody China—the girl bit back a moan. *Shit.* 'The truck will be here soon.'

'Truck?' The word snatched away on a gasp. Fists clenched, her teeth found her bottom lip as spasms wracked her slight frame.

But she didn't make a sound.

As she relaxed a fraction, as though the surge of pain eased, Nick finally allowed himself a breath. 'The doc said you should sleep. He'll skin us both if he catches you awake.' And he'd damn well skin Colley if the medic didn't get back, pronto.

A grimace shifted the bruised corner of the woman's mouth. 'He's a bit late to that party.'

Sweet Jesus. She was joking?

Maybe he'd misinterpreted, though, as her husky words were suddenly charged with panic. 'The children—?'

She surged forward, as though she'd get up, and he reflexively grabbed for her shoulders to restrain her. Winced at the dampness that wasn't all from his sweating palms. 'They're fine. We've shifted them under shelter.'

'Shelter? No, we're going home.' For the first time, she made eye contact, her pupils contracted with pain, the whites suffused with blood.

Bastards. Nick pulled his gaze away. 'Transport can't head cross country without full visibility. Even then, they're a couple of hours away. The shelters will keep us out of the sun until Kim—Major Kimber—gets the trucks in.'

'We have to go now. The parents will be frantic.'

She could barely move, yet she'd argue with him? Nick's tone hardened. 'You might have walked in here, but you're sure as hell not walking out. A few hours won't make any difference. In any case, the civvies' ETA at Murumalata is about the same as ours.' He leaned back against his rucksack and closed his eyes, hoping she'd take the hint.

Damn it. He could sense her watching him. With a grunt, he abandoned the pretence. 'Sun will be up soon. I'll get you over to one of the shelters.' *Shit.* She'd been locked underground for a couple of weeks and he threatened her with the *sun*? Real smooth. How the hell did he plan to get her to the shelter, anyway? That would entail touching her, and he had no idea where it was safe to put his hands. He only had to move, and she recoiled.

'What's your name? And the other soldier?' she demanded, like she needed to catalogue them.

The apparently random question disconcerted him, but he touched a forefinger to his wide-brimmed hat, a mock bow made awkward by his position. 'Captain Nick West. The medic is Lieutenant Steve Colley.'

She spoke quickly, as though she needed to fill the silence. 'Mikayla Petrovic. Kayla.'

'Mikayla, is it? They didn't tell us that.'

'If your names were an alphabet soup, you'd try to keep it quiet.' She tried for a grin, but pain twisted her face, her back arching from the rock. Her breath panted, harsh and fast.

He thrust an arm behind her back, protecting her from the stone. The other hand he dropped to her stomach, trying to immobilise her. 'It's okay, take it easy.' He fought a cowardly urge to yell for Colley. He'd noticed the medic's lips moving in silent prayer, as he worked over Kayla, and he knew that habit. Had seen it too many times on the battle-field. At best it ended with medevacs. More usually with flag-draped coffins. The woman's ragged nails bit into his forearm, and he tightened his hold, trying to impart his strength to her shuddering frame. Christ, why hadn't he assigned himself to the detail marching the abductors across the damn desert?

The seizure ended as abruptly as it began. Kayla's body limp, her pupils blown with shock.

He cleared his throat. 'Try and sleep. It won't hurt so bad then.' Meaningless drivel. But he had nothing else to offer.

The movement almost imperceptible, the girl shook her head.

His jaw twitched at the unaccustomed slap of outright defiance. 'Why not?'

The exhausted whisper barely reached his ears. 'Dreams.'

He knew torture. God knows he'd inflicted it often enough, unintentionally or otherwise. He knew the hopelessness of men lying in agony, calling for their wives, their mothers, their gods. But the end to their torment was in sight. This woman's single word hid indescribable suffering. And he didn't know how to respond. Within her grey eyes lurked something so dangerous, a chill rippled across his flesh.

The fear of fear.

He'd seen it before. He knew the terror it invoked, the dread that could cripple the strongest soldier.

But she wasn't a soldier. She was just a girl.

Kayla's words slurred, barely audible. 'Dreams hurt.'

Jesus. He wished he hadn't heard. Hadn't seen. His imagination, based on too much experience, left him struggling to contain the revulsion. 'Nobody can hurt you now. I won't let them. You're safe.' The bastards wouldn't even let go of the poor woman while she slept. They'd pay for this.

As the teacher's battered body shut down and she drowsed—or maybe slid into unconsciousness, how the hell would he know? —Nick focused on each locked muscle, willing the tension from his body. He clicked his jaw from side to side, trying to loosen it. His over-reaction unacceptable, he needed to talk himself down. Debrief.

Life revolved around deployment and danger. Excitement and challenges. Sitting in the desert feeling sorry for some half-drowned woman didn't rate. There was nothing for him here, no adrenaline-junkie high. The protective urge that had kicked him in the guts was simply a by-product of the mission's endorphin rush. He should recognise the signs by now. Overt masculinity. Aggression. Empathy. Pity.

And pity was not an emotion he could afford. Ever. Pity would rip him open, unlock the carefully sealed boxes he hid within.

CHAPTER 13

The glare of an overhead light shocked her into consciousness, and Kayla stretched out a protesting hand. Her fingertips brushed the cold coarseness of rock, and she shoved upright, pain ripping across her back.

Rescue had been a dream.

But the light, the bedding beneath her, made no sense. She glanced down.

Terror choked off her scream.

Floating in darkness far below, but closer by the second, Greaz's hair swirled in an unholy halo around his pockmarked face. Emotionless black pits stared into her soul.

He's not real. She closed her eyes. Still, Greaz drifted closer. A leer of evil reminiscence twisted his face, an Arctic wind across a violated graveyard. His filthy, jagged fingernails drummed a death march.

On the baseball bat.

His movement freed Kayla, and she flung herself from him.

Instantly captured and forced back on the blanket, she

screamed, lashing out with fists and feet, each contact jarring her body. Sobs tore at her throat, and she squeezed her eyes shut, shaking her head.

But she couldn't keep them closed forever. She had to face her fear.

On his knees, the captain gripped her wrists with one hand, the other pushed against her chest to restrain her. Face contorted, lines creased his forehead. 'Kayla?'

Her gaze darted frantically. The fractured images made no sense. She couldn't separate what was real and what was in her head. Greaz. The captain. Stone. Canvas. How could they be in a tent? She would be safer back in the cave, where she knew what to expect. Not here. God, not here with men *looking* at her.

Futile against the soldier's grasp, she tried to free her hands to cover her face, a coarse blanket slipping from her chest. *Naked*? She had to run. Again.

She lurched to her knees in the sand, but the soldier's arms locked around her. *Bastard*. He'd promised no one would hurt her, but his hands made lies of his words, pressed into the sticky heat of her back.

Sticky. Blood. *No one can know.* Mother taught her not to draw attention. Yet how could she hide this?

Coiled inside her the pain built, a screaming crescendo contained only by jamming her teeth together. She struggled to push to her feet, but the agony unfurled, blooming like fire until it exploded, shattering her into a thousand tiny pieces.

The soldier didn't move, holding her firm against his chest as the pain slowly ebbed.

A cool palm cupped her forehead, and the medic's voice came from behind her. 'Fever's broken. Hold her there, Cap.'

Water splashed in a bowl. Jesus, God, she was thirsty.

Colley's fingers trespassed, making their way over her shoulder. His touch pounded new fear through her. 'What happened here? Looks like a dislocation.' He pressed her mottled flesh, and she jerked rigid, a puppet controlled by strings of pain. 'Sorry, this is going to hurt. But I have to check it's not out of place, or you could lose the arm.'

'I don't need the damn arm. I need to be left alone.' Wasn't that how it was supposed to work? She said no, and they backed off?

But it never worked.

No never meant no.

Colley's fingers dug into muscle and, though she tried to suck it back in, a moan escaped. If she could keep quiet, play dead, they would leave her alone. Les had said so.

But the medic's examination moved to her back, stripping her bandages and her self-control. 'No more. Please, no more.' She didn't even know who she begged. Everyone who had ever hurt her. Her mother. Her lovers. Her abductors.

Her new tormentors.

KAYLA WINCED, the midday sun evaporating the moisture from her mouth and crushing her lungs. Only hours ago, she had longed to feel the clean burn on her face—but that was before she realised how the light would expose her.

As he carried her from the tent to the Land Rover a few metres away, Colley tried to make conversation. As though words could make any of this seem normal. But at least he allowed her to pretend that she'd not broken the rules, that she hadn't let them *know*. 'You're riding with Nick and me. Kim—you met him earlier?'

There had been a man in her fevered dreams. One among far too many. Grey hair. Pedantic.

The medic continued. 'Kim's gone on ahead in the truck with the kids, as it'll travel slower. I know you wanted to stay with them, but this will be a smoother ride. A little, anyway. We've rigged up the back so you can lie down.'

She snatched at the door he opened, the metal burning her palm. 'No.' Lying down left her vulnerable.

Colley hesitated, then slid her onto the front seat and climbed into the rear himself. The captain eased behind the wheel, avoiding eye contact.

She huddled into the corner, as far from either man as she could get. The engine roared to life, the machine's body shuddering awake. As did hers, the vibrations setting her teeth on edge. She stared at the desert. Willed the kilometres to pass.

Willed her life to pass.

Hours later, Colley leaned from the rear seat. His pitched voice indicated he repeated a question. 'Kayla, do you want a drink? Something to eat?'

She shook her head. Why did he have to speak to her? She needed to isolate herself, close out the unwanted intrusion of manufactured concern or curiosity. Concentrate on holding her breath through the cramp that gripped her abdomen and bent her in half. Oh Christ, it hurt so damn bad. She wanted to cry, to throw up, to pass out. Anything to stop the grinding agony.

It wasn't fair. The attackers gone, she shouldn't hurt anymore.

Though the pain Mother caused had never diminished with her absence.

'Kayla, you really need to—'

'Jesus, I said no!'

She closed her eyes, her fists clenched. She shouldn't have spoken like that. Shouldn't draw attention. If the men knew what had happened, they would judge her. No matter their words, deep down they would figure she deserved it. Like Mother insisted. Like every man in her past had claimed.

And they'd be right.

The contraction easing, she stared ahead with unfocused intensity, her arms locked across her stomach as she willed the heat to relax the spasms.

Nick spoke over her head. 'Put you back in your box, mate.'

'She's got to take some water. Her blood pressure is too low, and she's dehydrated. I need a push IV.'

When would they realise it no longer mattered? The kids had been her sole reason for survival. Now she didn't even get to make some pathetic attempt at amends by reuniting them with their families, she had to focus on a new problem. Or an old problem.

How to escape.

She had no option but to accompany the soldiers to Murumalata. That she'd never heard of the place meant it was one of the two-dog, dozen-house settlements that grew like mould on the plains. Despite no evident reason for existence, it would be serviced by an occasional Greyhound coach. Or she could thumb a lift out with a long-haul trucker. Either way, with the kids safe, once they got there she'd be free.

Free? That concept belonged to those not haunted by their past, those who had earned reward. Not those who did nothing but spread their legs and pray for salvation.

No matter how far she ran, she would never be free.

The men's conversation drifted into exhausted silence. Or maybe she drifted away as, when she squinted through the tinted windscreen, a horizon of sorts had moved to meet them.

The radio on the dash crackled and the captain picked up, his hand dwarfing the comm. 'Receiving.'

Kayla could barely make out words through static.

'Over.' Replacing the handpiece, the soldier jerked his chin toward the windscreen. 'Kim's waiting up ahead. Thought you'd like to roll into town at the same time as the kids.'

Yes.

No.

She no longer knew what she wanted.

The town melted in the afternoon heat, the edges of reality softened by writhing heat mirages. Like mushrooms after rain, identical prefabricated buildings sprouted along two streets bordered by stunted tree corpses. The solitary sign of life, a desert-coloured dog slunk across the road.

The vehicle halted before a long bungalow, the green-painted verandah lying about cool shade. Paint flaked like dried blood from the sign 'McNamara's Motel ~ Much Meals, Minor Money'.

People oozed from the bar. Slow motion. One, then another and another, until there were so many, they spilled from the verandah onto the dirt road. They gathered in a silent semi-circle as the khaki truck disgorged children mute with exhaustion.

Determined to pretend she was fine, Kayla slid from the Rover. Grimaced as her feet hit the powdered earth. Back hunched to ease the talons clawing at her stomach, she hid behind the open door.

A high-pitched keen broke the unnatural silence. Lily and Liam's mother rushed forward and flung her arms around her twins. Jacob's father buried his face in the boy's neck, his back heaving as his wife wrapped her arms around the pair. Ella's mum staggered forward but dropped to her knees partway, almost bowled over as the little girl bolted to her embrace. Clinging to his stoicism, Ryan hung at the back of the group, hands stuck in his pockets. But as his mum placed his pup, Benji, on the ground, he gave it up. The dog wriggled in his arms, licking at the tears he finally released.

It's done. Kayla sagged against the searing metal. *I'm done.*

Maddie broke away from her father and dashed around the vehicle, clutching at Kayla's legs. 'I didn't know where you'd gone, Miss P!'

No! She tried to pry the girl free, push her toward her parents as the crowd turned her way.

Arms straining, the child tightened her grip.

Kayla knelt slowly, snatching for breath as the pain flared. 'It's okay, Maddie. Camp's over. It's time to go home with Mum and Dad.'

Maddie pouted. 'I want you to come with us.'

'Mads, I've had you for days.' However many it had been. 'Mum and Dad want a turn. They need to hear all about your adventures. I bet, if you ask really nicely, they'll take you for ice-cream.'

Maddie's head bobbed enthusiastically and she darted

back to her family. 'Miss P said you have to buy me ice-cream.'

As though signalled, the other children swarmed her. Their embraces brought tears of pain and shame. She had done nothing to deserve their trust, and their love hurt, as Mother's love always hurt, hard slaps followed by contrite hugs and guilty forgetfulness in a bottle.

As the last child released her, Kayla stood unsteadily. The world see-sawed.

By her side instantly, Colley and Nick each took an elbow, shepherding her toward the building.

Don't let them know.

She forced herself upright.

Something inside her ripped apart, hot blood streamed down her thighs, and the world fell away.

CHAPTER 14

Don't panic. Kayla stared at the beige unfamiliarity of the ceiling, slowing her breath as she counted the spider-web cracks that crazed the paint. No cave. That had to be good. Beyond that, she couldn't recall what had happened. Memory played her false, pain the only constant.

Pain. Levering herself from the bed, she couldn't pinpoint the source. Everywhere hurt. Tubes snaked around her arm, attached to a needle. She ripped it out. Cool linoleum against her feet challenged the stupor, and memory tried to creep back in.

The cave. The tent. The soldiers.

No. She couldn't afford to remember. She needed to shower, get some clothes, and get the hell out of whatever new prison she had created.

Stiff bulkiness bound her back and thighs; the medic had dressed her wounds while she was unconscious. *What else did he do?*

No, he wasn't one of *those* men. She couldn't allow

thoughts like that. Or *of* that. She had to tuck them away with all the other forbidden memories.

The tiny room held two single beds. Eight stumbled steps took her to a dingy bathroom. She jerked back from her reflection in a full-length mirror, then edged forward.

Shrouded in a white gown that had come from God-only-knew where, her face floated, the features indistinguishable, melted into whiteness. She touched a finger to her cheek. Each livid scar screamed a story, forcing her memory. The jagged gash where Tomas dug his nail in and licked it clean. The balancing bruise on the other side from Les's fist. The shadow along her jaw that looked like black grease. Jesus, that was almost funny. Because she was pretty sure that one came courtesy of Greaz.

They'd branded her. She had to slough off the filth or be buried by it.

Her unbalanced stride slammed her shoulder into the wall as she lurched into the shower cubicle. Agony reverberated through her body. But it didn't matter. There was water and soap. She'd be clean. Normal.

Except, craving the water so desperately, she could barely struggle out of the damned dress-or-shirt-or-gown, or whatever the hell it was. Finally dropping the garment to the floor, bandaged hands clumsy, she grappled with the tap. Scalding water sluiced her body, but she didn't have the energy to temper the flow.

Hot was cleaner, anyway.

Her back to the spray, she leaned against soap-scummed tiles. Searing needles drove through her hair, setting her scalp on fire before sliding agonisingly down her back, splattering red and pink on the tiles in kaleidoscope patterns around her feet. She stood as long as she could, watching the filth and mud from her hair mix with blood. Then she slid to the floor, forehead resting on the knees she hugged to her chest.

Gradually, the water became softer, more soothing than scalding, drowning her sobs. If only she could drown herself.

With no idea how much time had passed, she ignored the knocking. Not that she had a choice. She couldn't move, even to turn off the tap that now ran cold.

'Kayla? Are you okay in there?'

One of the soldiers. She couldn't think which. It didn't matter. If she ignored them, they'd leave her alone. Their job also finished with the children's return.

The voice closer, the bathroom door opened a crack. 'Kayla?'

Nick. That was bad. He was less schooled in hiding his revulsion than the medic. She snagged the corner of a towel hanging from the nearby rail and clutched it against herself.

The soldier entered, crossed the small room uncertainly, and reached for the tap. Hesitated. 'Jesus, what a mess.'

She forced her chin up. 'Seriously? That's your best bedside manner?' Her voice cracked with pain, spoiling the effect.

The captain tugged at his ear. 'Unless this is a new variety of water bed, you've got a location problem. You want a good bedside manner, I'll get Colley.' He appeared ready to bolt—which would be great, except no way she could get off the floor unassisted. Her stomach cramped viciously, and it was all she could do to sit upright with the support of the wall behind her. 'No. Just pass me that nightshirt.'

One arm stretched into the cubicle, avoiding getting

closer, Nick dangled the limp rag. 'Can you get back to the bed?'

Towel pressed to her chest, she held in a moan. Waited a moment, until she had it under control. Forced a smile. 'Sure. Just kind of, you know, waiting for you to turn your back.' She gestured to the towel, indicating modesty prevented her from standing.

Lips thinned, Nick challenged her. 'I think not.'

The pain growing, she couldn't banter anymore. 'Leave me alone.' She flinched as he crouched alongside her. *Too close.*

He took the shirt and dropped it over her head. Waited as she slowly pushed her hands through the armholes. 'Listen, I'm going to give you a lift back to the bed, okay? Then I'll leave you alone. Promise.'

She nodded. If she spoke right now, she'd scream. Nick slid an arm around her back and the other under her knees, then stood in a fluid motion. Jaw clenched, she squeezed her eyes tight. He was too close, he was touching her, she needed him to get his damn hands off her.

'Colley!' he bellowed.

She clutched at his shirt as he lowered her to the mattress. Instead of recoiling, he tossed a sheet over her, then sat on the edge of the bed, his hand closed over her fist as the waves of pain crested.

The moment Colley entered, Nick disengaged though, retreating to the safety of the doorway. 'Can you get that morphine into her yet?'

Her arm out flat, Colley pressed for a vein. 'Told you, contraindicated by low blood pressure. I need to get fluids in first. Which,' his dark eyes pierced her, 'Would be easier if you didn't rip the drips out.'

Nick slammed out of the door as the medic cut away her nightshirt. 'I'll give you what I can and use a topical anaesthetic to clean you up. We'll hold off on the suturing until I've got your fluids up and can get some hardcore pain meds in the drip, okay?'

She pretended not to hear. Pretended not to be there, the sheets screwed in her hands as he mummified her thighs and back. Shouldn't have bothered with the shower. She sweated pain and fear enough to douse them both.

Sue Coulthard's strident voice accompanied a rap on the door. 'Kayla? You awake?'

Colley pressed a piece of tape onto her bandaged wrist and tucked the sheets tight around her. 'That's one of the mums? I'll leave you to it, then.'

Leave her to face the blame, he meant. Leave her to front up to the one person she considered a friend. Kayla crossed her arms over her chest, wincing at the movement. Trying to hold herself together.

Six years earlier, she had cut men—people, really—out of her life. Remaining insular meant she could never be disappointed. With country people notorious for their mistrust of outsiders, the remote teaching placement seemed a godsend. But, oblivious to Kayla's rebuffs, Maddie's mother had pursued friendship with the tactless enthusiasm of a Labrador. Despite Kayla's best efforts, Sue Coulthard had either found or created a chink in her armour.

Now she would use the opening to stab her.

As Colley headed out, Sue bustled into the motel room on a wave of Vanderbilt. She slapped the ancient Berber upholstery before dropping into the chair alongside the bed, her low-cut shirt straining across an impressive bosom as she leaned forward. Then she jerked back. 'Honey, what on earth happened to you?'

Kayla read her as quickly as a weekly magazine: *Revulsion. Pity. Judgment.* Everything she expected. She pressed her lips together. She wouldn't allow them to tremble, wouldn't show her shame. If only she'd been able to hide her arms, mottled with fingerprint-bruises, beneath the tight sheet.

The older woman's acrylic fingernails drummed a brisk tattoo on her meticulously faded denim leg, filling the silence while she found words. 'Maddie hasn't stopped for breath yet. All she can talk about is how awesome excursions are.'

The speed of the words proved her dishonesty, yet Kayla willed her to continue the lie. 'She's okay?'

The manicured hand swooped toward Kayla's bandaged fist, touched fleetingly, then darted away. 'She'll be fine. I think the excitement of the beach pretty much overshadows anything else. She said you promised to take her back—something about shells?' Sue's gaze ranged the room like she'd find the lost shells in a hidden nook.

Kayla focused on the peeling wallpaper opposite the bed. Her tongue cleaved to the roof of her mouth. She never apologised for anything; an apology was an admission of weakness. But she'd screwed up so bad. 'Sue, I'm sorry. I couldn't—I didn't—'

Sue held up a hand to stop her excuses. 'When Maddie ran up to me this morning, I...I...' Her voice nasal and muffled, she started again. 'When she wrapped those pudgy little arms around my neck, I thought I was going to burst. Honestly. My heart hurt so bad, but I've never been so happy in my entire life. Not even the day she was born.' She swallowed convulsively, her chin dimpling.

Shit. If Sue started to cry, she couldn't handle it. Kayla ground her teeth, seeking refuge in the pain spiking through her head.

Sue blew through pursed lips. 'I thought I'd lost her. Lost my baby. More than a week without her—you can't understand. I trusted my baby to you for three days, but then... Oh my god, *eleven days.* You have no idea how terrible that was.'

There were no words to undo the devastation she had wrought, yet anger chased Kayla's guilt; she had a damn good idea how terrible it had been.

Sue turned to the nightstand, fiddling with the pile of gauze squares, shifting the surgical tweezers that lay on a beige tray. 'I hated you. I hated you so much, I felt sick every time I thought of you. You took my baby from me.'

She'd never meant to hurt anyone. No-one but Mother, anyway. Yet she tainted every life she touched. Dad was dead. She'd ruined the careers of the men she'd used in her teenage search for affection. And now these six children were scarred, their families devastated.

Sue's hand dropped to the mottled orange quilt, close to hers, but not touching. 'For the first twenty-four hours, we thought you'd run off the road and all...all...' Her hot-pink lips quivered. She sucked in and rushed through the words, her voice growing louder as memory consumed her. 'I wanted *you* to be dead. Because I thought you'd killed my baby.'

The failure of Sue's wish was far worse than the knowledge that her friend wanted her dead. Kayla wanted it to be over. All of it. Her thumb gouged through the cover at the old scars on her thighs, as though she could force them open, release the pain and shame building and churning inside her.

'But then we got the ransom demand, and I was so bloody furious. I couldn't understand why you'd let anyone take our children, why you hadn't fought back.'

Eyes closed, Kayla concentrated on the repetitive clicking of a ribbon taped to the air conditioning unit. *Count.* Soon she could run away.

She startled as Sue's warm palm covered her hand, pressing it into the mattress. 'Honey, I know I lost my mind. I'm sorry. I can *see* you fought for my baby.' Sue's fingers twined with hers, squeezing until it hurt. 'You fought, and you brought her back safe to me, and there just aren't words to express what I owe you. I can never, never thank you enough.'

Brought her back safe? No, the soldiers had done that. 'It wasn't—' A shadow pressed on her lids, and Kayla shrank back instinctively.

Sue's breath smelled of sweet tea. 'Honey, is there anything I can get you? Anything I can do?'

'Clothes. Whatever you can find. I have to get out of here.'

'You know me, I never travel light. I'm sure to have something you can use. Have.'

She didn't miss the choice of word. Sue wouldn't want anything that had touched Kayla's foul body returned. Her leg jiggled beneath the cover. She couldn't control it, but the frenetic movement offset the growing pain. A little.

Sue gingerly lifted a lank tress of Kayla's hair. 'Tell you what, how about I fix this up? Nothing like a makeover to cheer a girl up.'

The kidnappers had touched her hair, wrapped it around their filthy cocks as they masturbated. 'Cut it off.' If only her skin could so easily be removed.

'Whoa, overkill, much? How about we try a comb, first? I'm sure I've got one in my bag.' Sue rubbed her hand against her sleeve. Removing the contamination.

As Sue methodically combed, Kayla fixed her gaze on the bottle of fluid dripping down the plastic tube and through the needle into her arm. Life pouring into her, even as it pulsed out through the sodden bandages. Funny how life could depend on a bottle.

Perhaps that was how Mother had felt. Maybe that explained why Father supplied the alcohol; without it, Mother would have died.

Thanks to Kayla, she'd died because of it.

The captain cleared his throat from the doorway. How had she not heard him approach? She needed to be more careful; inattention let secrets escape.

Sue stood. 'I'll pop back with those clothes later, Kayla, okay? You'll need them before we fly out, anyway.'

The soldier nodded to her as she left, then addressed Kayla. 'Colley's on the radio to the Flying Doc. Seems he's delayed—a couple of road trains crashed near the border.'

Anger forced Kayla upright, struggling against the imprisoning sheet. 'I don't need another doctor. I just need to get out of here.'

The captain shrugged. 'Colley's call, not mine. Speak of the devil.'

'And an angel will appear?' Colley said as he strode in. He slipped a cuff around her arm, pumping it tight. Clicked his tongue against his teeth. 'We're not winning. Still more going out than in.'

Why did he have to say that? Didn't he know they had to pretend there was nothing wrong? Dad always understood that.

Colley dropped to his haunches. 'Kayla, you want that morphine, you need to drink.'

'I'll get something,' Nick offered.

'I don't need anything, except to get out of here.' Her voice was slurred and odd, making it hard to talk. 'What did Sue mean about a flight? I'm going home.'

Colley shook his head. 'You're not going anywhere.'

She flinched.

'Shit. I didn't mean it like that!' The medic's hand moved to the crucifix around his neck. 'Sorry. I meant you can't go anywhere until I've stabilised your condition. Your blood pressure's critically low, there's a risk you'll go into shock. Plus, I can see you're in pain. If you drink, I can give you pain meds. Okay?'

She only had to drink, then they would let her go. But inadvertently, the medic offered her a more permanent escape. Drink killed her mother, and lack of drink would kill her. Such perfect symmetry. The promise of an end dragged resolve from deep inside, clipping Kayla's tone. 'I don't want anything.'

Colley thrust a hand through his hair. 'Don't you understand? If you don't drink, you could die.'

The men knew what had happened to her, but why didn't they realise that the way to deal with it was to pretend everything was fine? Her neighbours, her teachers, her counsellors; they'd all been happy to pretend. Mother's alcoholism disguised behind the thinnest façade, their hovel hidden behind closed doors, her broken bones and bruises explained by lies, she had learned how to present as normal, and the community had accepted her act with relief. Why couldn't these men do the same?

Fatigue ate into her bones. She needed them gone. 'Don't *you* understand? I. Don't. Care.'

Silence for a second, then Nick slammed a hand onto the table near her head. 'You'll damn well drink. It's not negotiable.'

'SERIOUSLY, CHICKEN SOUP FIXES EVERYTHING?' Kayla was torn between anger at the assumption and amusement at the absurdity, as the captain returned to the room carrying a steaming bowl.

He shrugged, placing the bowl on the bedside table, seeming to have forgotten the inexplicable fury of his exit. 'One of those cute twins bails me up every time I step outside. I swear he's set up camp on the verandah, waiting for you.'

Liam. Questions trembled on her lips. *Is he alright? Is Lily?* She had divested the responsibility for them, but still, she needed someone to tell her they'd be okay. That she hadn't failed completely. 'They haven't left?'

Nick stirred the soup. 'RAAF is flying you all to Adelaide tomorrow. Some form of civvy debrief, I imagine. Anyway, your kid's getting kind the dirts up about being locked out of here. Said he's waiting for you to take them home like you promised.'

'I brought them home.'

The soldier tugged at his ear. 'Guess he figures you're not quite there yet. How about I sneak him in for a few minutes, and you explain?'

'You can't!' She had promised the kids everything would be fine once they escaped the cave; no more falls, no more cuts and bruises. If Liam saw her hooked up to the medical equipment, unable even to sit upright, her lies would be discovered. And then the children might question their own safety. 'You don't understand.'

Dominating the small space, the captain rounded on her. 'You're damned right, I don't understand. I don't understand why those sadistic bastards hurt you so bad, but I also don't understand why you'd give in to them now. Don't give me that bullshit talk about not caring if you die.'

She cowered. The officer had seemed undemanding, prone to silence, avoiding looking at her as she avoided him. She hadn't believed his promise to keep her safe, but his attack shocked her.

He jabbed a finger at the curtained window. 'You care about those kids. You cared enough to fight and damn near die for them. And you stayed alive to bring them home, right? Well, it's not done: you need to finish the job. *Your* job.'

She held up bandaged hands to fend off his anger, fury dredging up the last of her energy. 'You don't know a damn thing. I didn't fight—' Not hard enough or long enough, but she couldn't finish the sentence.

'Then what happened to your hands?'

She tucked her hands under her armpits. 'Knife.' She gave the reply reluctantly, scared not to answer in the face of his inexplicable rage.

'You grabbed a blade? What, a dozen times?' His disbelief ricocheted around the room. 'Why the hell would you do that?'

If she gave him a little, would he be appalled enough to

leave her alone? Refusing to allow the memory, she uttered the words tonelessly. 'Trade. A slice down a finger for each promise they wouldn't touch a kid. And one for each time I cried out.' She bit her lip. She shouldn't have added the last sentence; now he could count her cowardice.

The captain's throat worked as he swallowed his revulsion. His hand rasped across the stubble of his jaw. 'And that's not fighting? You did that, but now you figure you'll roll over and die, let those sick fucks who abducted your kids get away with it?'

'No, I—'

'Bastards who torture and rape women?'

He said the word. He made it real. She couldn't breathe.

Condemnation quivered through the finger he pointed at her. 'You're the adult, the only one who can testify against them, yet you want to take the easy way out? You know what? *That's* the bit I really can't understand.' He turned on his heel, stalking to the door in disgust.

'The kids are safe now. That's what matters.' It was no defence, nothing but pathetic self-justification. But she'd tried, she'd tried so damn hard, the only way she knew how, and she needed one person in the world to recognise that. 'I couldn't find a way to get them out.' *Liar.* There had been ways. The rocks. The can lids. And the trade that she couldn't bring herself to make. Though there'd been nothing left to trade once she realised that the men were intent on taking what they wanted for free. Memory and shame quivered through her. 'I was too scared. I fucked up so bad.'

Nick's jaw twitched and he pinched at his throat. 'You had every right to be scared. But no way in hell did you fail. You brought the kids out unharmed.'

She shoved herself up against the bedhead, ignoring the pain. His lie fed her anger, and anger became strength. 'Unharmed?' She spat the word back at him. 'I know how screwed up those kids will be. You think I can live with that?' She swept a hand down the length of her mummified body, the aching evidence of her failure. 'Or with this?'

The soldier crossed the room in three strides, the mattress sagging under his weight as he restrained the hand she slapped against her chest. A waft of hot cotton and fresh sweat. No cigarettes, no beer. 'Kayla, you've been so strong for those kids, you can't cop out now. You *know* that would scar them worse than anything. They need you to get through this. I get that you want to chuck in the towel, but it's not an option.'

She recoiled as his other hand moved toward her face.

He jerked back, but his eyes locked to hers, and she couldn't look away. 'I know you hurt, though I can't even imagine what you lived through. Hell, truth is, I don't want to imagine it. But that's the key; you lived. You can't stop fighting now. And I'm sorry. I'm really fucking sorry. Because I *do* know how hard that is.'

Jesus. No. He wasn't accusing her of anything. He wasn't blaming her. *No, no, no!* His sympathy could undo her, she had to cut him off. She pointed at the bowl. 'I'll eat.'

CHAPTER 15

The woman's inexplicable surrender wasn't a second too soon. Faced with the anguish in her eyes, the surge of pity had caught him, a punch in the guts Nick hid behind loud words. He'd been far too close to losing his shit.

Even so, he wasn't about to spoon the soup into her mouth. Except it was bloody obvious that, weak as a newborn kitten, Kayla couldn't do it herself.

With a light rap on the door jamb, Colley rescued him. 'Got five, Captain? Sue will take over in here.'

'Sure.' He thrust the bowl into Kayla's cocooned hand. 'You okay with this?' Forcing himself to keep his pace measured, he fled, nodding to the brassy blonde who passed him in the doorway.

Colley hiked a thumb down a thinly carpeted corridor, decorated by numbered doors every three metres. 'End room. Kim had the seized phones downloaded. Usual procedure, run through the files, check there's no Ops footage. Feds are flying in tomorrow, so we need to make sure we're clear before handover.'

Nick squared his shoulders and thrust himself back into his role. His life. 'No worries.' Better than being stuck in the room with the woman. He'd persuaded her to eat. Duty discharged.

Scattered chairs and flyers advertising long-gone events bore testament to the use of the large room as a community centre. A sticker-adorned fridge struggled noisily against the heat, an ancient wooden drink trolley leaning drunkenly against it.

Nick reversed a hard chair, straddling it to face the television screen. Cracked his neck from side-to-side, then rested his chin on his folded arms. The other officers and senior non-coms scattered across the room in various attitudes of fatigue. The Flying Doc couldn't get here soon enough.

Someone clicked the lights off as a blurred image appeared on the screen.

The picture clarified, and Nick stilled.

Forty minutes later the lights flickered back to life. His men stared at the floor rather than meet the intimate knowledge in another's gaze.

'Gonna puke,' Sommers grunted. His chair skittered across the floor and he plunged from the room.

Nick stood unsteadily, reaching for the water jug on the trolley. His white-knuckled hand shook. He shouldn't have watched. He was no better than a fucking peeping Tom.

But he'd been unable to look away.

The brief, blurred image of the girl, a cautious smile on her unscarred face as she leaned toward the bus window, had intrigued him. And suddenly he'd needed to know exactly what happened to her.

So he'd watched every minute of the footage. Every sick second.

He rolled the glass between his hands, staring into it. He had to divorce himself from this. No matter what those bastards had done to her, she wasn't his problem.

Except, if he'd ordered the mission two hours earlier, maybe it would have made all the difference. His hand tightened around the glass and he ground his teeth. Hauled his mind from where it was determined to take him.

He was due leave; he'd head up the coast. To where the sand was golden rather than red, and the girls wore bikinis rather than bandages.

Not that he'd ever be able to forget what he'd seen.

With twenty years of military experience, he knew how to process brutality. Observe. Rationalise. Accept. And then lock away both the memory and the emotion.

But this was too damn big for any of his internal boxes.

He slammed his drink onto the table. 'Fucking bastards.' Dropped back onto his chair. He could shut his eyes, but he couldn't shut out the mental replay.

Muttered words of disgust and revulsion snowballed between the soldiers, growing into a maelstrom of impotent rage. Colley cut through the storm, zipping his crucifix along the chain. 'I don't understand how she survived.'

Not words you ever wanted to hear from a medic. *Fuck.*

Kimber stood, rising onto the balls of his feet as his gaze roamed the room, waiting for each soldier to connect with him. 'I'm sure we all agree Miss Petrovic has suffered an inordinate amount, and any mention of this footage would exacerbate that hurt. Therefore, such disclosure will not occur. Lance Corporal, ascertain whether the data has been forwarded or shared.' He glanced up at the drone of an aircraft, relief written across his face. 'Ah, sounds like the Flying Doc is on top of us.'

NICK REFILLED his mug of over-brewed coffee, then raised the pot in silent offering as Colley entered the conference room with the Flying Doc. Ninety-seven minutes it had taken them to patch Kayla up. Not that he'd been counting it off, reading and rereading the posters on the wall. Trying not to envisage the footage. Or what the doctors were doing in the room down the hall.

Thank Christ they were finished. Now it remained only to transfer responsibility for the woman to either the Flying Doc or the Feds, and they'd be shot of the whole deal. Not a damn moment too soon.

Kimber nodded toward the raised pot as he strode through the doorway. 'I will, thanks, Captain.' He turned to the doctors and inclined his head toward the corridor. 'You're done in there?'

Dr. Alec McGrath peeled off surgical gloves, turning them inside one another, then flicked them into the wastepaper basket under the table. He scrubbed at his face with both hands, his accent thick with the burr of Scotland, despite years in the Outback. 'So far so good. She's stable. A bloody mess though. And I do mean bloody. I've never seen the likes of that in my life. They tortured the wee lassie. You'll be wanting me to fly her to the base hospital?'

Kimber settled into a chair and shook his head over the brimming mug. 'I've been in touch with the Minister's office, and we have something of a problem. They deem it vital to limit the public perception of the harm caused to

Miss Petrovic. Accordingly, they prefer she not be admitted to the public hospital system. I've been asked to impress upon you, Dr. McGrath, the necessity for the bulk of the medical care to be provided before we depart Murumalata.'

Magnets showered the stained carpet as Nick thrust the milk into the fridge and kicked the door shut. 'No hospital? Where the hell's she supposed to go? Do they know how fucked up she is?' Kim would call him for being out of line, but screw that.

Kimber lifted an eyebrow but maintained his level tone. 'The Office is assessing appropriate respite care options. In the interim, under the auspice of providing "targeted support in extreme situations", the government has mandated Ms Petrovic remains under the umbrella of care provided by the ADF.'

'Last I heard, that mandate was issued for a pandemic. Not...this.' Colley seemed to share Nick's reluctance to name the crime.

'So we're not handing over to the Feds? She's our problem?' Nick blurted. 'This thing's been all over the news since day one, why the hell are they worried about closing it down now?'

Kimber took a slow swallow of his drink. 'Our *employers* are eager to avoid the opportunity for the pro-gun lobby to use this incident to call for repeal on our gun laws. They're concerned that excessive coverage of this matter will bolster a call for a bill, like that in Florida, to arm teachers. Given our gun laws, that's obviously not going to happen. But they are keen to avoid the controversy.'

'You have to be kidding. Someone has to be kidding. That woman—' he jabbed his finger at the doorway, 'Is messed up to shit, but the focus is on politics? They want to the Doc to patch her up and then toss her out?'

Kimber pursed his lips, staring into his coffee. 'The directive stands, Captain. Doctor McGrath, you'll be able to complete any necessary procedures with the equipment you have on board?'

Hunkered in a chair, the rotund Scotsman shrugged, the movement placing his shoulders near his ears. 'Should be no problem. It'll be a matter of keeping the drip in, fever down, and changing dressings.'

'My place,' Nick blurted.

Colley squinted in confusion. Kim waited silently.

Hell, he usually assessed every angle before tabling a plan. Nick shuffled his cup onto the table, buying time to school his thoughts. 'You need somewhere private to put her. She needs medical care. Colley can move in—he practically lives there half the time, anyway.' The tightness in his chest eased. He would still head up the coast, but this way he kept his promise to Kayla: she'd be safe.

Colley held up both hands. 'Hang on, Captain. Don't rope me in, I know nothing about the kind of care she needs—'

'It's basic nursing, laddie,' McGrath interrupted.

Colley ran his fingers around the inside of his collar. 'No, Alec. It's not. There's more. The physical injuries you've already addressed...well, that may be the tip of the iceberg.' He looked to Kimber, a plea in his dark eyes. 'Major?'

Nick's fists balled. *More*? Hadn't they fucking finished in there?

The major returned Colley's gaze, rubbing a thumb across the face of his silver wristwatch. Eventually, he nodded. 'Doctor, the perpetrators filmed what they did to

Miss Petrovic. We are, unfortunately, intimately cognisant of Ms Petrovic's ordeal.'

Colley's crucifix chimed against his dog tags. 'Except we have less than an hour of footage to represent over a week.'

Nick didn't need to think about that discrepancy, didn't need to wonder what horrors hid in the other hours. He stared unblinkingly at the fliers taped to the wall. Read them again, trying to ignore the conversation. Damned if he'd be complicit in disclosing Kayla's secrets.

'Lieutenant Colley, please apprise Dr. McGrath of the salient facts.'

That was it, then. Kim had made his call. The force with which his chair hit the wall did nothing to allay Nick's anger. 'I don't need a recap on this crap. Sir?'

Kimber nodded. 'Dismissed, Captain.'

He stalked from the room, yanking the door so it slammed behind him. Intending to turn left, out into the burning cleanse of the late-afternoon sun where Liam no doubt waited to accost him, his feet took him right.

At his nod, Sue left the room without a word. He dragged the chair closer to the bed and slumped in it, staring at Kayla. Trying to see the woman she had been.

She twisted and moaned in restless sleep, murmured something. So he reached for her bandaged fist. Snatched his hand back, glaring at it. *What the hell?* Years of training imbued a level of detachment that made him the perfect soldier, yet this woman's raw need stripped his professional array, negated his rigid programming. He had only instinct left to guide his words and actions. And that sure as hell wasn't good enough.

The two doctors entered and he thrust to his feet. Alec

forestalled his dash for the door. 'Nae lad, it seems we'll be needing help now.'

Colley moved to the table and unwrapped fresh rolls of gauze, stacking them on a tray and tossing the wrappers toward the bin.

So many rolls.

The medic shot him a glance. 'Smithson's down the hall. Send him this way.'

Nick eyed the door. So close to escape. He could easily fetch the junior medic. 'I'll bloody do it.' Nobody else needed to be privy to Kayla's secrets.

CHAPTER 16

Pressure on her shoulders woke Kayla.

Nick. For some obscure reason, she felt safer with him nearby. Maybe because it seemed his daunting size would keep all other men away.

Hands gripped her ankles. Betrayal flashed cold through her, the breath choking in her throat. She lashed out, despite the pain. No! She wasn't going to allow this to happen.

Never again.

Out of sight, Colley's words were muffled, disjointed by her frantic kicks. 'Kayla, it's okay. Remember, this is Doc McGrath of the Flying Doctors. He's going to finish up, so we can get you home. Do you understand?'

The doctor. She understood doctors, knew what they thought, what they chose not to see.

Tired, dark circles under his eyes, the doctor groans under his breath, squinting at my shoulder. I must remember to say it was an accident. At gymnastics. Nowhere near Mother.

The soft pyjamas he pulls aside are covered in tiny pink flow-

ers. *They're so pretty, I've never had anything so nice. Mother said I must wear them, to look decent for the doctor. I blink, forcing back tears. Not because of the pain; that never makes me cry. But because the pyjamas were to be my Christmas present next week, and now there'll be nothing.*

Dad looks worried. He doesn't need to. I won't cry, and I always know what not to say.

Why couldn't these doctors be the same? Disinterested, uncaring, completing their job by rote and clocking off? She didn't want them, didn't want anyone looking at her, exuding sympathy and revulsion. *Knowing.* She squeezed her eyes tight, latched on to the only word that offered reprieve. 'Home? I can leave?' Damn, she was begging for freedom. Again.

The grip on her ankles released and Colley appeared alongside her. His hand cupped the side of her face. She shrank back, but he wasn't forcing her. Or striking her. Or hurting her. But he wasn't letting her die, either, and she wouldn't forgive that.

'Sure. Home. But Kayla, listen.' Even his voice was gentle. 'Do you hear me? You have to try and relax, okay? No one's going to hurt you.'

She heard. She wanted to believe him. But no way in hell could she relax.

One hand resting on her knee, the Flying Doctor displayed gloved fingers, his accent thicker than it had seemed earlier. 'Now, wee lady, I'm going to do a quick internal and check nothing's badly damaged. It'll no' hurt, the pain killers will take any sting out, so you've no' got tae be frightened.'

Men inside me. Christ, no. No amount of sedative could protect her from this. Colley nodded and the pressure on her shoulders returned. She jerked her head back, pressing into the pillows. Nick stood slightly behind the bed, his hands lightly on her shoulders. 'No,' she whispered. *Don't touch me. Don't let them touch me.* She'd trusted him. Told herself she was safer with him there.

But now he held her down.

Nick released her shoulders and stepped away. The blankets trembled as Colley took her ankles, drawing her legs apart. She needed to concentrate to understand McGrath's combination of suddenly soft voice and strong accent. 'Okay, Kayla, I want you to take a deep breath and let it out slowly while I count to five. One. Two. Three—'

She choked, unable to draw the oxygen past her spasming throat. She had rights. She could stop the men. But how, when fear strangled her and she couldn't even speak?

'Try again. One. Two. Three. Four. Five. Good. And another. That's it, good girl. Nice and slow. Keep breathing like that.' McGrath displayed a tube of lubricant. 'On the next breath, I'm going to slide two fingers in.'

She tried to breathe, she tried so hard, but the doctor bent over and, oh God, she could feel the warmth of his body between her thighs. Then his fingers. A whisper of sensation, he hadn't really touched her yet.

But he was going to.

She screamed.

Desperately kicking away from him, hysteria snatched at her. 'No, no, don't touch me!'

The captain reappeared, leaning across to hold her down. 'Nick. No. Please.' She writhed and bucked against McGrath's touch.

The doctor grunted and Nick released her shoulders instantly, like he couldn't stand to touch her. 'Finished?'

McGrath snorted.' 'Nothing like. Can ye hear me, Kayla?'

Jaw paralysed in terror, she panted between clenched teeth.

'Lassie, I need to push this time. It'll no' hurt, I promise. But you need to relax. Got her, laddie?'

McGrath didn't understand. It wasn't pain that scared her. It was the memories he awoke.

Nick replaced his hands on her shoulders, and she grabbed at them, adding to the pressure keeping her on the bed. Nick's hands. Real. Not nightmares. Nothing to be afraid of. He and Colley both promised nothing would hurt her.

But Dad had promised that. So many times.

The doctor bent forward. Kayla's muscles tightened and her back locked. Her teeth ground together, her broken nails gouging Nick's hands.

McGrath grunted. 'Amazing those buggers got anywhere, even wi' the pack o' them.'

'Jesus,' Nick choked.

No, not those numbers, she mustn't count those ones! She arched up, away from McGrath, as memory spun the room into blackness, her hands sliding from Nick's.

White, why was his face so white...

FEAR POUNDED through her as she startled awake.

Nick leaned against the door, consulting his phone. Colley, in a chair alongside the bed, yawned and stretched, linking his hands and reversing them to crack the knuckles.

How long had they watched her sleep? And why?

The medic stood. 'Hey. Nice timing. We're moving out shortly.'

Blood coated her teeth, fouled her breath. Hot and salty. Like...no. Don't think. She swallowed convulsively, licking at her cracked lips, pieces of dislodged skin sticking to her tongue. 'Home?'

'Sure,' Nick said as Colley detached tubes from the needle in her arm.

'Where's the doctor? The other one.' She needed to know. To make sure he wouldn't touch her again.

The medic taped gauze over the needle, keeping it in place. 'Had to fly back to base. But he left the name of a good gyno in the city. Said he'd email a referral.'

'No more doctors.' She was going home. She'd done nothing wrong. Nothing they knew about, anyway. They couldn't hold her.

Colley coiled the IV line. 'Not a doctor. Specialist.'

'No.' He couldn't force her to do a damn thing.

The other men did.

But that was over, now. She'd never be that weak again. She only needed to work out how to forget, how to erase it from her mind, like she had done with everything in her past.

Except that wasn't true, because all the denied memories had crowded back; her mother, her father, her lovers jockeying for position in her brain. All current and painful, stealing her focus.

Colley twisted closed a garbage bag of hospital waste. 'I'll dump this and grab you a drink.'

'I'll go—' Nick spoke too late, the door latching with a muted click behind his colleague.

After what he'd witnessed, Kayla wanted Nick gone

every bit as much as he wanted to escape. But, the memories unleashed, she had to find a way to control them. Her history she would somehow shove back down inside, try and contain it. But the kidnappers...Tomas had threatened he'd never let her go. She needed to know where he was.

The captain's hand covered hers. 'What is it?'

The words locked in her throat. He had big hands. Bigger than her father's. Stronger. 'The men—'

His grip tightened. 'Under guard, on their way to the city. By road. My sergeant's a hard-ass. Those bastards will be glad when he hands them over to the cops. Don't worry. You're safe.'

She didn't struggle from his grip. The warm pain tied her to reality. Briefly kept the darkness at bay. Between that, the morphine coursing her veins, and knowing the men would be punished, perhaps she could survive.

Twenty minutes later, Nick slowed the truck around the sole corner in the town, cursing it over the bumps.

Kayla perched on the edge of the seat, inhaling hot plastic and dust—far better than the iron tang of blood and antiseptic that permeated the motel room. Lips compressed, she strained to counter the sway of the vehicle without touching the man on either side of her. It was like the game she'd played as a kid, treading carefully to avoid the cracks in the pavement so the elephant waiting around the corner wouldn't crush her. Only now, the men were the cracks, and pain the elephant.

Within seconds, a dusty paddock spliced by a pot-holed blacktop surface came into view. A plane sat on it like a discarded child's toy. Nick pulled up twenty metres from the aircraft and jumped out, then strode to meet Kimber partway across the strip.

A wave from the major and Colley also clambered out, holding up a cautionary hand. 'Don't move till I come back.'

She could barely keep upright, but morphine provided enough of a cushion to find humour in his order. 'You're kidding, right?'

'Ah. Yeah. Sorry.' Colley flashed a commiserating grin, then headed across the paddock.

The three men conferred, glancing from her to the squat plane. Nick dropped to his knees on the melting tarmac, investigating something from beneath the protection of the plane's pregnant belly, then stood, licking at burnt palms before shading his eyes to stare into the distance.

Warmth trickled between Kayla's shoulder blades. God, let it be sweat.

Colley swung open the door. 'The press are interviewing on the other side of the plane. We'll get you settled in before they spot us. Captain, I'll pass her down. You carry her over while I grab my kit.'

'Like hell. I'm walking.' Couldn't they see how it would look if they carried her? Like there was something wrong with her. And there damn well wasn't.

Colley shook his head. 'It'll be faster this way.'

'No.' She was sick of people telling her what to do. It was like being a child again. And nothing good ever happened when she was a child.

Kimber glanced back toward the plane. 'We need to move now, gentlemen.'

Colley shook his head. 'This is a bad idea. But let's go.'

He helped her down and, sandwiched between the officers, she hid her wince with each slow step across the tarmac.

They almost made it to the plane before the journalists rounded the nose of the aircraft, barrelling toward them.

Nick tensed. 'Shit.'

Colley took a step backward. 'Hell.'

She teetered in the no-man's land of their indecision, her balance shot. Camera flash set fire to the desert and Nick scooped her up, bolting for the boarding steps and up into the plane. He lay her on a narrow stretcher in the sectioned-off fuselage, and then whirled to face Kimber. 'If the government wants it kept quiet, what the hell are those vultures doing here?' Knuckles white, his hand wrapped the edge of the stretcher.

Odd he seemed so angry. She wasn't. She drifted in a pleasant, painless haze.

Kimber drummed his fingers on the bulkhead. 'As it was judged inflammatory to order a media blackout, a very select presence has been condoned by the Government.'

'Christ—'

'Captain.' Colley squeezed into the cubicle and jerked his chin toward her. 'Cool it. Let me get Kayla settled and a drip set up.'

Nick cast around for a moment, then ducked through the opening in the particleboard. Head twisted to one side, Kayla watched him through the small window. He shouldered past journalists and photographers and strode across the tarmac. Toward what? The burning nothingness of the desert? There was nothing to run to. She could tell him that. Life was all about running away.

CHAPTER 17

'Green stuff.' Nick stared out of the window, not to admire the verdant outskirts of the city appearing between the puffs of cirrus cloud below them, but to avoid looking at Kayla.

He tugged at his shirt, pulling the cotton from his chest. Could smell his own sweat. Striding around the airstrip to walk off his anger had been an exercise in futility. The need to do so proved he was way too invested in this mission. The team had retrieved the kids: that should've been his cut-off. What the hell was different this time?

Shooting his cuff, Kimber timed the pilot's precision. 'Another seven minutes and we'll be down.'

The hairs on Nick's arms prickled as Kayla moaned and rolled her head where she lay on the stretcher. Pale as paper, inked by bruises.

Forehead furrowed, Kimber glared at her. 'Captain West, given the Government directive regarding the shaping of public knowledge, you'll accompany Lieutenant Colley as he transitions Miss Petrovic to the recuperation facility. It's incumbent upon us to make certain tabloid exposure is limited.'

'Sir.' Maybe he should use Kim's label on his letterbox. *The Recuperation Facility*. Kim had run with his idea, effectively honouring Kayla's wish to limit her exposure to other medical staff. Nick couldn't get her home, not yet, but he could at least give her his.

Colley cradled the girl's face between his palms. 'Kayla, are you awake?' Her eyes rolled unwillingly open but didn't focus, and his tone rang urgently. 'Can you hear me?'

Her hand twitched in vague acknowledgment.

They surged through a pocket of turbulence, and Colley frowned as Kayla's jaw clenched, shifting beneath the bruises. 'The morphine is wearing off.' He rubbed his crucifix with his thumb. 'I'm not happy with the way she's responding. We're past the walking-by-herself farce. We'll unbolt the stretcher, take her to the transport on that rather than keep shifting her.'

On his feet the instant the tyres screeched onto the runway in a melt of hot rubber, Nick squatted and wrenched free the last couple of bolts securing the bed. Aware of Kayla's short, sharp breaths, he kept his eyes on the job, tried not to look at her face. Remembered the pretty, unscarred girl from the film, instead.

He skidded a bolt across the floor. Why the hell was he thinking about what she *had* looked like?

Kimber stood, every one of his sixty-two years unusually evident in his bearing. He pulled aside an edge of the fabric dividing their section from the main body of the aircraft. 'Good. The press are disembarking. I was concerned they might try and wait us out.' He bent across the small space toward the thick window. 'Goddamn it!' His fist pounded the glass.

Nick stared. Kim never lost his cool.

Just like he himself never…never what?

Never allowed pity to intrude. That's what was screwing with him, pure and simple. He had to get a grip. The mission practically over, it was time to debrief and then get back to punishing physical routines and paper mountains. Everything neat and orderly, no room for emotion.

Or for thoughts he shouldn't have.

Kimber leaned his forehead against the window. 'This is a regular bloody circus. There's an entire fleet of ambulances out there.'

'I thought the government were keeping it quiet?'

'Keeping her condition quiet,' Kimber tilted his head toward Kayla, his tone unusually acerbic. 'But there's no need to downplay their concern for the children, given that they all appear to be fine.'

'Looks like more media, too.' Colley peered beyond him. 'Maybe if we wait a while—'

A sharp grunt of pain echoed in the tin can, Kayla's eyelids fluttering as her pupils rolled backward.

Colley grabbed the IV line. 'Fuck. Vein's collapsed. We need her in ICU immediately. Hold one of those ambulances, Major.'

'On it.'

'What the hell?' Nick grabbed Colley's wrist. 'You said she'd be okay now.'

Thumbs pressing urgently along Kayla's arm, Colley shook him off as he tried to raise a vein. 'I've got a fucking stethoscope, mate, not a magic wand. I need a cardio team. Look at the colour of her lips.'

He couldn't.

But Colley wasn't working the crucifix. He wasn't silently praying. It'd be fine.

It had to be.

Colley tugged a corner of the sheet to cover Kayla's pale face. 'Let's go.'

The stretcher in a death-grip, Nick backed down the steps, refusing to look at the slight form hidden beneath the sheet. Shrouded. Like a corpse.

Journalists closed around them before Colley had negotiated the last step. A manicured claw stretched from the crowd and tweaked aside the sheet, exposing Kayla's bruised face.

'Get the hell out of the way!' The bellow stripped his throat. But it momentarily deflected the stunned journalists, the crowd reflexively retreating.

Colley dropped his end of the stretcher into the nearest ambulance and Nick slammed it home, then lunged aboard. Kayla wasn't safe without him.

Siren blaring, the trip from airport to hospital took only minutes. The longest minutes of his life, as the ambo and Colley worked over Kayla's prone, silent form.

Her bed piled with equipment from the ambulance, they jogged through metres of stark hospital corridors, but still didn't evade the supposedly-forbidden media. Journalists crowded the doorway the panting nurse indicated, proving the government had failed to exercise their authority effectively. Well then, he had every damn right to see them off. He angled toward the journos, but Colley's hand tightened on his upper arm. 'Not our fight anymore, Captain.'

The medic was right. He was off the hook. As the orderlies trundled the bed into a private room, medical staff flocking around Kayla in a flurry of white coats, he should be relieved.

Yet that wasn't what he felt.

Christ, he wasn't supposed to *feel* anything. 'It's not right,' he muttered. 'She deserves better than this.' They had stolen the last of her privacy.

Privacy he'd already breached by watching the footage.

'You heading to the barracks for debrief?' Colley said. 'Tell Kim I'll be along when Kayla's settled.'

His jaw was stiff. 'Roger that.' He twisted the slouch hat between his hands, fiddled with the golden crest on one side. Shot a glance at Colley. The lieutenant always saw far too much. Knew him better than any man alive, since Dad died. Saying anything was a risk. 'Just...take care of her, okay?'

He elbowed between hospital staff and crossed to the bed. Kayla lay unconscious, dwarfed by machines. Utterly defenceless. Taking her hand, he squeezed it gently. Chest tight, his throat ached.

She'd wanted to die. And there was not a damn thing he could do to prevent it now. 'Promise me you'll hang in there, Kayla.' The humming of machines and clicking of cameras made his words inaudible to anyone else. Probably even to her.

Hat pulled low over his eyes, he strode from the room.

He hated when he didn't have control of a situation.

CHAPTER 18

K ayla's arm tingled unpleasantly, the borrowed blood coursing sluggishly through collapsed veins. Her eyes flickered open, then closed again. Once. Twice.

The smell of the hospital gave it away. She remembered that smell. And the dead body in the bed. The fried corpse they said was her dad.

With unsteady fingers, she tugged the needle from her arm and ripped the monitoring pads from her chest. Shoved aside the bleached sheets. Fuck this. She was going home. 'He agreed, he bloody agreed.'

Her knees buckled when her feet hit the floor, and an iron grip crushed her chest. Hand clutched to her stomach, she crumpled to the scuffed linoleum, sobbing almost soundlessly.

The squeak of rubber footsteps intruded, and blue hospital uniform pants hove into view.

She had to cling to her anger, deny any other *feeling*. 'Leave me alone.'

'Okay,' a disembodied voice replied agreeably. 'I only

dropped in to introduce myself. I'm R.N. Scotty McGrath. The Flying Doc's son, in case you're trying to place the name. Lieutenant Colley phoned through to say he'd be here in about ten minutes, if you looked like waking. See ya.'

If Colley found her like this, she stood no chance of escape. Acid licked at her belly, the bile of asking for help clawing its way up. 'Wait. Give me a hand getting back on the bed? Damn thing's so high, I need a ladder.' *Keep it funny. Don't let him suspect.*

'No sweat.' The nurse easily lifted her.

Another strange man pawing at her. *Get your hands off me, get your hands off me, get your hands off me.*

His voice boomed in her ear. 'You've pulled some stitches through. I'll call in a doc.'

Too close, too close. She blinked at his uniform. 'Who did you say—' The ache in her chest blossomed, exploded into a roar that drowned out her thoughts. The nurse's face faded in the smoke-filled room.

She had to tell him not to go toward the fire.

Except...what fire?

The campfire.

She needed to warn the children. 'Ryan?' Her voice rose. God, she couldn't see them, where had they gone? 'Ryan, keep the kids away from the fire!'

Who? The names disappeared from her lips. Regardless, they were in danger and only she could save them. She flung herself onto the embers, smothering the flames. The smell of charred flesh and weeping blood strong in her nostrils, fiery tongues licked up her thighs. Only now the tongues weren't of clean, cauterising fire. They belonged to the faces crowding her. She screamed, fighting free of the hands that restrained her, the open mouths that yelled silently at her.

The smoke cleared and Nick was there, swearing to keep her safe.

But he'd vanish, like the children had, leaving her alone with these strangers.

God, she didn't want to be alone anymore.

CHAPTER 19

Nick broke into a jog, the ominous strobe of the light outside Kayla's hospital room surging adrenaline through him.

Colley matched his pace, but swung in front of him, blocking the doorway. 'Wait.'

Medical staff surrounded Kayla's thrashing body. More streamed along the corridor, pushing into the room and elbowing for space. The bed rocked, in danger of tipping as Kayla convulsed.

He shook Colley off and pushed through the nurses. Cradling Kayla's face between his hands, he forced her unfocused gaze to him. Jesus, he should never have left her alone hours earlier. She'd made it clear she was terrified. And he'd made promises. 'Kayla. It's me, Nick. Kayla, listen to me.'

Recognition flickered within the grey eyes. He slid an arm beneath her shoulders. 'It's okay now. Settle down. We're taking you home.'

Kayla clutched at him, twisting a hand in his shirt, her pupils huge. 'Nick!'

'Yeah, I'm—'

She arched back in his arms, suddenly rigid.

'Out of the way.' A white-coated doctor pushed him aside and ripped at Kayla's hospital-issue gown.

Colley seized his shoulder. 'Captain, stand down! She's flat-lining.'

No. She was okay now. The danger had been in the desert.

'Nick! She's in cardiac arrest. Back the fuck off!'

He shook off the medic. Colley was wrong. He needed to take Kayla home like they'd promised. Keep her safe. She'd be fine.

One hand across the other, the doctor brought his weight down on Kayla's chest. Blood oozed between his fingers as scars ripped open beneath the pressure.

Each compression crushed Nick's own chest.

The ER doctor watched the monitor. 'V-fib. Give me the paddles. Charge. Clear.'

Kayla's body jumped under the defibrillator.

Nick held his breath.

'Clear.'

Life registered on the monitor. The peaks small and far between, the valleys deep and elongated; but definitely life.

He sagged against the wall, seeking solidity. Long minutes passed, but he couldn't move. Could only watch as the medical teams stabilised Kayla, taped her to machines. Imprisoned her with wires.

The doctor checked the drip, then peeled off bloodied gloves. 'She'll be fine now, providing she keeps calm. Don't worry, she's all hooked up. We can hear the alarms at the station.'

Colley nodded at the doctor's retreating form, then turned to Nick 'You okay?'

He grunted, then shook his head, sliding down the wall until he rested on his haunches. 'Jesus,' he muttered. 'Jesus Christ.' He stared at his hands. Capable of caressing a lover, building a wall, stripping a gun. Hands capable of killing a man. But fucking useless hands, incapable of protecting a young woman.

Colley indicated the heart monitor. 'She's all right, mate. Lucky it happened here, not back of Burke. Christ knows what triggered it now, though.'

'I know.' A nurse remained on the far side of the bed, his expression almost guilty. 'I came in twenty minutes ago and she was on the floor, swearing like a trooper. Saying something about a promise. Only agreed to get back in the bed when I mentioned you were coming in.' Freckles stood out in orange blotches on his pale face. He waved an unsteady hand. 'She's talking, then suddenly her eyes roll back and she starts to shake and cry.' A shadow crossed his face and he finished the sentence on a mutter. 'Jesus, she looked so scared.'

For the first time in ten years, Nick craved his dad's advice so bad it hurt. He'd fucked up big time and didn't know how to fix it. Dad would've taken the facts, noted them down, carefully unravelled them. Probably made some sort of diagram or chart. He'd have talked Nick through, quiet and calm, helped him see where he'd gone wrong and find the solution.

But he knew where he'd gone wrong: he'd lied to Kayla. Told her she was safe, told her she was going home. Yet why did he care? She wasn't his responsibility, he should be able to dismiss her as simply another victim. He'd seen plenty. Why the hell should she be any different?

Dad would say the *why* didn't matter, only the *how*. How would he fix his mess?

Nick forced himself upright. Refrigerated air burned through his flared nostrils. His chest ached with the massive intake of oxygen. Good. He needed the focus. 'We have to get her out of here.'

Colley's eyes hardened. 'First I need Yarrow Place to come in and handle the sexual assault side of things. And I told you, it'll take a couple of days to run tests. Yeah, I know.' He intercepted Nick's objection with a raised hand. '*No more doctors.* But I'm not a gyno, and I'm so far out of my depth I need water wings. We need a sonographer for a transvaginal ultrasound—an internal,' he clarified, as though determined to spell out the worst-case scenario while he could negate Nick's objections. 'She's too dehydrated for a standard pelvic ultrasound. I want a complete set of MRIS, and I need to make certain her heart's not going to do backflips again.'

Nick moved his head minimally, restraining his anger. Colley would question it, and he sure as hell didn't have an answer.

Colley dug his hands into his pockets. 'It's the best I can do, Captain. Your house might offer the desired privacy—though it's like we're trying to shut the bloody stable door after that debacle—but my primary concern has to be whether I can provide the care she needs. I'll only transfer Kayla when I'm certain she's stable. It won't be for a few days—and that's assuming I can get her in to the specialists without delay. You know how backed-up the arse the hospital system is.'

'There will be no delays.' Entering the room, Kimber returned their salutes. 'You give me the names, the specialists will be available immediately.'

'I'll get on to it, sir,' Colley said. 'Alec mentioned there's potentially a couple of operations to minimise internal bleeding. I can't get her out of here until that's dealt with.'

Jesus. Nick mashed his lips together, staring at the ceiling until he'd regained control. 'She can't be left alone again.'

Colley had his phone out, thumb scrolling. 'Captain, I can't be everywhere at once.'

'I know. I'll take the leave I'm due. I'm staying.'

Kimber's gaze bored into him. 'No need to take leave, Captain. Miss Petrovic will remain under ADF protection. You and Lieutenant Colley will roster.'

CHAPTER 20

'Hey there.' Colley lifted her wrist from the mattress, checking her pulse. 'How are you feeling?'

Kayla massaged her chest with the other hand. 'Flying on morphine. I think I may be addicted.' A life raft, drugs had kept her head above water the last few days, yet the pain could still snatch at her, drag her into the inky depths.

Colley nodded. 'Morphine's good, but not magic. Before we can bust you out of this place, we have a few things to get through. That DNA I mentioned?'

Kept mentioning, more like. DNA tests were for suspects. Perpetrators, offenders, criminals. Why the hell should she allow someone to hunt her body for traces of....She shuddered, rolling her head away from Colley on the flat hospital pillow. She had rights, and if this was the only one she could exercise, she bloody well would.

'Kayla, I promise the DNA collection is painless.'

Physically, maybe. But he wasn't allowing for how demeaning the constant parade of *interested* medical staff was. The tests and procedures he'd already forced on her had been excruciating. Humiliating.

'Optimally, it should have been done within seventy-two hours.'

Seventy-two hours from what? The last time they'd assaulted her? The first? She was trying so damn hard to convince herself that she'd scrubbed their filth from her body, yet Colley seemed intent on pointing out the impossibility.

'Our window is about closed.'

'Then bloody lock it,' she ground through clenched teeth. 'Last I checked, South Australia supports the right to bodily autonomy.' Considering her current position, the statement was laughable, but instead her lips trembled with sobbing betrayal. 'They kidnapped the kids. There's no need for DNA proof.' Obstinately, she clung to the inference that kidnapping was all the men had done. If her mother, her father, had created their own truths, why the hell shouldn't she?

Colley sighed. 'All right. We'll cross that bridge when we come to it. Let's just get the paperwork signed off, shall we?' He paused, as though he expected her argument. But she wasn't capable of speaking again yet. Not without giving herself away. Anger could only carry her so far.

'I'll read through what I've got, stop me if it's wrong. Name, height, weight, I've pulled from the admission form.'

As he ran through the basic details, she neither commented nor corrected. Days of experience with the probing, prodding specialists had taught her the less she spoke, the sooner they left her alone.

A minute later, Colley flipped to the second page of the questionnaire and read silently. Lines furrowed his forehead. 'Sorry. These are pretty invasive.' He glanced up as a trolley squeaked along the corridor, teacups rattling. Waited for the steps to recede. 'Right. Were you a virgin when this, uh, this incident occurred?'

Shit. Actual questions. She responded to the wall over his left shoulder. 'I'm twenty-four. What do you think?'

'So that'd be a no, then? When—' Colley swiped a hand across his mouth. 'At approximately what age did you lose your virginity?'

She elbowed up in the bed. 'You're kidding me, right?' No way could he handle the truth. At fourteen she had come home with an experimentally traded love-bite, and Mother added 'slut' to her labels—so she spent the next five years earning the title. She knew sex, in so many forms: Currency. Apology. Bribery. Gift. And a constant attempt to fill the emptiness inside. Men made love to her, but she simply fucked them, rejecting their emotional needs. And despising her own.

Because love was weakness.

'Sorry. These questions are intense, but apparently they're standard form for the sexual assault forensic exam. The detail might also help with your victim impact statement.'

Her jaw tensed. 'I'm not a victim.'

Colley lifted an eyebrow and waved his pen the length of her sheet-covered body.

'I'm not a victim.' She said it louder, like she could cement the fact. 'I traded to keep the kids safe.'

Colley's breath escaped in a sharp explosion. 'Jesus. Kayla, I—'

'What was the question?'

She waited for him to repeat it. Then she lied. 'Eighteen.' The government had no right to her buried past.

A few minutes later, Colley's cheeks chipmunked with relief and he set the clipboard on the bed. He pulled on gloves. 'Okay, then. Physical assessment and we're done.' He moved careful fingers across her ribs. 'Does this hurt?'

Nostrils flaring, she stared past his ear. 'Not too much.'

'Scale of one to ten, how much is 'not too much'?'

She shook her head, refusing to quantify the pain, to validate it. But her heart pounded with the fear of surging memories. '*Does it hurt, honey? Did you make Mummy mad again? Tell Daddy, then it'll be all better.*' But there was never an answer that diminished the sting of her mother's loathing. 'Ow!'

Colley snatched his hand back. 'That much, huh?'

'Not until you whacked it.'

'Sorry. This wound's deep, and bruised up real bad.'

'Thanks, I think I could probably have figured that out by myself.' She had to keep it funny, but her words came out jerky. Dammit, Colley should dose her up before he did this. Dose her up so that she didn't have to think about his hands on her body, his too-intent gaze on her flesh.

He prodded again, probably gently, but a bolt of pain lanced through her. She grabbed the sides of the narrow bed, jerking upright as agony mushroomed within her.

His hands on her shoulders, Colley pressed her back against the pillow. 'Okay, try not to move around, or you'll rip the stitches. Breathe through it, Kayla. Just breathe.'

How bloody ridiculous was that direction? Her pent-up breath sobbed out as she subsided.

The pen scratched across Colley's notes. 'Continuing the course of antibiotics. The whole area's infected.' He set aside the pen and scrubbed a hand across his face. 'You know, this would go a lot easier if you'd give me some feedback.'

'Easier for whom?'

Colley pulled a wry face, though deep creases grooved his cheeks like he'd not slept well. 'Right now, I'd settle for either of us.'

'No free passes. You dragged me back here, remember?'

He snorted. 'Nick doesn't let me forget it. But if you just let me know what hurts?'

'Nothing.' She wasn't stupid, she knew Mother's insistence that she camouflage injury hadn't stemmed from a maternal desire to impart strength. Yet denial had become habitual.

Colley dropped his clipboard on the bed with a defeated sigh. 'After what those bastards did to you, I don't believe that.'

'I can handle it.'

'You're not handling it, you're hiding it.' Colley pointed at her torso. 'If you don't talk, those scars won't be your worst ones.'

'Seriously? You actually use that line?' Then he knew nothing about pain, physical or mental—because sometimes, hiding was the only option. 'Talking doesn't make anything any better. It makes it *real*.' She daren't let herself think, for even a moment, that someone actually cared. There had been plenty who pretended, but they always failed her.

Colley pulled a crucifix from within his shirt, and she shook her head warningly. She'd said her share of prayers but it was clear that pleas uttered so deep within the bowels of the earth couldn't reach the ears of the Almighty. 'Leave me alone.'

'I know they hurt you, in ways that don't show in bruises and scars. Ways that can't be treated with antibiotics and morphine.'

Liar. 'Psychology's a load of crap. Unless you're on TV, making millions.'

He reached for her hand. 'That's not what I mean. Kayla, when you're unconscious, or asleep, you…talk.'

Her eyes grazed Colley's. Read the unpalatable truth. Her stomach lurched, her fingers turning to ice as she wrenched her hand from his.

'Kayla, it's like everything you're bottling up is fighting for release. You have to let it out.'

Her voice cracked, muffled by her hands. 'Leave me alone! I don't want to remember.'

He stroked the hair back from her forehead.

No one had ever done that.

'You do remember, Kayla, that's the problem. You don't get to shove fear and pain into a little box and lock the emotion away. That never works. It grows inside you, like a cancer.'

The hand on her hair paused. Maybe he would stop talking. Now, while she could still keep it together, holding her breath to stop the tears, trying not to hear the lies that whispered perhaps she didn't have to do this alone.

His words tore at her defences. 'You have to expose the memory. Talk about it. Not just once, but until it no longer has any power over you. Give it conscious thought. Get angry. Get sad. Anything, just stop internalising.'

She shook her head, her heart pounding in her ears.

'What is it that terrifies you so much that even asleep you beg for it to stop?'

She couldn't risk thinking about it, needed him to leave,

now! Her hands hid her face, but her words, too small to encompass the enormity of the pain, snuck out. 'They hurt me.'

Colley's arms were around her instantly. Securing and protecting her. Only he didn't hush her like the others had. Teachers, neighbours, counsellors, cops. They'd pretend to care. Maybe they really did. But they couldn't *do* anything other than utter platitudes. Ultimately, she ended up alone with Mother, paying for her betrayal.

She desperately tried to retract the admission. 'But it was only sex. It meant nothing.'

Still Colley simply held her, like he knew he had breached the dam, and waited for the truth to spill.

She sucked in a ragged breath. A whiff of hand sanitiser and cologne. Not blood and shit and sweat. Her body trembled, impermissible emotions fighting for escape. Maybe there was catharsis in talking, maybe someone could share her pain, maybe Colley *could* help.

Because someone had to, she couldn't bear this alone.

Her armour cracked, and the words poured forth. 'Oh God, it hurt. Make it stop hurting. Please, please make it stop.'

CHAPTER 21

'Shit.' Nick pulled the khaki wagon to the kerb, his mouth dry. Why the hell hadn't he foreseen this? It wasn't like the government's attempt to bury the story had succeeded in quieting the outspoken reactions of the well-funded gun lobby, which had, predictably, further inflamed public interest. Nor did the media hide their obscene interest in the girl. But he'd had no choice. Earlier, he had stood outside her room. Heard her pain, watched her sob herself into a drug-induced sleep. His gut had twisted with something like...jealousy? No, that made no sense. Why would he care that she found momentary comfort in Colley's arms?

But he'd needed to get her out of the hospital. Perhaps, away from the smell of antiseptic and anaesthetic, she could begin to forget. Because Colley was wrong; sometimes, locked boxes were the only way to cope.

Beside him, Kayla lifted her chin from her chest, assessing the scene two hundred metres ahead. Emblazoned with logos and prickling with antenna like metallic beetles, vehicles bottlenecked the street. Deserting the stately security of their bluestone houses, residents stood between elegant iceberg rosebushes, peering through wrought-iron railings at the milling crowds. A group of cheering, flag-waving schoolchildren heightened the carnival atmosphere.

Kayla's tongue traced her lips. 'Don't tell me this is your place.'

'Okay, I won't tell you. But my neighbours are probably coming for me with pitchforks.' He flicked off the whining air conditioner, then clenched the steering wheel again. His knuckles gleamed white as the human tide swept toward them. 'Keep your head down.' Revving the engine, he released the clutch with a jerk, slammed his palm on the horn, and then anti-climactically crawled through the journalists who blocked his tree-lined driveway. Immune to the cavalcade of camera flash, the garage door ponderously retracted. Kayla shrank in the bucket seat alongside him. 'Shit, I'm sorry,' he managed. 'We should have done this at night.'

Tyres squealing, he hit the ramp into the garage and was out of the car, vaulting the hood of the wagon almost before the engine stopped turning. Opened Kayla's door as the garage roller slowly descended.

Too slowly.

'Nick, Nick, Nick.' The chant fell apart amid squeals and screams.

'Jesus.' He fumbled for the house key as he helped Kayla the few paces to the door.

'You regularly come home to a fan club?'

In the days since the RAAF retrieval flight landed in Adelaide, he and Colley had been dogged by journos and a growing crowd of enthusiastic followers. Until now, the phenomenon had only vaguely irritated him. He shoved the door. 'Only when I'm trying to create an impression.'

'Money well spent, then.'

The thick stone walls muffling the chorus, he guided Kayla through the vaulted entry hall, resisting the urge to lift her down the three shallow steps to the sunken lounge. She'd made clear her feelings on that kind of nurse-maiding.

He eased her onto the worn burgundy leather Chesterfield and piled up the cushions. Like he could hide her.

Bit bloody late.

Then he stood back, tugging on his ear. Why the hell did he feel so unprepared? A clerk from the barracks had volunteered to help sort the place, made fresh beds and stocked the fridge. She'd been less keen on the job when he made it clear his bedroom didn't require her ministrations. Sue had dropped off boxes full of—whatever, female stuff—and Colley set up what looked ominously like a full-blown surgery in one of the guest rooms.

Everything was in order.

Everything except his mind.

Fact was, no amount of physical preparation could mentally equip him to deal with the assignment. Now he had Kayla here, Nick had no idea what he should do with her. Damn it, maybe Colley was right; the hospital would have been the best place for her.

But she didn't want to be there.

He gestured toward the kitchen, separated from the lounge room by a granite bench swirled through with the browns and ochres of the Flinders Ranges. 'Would you like a drink or something?'

'No, thanks.' Kayla scrutinised her knees with tongue-tied intensity.

He cast around the room for an icebreaker. Considering how fast he was sinking, he'd more likely find an iceberg. 'Colley should be here soon.' Not soon enough.

Kayla rubbed her shoulder with a bandaged hand.

He tucked another cushion behind her. He doubted he'd ever used one of the damn things, before. They were a relic from mum's decorating. *Mum*. If she'd been here, it would have been so much easier. But that pretty much encompassed his life. 'Shoulder giving you trouble?'

'Aches a bit.' Kayla followed the admission with a grin, a flash of brightness in his direction. 'But I'll take a raincheck on a massage.'

Jesus. How did he respond without it seeming that he trivialised her pain? The deafening silence stretched. He thrust his hands into the pockets of his fatigues. 'Sorry, I'm not used to this.'

'What, entertaining strange women in your home?' Kayla quirked an eyebrow, though her grey gaze flickered past him, as though landing would be dangerous.

'Entertaining strange women in my lounge room.' *Shit*. Glib reply, like she was one of the guys from the squad. Could he get it any more wrong?

She dipped her chin. 'Touché.'

The breath trapped by his ignorance escaped in a rush. Kayla wasn't high maintenance or precious. Her sense of humour, though disconcerting, could make things easier.

Or so much worse, because it was something else those bastards had damaged.

He balanced the television remote on a cushion alongside her. 'I'm going to change, then catch forty winks.'

Strode down the hall to his bedroom. Polished boots kicked under the bed, he dropped his uniform to the floor and stretched, angling his back to crack each vertebra individually. The tension dissipated. It wouldn't be so bad. Kayla could watch TV and he'd do his own thing.

He pulled on a pair of faded jeans and padded back to the kitchen to rummage through the unusually well-stocked fridge. 'Sure I can't get you a drink?'

Across the bench, he caught the negative movement of Kayla's head. Beer in hand, he closed the fridge, then changed his mind. Opened it, and poured a juice. He placed the glass on the wooden trunk in front of Kayla, and then sank into his favourite armchair, sliding down so his shoulders were level with the back. From the corner of his eye, he caught Kayla's glance.

Not at the juice. At him.

Her hands clenched.

Fuck.

He counted off the endless seconds, trying to appear unhurried as he drained his beer. Damn stuff wouldn't go down quick enough. 'Colder in here than I thought. Better grab a shirt.' He unfolded from the chair and paced each step, casual and calm. Teeth gritted.

Slammed the wardrobe door. Yanked a long-sleeved henley over his head, and tugged it roughly into place. A big part of him wanted to be pissed that he couldn't relax in his own house—but he knew that was a cop out for his thoughtlessness. What the hell should he say to Kayla? Anything? Nothing?

Returning to the lounge room, he dropped an unnecessary rug across her knees. Reclined with a groan and propped his feet on the coffee table. 'Throw a cushion at me

if you need anything. Or if I snore.' With Kayla safe, at least
he'd finally be able to sleep.

Stupid. There'd never been a reason for him to lose
sleep: she wasn't his responsibility.

NICK'S cramped shoulder demanded he wake. Yawning, he
stretched his arms. 'I needed—'

Face pale in the flickering light, Kayla stared on the TV.

'What's up?' She didn't respond, and his gut clenched.
Shit. She was having some kind of medical episode. Bare
feet cringing on the floorboards, he strode to her side and
grasped her chin, turning her face to him. 'Kayla?'

She blinked, refocused to meet his eyes, then let her
gaze slide. 'Nothing. Only—' Jaw tense against his palm, she
swallowed. 'They know, don't they?' A flick of her hand indicated the television.

He shook his head groggily, trying to tune his ear to the
news item. He was missing something. Something important. 'About the drugs in prison? No brainer.'

'About me.'

His lungs squeezed, forcing him a half-step back. 'Well,
the kidnapping hit the news from day one.'

Her eyes sparked anger at his dissembling. 'They *know*,
don't they?'

He yanked on his ear. 'Gutter journalism. They'll make
up crap for a ratings grab.'

'You're right. There's no proof.'

No proof? She hadn't looked in a mirror.

Or at the footage.

A dimple appeared and disappeared with hypnotic

rhythm beneath the long scar on Kayla's cheekbone as she bit the inside of her cheek. 'They'll forget about me, right?' Her anger evaporated, she was pleading. Her need drew him closer, a spider trapping him in her web of pain.

No. What the hell was he thinking? The girl simply wanted reassurance.

Which he couldn't offer, not unless he lied outright. Because before she could slide back into obscurity, she was to be prime political propaganda at a bullshit official function. He ground his palm against the knot in his chest. Why did the thought of her leaving bother him?

Probably because any idiot could see she couldn't manage alone.

Yeah, that was the only reason.

At least once she escaped back to wherever the hell it was she came from, there would be no risk of her learning the true extent of her exposure.

CHAPTER 22

K ayla rested her elbows on the windowsill, the chink beneath the blind allowing a letterbox view of the courtyard behind the house. The garden held a hidden allure, although she would never bother exploring the interior of Nick's home. Long ago, in a different lifetime, she had become accustomed to the unfamiliarity of strange men's houses.

Who was she kidding? It wasn't a different lifetime. Despite her years of abstinence, her denial and pretence, she was no different than she had been. No better.

'Morning.'

Blood prickled her chest as it drained from her face. Nick's military training lent silence to his bare feet. She covered her reaction with a smile. 'Hey.'

'Sorry. Wasn't thinking.'

'I'm not *that* fragile.' She turned back to the window, pressing her fingertips to the frosted glass. Winced at the movement. Despite the warmth of the room, goosebumps rippled across her skin, a rash of wake-up reminders to any part of her that forgot to ache. The passing twinge meant the narcotic buffer was wearing thin.

Her heart raced, but she refused to check the time on the grandfather clock ticking behind her. Colley would be here soon enough.

No, it was never soon enough: but he'd be there when it was time. Then she would trade carefully selected secrets— so he'd believe she didn't need a counsellor—for the relief he carried in his medical bag.

Until then, Nick would remain alongside her, despite knowing that when her self-control evaporated, she'd be pathetically sobbing for the oblivion only the drug could provide. When the physical torment became too much he'd take her hand, as though he would absorb her pain. And she'd convince herself that if she clung to his silent strength it would be okay, she'd get through another hour.

With the fresh morphine flowing through her veins, Colley would start the questionnaire and Nick would retreat, never remarking on the predictability of her shameful dependence, her need every bit as pathetic as Mother's alcoholism.

Her fingertip leaked tears on the rising sun she had drawn on the window. Nick didn't judge her based on past behaviour. Instead, he approached each new day as a clean slate, never carrying forward the broken pieces of yesterday.

Her entire life consisted of broken yesterdays.

CHAPTER 23

Nick wanted to leave the room, to start the day again. He'd already fucked this one up.

Despite the media presence lurking outside his house, the hours had passed slow and quiet. His awkward attempts at assistance thrown back in his face, it was days before the realisation hit him like the blast wave from a scatter mine; Kayla didn't require conversation or entertainment. She would ignore his existence if he had the brains to extend her the same courtesy.

Which would represent the perfect level of involvement for him, except that he remained ridiculously aware of her every movement; listening for the gasp that signified pain, tracking the slow footfalls crossing to the shower, counting the minutes she was in there, debating whether to check if she was okay.

At the end of the week, as Colley made his twice-daily round to dress Kayla's wounds and run through the pain-ratings that Nick tried not to hear, he bailed the medic up.

'Have you noticed how much she sleeps? Do you reckon that's normal?'

Colley lifted one shoulder. 'Partly the painkillers, but more like her body can only repair while her external functions are closed down. Just let her be.'

'She'd need to sleep more hours than there are in the day.'

Colley sighed heavily. 'Not arguing.'

Nick tugged at his ear. He wasn't breaking Kayla's confidence by talking to the doctor. 'Thing is, she never gets an unbroken sleep.'

'Nightmares?'

He nodded. She avoided the bedroom he'd allocated, preferring to curl into a deep tub chair by the lounge room window, the manoeuvre clearly painful. The book on her lap—author irrelevant, as the pages never turned—would slide to the floor as exhaustion claimed her. That should signal his reprieve. Instead, he'd rescue the book, and then watch over her as she muttered restlessly. When the terror seemed too much for her to bear alone, he held her hand.

Bloody useless, but what the hell else could he do? He'd pray for her to wake, to escape the demons he couldn't fight for her. But when her eyes flickered open, forcing an uncomfortable awareness of what had been damaged in that subterranean hell, he'd wish she slept. Never more so than when the damn morph wore off. Each morning, he'd pretend not to notice her vulnerability, to have forgotten her desperate grasp of the previous day, and the secrets she'd sobbed as agony tore her apart.

Christ, if only he was able to forget, instead of staring at his ceiling all night, dreading the fresh day that would bring her more pain. The best he could do was compartmentalise and move forward; a skill hard-won in the deserts of Afghanistan and Iraq, necessary armour against the horrors witnessed in seven tours. But he never forgot. Anything.

The memory of each child he'd cradled as they bled out in the dirt of a distant land, each hand he'd held as a soldier breathed his last, each grieving parent he'd saluted over a flag-draped coffin, remained locked inside him.

He sucked in a heavy breath. If Kayla wanted to pretend normality today, good. Because he needed her to be strong.

He leaned across, lifting the blind a little higher, and she gravitated toward the window, like metal to a magnet. He hesitated, inspecting her doodle on the steamed glass. 'Fancy five minutes in the back garden? I think we could beat the media.' He'd never invited anyone into the small courtyard that held the last unadulterated traces of Mum.

'Really? I don't think I've ever been locked up for so long.' Kayla's lifted eyebrow invited his comeback.

Though he welcomed her dark sense of humour, he was never sure how to respond. 'Me either.' Jesus. Like he had anything to whine about.

Kayla touched his arm in apology, but her fingertips brushed his skin and she recoiled.

His jaw tightened, stomach twisting in a manner that was becoming far too familiar. Each time a memory triggered she disengaged from him, physically and emotionally. And he resented bitterly the harm that caused her to withdraw, hiding all she might have been.

CHAPTER 24

The scent of jasmine thick in her throat, Kayla surveyed the paved courtyard. Bougainvillea fought in a riot of purple and orange for possession of an old red-brick wall, and lemon trees starred with tiny white blossoms hedged the far side. The mate of the willy wagtail she'd watched from the window perched on the side of a moss-edged pond, accepting his accolade.

Gardening was a mystery. Seeds were planted, grew, and died. A pointless perpetuation. Like love, it would always end in death. Yet the existence of such unexpected beauty so close to her dark world stirred the familiar yearning. The longing to have her emptiness filled. She spoke quickly, over-talking the impermissible emotion. 'This is beautiful. Did you do it?'

Nick guided her to a park bench. His hair stood in blond spikes as he ran a hand through it. 'Mum planned and planted. Watering and weeding are pretty much my input, though I barely manage to keep it alive. When I'm not deployed, I head out here for a morning coffee, get my head straight.'

If only getting her head straight were that simple.

Koi schooled beneath her shadow, fighting for non-existent crumbs as her fingers trailed in the waterfall.

'Kayla.'

Something about Nick's tone...she turned to him, her fingers curling over the edge of the seat.

He stared at the koi. 'I don't know how to make this any easier on you, so I guess I'll just say it straight.'

Still he hesitated, and her stomach lurched. 'What is it?' The early-morning air wasn't chill enough to account for the tremors that rippled through her.

Nick's toe gouged at the carpet of moss. 'There's been no committal hearing yet, but the DPP is confident the case will go to trial.'

She frowned: she didn't care about the legalities, and had no interest in the court infrastructure. She just wanted the four men locked away. Forever. 'And?'

'They'll need to put you on the stand.'

The words dropped heavily, stones into a pond of tranquillity, ripples growing and forming waves. She absorbed the pronouncement, an icy hand gripping her heart. 'Why?' *Good.* The word sounded calm. Self-possessed. Almost disinterested. She could fake this. Had to fake it. Because she couldn't deal with it, couldn't allow the meaning of his words to penetrate her façade.

Nick's shoulders slumped, and the wooden slats of the bench bowed as he sat heavily. 'Something to do with making sure those bastards are put away for more than abduction of minors and deprivation of liberty.' Apparently falsely encouraged by her demeanour, he added swiftly, 'It'll be an open court.'

Her knee jerked uncontrollably. 'But if I refuse, they'll still be locked away, right?'

Nick's hand bunched on his thigh. 'It's not optional. You'll be subpoenaed.'

'I don't want to remember—' She hated herself for the weakness of the whispered admission. But she had to be vigilant, actively blocking the memories.

'I know.'

Her fingers and toes numb, black spots waltzed before her eyes, the beauty of the garden evaporated. Beyond the high brick fence, the rest of the street woke. Dogs barked, children shouted, someone hawked phlegm onto the pavement. Jealousy seared through her: their life went on. 'Can we go inside?'

Nick helped her to the sofa, knowing her legs wouldn't support her. 'I'll get you some breakfast.'

The plate was on her knee before she'd formed a coherent thought. She picked at the toast, struggling to retain control. For days, all she had ever asked was to be allowed to go home.

Nick spoke, but she couldn't listen. Had to concentrate. Keep the panic under control. Count. Count his words. Count the crumbs on the plate. *They're going to expose me.*

Colley arrived early. Morphine and the daily assessment. She counted the times he tapped his pen. *Keep it together.*

An hour later, when George Kimber knocked at the door, she had regained control. Could maintain it, providing she didn't think about what lay in her future, what they planned to make her do. How they would expose her. She counted the number of times he fiddled with his watch. *Don't think.*

Adam's apple bobbing as he cleared his throat, Kimber unnecessarily smoothed his trimmed hair. 'Miss Petrovic. Kayla. I've something rather unpleasant to ask of you.'

'No. Nick already told me.' They didn't need to discuss it. It was there, in the back of her mind, with all the other nightmares. Hidden behind counting.

'Told you?' Kimber's freckled features creased as he glanced between Nick and Colley. 'He couldn't have. I've only recently been informed of this development myself.' He took a step toward a chair, then evidently decided the delivery would be better made standing. 'The perpetrators had been remanded without bail.'

'*Had* been?' Nick said, dangerously low, and Kayla startled. She was counting George's words. Trying not to listen.

Kimber's arctic gaze slid to the captain, then he addressed Kayla's feet. 'Their legal counsel is pushing to have the bail application reassessed. In the normal course of events, this would be extremely unlikely. However, there is a slim chance they could win temporary release on a technicality.'

Release? No. She misunderstood Kimber's words. The four men couldn't be free, not ever. Because she would never be free. But if she misunderstood, why were Nick's fingers digging into her? She tried to ease from his grip.

'Sorry.' Nick's hand loosened but remained warm on her shoulder. 'What the hell, Major?'

'Before the matter can go to a committal hearing to have a trial date set, the DPP requires a signed statement from Kayla. As the perpetrators were never formally identified, there's a risk their counsel may argue there weren't justifiable grounds for their bail refusal. I can't stress enough that this is an outside chance, given that presumption against bail should prevail. But obviously we want to be certain all our i's are dotted and t's crossed.'

Nick's fingers tightened again. 'Bugger a statement: there are ten men who can attest that we seized those bastards in the cave, not a hundred metres from Kayla and the kids.'

Kayla didn't like them talking about her. Over her. But it was far better than them talking *to* her. As long as they didn't include her, she could block the images their words conjured.

Kimber shook his head. 'I don't know the intricacies of the legalities, but I assume their counsel may argue that proximity doesn't equate to guilt. Be that as it may, the committal hearing is scheduled in three days. To forestall the release of the accused in the interim, it is strongly suggested that Kayla lodge a signed statement and formally identify the men who hijacked the bus, abducted the children and, ah, assaulted her.'

'They're not *the accused*. We all know what they did,' Nick growled. 'This is bullshit. Surely someone else can take care of it?'

'Who? The minors?' Kimber's retort didn't invite a reply.

Minors. Her students. The ones she was supposed to protect. 'They can't get out. I promised the kids.' Her voice sounded strong.

Kimber nodded approval—or perhaps relief—at her composure. 'Excellent.'

'When?' This time the word stuck in her throat, and Colley took a half step toward her.

Kimber met her gaze. 'Now.'

Now? The urge to flee cramped her stomach, but she had

nowhere to go. Hell, she wasn't even capable of *going*. But this time, she could keep the kids safe. 'I'll get dressed.'

Her back as rigid as her voice, she concentrated on putting one foot in front of the other, Nick supporting her weight until she reached the bedroom.

Nine unsupported steps to the wardrobe. Five to the bed.

She drew on her clothes, one leg, then the other. One arm, then the other. No thought could intrude.

'Kayla?' She could tell Nick leaned his forehead against the closed door. 'Are you okay with this?'

She concentrated on applying hand cream. 'No choice.' One hand, then the other. Back to the first hand.

Again. Again. Obsessively. Compulsively.

Controlling every movement, every breath.

Eight steps back to the door, where Nick waited. Waited to take her to them.

Don't think of that. Count.

Nick assisted her to the khaki station wagon parked in the garage.

Forty-two steps.

He helped her into the back seat, and Colley clambered in the opposite door, buckling her belt like she wasn't capable.

He was right.

The wagon reversed out, following Kimber's Land Rover. She didn't need to watch the media contingent fall into line behind them. Could count them in her imagination.

In silence, they drove to the Holding Centre.

Colley massaged her cold hand.

She counted the passing vehicles. No room for thought.

In silence, they waited for Major Kimber to cross the bitumen, direct them to the interview room.

In silence, she pushed back her cuticles, first one, and then the next and the next, one hand finished, start the other one...back to the first.

Nick's murmur broke the silence. 'You're strong. You can handle this.'

In silence, she loathed his words. A lie that made it harder to admit her fear.

Concentrate.

One breath must follow another.

Spartan room. Shake hands with the prison officer. Don't make eye contact. Avoid the disgust on his face. *He knows what I did.*

A large window dominated the room, her side darkened, the other illuminated.

'Jesus, I thought this stuff went out with the Ark,' Colley said.

'Don't worry, they can't see you,' Nick soothed.

She knew. She'd seen the movies.

Men filed in, one after another.

Her heart stopped beating.

Control.

Now it was them that she counted.

Three times, five men filed in.

She uttered only the number held by each of the men she recognised.

The men who assaulted her.

Tortured her.

Raped her.

Greaz. 'Three.'

Fatty. 'Five.'

Les. 'One.'

Then Nick was at her side, applauding her self-control, her strength. 'Come on Kayla, that's it. Let's go home now.'

And she began to tremble.

It started in her feet. Moved up through her body, sparking the latent pains that lurked. Climbed until her teeth clashed together, her hands shaking uncontrollably. She forced herself to meet Nick's gaze. 'The other one.' Her voice devoid of emotion. Of life. 'Where's the other one?' Pitch rising.

Keep control.

Nick tried to guide her from the window. 'You identified all three. You're done.'

Oh fuck oh fuck oh fuck.

An hysterical sob escaped her lips, her head shaking faster and faster and faster until the words worked themselves free. 'No. No, no, no!' Her scream echoed from the walls of the cave.

Colley moved to calm her.

To silence her.

She drove her hands through her hair, as though she could force the horror from her brain. She had to make Nick understand. He'd promised to protect her, but now nobody could keep her safe. And the kids, oh God, the kids.

She grabbed at Nick's shirt, screwing the fabric in her fists. 'There were four men, Nick! Four!' Her heart lurched and seized as she forced out the name. 'T-T-Tomas.'

CHAPTER 25

He caught Kayla as she collapsed, but Colley pulled her from his arms and lowered her to the industrial carpet. Nick's breath expelled in a rush as Kayla's screamed, almost incoherent words sledge-hammered into him.

Four.

They'd missed one. He staggered backward, brought up short by the plate glass. Shook his head, trying to deny what he'd heard.

'C'mon, Captain, let's go.' Kimber urged him to the door. 'Lieutenant, you have Miss Petrovic?'

They couldn't run from this. They had to do...something. 'No, she was trying to say—'

Kimber blipped the fob remote as they exited the building at a jog. 'I know. Not here.' He yanked open the car door and Colley slid Kayla in and snagged a seat belt over her.

Nick's fingers twitched around an imaginary rifle stock as his eyes raked the parking lot. Caught off-guard, journalists scrambled toward them. Any one of them could be this

Tomas. He scanned their faces, probed the shadows beneath bushes, searched every vehicle. He'd let one get away. He had to find the bastard. Fix his failure.

Colley started the engine and Kimber smacked a palm on the roof. 'Go. Captain, my car.'

Nick dropped into the Rover's seat, staring out of the window. Kimber concentrated on the road in tense silence. They'd fucked up so bad. The prick was out there, somewhere, and they didn't even know what he looked like.

The drive from the Holding Station took twenty minutes, yet when the Rover pulled into the driveway it seemed mere seconds had passed. Not long enough to come up with a solution.

Nick slammed inside. Faint noises from the bedroom marked Colley and Kayla's whereabouts. He crossed to the chair Kayla had used only hours earlier. When she'd been watching the birds in the garden. Smiling. Joking. Finally a little stronger.

Colley's footsteps echoed on the floorboards. 'She's asleep. Well, sedated. Jesus. What a mess.'

Leather creaked as Kimber dropped into a chair. 'We had the footage. How in God's name did we miss one?'

Crossing to the kitchen, Colley rooted through cupboards. 'Don't know about you, but I wasn't scrutinising faces. When I managed to look at all.'

Kimber swiped an age-spotted hand across his face. 'We have to view that film again.' He pinched the bridge of his nose. 'Have his picture broadcast. He's probably not even in the bloody country by now, never mind the State. Damn it to hell!'

Coffee wafted strong from the mugs Colley carried into the lounge. He passed one to Nick. 'Captain. Thoughts?'

Jesus. They sure as hell didn't want to know his thoughts. Unarmed on a battlefield unlike any he'd ever known, he shook his head, clenching and releasing his hand as he waited for words that didn't come. For a plan that didn't exist.

Colley's eyes narrowed. 'Take it easy, Cap. You've done everything you can for her.'

'Less use than piss on a bushfire.' He stood, slamming the mug onto the table. Colley and Kimber couldn't understand, they didn't know the unkeepable promises he'd made. He needed to get out of the room before he blurted something stupid.

Fuck protocol. He lurched into the hall without waiting to be dismissed.

The cool stone wall against his back should have calmed him—except he halted opposite the open bedroom door. Guilt churned his stomach as Kayla tossed restlessly, a fragile raft amidst a tumbled grey sea.

He stumbled to the bed and dropped clumsily onto the mattress. His hand covered her icy fist where it lay on the pillow. 'I'm so sorry.'

Kayla's fingers interlaced with his, clutching on like she was drowning.

His heart kicked. He grunted. Rubbed at his chest. Hesitated, then lay on top of the counterpane, his eyes on Kayla's face, fingers still entwined.

CHAPTER 26

Kayla's body trembled with the last vestiges of a nightmare, but that wasn't unusual. Disoriented and dimly aware of a sense of foreboding, her drug-clouded mind didn't question Nick's inert form on the bed.

Until she remembered.

Fear clawed up from her stomach. She reared upright, her knuckles stuffed into her mouth to stifle the scream.

Nick jerked awake, a lithe movement taking him instantly to his knees as he wrestled her bloodied hand down to the covers. 'Kayla? It's all right, you're safe. He can't hurt you anymore.'

Really? Then what the hell was this terror that ripped her open? She wanted so desperately to believe Nick could save her. But he lied. Every man she'd ever known lied. 'No!' She thrust him away, her words jerky. 'He's out there.'

'Listen.' Nick seized her shoulders, his voice vibrating through her core. 'You have to stay strong. We'll fight this.'

'Strong?' All of her strength and resilience had dribbled from between her legs, contaminated with the wet foulings of evil men. She wrenched free. 'I tried to fight. I tried and I fucking *lost*. Don't you see? I *let* this happen.' She pounded her chest. 'Everything. It was all my fault.' The kidnapping, the torture, the rape, the childhood beatings. She'd caused it all, and now she had to run. Again. But where, this time?

Because the danger wasn't only outside. The nightmares, the daylight terrors, the memories that struggled to surface; Tomas had told the truth when he said he'd never let her go. He was under her skin, inside her head. An intrinsic part of the fractured jigsaw that formed her.

She lunged for the side of the bed, but Nick captured her. 'Colley!'

The medic responded to the captain's bellow at a run. 'Lie her down, mate.'

Nick tried to lay her back on the bed, but she clung to him. If he wouldn't let her escape, she wouldn't let him leave her. 'Kayla, it's okay. Relax.'

He didn't understand. Nobody could understand. If she relaxed, she'd let the fear in and the memories would drive her mad.

Colley seized her forearms.

She wanted to grab onto them, anchor herself between the two soldiers, but hysteria erupted inside her like a volcano, her entire body trembling, her teeth clashing together.

'Kayla, don't let this flip you out. Wherever this guy is, we'll get him. The police have been alerted in every state. The entire strength of the army is behind you. Kim will make sure of that.'

She fastened her eyes on Colley, tried to speak. To tell him he was wrong. But only a high-pitched, terrified keening came from her mouth.

'You're safe, Kayla. Do you hear me? Don't let this screw with your head.'

His words couldn't prevent *it* happening.

Deafened by her jagged breathing, she focused unseeingly on the window. Something monstrous approached. Her dread dragged Nick's gaze to the curtained expanse, but he searched for a physical presence. He wouldn't be able to see *it*. Nobody could. Madness lurked invisible.

Colley moved into her line of sight, blocking the window.

How could she be ready for what was coming, if he stood in the way? She shook her head furiously, unable to form words. Unable to do anything but whimper.

He grabbed her chin, forced her attention to him 'Kayla, the one we missed. He had the baseball bat?'

She gasped, jerking back.

'What the hell?' Nick's hand slammed into Colley's shoulder.

Colley staggered. 'She's losing it. I need her to stay with us. Grab a bucket or something, quick. Kayla, you talk in your sleep, remember?'

No. No remembering. The temptation of insanity lay within reach. There would be no pain, no failure, no judgment in the velvet embrace of madness.

His face too close to hers, Colley's palms were damp on her cheeks. Sweat beaded his forehead. 'Kayla, tell me about that bastard. What was the bat for?'

'Jesus, mate, her heart—' Nick shouted.

Colley stole her escape. She couldn't slip away, hide from Tomas in the recesses of her mind, while the medic yelled at her, demanding she focus, remember, oh Jesus, remember what they'd done to her, remember the pain, remember the shame, remember the fear. Memories exploded in her brain, allowing no room for the darkness.

Colley thrust a basin in her lap. 'The bat, Kayla. Tell me about the bat. Come on, you're not checking out on us. Tell me about it. Remember, you have to tell me what you're feeling.'

The bat the bat the bat. Her mouth filled with saliva. She swallowed convulsively, acid climbing her gullet, stinging the back of her throat, watering her eyes. *The bat the bat the bat.*

As she doubled over, Colley scooped back her hair. 'That's it, good girl.'

Retching and gasping for breath, still she couldn't miss Nick's expression as he staggered backward from the room.

This, he wouldn't be able to forget. There could be no new day.

CHAPTER 27

Nick forced himself from the leather chair and padded barefoot to the kitchen. The harsh burr of the grinder blurred his thoughts for precious seconds. He ran it until the portafilter overflowed. Then he stood staring at the growing pyramid of shattered beans on the counter. *Get a grip.* 'Major. Coffee?' One a.m. Kim wouldn't touch caffeine now.

Major Kimber stretched, leaning to peer toward the kitchen. 'Thanks, Captain. I don't think anyone's sleeping tonight.'

Colley didn't shift from the sofa he sprawled on, his dark gaze locked on the ornate ceiling rose, his fingers working his crucifix. 'This is bloody stupid. We achieve nothing by sitting here waiting for someone, somewhere, to call and say they've picked him up.'

Nick scowled. He understood Colley had forced a physical reaction from Kayla to override her frantic mental activity. But he couldn't forgive him for it. Not yet.

'I must ring Lorraine, let her know I won't be back

tonight.' Despite his words, Kimber didn't make a move but stayed slumped in the chair, his hair awry. Nick had never seen him anything less than militarily upright.

None of them deserved sleep. Not that it'd help anyway; the fatigue that ate into him went far beyond the physical. He could barely imagine how Kayla felt. And he didn't want to try.

The silence thickened. Like him, the other soldiers no doubt trained their ears on the bedroom, registering every restless movement within. Each accusation of their incompetence.

Kimber straightened and tugged his uniform into place. Twisted the silver Rolex on his freckled wrist, peered closely at the face, then cleared his throat. 'Will she be fit for Saturday?'

'Saturday?' Colley raised his head. 'Oh, shit. The Lord Mayor's do, right?'

'The official thank-you.' Kimber's tone dripped sarcasm.

'Doubt it. Can't see her agreeing to leave the house unless that bastard's picked up within the week.'

Crossing to park his empty cup on the counter, Kimber addressed the kitchen. 'She's the guest of honour. If she doesn't show, I wouldn't put it past that mob to descend on you here.'

Nick snorted, turning back to the grinder. 'I'd like to see them try.' He wouldn't let anyone get close to her. Again.

The C.O.'s polished shoes appeared in the periphery of his vision. 'I'm serious. With the election campaign starting up, the government is keen to convey that their handling of this saved millions of taxpayer dollars, with minimal adverse outcome.'

'Jesus.' Colley's lips thinned into an angry white line,

stark against his dark skin. He jabbed a finger toward Kayla's room. 'Does that look like minimal adverse outcome? Oh, and that reminds me, the gyno said those bastards fucked her up so bad, there's a chance she'll never have kids. You want me to tell her that, then send her off to party with a load of suits intent only on saving their own jobs?'

Nick shoved his cup across the granite bench. Pushed a fraction too far, it plummeted, shattering on the slate floor. 'Why should Kayla be part of their bullshit circus? The kids will provide enough good PR.'

Kimber's audible exhale signified he had already argued every point they made. 'Without Kayla, the spin lacks credibility. And, in all fairness, people want to acknowledge what she did.' He shook his head, his voice dropping to a mutter. 'Not that they'll ever know the half of it.'

CHAPTER 28

'I'm sorry, Kayla, we need a description.'

Though Colley had warned her he'd bring the police artist around, she shrank back as he ushered the man into the lounge room. She forced a nod. Had to do this. Had to make sure Tomas was caught.

The plainclothes officer took a seat and pulled out a tablet, keeping his gaze on the screen. Colley sat beside her on the leather lounge. Nick stood in the doorway, arms folded across his chest, glaring at the cop. Despite her hysteria two days earlier, still he didn't treat her any different. He remained calm and solid, an anchor.

Even though she knew the danger of allowing herself to depend on anyone.

The officer tapped his screen, and she focused. She had to be careful not to think. To provide a generic description that didn't evoke any memories, but enabled the police to locate and arrest Tomas.

Except it wouldn't do her any good. Tomas had warned he'd never let her go.

As the officer sketched the details she provided, he occasionally turned the screen toward her for verification.

Fear bubbled in her chest as the face became familiar. She wanted to lie, to change the picture so she didn't have to view it. Instead, she spoke quickly. 'Thinner eyebrows. Hairline further back. Smaller eyes.' Tried to stop her hand convulsively leaping in Colley's.

He tightened his grip. 'It's okay, Kayla, take it slow.'

She shook her head. 'No. Get it done. His tongue…his tongue was split.' The artist glanced up in sudden interest. 'Like a snake.'

Nick grunted and dropped his arms, taking a step toward her.

'Like this?' The artist altered the picture and held it up. She jerked back. Caught herself. Remained tremblingly rigid as she nodded.

'Any other distinctive features?'

'No. Yes. His nails. They were long. Pointy. Painted black.' Except when they were covered in her blood, caressing her flesh. Bile rose in her throat and she pushed to her feet, ignoring the spearing pain. 'Is that enough?'

Nick was alongside her, there if she needed to lean on him. 'That's plenty. We'll get him. I promise.' His thumb rubbed over the back of her hand.

She snatched at his hand. 'You have to. He'll come back. He said so.'

'It's okay. You're safe here.'

'That's the problem. If he can't get me, he might go for the kids.'

'They've all got protection. They'll be fine.'

She shook her head, biting at her lip. 'I should make it easy for him. Then they'd be safe.'

'Use yourself as bait, you mean?' Colley said.

Nick tensed. 'That's not happening. You've done more than your share.'

She blinked back tears of relief and gratitude; he'd take responsibility and allow her to be a coward.

THE DEEP-THROATED tick of the grandfather clock echoed through the emptiness, counting her slow steps.

Seven in the morning, and seven days since she'd made a fool of herself. No, that wasn't true; weakness still betrayed her daily. But seven days since she discovered Tomas was free. Seven days she'd hidden indoors, never moving more than a room from Nick's silent strength.

And on the seventh day—what? On the seventh day, she had to face the world. Exposed. Alone. Vulnerable.

But not alone enough, because Tomas would be watching her. Wanting her.

She gravitated toward the courtyard. Nick would be there, and she'd feel safe, if only for a few moments. But she'd bite her tongue, not beg him to explain—again— why she had to front the dinner tonight. She only protested and questioned when the morphine wore thin, when she couldn't hold back the fear any longer. Because she knew the truth that none of them spoke: if she didn't make the appearance the government required, they'd withdraw the ADF protection. And without Nick, Tomas could get to her.

Nick dwarfed the area as he tossed feed to the birds flitting over tufts of black mondo grass to crowd his feet.

Frozen in the doorway, Kayla pressed a hand to her

chest. She'd seen Nick shirtless before. What struck her different now? And, Jesus, *why?*

He smiled a characteristically asymmetrical welcome. 'Wasn't expecting you to surface yet. Planning to knock them dead in that, tonight?' He gestured at her camouflage castoff, fresh soap wafting with his movement.

She pulled the shirt closer, the coarse cotton of his uniform a habitual reassurance. 'Would have been my choice, but Sue's shopping for something she considers more suitable.' If she was careful not to associate imminent reality with his words, she could conduct a conversation almost like a normal person.

Nick tossed the last of the crumbs and headed toward the house. Toward her. 'Could be worse. I'm forced into dress uniform for these gigs.'

She retreated as he advanced. Didn't blink. Scared to take her eyes from this unexpected new threat. 'I...ah... you're right. It's early. I'm going back to-to bed.' She limited the time she spent in that playground for nightmares, but now she had something worse to hide from—and nowhere to run, because this new monster resided inside her. Her toxic awareness of Nick's masculinity proved Mother right; she was a slut. Worse than that, she was sick. Both body and mind. Because she wasn't looking at Nick like she *should*. She wasn't sickened or repulsed.

She crawled into the shelter of the bed. Hid under the covers. Sue would be here in a few hours. She needed to block her thoughts until then. Hours of not thinking. About anything. Because nothing was safe.

Except Nick.

The truth was, she only dared close her eyes when he was near. Each day, he literally held her pain at bay: when she woke from a nightmare he'd be there, silently holding her hand so she would know that fear belonged only in her memory and imagination.

She blew out a shaky breath, lowering the covers she had drawn over her head. Her pulse settled as relief relaxed her muscles; it wasn't desire that had surged through her, but a longing for protection. Primitive instinct drew her to Nick, because he unquestioningly lent her his strength.

Still, she'd stay in her room until Sue arrived.

ELEVEN HOURS LATER, sweat prickled Kayla's armpits, and her pulse pounded like a Japanese drummer. In an hour, she'd front a room full of unfamiliar faces.

Worse would be the familiar ones.

Sue jerked the loaded contour brush back. 'Yikes, don't screw up your face.'

'Sorry. Are you done?'

Excess powder clouded the air, and Sue waved it clear. 'Patience. This is no easy task, you know.'

'No kidding.' Years of practice had honed Kayla's ability to pretend: she had created a facade that allowed no hint of her reality. A specially constructed prison that enabled her to view the world, but hid her from display. But now, could her paint ever be thick enough?

Her own air-brushed perfection quickly assessed in the mirror, Sue gave Kayla a one-armed hug. 'Okay, chick, you're all done. Gotta fly. I'll see you at the dinner. Kisses.'

She had only minutes left. Seconds to find an excuse not to attend the official dinner. Seconds before she was exposed. Seconds before she had to step beyond the locked door, into a world in which Tomas lurked. Watching her. Desiring her.

Nick cursed a cufflink into the sleeve of his linen shirt as he filled the doorway. 'Need to be a damn octopus to put these things in. Can you give me a hand?' He glanced up. 'Nice. Good thing you were banned from cams.'

But not a good thing that he'd been ordered out of them. Nick appeared different in the white dress uniform. Hard-edged, stern and official. His sudden unfamiliarity made her pulse skitter.

But it wasn't with fear.

She looked down, her hands crushing the loose fabric of the black chiffon pants which tapered to her ankles. Teamed with a high-necked silver tank under a lined jacket, almost all of her scars were hidden. But how did she hide this new mental aberration?

Nick's wrist appeared, and her fingers trembled as she threaded silver through fabric. Trying not to touch him.

Wanting to touch him.

The need that surged through her was dangerously familiar. The longing to have a man desire her had nothing to do with seeking protection. It had always been about power, proving she could make conquests, put notches on her bedpost. Proving wrong her mother's opinion: she wasn't unlovable.

She didn't want to get out of the limousine when they pulled to the curb in front of the venue half an hour later. The locked car doors promised security, despite the presence of the chauffeur. He wasn't Tomas, disguised beneath a suit and thick-rimmed glasses. She'd checked. Scrupulously. And, if she kept her gaze on the plush leather interior, Nick's presence was still familiar and safe, quiet strength wreathed in the particular mix of cologne and soap she would always associate with him.

Her fingers tightened on the door handle, her heart pounding as she surveyed the shadowy forms milling outside. For a brief moment, she could be the one staring at the world through the tinted window, instead of contained in a fishbowl with everyone's noses pressed to the glass. Eventually she would have to leave this pseudo-security—but with Nick alongside, maybe she could endure this new hell.

Cameras flashed.

Or maybe not. 'You know, if you're working on some brilliant plan to save me from this, now would be a great time to share.' She mashed her lips together to stop them from trembling.

Nick stared out of the window. 'Believe me, I've got nothing.' His tone rang uncharacteristically bitter. 'But your kids will be waiting in there.'

The words were offered as enticement, but he couldn't realise they increased her apprehension. If the kids had changed, if they weren't the mix of obnoxious and gorgeous she'd dragged into that damned desert, Kayla would be forced to face her failure.

Nick's hand closed around his door handle. 'Ready?'

As he unfolded from the vehicle, a murmur rose from the crowd. A smattering of applause, breathy cries from his fan club.

Kayla's mouth went from dry to madly salivating.

Nick reached her door before the chauffeur, letting in a rush of chilled air. He offered his hand and a tight smile of commiseration. 'We'll get through it as quickly as we can.'

'The crowd or the dinner?' she murmured. It was irrelevant. She knew that, just like fronting up at school with smiles covering her bruises, she was expected to put on an act. That was the price of her protection from Tomas.

She ducked her head, hiding behind a curtain of hair. The crowd roiled around them, jostling for a better view, but Nick cheated them of the opportunity. Hand warm against the small of her back, he ushered her across the few metres of cement sidewalk, up the shallow steps, and into the chandeliered foyer as quickly as her unsteady pace allowed.

The coldly-marbled entry hall almost empty, Kayla quailed at the sight of a flight of stairs, but suited valets directed them toward an elevator in the rear corner. A few people circulated; late arrivals, handing jackets to the coat check, or red-cheeked with cold after ducking out for a cigarette. Without exception, they stared.

She moved closer to Nick, trying to hide. He didn't pull away but slid a hand around her waist. His breath stirred her hair. 'Kim's had them hold the guests in the main auditorium upstairs, so we have a moment to regroup.'

As they exited the lift, even the solid stone walls failed to disguise the churn of voices from the closed room in front of them. She hesitated, glancing along the corridor that led to the stairs. Tomas could be amongst the crowd that milled below. The door before her caged more terrors—but Tomas couldn't hide in there. 'Remind me again why I have to do this?' Damn, she'd promised herself not to beg for reassurance.

'Closure.'

'Over-rated.' There could be no closure for her. But perhaps for the kids' families? She owed them that much.

Striding toward them, Colley indicated Nick's dress whites. 'Captain. Bit of a dog's dinner.' His olive skin glowed dark against his own uniform. 'Trying to live up to your media image?'

'Compensating for the sloppiness of certain junior officers, Lieutenant. I, at least, am suitably attired to escort a beautiful woman.'

An easy lie, she should be angry at Nick's flippant tone. Instead, she would pretend it held some truth, because then she could focus on that fantasy rather than think about what lay beyond the highly polished double doors through which Major Kimber had appeared.

Noise ebbed as ushers tugged on huge brass rails to close the doors behind him. 'Sorry to disappoint you, Captain West, but in the absence of my own good wife, I intend to claim that particular honour for myself.' Kimber proffered an arm.

It didn't matter whose arm she held, as long as they didn't leave her alone. She rubbed sweating palms against her jacket, then gripped Kimber's tailored sleeve. Her flat pumps sliding on the royal blue carpet, she concentrated on individual muscles, willing her legs not to fail.

In the slow motion of a nightmare, the doors swung open, inviting her into the maw of this new hell.

The rustle of expensive finery and shuffle of feet in the cavernous room suspended, creating a momentary breathless hush. Then noise and movement exploded toward her. Cameras clicking like furious death-watch beetles, journalists rushed to chronicle the moment. Dignitaries craned toward the entrance.

Toward her.

Too many people. She couldn't assess them all. Maybe Tomas did hide in here. She jerked back.

Kimber bent his elbow, trapping her hand to prevent her flight.

Nick stepped up, buffering her between him and the major. Decorum forgotten, journalists vied for her attention, thrusting cameras toward them.

Kimber kept his voice low. 'Keep moving, Captain.'

Fear pumped through her. One arm crossed over her stomach, she stretched her fingers toward Nick's hand on her waist. She could never tell him, but she needed him.

His grip tightened.

The media backed off as Kimber hustled her toward the dignitaries, though the camera flash and shutter noise still drowned the music from the small orchestra.

The face at the head of the line frequented the TV. The Premier. Perspiration rolled down the sides of his flushed face.

Nervous? Or revolted? Every person here had formed an image of what she'd done. What she was.

The Premier effusively enclosed her hand in both of his. His greeting smooth and practiced, he had no cause for nerves. But he had to touch her, for the cameras.

His wife smiled with too many crooked teeth, even for her over-generous mouth. 'You're so thin, dear. I thought it was the photos. You really must eat, you know. Best thing after an illness.'

An illness. That was one hell of a euphemism.

'It's such a blessing the Good Lord chose to spare and protect you.'

He could have pulled his finger out on the protection part. If she voiced the irreverent thought, Colley would psychoanalyse her, Kimber would tighten his lips, and the fine lines around Nick's eyes would crease in encouragement.

But she couldn't speak. She needed morphine. Not for the pain, but to dull the reality; to avoid the knowing looks, block the too-interested questions, erase the whispers that trailed her passage. Did they think her injuries made her deaf?

Expressionless, she moved down the greeting line. Shook hands. Feigned interest at introductions to people who shouldn't know or care that she existed. Pretended to accept their pretend sympathy.

The end finally in sight, more than exhaustion slowed her step.

The children. Her gaze ranged over them, measuring and assessing, desperately searching for signs of damage. Terrified of what she'd find, what she had caused.

Jacob. Lily and Liam. Ella. Ryan. Maddie. *They look all right.* But so had she, the childhood injuries hidden beneath clothes. And deeper.

Her nails bit into her palms. She had deserted the kids, she should have been at the school, easing them back to normality.

But she no longer had a normal.

Shrugging from her escorts, she held open her arms. Crucified and alone, a millisecond stretched into eternity. Her last chance at forgiveness. Then the children rushed into her embrace like boisterous puppies, loud and exuberant.

Hope rippled through her. Had they, somehow, survived the horror unscathed? Or did she lie to herself?

Maddie wriggled from her grasp. 'Are you coming back to school now, Miss? Jacob's had Roger Rabbit forever and he won't share him. It should be my turn. You said we each get a weekend to take him home.'

Jacob fisted his hands on his hips. 'Yeah, but I'm not home this weekend, stupid, so it doesn't count.'

They were...normal. Lily's hair hid the dry sob that tore from Kayla's chest.

Her face scrubbed to shining, Lily pulled back. 'Do you want my hanky, Miss? I've got a new one. And a new dress.'

Kayla's grin wobbled. 'No. I'm not crying. And that is a really pretty dress.'

Ryan's blue eyes challenged her. 'You're not going to cry anymore? Because you cried heaps. I didn't cry, because I'm a boy. Maddie cried, too.' He turned to include the adults in the conversation. 'But Miss P stopped her. When *she* wasn't crying.'

God. She ruffled Ryan's hair, trying to distract him. He'd always been the quiet kid, now he found his tongue? Her face burning, she reluctantly straightened and turned to the parents. Her chest ached with her sudden inability to breathe. Sue had come to terms with her evident corruption and hid her disgust well. But the other parents—what would they think? What had their children told them? Did they hate her, as Sue had?

Sue tugged her into an embrace, then laughingly accepted Lily's handkerchief and wiped her eyes, pushing Kayla toward the twins' father. Gruff and somehow smaller without his customary layer of grease, Phil smacked broad lips against her cheek. 'Kayla. Good job.'

She sucked in a great breath as Phil propelled her gently to the next parent. Surrounding her, they would keep Tomas at bay. Protect her, even though she had failed to protect their children.

As the last of the parents murmured their misplaced

gratitude, Liam turned, hero worship lighting his countenance. He executed a wonky salute toward Nick.

A grin flashed across the captain's face, then he schooled his features and returned a crisp salute. He caught Kayla's gaze and edged through the group. Spoke low as he guided her across the room. 'The kids needed to see that you're okay, every bit as much as you needed to see them. And they're fine. You did your job.'

He understood. She managed a tremulous smile as he seated her, a gilt-edged name card placing her between the Premier and the Lord Mayor, with George Kimber opposite. Each face around the long rectangular table warranted covert examination. She searched for narrow features, coal eyes and overfull lips.

Polished ebony nails flashed against the white tablecloth and she tensed, but the hand disappeared into long blonde hair. Maybe Tomas's nails would be a different colour now? Kayla's gaze raked the hands. Fingering glasses, reorganising cutlery, punctuating unheard sentences. *Jesus.* She didn't know what to search for. Tomas would find her long before she found him. Panic fluttered dark inside her, blackness crowding the edge of her vision.

'Kayla, remember the dinner is invitation only.' His hand on her shoulder, steadying her, Nick's words were calm as she pushed her chair back as though she could leap up and run. 'The Feds have every entry covered. There's no way anyone else can get in.'

He'd told her that earlier. But none of them understood Tomas as she did. They looked for logic where there could be none, and didn't believe he would come back.

Colley signalled, indicating a place setting—at a

different table, acres of snowy linen away. Nick squeezed her shoulder gently. 'You'll be okay?'

She wanted to beg him not to abandon her. But she needed to stop being so pathetic. Relying on a man—on anyone—was always a mistake.

The evening seemed endless, the numerous courses delivered with military precision to the elegant banquet tables, interspersed with guests circulating in kaleidoscoping groups of noise and chatter. Kayla slumped in her chair, then straightened, craving a position that would relieve the ache that inched down her spine and through her kidneys. Conversation swelled then stuttered to an uncomfortable death in the face of her monosyllabic replies; speaking encouraged questions, and answers revealed secrets.

Her full plate cleared and replaced by another offering she wouldn't taste, steak swam in a pretty pink pool, the bloodied jus dripping from the tines of her fork onto creamed white potatoes. Was that how her back appeared, scarred and raw? She'd never know. She would never look.

Seizing her silence as an invitation to chat, the Premier's wife exchanged seats with her husband. Having exhausted the topic of invalid food preparation, she embarked on a vitriolic diatribe regarding suitable dress for the function.

Nodding disinterested agreement, Kayla smiled mechanically. She wanted to go home. To Nick's home. Her attention strayed toward the officers.

A sinuously attractive blonde draped herself over the captain, her arm stretched along the back of his chair. Receiving scant attention, she turned to flirt with Steve Colley. More receptive, Colley threw back his head in laughter, his finger tracing the woman's smooth forearm. The woman giggled as his hand covered hers on the white table-cloth. She layered her other hand, and Colley completed the stack. Pretending to struggle, the woman swayed away from Colley, her breast brushing Nick's arm. She simpered, leaning closer in contrived apology.

Kayla's fingers curled into a fist as she watched the flirtatious ballet.

Nick's eyes caught hers, and he raised his glass, one side of his mouth lifting sardonically.

Shit. Kayla ducked her head. Chased a caramelised fig through a moat of cream. Didn't he realise she coveted the woman, not him? She lusted after her uncontaminated health, her right to assumed virginity. Her past and her future. She wanted to exchange herself for that woman.

And then maybe she would have a right to look at Nick.

The Lord Mayor tapped her fork on the side of a crystal glass as she stood. Brandy splashed the tablecloth, spreading like a malevolent cloud. 'Ladies, Gentlemen, we come to the most important part of this wonderful evening.'

Teeth clenched, Kayla scrunched the fabric napkin in her lap. Counted the individual threads. Tried to pretend every head hadn't swivelled toward her.

Intent on holding centre stage, the mayor waffled, thanking the decorating corps, the catering staff, the gods of all denominations. The premier's wife nodded sagely, as though she had orchestrated the Divine Intervention. In a lather of spittle-flecked enthusiasm, the mayor threw one arm wide. 'And, above all else, we must surely thank Miss Petrovic.'

Invited to gawk, applauding guests craned to catch her reaction.

The noise reached her in disjointed bursts. *Nowhere to*

hide. Her head spun. Too much wine, too little food. And not enough pain killers. Never enough. She could still *feel.* Eyes burned into her, trying to search out her secrets. She smiled woodenly, dropping her gaze to her hands, shoving them under the table as the scars advertised her lack of control.

The premier stood to take his turn at exposing her.

She wound the napkin around her hidden hand. Pulled it tighter and tighter, staring with fierce concentration as her fingertips turned red, then slowly blue.

The premier's measured pace increased, passion infusing the tale he recounted. His warped version of the truth. 'We cannot truly fathom the incredible bravery and tenacious strength displayed by this young woman, in the face of cruel and unnatural torment. I promise you here and now,' he pounded the table for emphasis. 'This government will ensure the perpetrators are duly punished.'

She wished him dead.

Much throat-clearing warranted the deployment of a navy handkerchief before he found himself able to proceed. He dropped a hand onto her shoulder, and she recoiled at both the contact and the jolt of pain. 'Ladies and Gentlemen, please charge your glasses once more. At immeasurable personal expense, Miss Petrovic has returned to us the lifeblood of this great nation.'

The idiot made it sound like she'd offered herself up as a sacrificial virgin.

The storm of applause and scrape of chairs startled her, and she made to rise along with the other guests. Major Kimber unobtrusively signalled her to remain seated. She bit the inside of her cheek and focused on a cube of ice floating in her water glass. Counted the myriad scars on its surface. Eventually, they'd connect. A tiny explosion, unnoticed in the world, would leave the shattered fragments irreparable.

The guests sat. Louder, more joyous now.

More drinking.

As some wit at the table proposed yet another toast, Kayla cast around for means of escape. The hot room, noise, too-bright colours, closed in on her. Surrounded, yet completely alone, fatigue crawled up her spine and her neck ached with the strain of holding her back rigid. Inexplicable tears pressed against her briefly-closed eyelids, and she longed to give in, to feel the cathartic release. But she wouldn't cry; it proved weakness.

She startled as Colley spoke, then twisted to face him, hiding her wince. 'Sorry, what?'

He frowned and indicated the full glass by her hand. 'Remember I said take it easy on the booze. Anyway, I asked if you'd like to head home? Seems the official bit's all over, we're off duty and I'm, uh —' his head inclined toward the blonde across the room. Purse in hand, the woman's hard eyes assessed the potential competition, one stiletto-heeled foot tapping a warning. 'I'm invited out for the rest of the evening.'

Kayla looked away from the blonde intimidation. 'And you'd like to dump me? Real nice.' She had already eased her legs from under the table. 'Can we sneak out?'

Nick's voice rumbled behind her. 'Not without me.'

Colley's long fingers kneaded the nape of her stiff neck, and the urgency of his date's Morse code increased. 'You're invited for a drink, too, Captain. Drinks only, mind, then I'm ditching you. See Kayla home then catch up with us at the club. You'll be all right, Kayla?'

'Of course.' She wasn't a teenager, trusted to stay home alone for the first time.

Alone. The word, the actuality, snatched her breath. No, she wouldn't be alright. She didn't want to be alone. Ever again.

'You're on your own, mate,' Nick said. 'I've hit the drink a bit too hard. Not up for a party.' He sounded completely sober. 'You organise the limo, we'll be there in two shakes.'

Her stomach clenched. Being alone with this new Nick, with her recognition of him as a man, held its own terrors. She pushed to her feet, staggering a little.

'A slow two shakes,' Nick added, dropping his arm to her waist.

Seated, she hadn't realised the true extent of her fatigue. Now she could barely find the energy to slide one foot in front of the other, despite leaning against the captain.

By the time they reached the hollow iciness of the foyer, populated only by policemen, her feet no longer touched the ground. She had given up any pretence of walking, instead drifting in Nick's one-armed lift.

He scanned the room. 'Journos outside, Lieutenant?'

Colley's levity disappeared. 'All clear, Cap. Transport's waiting.'

Nick scooped her into his arms and exited the building, half-a-dozen strides taking them to the limo. He lowered her into the plush interior as the chauffeur held the door.

She didn't protest. Didn't even check the chauffeur's face.

Everything hurt. Even her teeth ached.

But it was all over, now. She was one step closer to home.

To being alone.

And now, her heart hurt.

CHAPTER 29

Nick tugged at his ear as he leaned over Kayla. She moaned, muttering something incomprehensible. Her eyes closed, the words nothing but a whisper of sweet breath. He pulled her seatbelt into place, latched it, then nodded at the driver.

The heater blasted their feet. She would stop trembling soon.

But he'd been telling himself that for weeks.

A strand of auburn hair tickled across Kayla's face in the warm draught. He caught it, wound it around his finger, and tucked it behind her ear. Shot a glance at the rearview mirror to make sure the driver hadn't caught him.

Kayla's skin soft and cool, he stared at his hand. *Jesus.* He had to keep his mind blank. Anything he thought right now would be wrong. So wrong. He held his breath, hoping the rush of blood in his ears would drown the illicit thoughts.

Kayla moaned again, swaying toward him as the car cornered.

Loosening her seatbelt, he slid an arm around her shoulders. She curled into him, her face and one hand against his chest. Chin resting on top of her head, he breathed in her honey and vanilla. Stared at the neon city flickering by. A motorbike zipped close, slowed, moved up on the other side of the limo, and then sped away, leaving only the pounding of his heart to fill the silence.

He needed to talk to Dad.

Get a grip, man.

He shouldn't have moved toward Kayla. His mandate was to provide her with security, not comfort. Not anything else. There was a line he could never cross.

Not even in his most private imaginings.

CHAPTER 30

Colley didn't bother to hide his grin behind the newspaper. 'Get a grip, mate. You can't sue the papers for printing what they see.'

'The hell you mean "what they see"?' Nick mimicked savagely. The generous proportions of the lounge room seemed suddenly constrictive. 'There's bloody well nothing *to* see!' Not unless they got inside his head.

'C'mon, Nick. It's obvious you guys have a connection.' Colley lowered his voice, nodded toward where Kayla slept down the hall. 'But it's not like anyone's pulled out the 'L' word.'

Nick snorted: the lieutenant hadn't seen the online pieces from the trashier mags. He prowled the room, tossing cushions into the chair Kayla favoured. Moved her book closer. Controlled his movements, defying the urge to slam something, hit something. Colley had better tread carefully. He'd been able to disregard the steady drip of moronic insinuations that had started with the medevac landing, but today's paper...they'd really done a number on him. The paparazzi had managed to get pictures of Kayla curled into the crook of his arm in the limo. Fuck knew how. But Kayla would see that she'd been asleep and he'd taken advantage.

'Connection?' he snarled. 'Christ, hasn't Kayla done enough that maybe she could be afforded a little common decency? Did anyone stop for one second to think about the repercussions of printing this shit, of what it could do to her? She's fragile. She doesn't need speculation about her private life. Hell, she barely has a *private* life.' Nor did she need to be led to doubt his dedication to protecting her. He'd made her promises. He would keep them.

Colley frowned. 'That's a whole lot of denial right there.'

He should have kept his cool. Colley always saw too much.

The medic rubbed his chin thoughtfully. 'Okay, so there's no connection. Nada. Zip. What's with blowing off the party last night? And this?' He gestured toward the cushions, the book. 'This isn't you.'

That was a dirty strike. Nick treated women well but, as with everything, he laid out rules, kept control. Never invited them into his life. Kayla was different. She didn't need to conform to his regulations. Wouldn't conform: from the first, she'd challenged his orders.

He maintained a harsh-breathed silence, snatching cups from the cupboard. Slammed them onto the counter. Better he didn't speak. Didn't think.

Colley rose and closed the door into the hallway, then crossed to the kitchen. Braced his hands on the counter. 'C'mon, Nick. I know you don't want to discuss anything *emotional.*' He made air quotes. 'You'd rather bury issues than deal with them. But at least admit it to yourself. Kayla does something to you.'

Nick shoved a mug toward him. 'What sort of jerk wouldn't feel sorry for her?'

The stool Colley pulled from beneath the counter scraped across the floor. He counted spoonsful of sugar into his cup, clearly buying time to choose his words. 'Sure. I misread the situation, and so has the rest of the country, thanks to the Sunday rags. You're incapable of anything approaching a normal human emotion, so of course there's no way you could actually care for her.'

'That's bullshit and you know it. You literally just accused me of caring too much, now you're having a go at me about not caring?'

'I said care *for* her, not about her,' Colley said precisely.

'*Jesus!*' Coffee splashed as Nick's arm jerked with the cold rigidity of shock. 'What kind of sick bastard do you think I am?'

'Mate, you know I'd generally be first in line to give you that label.' Smart enough to give him space, Colley headed back to the lounge. 'But not this time. Kayla's not the sum of what happened to her. That's a sad, fucked up equation. She's so much more.'

'Of course she is. Doesn't have anything to do with me, though.' Could never have anything to do with him. The strength of spirit behind Kayla's physical frailty both awed and humbled him. She was so far out of his league.

Not that he was interested in that way.

Colley slumped in a chair. 'You're right.' He flipped the newspaper onto the floor, the front-page photo of Kayla in Nick's arms an unstated accusation. 'What bloke in his right mind would be into a girl half the country has had a poke at, and the other half knows all about?'

Nick slammed his fist onto the sink so hard the steel

dented. 'What the hell—?' For the first time in his life, the rage that trembled through him felt uncontrollable.

'I mean, she's completely fucked up, isn't she? Anxiety attacks, PTSD. Coming up near two months, and she's still afraid to sleep with the lights off—hell, she's scared to sleep, period, right? And now she's convinced this bastard's stalking her. That's some seriously messed-up paranoia.' Colley shook his head. 'Then there's all those scars and shit. And I'll tell you something,' he leaned forward, elbows on his knees. 'Those aren't all new. She's a cutter, Nick. There's crap gone down in her past, too. You're right, she's pretty much the ultimate in soiled goods.'

Nick vaulted the bench. Every muscle quivered like an overstrung bow as he struggled to contain his fury. 'You bastard! There's bloody well nothing wrong with her. You get the fuck out of my house.'

Colley hunched one shoulder, anticipating the strike. Yet he didn't move away.

Nick's fists clenched tight enough to split the knuckles as he held himself back, though every fibre in his body ached to land the blow. To defend Kayla. This wasn't the man he knew, his brother. The guy who would shit the entire crew off by insisting that most everyone had at least one redeeming feature. Hell, the guy didn't even talk trash on his ex.

Nick lowered his fists a little, though his chest still heaved.

'Nothing wrong with her? How do you figure?' Colley said. But there was something else in his tone, now, not derision. Satisfaction?

Nick forced his fingers to uncurl, stiff with anger as he pointed toward Kayla's bedroom. His voice ragged, the words came out jerky. 'You know her. Better than anyone, Colley, you bloody *know* her. You know what she's been through. How can you take what those bastards did, pin it on her, make it her fault? Where the fuck do you get off measuring her by what was done *to* her? She deserves so much better. She deserves to be...to be...' Fuck. He couldn't say it. Shouldn't say it. Mustn't even think it.

Colley let go a long breath. 'I don't give a flying fuck what label you put on it, Nick, but maybe keep that *emotion* in mind next time you try to give me some bullshit spiel about how much you don't care.'

He could still take Colley. Pound some sense into him.

Except maybe Colley was the one who was making sense. He needed time to think.

Colley angled his head toward the hall. 'I suggest you get rid of your newspaper collection before Kayla sees it, and go cool off in the shower.'

THOUGH HE'D SPENT time in the courtyard trying to untangle Colley's words, Nick was still confused as all hell. The *emotions* threatening his control were neither right nor normal. He stalked back into the house.

In front of him, Kayla stepped from the bedroom. She paused on the edge of the living area, where Colley sat with his head in his hands, and glanced at the clock. 'Ugh. You're here revoltingly early.'

She was usually eager for the meds. Maybe he should take that as a good sign? Kayla rubbed at her sleep-crumpled face, avoiding the scar along her cheekbone, and his hope evaporated, anger surging too easily. He hung back in the hall, striving for control.

Colley looked up. 'Did you leave the other five behind?'

'Other five?'

'Yeah, that's Sleepy and Grumpy accounted for. Where are the other five dwarves?'

Kayla snorted, crossing to the kitchen. 'Hilarious. You came by early just to share that line?'

Colley waved a mug. 'No, I've plenty more where that came from. I'm guessing Nick introduced you to one of his prized reds when you got home last night?'

Kayla screwed up her face. 'I don't even remember getting home. Anyway, I had enough sour grapes at dinner to do me for a few years. I'm not into hardcore stuff. Mother, y'know.'

Nick scowled at the inference that Colley knew her history more intimately than he did. But he chose not to listen to the secrets Kayla shared in exchange for the medic's drugs.

'Lolly water is more my thing. Nick's a wine snob?'

'Yep, that's me.' He strode into the room, pretending he hadn't lurked. Shrugged into his leather jacket. 'Though I prefer the word connoisseur. Fancy wine, shiny cars, fast...'

'Women?' She looked disappointed with his predictability.

'I was going with food. It's freezing outside. Feel.' He pressed his fingers to her cheek, careful to approach slowly.

She didn't flinch.

But he was imagining shit if he thought she leaned into his frigid touch. 'Anyway, how about we get out of here? I figure the press would have had their fill last night and might back off a bit. Or at least make a late start. We could take a drive through the Hills, maybe grab lunch at Hahn-dorf.' His words came out too fast, giving away that he'd rehearsed while he showered. 'We can probably find some decent *lolly water*. Colley, you in?' Still pissed at Colley, he begrudged the invitation. But it'd be safer that way.

Colley eased back in his chair. 'Raincheck. It's a daddy-day, and the zoo and Macca's are more Sara's idea of fun.' He clasped the mug to his chest. 'And coffee, I hope. Lots and lots of coffee.'

Kayla shook her head, her words too quiet. 'It'd be better if I just hang out here.'

'Better?' Jesus, he'd kill Colley if she'd overheard their argument. '*Better* in what way?'

She lifted one shoulder, examining the red scars that crisscrossed her palm like ribbons of valour. 'Just...safer.'

He scowled at Colley, a silent accusation Kayla wouldn't understand. 'You'll be safe with me. I promise. Come on, I'll warm up the car.'

Colley hauled himself up. 'You'd best get a move on, Kayla. You don't want to see what the Cap's like if you disobey orders. We'll skip the once-over, but I'll give you some extra painkillers to take with you. Just in case.'

Nick winced. Painkillers. 'Should she not go?' His voice came out harsh. He tugged on his ear, staring Colley down.

The medic eyed him levelly. 'I wouldn't let her do *anything* that I didn't think was in her best interests, Captain.'

Colley had manipulated him. And he knew why: the medic took exception to his almost pathological rejection of emotion. But Nick wasn't a talker, and their friendship—forged in blood and violence—didn't lend itself to intimate sharing: he'd shoot Colley down before he got five words out. Yet by goading him, Colley had made his point. At the risk of a beating.

Which Nick still wasn't certain he wouldn't dish out.

Covered neck-to-wrists-to-ankles by jeans and a sweater, Kayla appeared in the garage doorway as he folded the car cover. 'Impressive. You dress quicker than any woman I know.'

She shot him a sideways glance. 'Maybe they thought you weren't offering much incentive.'

As always, it took him a hot second to realise she joked —or was there an implicit compliment? By then she'd reached out to caress the Jag's black duco, but froze, like she expected a reprimand.

Tossing aside the cover, he took Kayla's hand and planted it firmly on the paintwork, her bones bird-fragile beneath his palm. 'She's a classic. You won't hurt her.' He wasn't making an excuse to hold her hand. He regularly invited people to smudge the painstaking wax job.

Kayla pulled free. A flush dusted her cheekbones, dragging his eyes to that scar. 'Might have to sign up if the Army pays this well. And provides camo uniform into the bargain.'

'The cams are a given, but it's not great pay.' He helped her into the low seat, holding his breath. Like that'd ease her pain. 'The car was a gift from my folks when I finished officer training. Doesn't get run much now, she's a bit flashy. I prefer the bike.' He hiked a thumb toward the Ducati Multistrada occupying the third bay.

'Your parents are generous.'

He reversed out of the garage. He'd been right about the media. No vans lurked in the street 'Were. They died a few years back.' Like always, the words cut him with renewed loss, slashes too fine and numerous to ever heal. Stupid. He was sure as hell old enough and big enough not to need his folks. But it would've been good to chew his old man's ear off, debrief to someone other than Colley.

Maybe it hurt worse because he'd never told them how much he...*appreciated* their support. Yeah, that emotion he could allow. But telling them wouldn't have made any difference. The damn truck driver would still have been on the wrong side of the road at the wrong time.

'You're an orphan, too?'

He grinned. 'I don't know about that. Orphan fits you just fine. Y'know, being small and helpless. But me...?'

Kayla turned to the window and he knuckled the leather steering wheel, the bruise from belting the sink swelling. *Helpless.* Why had he chosen that word? Her strength intimidated and awed him. Jesus, did he say it so she'd rely on him, allow him to play at being a knight in shining armour? Because that'd be a total bastard move.

Few residents of suburbia prepared to be out of a warm bed on a cold morning, the Sunday streets were sleepy. Kayla scanned the pavements, and Nick's mouth twisted into a bitter line. If he'd done his job right, she wouldn't need to do that.

Despite neglect, the car handled well, hugging the road up the steep grades of the hills to the east of the city. The heater kicked in, and the leather interior filled with Kayla's scent. Honey and something smooth. He should flick over to external air, let in the raw smell of the eucalyptus leaves crushed beneath the tyres. Instead, he dropped a gear, cornering harder than necessary. Kayla swayed toward him. He inhaled deeply. Vanilla.

Christ, man, get a grip.

The old-school tape deck cranked, Kayla's fingers beat

time on her denim-clad knee. With the doors locked and the city spread below them she seemed less wary, her features softened. Still, she clearly wasn't the type to waste time on the tanning bed or the nail salon.

What the hell? Why was he comparing Kayla to the *type* of women he dated? Damn Colley. He wasn't *interested* in her. She intrigued him. That's all there was to it. Her grave reserve, interspersed with flashes of ironic black humour, and the pervasive sense of loneliness made him want to know more.

Which was completely fucked up. He never needed to know anything about the women in his life.

He forced his attention back to the road. 'You like Meatloaf? Feel free to sing along.'

'I'll spare you. My warning label reads 'strictly air singing only'.'

He lifted an eyebrow to prompt her. Thank God the road narrowed, and he needed to keep his eyes on it.

Kayla hesitated, then spoke fast, as though unaccustomed to sharing her thoughts. 'You know, air singing, like playing air guitar...only, singing.' She waved a hand to clarify. 'My musical ability exists entirely in my imagination.'

Long-forgotten memory flashed through him. 'I know exactly what you mean. When I was a kid, I begged Dad to buy me a guitar. I was on his case for months, telling him I'd be the next Chris Isaak. No, bugger that. I reckon in my mind I actually *was* Chris Isaak.'

They hit a hundred metre straight and he risked a glance sideways. Ripped his focus back to the road. Watching him, she was all huge grey eyes and soft silence. The rest of his story stammered out. 'As it turned out, I could barely get to grips with the basic chords.' Real smooth. A good decade or more younger than him, Kayla would have no idea who Chris Isaak was.

Focused on the windscreen, she bit at her thumbnail, frowning. Her lips curved in sudden delight and his chest tightened as she turned back to him. 'Wicked Game. Right? That's the song that sucked you in?'

'You know Chris Isaak?'

'The boxer who stayed pretty? Every girl knows Chris Isaak,' she laughed, all pretence and defence driven from her face.

Shit. It wasn't only his dad he needed to speak to. Mum would've had an explanation for why he suddenly couldn't breathe.

Not necessarily an explanation he'd want to hear, though.

CHAPTER 31

Kayla hunched deeper in the seat as Nick pulled the car up against the stone-paved gutter. Lined with whitewashed, shingle-roofed shops offering a range of goods from charcuterie to candles, they could have been in an alpine German village from an earlier century. Except for the tourists.

The doors clicked as Nick unlocked from the central console. 'Fancy a bit of a walk before lunch?'

No. With no money and no mates, Tomas hadn't made a run for Bali, despite what the police believed.

Nick skirted the hood and opened her door, then leaned in to snag a stray leaf from her hair as a chestnut tree showered them with gold.

A tremble coursed her body.

He misunderstood. 'Can't believe how quick the weather's turned. Autumn always catches me out. Here, take my jacket.'

'I'll look like a mushroom buried in all that leather.'

'You'll look cute.'

Her smile froze. *Don't read anything into it.*

They meandered along the footpath, Nick taking the roadside edge. Pausing in front of each shop, she stared at the small panes of rain-washed glass, scrutinising the liquefied reflections of people wandering behind them.

She caught Nick watching her in the wavy lines of the glass. He spoke low. 'I've got your back, Kayla. You can relax.' He angled his head toward the door. 'Do you want to go in some of these places, or shall we just press our noses to the windows?'

Would they be hidden from Tomas? Or could he corner her? 'Sure. This place is perfect. I need to grab a gift for Sue.'

It was warmer in the shop, and it took her only a moment to assess and dismiss the other two customers. She lifted candles, sniffed at the base. Sue had an affinity for anything musk.

Sneezing repeatedly, Nick took the bagged purchase from her and hurried toward the exit. 'How is it you're not sneezing? The smell has to be a whole lot stronger down there.' Only the left side of his mouth ever responded to his humour. The other side remained firm and straight, as though he held something in reserve.

'Short jokes, is it now? If this sets you off, you're about to be in all kinds of trouble. I noticed a soap-maker down the street.'

Nick swiped his eyes with the back of his hand. 'How about I wait outside?'

A cloud of fear eclipsed her brief pleasure. 'It's fine, I don't need to go in.'

Nick held the door. 'Actually, I need to get a gift for Colley's kid.'

Though she heard him, the need to stay vigilant stole

her focus, and she peered cautiously into the street before stepping from the candle shop.

She couldn't keep acting like this. Colley already watched her as though concerned she'd slip back into the brief madness conjured by the discovery of Tomas's freedom. And Nick couldn't treat her like she was normal if she didn't act normal. They both needed to be invested in the lie —she remembered that from childhood, when they'd all had their part to play. Her, Mother and Dad.

A jerk of Nick's head indicated the wrought-iron framed sign above the next shop. 'Maybe I can find something for her in here? I've no idea what girls like.'

Act normal. 'Oh, sure.' She drew out the last word.

He grinned. 'Ouch. I said *girls,* right? Emphasis on the age.' He ducked beneath the wooden lintel, his shoulders blocking the doorway as he reached back to guide her down steep stairs.

She slid her hand into his and stepped down. 'How old is—'

The cellar lurked in gloom, the shadowed corners impenetrable after the wintry brightness outside. Lanterns chased flickering wraiths across the dirt floor and up rough faux-rock walls, studded with semi-precious stones. The fake mining tunnel reeked of damp soil and darkness.

And suddenly of smoke and sweat and fear and shit and agony.

Shock stole the blood from her hands and toes, pumping it to her overworked heart. The surge of adrenaline urged her to flee, but she could only stare over Nick's shoulder as every muscle in her body tightened into an unbearable tangle of pain.

'Christ!' Hands on her waist, Nick lifted her up the single

step like a ragdoll and strode to the shelter of a huge elm on the footpath.

She blinked furiously. Mustn't cry.

Nick's mouth contorted. 'Jesus, I'm sorry, Kayla. I should've realised.' He pulled her against his chest, hiding her from passers-by, his chin resting on her head.

Covered her. Protected her. Waited for the trembling to pass.

She snatched shallow breaths, fighting the memories. But she didn't cry. The terror brought nausea, and she focused on that. Like Colley showed her.

Gradually her pulse slowed, and she fought to relax her muscles, one by one. She could smell the dubbin on Nick's jacket, his aftershave, the nearby bakery. So many things that weren't a cave. Teeth gritted, she masked the trembling. Tried to cling to the reality of this moment, blocking the memories.

Nick spoke without lifting his chin. 'Wait here. I'm going in there—' He freed a hand and indicated the shop. 'But I'll still be able to see you, okay?'

He meant he'd be able to see Tomas.

Tomas, who belonged in a cave. Tomas, who said she was the best he'd ever had. Tomas, the nightmare she would never escape—because he was so much more than a figment of her imagination.

She didn't want Nick to let her go. His arms shielding her, he was clean and safe and strong.

And forbidden and untouchable and taboo.

She dug her nails into the smooth trunk of the tree behind her as Nick disappeared into the darkened doorway. Kept her eyes fixed there, glancing neither left nor right, terrified of what she would see. Held her breath until he reappeared.

Nick eased her hand from the trunk, prying open her fingers. She should uncurl them herself, but couldn't spare the energy. Every fibre of her being, every breath, every heartbeat, had to focus on blocking the memories attached to the scars he revealed.

He slid a fine gold band set with a small opal onto her finger. The dark-blue gem flashed red and green in the wintry sun. 'That bloody desert owes you something.'

What should she say? She had no frame of reference for accepting a gift not couched in expectation and innuendo. Her hand reflexively clenched, capturing Nick's, but he didn't pull away. Instead, his thumb stroked her whitened knuckles, his words warm against her face. 'Do you want to go home?'

Her brittle laugh crackled with deceit. 'Didn't you promise me lolly water?'

'Are you sure?'

No. She was only sure she didn't want to lose time that could be spent with him. Going home now would bring them a little closer to the court case, when she'd give her deposition, then walk out of Nick's life. But that's how it had to be. Her history made it vital she didn't rely on anyone. But surely she'd earned these few minutes?

She pushed away from the tree and walked ahead, determined to prove her independence. The wind cut to bone, tugging at her hair, leaves skittering like frightened kittens around her feet.

Nick fell into step, an arm loosely around her shoulders, fingers spread as though the less of her exposed, the better he could protect her. Squeezing between redgum tables and the stone frontage, he guided her toward a pub. 'I have to warn you, this place doesn't look much from outside. But they make the best chicken Kiev in the state.'

'We'll have to see about that. There's a truck stop out Oodnadatta way...'

Nick placed a hand on the planked timber door. 'I'll make you a deal. You try mine and next time I'm up north, we'll check out your roadhouse.'

The harsh jangle of the doorbell killed the illicit thrill of his teasing as the aroma of stale beer and deep-fried schnitzel cloaked them. The clink of glasses stilled, the hum of conversation drifting to a discordant halt as patrons at the bar swivelled to check out the interlopers.

Typical country pub.

Normal territorial behaviour.

Except for the greedy flare of recognition in their eyes, the ducking of heads and not-so-quiet whispers of interest. She wanted to hide from them, from their knowledge and curiosity. But she couldn't. She had to inspect each person, had to check, had to be *sure*.

'Don't worry. We're not stopping here,' Nick said quietly. He drew her through a narrow passageway and into a small dining room, the tables made private by the high backs of roughly-hewn wooden benches. A vaulted timber ceiling soared above stone walls. Blue smoke from a log fire hazed the air, the smell of well-seasoned gum sweet and deep, like a mellow cigar.

Nick scowled as he slid onto the bench opposite. 'These seats look awesome, but they're damn hard. Never noticed before. I'll get some cushions.'

She bit the inside of her cheek. 'No, don't bother. It's fine.' He didn't know the rules of the game of pretend.

He'd already stood. 'You're sure? We'll sit in the regular dining room if you prefer?'

She waved him down. 'No, this is...nice.'

A jeans-clad waiter handed them parchment menus. 'Grab your drinks at the bar, mate.'

'No worries. So, lolly water?' Nick's cheek creased. 'I'll see what they can do, but don't shoot me if I end up with one of those triple-colour kids' drinks. Back in two ticks, sweetheart.'

Sweetheart. He'd used the term a few times. Obviously a habit. It meant nothing, yet longing trembled through her body.

Craning around the seat, she watched as Nick leaned on the polished slab of wood, as wide as a car, which ran the length of the room. The barmaid held the glasses, rather than slide them across the counter, relinquishing them only when Nick's hands brushed hers. Nick flashed a smile at the flirtation, and Kayla grunted as a flare of jealousy stabbed the pit of her stomach. Her fingernails dug into her scarred palms. The gold band pinched. She stared down at it. The ring Nick purchased to divert her. A forbidden treat under the door.

He returned with two glasses. 'Yours is Howard's Vineyard Rosé. Tell me if it's not sweet enough.' He paused as the waiter deposited a basket of rolls on the redgum slab. 'You trust me on the Kiev?'

She nodded.

He held up two fingers to the waiter. 'Two of the specials, please.' Nudging the wine toward Kayla, he settled back with his glass. 'So, your turn.'

'My turn?'

'Sure. You copped my tales of yore. Tell me a happy story about your childhood.'

Her fingers tightened on the stem of the glass. After weeks of companionable silence, she hadn't expected the third degree. She had no story to tell. None that should be told, anyway. 'Happy?' She lifted one shoulder. 'Childhood was short.'

The hard planes of his Nick's face shifted as though he clenched his teeth. 'Okay. So, skip ahead. Why teaching? Guess you love kids?' He flinched, like he'd spoken amiss.

The glass left a wet circle as she used finger and thumb to twirl it, faster and faster, never spilling. 'The only adults I knew were teachers.' *And the men in my bed.* The men who left money on the bedside table. At first, she had refused the cash, knowing what it made her. But then she realised that, their love a lie, their money was real. Taking money added to her power and paid for her escape.

'Your parents were teachers?' Nick took a hot roll from the basket. Ripped it in half, arranged thick slices of butter, like cheese wedges, and passed it to her. Grinned at her expression. 'German style.'

Butter melting on her fingers, she shredded the bread, dropping it to her plate. 'No. They'd been dead three years when I got into uni.' She should admit she had killed them, save him the standard declaration of sympathy.

His knife hovered over the creamy yellow curl. 'How old were you when they died?'

'Fifteen.'

'You lived with other family?'

'State care.'

'And then teacher's college?'

'Uni.' He seemed determined to piece together her life.

'Figured I'd teach for a few years while I decide what I actually *want* to do.' She buried the surge of bitterness beneath a smile. 'Guess it's time to come up with that plan B.' Yesterday, she'd turned on the cell phone Sue provided. Her heart racing in fear of exposure and confrontation, she avoided social media and news apps, but checked her emails. Carefully hidden between departmental protestations of concern had been the formal notifications.

'Plan B?'

'My job's been reassigned and my house re-let.'

'What?' Nick's monosyllable ricocheted around the booth. 'Why?'

Conversation from the neighbouring tables faltered and Kayla lowered her voice. 'The Department had to get another teacher in.'

Butter congealed on the table, the roll hanging forgotten from Nick's fingers. 'You're still getting paid, though?'

Kayla's thumbnail blanched the denim across her thigh. She wouldn't be caught begging sympathy for this new injustice. She shook her head. 'I'm out of sick leave. Shared Services suggest I apply for workers compensation—though they can't say whether my claim is likely to be approved.' She forced a grin. 'Seems there's a shortage of precedents.'

The flatware jumped as Nick slammed the table. 'That's ludicrous!' Customers peered around the edges of their booths. Her hand reflexively flashed across the table, trying to calm him, and he captured it. Leaned closer. 'I'll get Kim to have a word with someone. He's good with bureaucratic bullshit. He'll sort it out.'

His thumb stroked across the back of her hand and the words stuck in her throat. 'D-don't worry about it. I'll wait a couple of weeks. If nothing happens, I'll go to the union.'

His grip tightened. 'It's not bloody right. You've enough on your plate without this crap.'

'Speaking of plates...' She slid from his unintentional caress as their meals arrived.

Nick's fingers briefly stretched toward her retreating hand, then curled quickly around his wineglass.

Half-an-hour later, having devoured most of her meal along with his own vast portion, Nick pushed the plates aside. 'Coffee?'

She'd drink poison if it would prolong the moment of make-believe. Nick had dropped his interrogation while they ate and, with no ebb and flow of customers at the other tables, she didn't need to keep checking the room.

Nick flagged a waitress and ordered, before turning back to Kayla. 'So, after we're through with court and all this business is over, what is Plan B?'

Her leg jerked involuntarily at the reminder, knocking the underside of the table. She rubbed her kneecap. 'Seems like it'll never be over.'

A shadow crossed Nick's face, probably irritation at her whiny tone. 'But the department will reinstate your contract?'

'No. I've been terminated.' If only the word encompassed the complete truth. Ended. No more pain. But then there'd also be no more joy. It hadn't figured much in her life, yet this moment, mellowed by wine, warmed by the crackling log fire, rated as pretty huge.

Or hugely pathetic, given that it was all in her mind.

'But they'll relocate you? A new contract?'

She straightened her back, the pain a reminder, a warning. Tempted to allow him under her armour, she shared too much. 'I'm not interested.' She'd never teach again. Which would be fine, except she'd only ever been good at two things: teaching and fucking. And they'd both screwed her over. 'I won't be responsible for someone else's life.'

Nick's leather jacket creaked as he leaned closer. 'That would never happen again.'

She should have accepted the loan; being wrapped in his jacket would be close to being in his arms. She had become accustomed to—*dependent on*—him holding her when she couldn't face the present or the future. Now, the longing to beg for consolation, for comfort, for promises that would be broken, swelled within her. 'It wasn't exactly in the job description this time around, either.'

'What do you want to do?'

She shrugged and reached for her coffee, drank with a deliberate air of finality. But the words wouldn't be drowned, so she strangled the mug, trying to at least censor them. She didn't look at Nick. She could either talk or look at him. And neither was advisable. 'I used to dream about what my life would be, like I could achieve something, become someone. I thought there'd be a purpose, something exciting, meaningful.'

She knuckled her mouth, but the words sneaked around her fist. 'But people like me, we don't deserve to dream. Instead I live a nightmare, so damn scared that *this*—simply surviving—will be as good as my life gets.'

Nick's eyes glazed. His throat working convulsively, his disgust was obvious.

Had the other patrons overheard her secrets? Kayla nailed her gaze to the wet-ringed table. Conversation swelled reassuringly around them, the scrape of cutlery a comforting backdrop.

Pushing aside their cups, Nick reached across the table

and captured her hands, squeezing until she looked at him. Twice he raised his head, his mouth working. Then he released her, flicked open his wallet, and tossed notes onto the bill platter. 'I'll take you home.'

Cold seeped through her. Men paid for her meals often enough, but they always expected—and received—fair compensation.

She had nothing Nick would want.

CHAPTER 32

Although Kayla tried to recapture their easy companionship over the following days, her pathetic outburst had altered the dynamic. She had finally challenged Nick's ability to start each day with a clean slate. Now he watched her with a slight frown, the quality of his silence altered, fraught with unasked questions. Did he feel trapped by the admission of her homeless, jobless state?

He took her phone from the granite bench, his fingers sliding across the screen. 'I won't be long. If I don't get something to eat, I'll start gnawing on the bookshelves.'

She hunkered in her chair, squashing the surge of panic. She would be alone. Both George and Colley were adamant that she was safe, Tomas had nothing to gain by seeking her out. When she insisted they were wrong, their reassurance hid pity. She didn't need Nick to look at her that way.

He handed her the phone. 'My number's programmed. Leave it on that screen, swipe if you need me. Okay? I'll be, seriously, less than ten minutes away.'

Ten minutes. She knew what could happen in ten

minutes. How many times it could happen. She had counted off the seconds.

She wrapped her fingers around the sliver of plastic and metal, careful not to change the screen. 'Yeah, of course. Take your time.'

Nick headed for the door but pulled up short. 'No, wait.' He tugged his own phone from his pocket. Dialled. 'Yeah, hi. Two large nachos to go.' He angled the phone away from his mouth. 'Are you sure you don't want anything?'

She shook her head. He'd heard her silent plea; he wasn't leaving. Relief and guilt battled within her. No wonder he felt trapped. But it was another day Tomas couldn't reach her.

Nick addressed the phone again. 'Plus two chicken quesadilla and a beef burrito. Pick up.'

Her throat closed.

He slid the cell into the pocket of his faded jeans. 'I'll make you a drink, first.'

As he clattered in the kitchen, she shrank back into the chair. He would be gone only a few minutes. She had to stop being so pathetic. Soon enough, she would have to live without his protection.

Or die without it. Death held more promise than threat, her fear not of what Tomas would do, but how slowly he would do it.

Nick placed a steaming mug on the chest. 'Can you reach? Want me to pull the table closer?' He rubbed absently at a scorch mark on the wooden surface. Checked his watch. 'Probably not ready yet. No point going too early, just to sit and twiddle my thumbs. Do you like hot sauce? I'll get extra.'

Good, the hands she wrapped around her mug didn't

tremble. She could do this. 'You better get going. Soggy cornmeal is pretty unappetising.'

Nick chewed at his lip. 'Yeah, right.' His fingers drummed the back of the chair, then he smacked his palm on the leather, turned, and headed toward the door. 'I'll lock up, but shoot the deadbolt, okay? You'll feel safer.'

She followed, shoving the door closed, grimacing as it snagged Nick's heel. Twisted the deadlock and slid the security chain across.

Her back braced against the door, holding the world at bay, the house threatened to swallow her, echoing in vast, dangerous silence. She'd had little interest in her surroundings, content simply that it wasn't a cave. Or a hospital.

But now it represented Nick.

She forced herself from the door and moved to the oak bookcases.

Jerked around as something scrabbled near the unguarded door.

A sinister rustle, fingernails on wood.

Could she make it to the kitchen, grab a knife?

Not without taking her eyes from the door. And she couldn't do that.

Mail dropped through the hatch, a slot too narrow for a black-nailed hand to squeeze through.

Her knees sagged and she wilted against the shelves, waiting for her heart to steady before she turned to the books.

Stared at their alphabetical organisation.

Couldn't focus.

Panic churned in her gut, clawing higher.

She needed to distract her mind from all the places it was prohibited.

A pair of paintings hung on the wall, but as she crossed to scrutinise them, the drapes caught her eye. Nick would keep the windows locked. But maybe she should check? Yet that would mean pulling aside the curtains, confronting whatever peered in— she stumbled across the room, putting the heavy furniture between herself and the windows.

The hallway, jellied red and blue by leadlight skylights, led to the safety of her room, made masculine by a large bed, wooden dresser, and huge wardrobe. Had Nick given her his room? Did she hide beneath his covers?

She slid one foot forward. She could find out. A frequent overnight visitor, Colley also had a room somewhere along that unexplored hallway, and further down was the bathroom the men used.

There would be razors.

Her pulse quickened. She took another step.

Her left hip was virgin territory. Two swift slices and she could release the anxiety that bubbled within her. With fear and self-loathing oozing across her skin, she would be back in control. She hadn't cut in five years but, God, she never stopped craving the release.

Another step, her need growing.

But surrendering meant leaving the door undefended.

She had to watch it until Nick returned to guard it for her.

Car tyres spun on the driveway, and she raced back to the door, slammed into it as though she could hold it closed.

Nick couldn't be back yet.

Colley rode a motorbike.

Fingers trembling, she shaded the privacy panels alongside the door, squinting but afraid to lean close in case something leaped toward her.

A khaki wagon, George Kimber's distinctive rolling stride. Relief fogging the glass, she fumbled with the locks.

His overhanging brows at odds with an otherwise immaculate appearance, Kimber pursed his lips. 'Didn't expect to find you opening the door. The lads all deserted you?'

She had survived. Minutes only, a baby step, but she'd done it. 'Nick's out grabbing food. Steve's not here yet.' She reached around George, relocking the door.

He waved a folded bundle of junk mail as they moved to the lounge. 'This was on your step. Captain West is shopping? Seems you have domesticated him. It's somewhat reassuring to discover the tabloids don't fabricate everything they print.'

'The tabloids? What do you mean?' Giddy with relief and achievement, she couldn't make sense of his words. She took the mail, making a grab for the local rag as it fell from her grasp.

George turned back to the door. 'Sounds like Lieutenant Colley's bike.'

As he crossed the foyer, Kayla bent to pick up the papers. The newspaper unfolded, the front-page photo leaping out at her. *"Romanced by Rescuer!"*

A chill swept from her feet to her soul. Her legs gave out, and she slumped into the nearest chair.

'Hey, Major Kimber tells—what's wrong?' Colley leaped down the three steps, landing on his knees in front of her chair. His fingers went automatically to her wrist. 'Kayla, talk to me. What is it?' He cast around as though he expected to find an assailant, and his eyes lit on the newspaper. 'Ah. That.'

'You've seen it?' she whispered.

Kimber sat, smoothing his carefully creased pants. 'I'm sorry, Kayla. I wouldn't have brought the mail in if I'd realised you weren't aware of the press.'

Her mind spun. Teeth chattering, she wrapped her arms across her stomach. 'Why would they print such crap?' She couldn't bring herself to look at the paper, but she needed to move it. Destroy it, before Nick saw it.

Kimber grunted. 'Nature of the business. And Captain West's wise refusal to comment is driving them into a frenzy.'

Her heart stuttered, and she slammed a hand to her chest. 'You mean, he knows?' No razor cut deep enough to fix this. 'How could they do this to him?' She was blaming the journos, but it was her fault, all hers.

'What do you mean?' Kimber frowned.

'Doesn't the Defence Force hold integrity as a core value? They'll destroy Nick's career.'

'I don't see how.'

'He hasn't...he didn't do...this.' She pointed at the paper. 'It's my fault. I thought—I wanted—' Each of the words scraped at her throat, unwillingly torn free. 'But I never said anything, I don't understand how they found out.' Humiliation manifested as pain, and she hunched forward, struggling to breathe.

Colley gripped her hand. 'Kayla, calm down.'

The major thrust himself up, pacing back and forth. Stopped, as though summoning a thought, then paced again. 'I don't really know what to say.'

Of course he didn't. She was sick, corrupt in body, mind, and soul.

'Lieutenant Colley, I'm sure you can arrange some appropriate help if Ms Petrovic feels she needs—'

The counselling talk, again. 'Jesus, how is anyone supposed to help? They can't change who I am, what I've done!'

Kimber shook his head. 'I'm sure you have no cause to judge yourself so harshly.'

'Don't you understand? It's my fault they're saying that shit about Nick. They'll judge *him*, and they have no right to.'

'Judge him for what?' The major managed to make his confusion sound genuine.

Kayla rubbed both hands across her face. 'You don't know me. You don't know what I've done.'

'I do,' Colley said bluntly. 'And I don't see the problem.'

'I didn't tell you everything. I'm not a good person. Th-this court case. If they find out who I am, what I am...it doesn't matter to me. But Nick can't be associated with me. Not like this.' She jabbed a finger at the papers.

'Who are you, Kayla?' Colley said. 'What is it you've done that's so terrible?'

She couldn't tell them everything. But she had to make them realise they needed to protect Nick. She twisted to face Kimber. 'I killed my parents.'

She expected to see shock, perhaps disbelief. Instead, he nodded. 'Your parents died in a vehicle accident.'

'I gave my mother alcohol. I wanted her to die.'

'Your *mother* never was one,' the major said, an unusually sharp note in his usually well-modulated voice. 'You were fifteen. An abused child. Your mother had issues of her own.'

'How do you know that?'

'Matter of record.'

Colley hadn't released her hand. 'It wasn't your fault, Kayla. Your mother chose to drink. She self-destructed.'

'I enabled her. But my dad. I didn't mean for my dad to die. They never went anywhere together; he wasn't supposed to be in the car.'

'Still not your fault, Kayla.' The major's tone was again imperturbable. 'And I fail to see how this reflects on Captain West.'

'There are other things.' How much had she told Colley? She couldn't remember. Desperate for the drugs, she could've traded any information.

Kimber patted clumsily at her arm. 'You don't have a criminal record, Kayla. Anything that you believe you've done wrong is measured only by your own moral value.'

Colley rounded on him. 'She's done nothing wrong. She survived a shit childhood by making the best of the situation.'

'Making the best of it?' She shook her head exhaustedly. 'I sold myself.'

Kimber nodded. 'And if that's what you had to do, that's what you had to do. That's an indictment on our society, not on you.'

Her head and heart hurt. 'The excuses don't matter. Nick is tainted by being associated with me.'

Colley jerked to his feet. '*Tainted?* Hell, Kayla, I'm not even going to buy into how wrong that word is, but don't you think it should be his call?'

Sudden fury lanced through her. 'He didn't get to make that choice. They already printed this bullshit!'

The major folded his hands between his knees. 'Excellent. Embrace that anger, Kayla. Anger will serve you far better than shame or guilt. Just don't let it change who you are.'

If only she could change who she was. 'You. Don't. Get. It.' Her fist pounded her chest with each word. 'It's fucking disgusting. They're suggesting Nick would want to be with someone who...who...' Her chin trembled and she bit off the word.

'Was raped.' The major's tone was firm. 'Kayla, that's the only crime in your history, and it was committed *against* you, not by you.'

How stupid could he be? The truth ripped from her like a sheet of flayed skin. 'It's not rape if I said yes. It's not rape if I traded. It's not rape if I deserved it.'

The major jerked back like he'd been slapped. 'Deserved it? Are you mad?'

Still on his haunches, Colley folded a hand around her shaking fist. 'Whether they coerced, persuaded, traded, bought, or whatever the hell else you want to call it, those bastards forced themselves on you, Kayla. That's rape. There is no other word for it. They did unforgivable things to you, things that no-one could ever deserve. But let it end there.'

She snatched her hand away. If she allowed them to use the label *rape,* they stole what little control she retained over her life. Forced her to be a victim. How could they think that stigma didn't change who she was, who she could be?

The sole of George's polished shoe squeaked across the floor as he shifted. 'Kayla, they tortured you. Don't torture yourself. You deserve better than that.'

Her bitter laugh almost escaped. They thought they knew her, but it would only ever be a slivered fraction of the truth. They knew nothing about what she deserved. But she nodded, because agreement was easier than trying to explain.

The familiar tone of the car purred up the paved drive-way. She clambered to her feet, brushing aside Colley's assistance. 'Tell him I'm asleep.'

Kimber stood. 'I'll tell him you're getting changed. I assume, like any female of my acquaintance, you require several hours? My wife directed me to invite you to dinner. There are a few points I wish to discuss before the hearing, and Lorraine's keen to meet you. I believe you've attained something akin to celebrity status in the magazines she favours.'

'No—' The refusal trembled on her lips. But Nick's key twisted in the lock. She fled.

CHAPTER 33

She barely spoke to Nick on the drive to the Kimber home. She'd heard the low voices in the lounge room, the sudden punctuations of incoherent anger. He knew that she knew. And neither of them could expose that knowledge.

Nick leaned forward, reading the house numbers, indistinct in the gathering dusk. He pulled up before a stone cottage, the white painted walls offset with blue trim on the windows and eaves. 'Looks like this is it.'

She forced the words. 'You've never been here?'

He toggled the handbrake. 'Twenty years, never rated an invitation. Though I've met Lorraine at functions. She's a sweet old bird. You'll love her.'

Sarcasm? Kayla couldn't imagine the austere officer's spouse being 'sweet'. As she stepped from the car the rhythmic wash of waves breaking on the sand accompanied the taste of salt on her lips. Last time she'd been at the beach, everything had been...different.

Nick unlatched a picket gate and guided her along a rose

bordered path. The last few ice-white blooms of the year nodded in a brackish breeze.

A short, plump woman stood outlined in the light of the open door.

Nick murmured 'You know the nursery rhyme *Jack Spratt could eat no fat?* Well, prepare yourself.' His body vibrated with laughter as they entered the pool of light on the porch. 'Lorraine. How are you?'

The woman stood on tiptoes, but still the captain had to bend for her to peck at his cheek. 'Nicholas, how lovely to see you. It's been far too long.' She turned faded blue eyes on Kayla. 'And you must be Kayla. I've been longing to meet you. George tells me you are quite the most amazing young lady.'

That didn't sound like anything that would have come from Major Kimber's lips. Kayla stiffened in the woman's lavender embrace.

Lorraine's hug slid away, though she kept hold of Kayla's hand and drew her inside. 'Come in, you're half frozen. George is in the study, he'll be out in a moment. Oh!' Her fingers located the scars on Kayla's palm. 'Oh, you poor thing. Nicholas, you wander down to the dining room— that way—and pour us drinks. Everything's on the sideboard. Kayla, come with me. I have something that will help with those cuts.'

Silently beseeching Nick's rescue, Kayla fought her instinct to pull away from Lorraine's warm, soft hand. Conversation with the captain would be better than working out how to respond to this woman.

Nick's eyes glinted as he saluted Lorraine. 'Yes, ma'am.'

Reluctantly, Kayla followed Lorraine.

Like the woman herself, the Kimber house was decorated in shades of pastel. Floral and homely. At least, it was what Kayla imagined homely to be.

The muted peach walls of the hall were hung with framed photos, and Lorraine caught her staring. 'My boys.' She caressed a frame. 'All three of them in the forces, like their dad. Mind, not one of them has settled down yet.' She sighed. 'The way they're going, I'll never be a grandmother.' She moved on. 'Just in here, love.'

Kayla halted in the doorway of the bedroom Lorraine entered.

'Come in, come in,' Lorraine fussed toward a white dressing table. 'Sit yourself down on the bed.'

Covered with a fluffy white comforter, the bed was too beautiful to sit on. Dusky pink floral curtains closed a huge bay window, where a fat spaniel lay ensconced in a white wicker basket. No empty gin bottles or discarded medication packages. No crumpled tissues or filthy clothes. The room smelled of lavender and fresh linen. Not of vomit and sweat.

'Sit,' Lorraine repeated.

Kayla perched on the very edge of the bed, stiffening when Lorraine took her hand and squeezed cream onto it. 'I can do that.' She tried to snatch her hand back as Lorraine smoothed the lotion in, her thumb working firmly over the scars no one should have to touch.

Lorraine tutted comfortably. 'Nonsense, it's much nicer if someone does it for you. That's why we all love spa treatments, isn't it?'

Kayla remained silent; she wouldn't know.

Grey head lowered, Lorraine peered closely at her work. 'Oh, that's such a pretty ring. Coober Pedy opal?'

'I-I don't know. Nick bought it.' *Shit.* He wouldn't want anyone to know.

Lorraine's movements paused. 'Did he now? Well, that's lovely. This cream is wonderful for scars. Full of vitamin C and E. I get lots of scratches tending the roses, but they disappear overnight.' She held up the tube so Kayla could read it. 'George said you have a friend doing your shopping? Perhaps she can pick some up.'

'I'll ask next time she comes down.' She shouldn't stare at the room, but it was a magazine spread. Or a fairytale. That was it, Lorraine reminded her of the Fairy Godmother in the animation the kids watched for an end-of-term treat. Small and grey and sweet. Jealousy spiked: her sons were lucky.

Lorraine squeezed more cream onto her index finger, then turned to place the tube on the dressing table. 'Comes down? You mean she's up north?'

Hands hidden in her lap, Kayla massaged them together, trying to recreate the sensation. 'Yes. She'll be down for the c-court case.'

A frown puzzled Lorraine's forehead. 'But who's picking up all your little bits and pieces? The men can't possibly understand all the things you *need*. Oh, you poor thing.' Lorraine reached toward her face.

Kayla recoiled.

'How dare you come into my bedroom?' Mother's hand slaps across my cheek. 'How dare you go through my belongings?'

'But I need—' I indicate the packet of sanitary towels lying amongst the tumbled mess of the open drawers. School made it clear I can't keep asking for handouts at the office.

'You need?' Mother picks up one of the pads, exerting herself to shred it and dropping the wadding like confetti. 'You don't need

anything. You're not a woman. You never will be. You can use toilet paper. And don't you ever come in my room again.'

I know how to get the money to buy what I need. But I hate doing it.

Lorraine's index finger smoothed cream along Kayla's cheekbone. 'George should have told me that you're all alone. That's really just not good enough, I'll have a few words to say to him later. Well, you'll take this tube with you today, and I'll shop for you tomorrow.'

Get a grip. She couldn't cry. 'No. There's really nothing I need.'

Lorraine tutted through her teeth. 'Well, you can tell me what you need, or I'll go and buy lots of things that perhaps you don't need, but I think you should have.' She smiled comfortably. 'Now, let's go and turf that husband of mine out of the study. I didn't know which you'd prefer, so I've done both lamb and chicken for dinner. I'm sure Nicholas will eat anything. If he's like my boys, the issue is trying to fill him up, not finding what he likes.' She threaded her arm through Kayla's and guided her to the dining room.

'You sit next to your young man.' Lorraine indicated a seat that was far closer to Nick than it needed to be, given the size of the lace-covered dining table.

Kayla sat, her gaze on the silverware rather than register Nick's reaction to Lorraine's words.

The older woman perused the table, tapping a forefinger on pursed lips. 'Nicholas, you found the drinks? Be a dear, pour a scotch for George. I'll have sherry. I'm sure you can sort Kayla out.'

Lorraine left the room, and Nick murmured, 'Quite a force to be reckoned with, isn't she? You do realise that now every time I say Jack Spratt, you're going to lose it?'

As he stood, she risked a glance at him. 'I'm sure it works both ways. And I won't be court-martialled for insubordination.'

'End my career, would you? Then you'd be stuck with me full time.'

She frowned. Mention of his career reminded her of the headlines. She could apologise, but nothing she said would mitigate the humiliation. Like so much in her life, it was better to pretend it had never happened.

Nick turned to the sideboard. 'Now, drinking? Or meds?'

She screwed up her face. 'Can't I have both? Not tell Colley?'

He swivelled back, eyes locked to hers. 'I'll give you anything that makes you feel better—'

'Ah, good, you're here.' Kimber marched into the room like he crossed a parade ground.

It had been hard to imagine the major belonged in the snug house. Though Kayla had greedily scrutinised the fripperies and mementos of *normal* lives, nowhere had lurked evidence of his service in a disciplined and violent career.

'Major.' Nick surged to his feet.

Kimber waved him down. 'Not on duty tonight, son. Relax. I think we could all do with it. Where's that lovely wife of mine?'

Kayla started guiltily. 'The kitchen. I'll go and help her.'

Kimber dropped a hand onto her shoulder, patting clumsily. 'You'll do no such thing, young lady. You two entertain yourselves, I'll see if Lorraine needs any assistance.'

As the major left, Nick pulled his chair closer. 'Do you think we slipped down the rabbit hole?'

'Curiouser and curiouser?'

A line creased between his eyes. 'Sums up my life, at the moment.'

Bearing aromatic platters of roast meat and vegetables, Lorraine and George re-entered. Lorraine fussed around the table, piling Nick and George's plates high and selecting the choicest cuts of meat for Kayla.

As his wife finally took her seat, George reached for her hand and pressed a kiss on her knuckles. 'A wonderful feast, my love. Thank you.' He glanced at Nick and Kayla. 'All right, don't let it go cold, you two. I happen to know it's apple crumble for dessert, and I'm eager to get there.'

In the easy company of the small gathering, it seemed the captain treated Kayla as he had before their outing. Like a normal person. Her concern over the tabloids slowly dissipated. Survival had always meant choosing her battles; if Nick knew about the reports, but chose to ignore them, could she do the same?

The tension in her chest uncoiled a little, her guard dropping.

Despite his stated reason for the dinner, Major Kimber didn't bring up the court case. Although she barely joined in, Kayla followed the conversation as it flowed naturally from current affairs to cooking, soldiering to sewing.

Maybe this was what having a real home was like.

The emptiness inside her hurt.

CHAPTER 34

The sun had not yet risen in the ominously leaden sky, the air acrid with the promise of rain as thunder rumbled over the steep ranges surrounding the coastal city.

'Fitting, huh?' Kayla forced an approximation of a grin, then wrinkled her nose at the warm smell of fried onion filling Nick's kitchen.

Colley handed her a glass of juice and turned back to the stove. Worked a spatula under the edge of an omelette. 'Nick's in the shower. Trying to drown himself, I think. Did Sue get the gear you need?'

'Yeah.' She exhaled forcibly, shaking her tingling fingers.

The pan squealed as Colley slid it off the burner. He walked around the counter and grasped her hand, stilling her agitated movement. 'How do you feel?'

'What, no clipboard? Winging it, Doc?'

Colley's dark eyes locked to hers. He would stay silent until she replied.

She blew a breath from the corner of her mouth, lifting

her hair. 'Emotionally or physically?' Always question a questioner. Distract the inquisitor.

Colley wasn't fooled. 'Both.'

'Fine, thanks.' She forced a smile as Colley parroted her standard passive-aggressive response. She stuck with it because she was too much of a coward to admit the truth. Or maybe because admitting the truth wouldn't change it.

'Kayla...?' Colley wasn't letting her off, today.

She rolled her eyes, tempering the frustration with a half-smile. 'Remember falling out of bed when you were a kid? Half-asleep, you know what's happening, but you can't prevent the inevitable?'

He nodded.

'Well, like that. Except, I'm stuck in the freefall bit—and scared shitless of the impact.' A crack of thunder rattled the roof tiles. She set her glass down with a clunk, licked juice from her fingers.

Colley's hand moved to the small of her back. 'Moretti's certain the case will be straightforward. Thirty years in the business, I reckon we can trust his judgment.'

'Easy for you to say,' she muttered, wedging her hip against the counter so the medic wouldn't feel he had to steady her.

'This early, nothing's easy to say.' Nick prowled into the room, towelling damp hair. 'Morning, all. Why does my head feel like an entire tribe of pygmies danced on it?'

Colley moved back to the hotplate and retrieved the spatula. 'Could have something to do with the amount of booze you knocked back at Kim's.'

'You didn't exactly abstain, how come you're so bloody chirpy? Anyway, what's with all these invitations to the Kimbers' place? In twenty years, I didn't rate. Now it's three times in ten days.' Nick pointed at Kayla. 'You've turned Kim soft.'

After the Kimber's initial dinner party, George had decided that meeting with the barrister there would be opportune. Kayla hadn't protested. As Tony Moretti drilled her on what to expect, Lorraine's distant presence, although always carefully out of earshot, provided comfort. And cups of tea. Apparently, Lorraine believed strongly in the restorative powers of tea.

Colley held a jar of Vegemite toward Nick. 'Whack this on your toast. A mega dose of vitamin B will fix a hangover —I only have one naked tribesman. The alternative is to learn a little self-control, like Kayla.'

'Not self-control, I'm just a cheap drunk. I mean, cheap to keep.' Her voice rose as she floundered, realising it sounded like she was begging for somewhere to live. She'd done that plenty of times, but always had something to trade for the roof over her head. Cheeks flaming, she brushed past Nick. Fled to her room.

Seated at the dressing table, she stared at the wooden surface, rather than face her image. New clothes, courtesy of Sue, hung from the wardrobe door. Tailored black pants, white shirt with a high mandarin collar, and a heavy jacket. The same pumps she'd worn to the formal dinner. Metres of fabric to conceal her scars, only her hands and face would be exposed.

And her privacy.

She shuddered. Grabbed a brush and braided her hair over one shoulder.

Her eyes flicked to the mirror, and she tore her hair free of the plait and raked it into the familiar curtain around her face instead. Her shaking fingers caressed the charm

Lorraine had given her, along with a plethora of other items she apparently needed. A jewelled bluebird, Lorraine said it would bring good luck. The gift was so much more than she'd ever received from her own mother.

She picked up her makeup brush. Face powder floated like dust to the table. God, she had to control the trembling. Focus on breathing, Colley said. Count in. Count out.

No reason to panic.

Tony Moretti had spent hours locked in George's study, trying to desensitise her to the admissions she would make, the words she must use. Trying to convince her the whole thing was an act, a charade. She only had to play her part, speak her rehearsed lines.

The diagram he had drawn to familiarise her with the courtroom lay on the dresser. She traced it, measuring the distance between the square labelled 'accused' and the x marked with her name.

Nothing to fear.

Except *they* would be there. And Tomas wouldn't.

CHAPTER 35

Nick picked up Kayla's discarded glass and lifted an eyebrow at Colley.

The undercooked omelette squelched as Colley dropped it onto a plate and slid it toward him. 'Go easy on her, mate. She's nervous.'

Tossing back the juice, Nick straddled a barstool. 'Blame her?'

'Nope. Wish there was some way round this instead of putting her on the stand. The shirt's organised?'

Nick rolled the glass between his palms, nodded reluctantly. 'It is. But I'm not on board, mate. Moretti's wrong; he needs to tell Kayla his plan.'

Colley glanced toward the hallway, lowered his voice. 'Moretti said that sexual assault is statistically one of the most difficult offences to successfully prosecute. With Kayla refusing to have medical evidence taken, he needs a back-up strategy.'

Nick stabbed his eggs. He didn't want to think about exactly what the *medical evidence* entailed, or recall Kayla's vehement refusal to be assaulted, even under that guise. The barrister's proposal was all kinds of screwed, but he didn't have an alternative. This was no military manoeuvre with an enemy he could outfox. 'It's another bloody secret.' He already kept too many. 'It better provide the insurance Moretti expects.'

Colley stared at the skillet, the fork he tapped in an agitated rhythm driving spikes into Nick's head. 'Moretti said he has a prosecutorial burden to go for the highest possible charge. Once the jury *sees* what those bastards did to Kayla, defence will find it hard to argue down from attempted murder.'

The eggs were sawdust. 'A few years back, some bastard slit a girl's throat and left her for dead. The judge reduced the sentence because he figured, being unconscious, the girl hadn't suffered. Where the hell does that leave us? Can the defence assert that the level of v-violence makes no difference?' *Fuck.* Had to hope Colley didn't notice that one. He could get his head around the fact Kayla had been raped, but the extent of the brutality left him gutted.

'You've spent too long on the computer,' Colley cautioned. 'It's not going to help you, or her. Just let Moretti do his thing. In any case, I think there's been rape law reform since then.'

'You'd bloody want to hope so. But how fucking pathetic are we as a society that, instead of enacting laws that are patently just and fair, we spend years debating and trawling them through parliament? No wonder the system continually fails women. You know that less than two percent of sexual assault cases result in a conviction? And that's after more than eighty-seven percent of rape accusations are pulled without even making it as far as trial. Because there's no damn point.' Colley was right, he'd put too much time into researching the stats. No matter where he looked, there was no good news.

Colley shook his head. 'Like I said, that's where this insurance comes in. Christ, they beat Kayla to within an inch of her life: the attempted murder charge should stick. But if not, there's no way they can get off on the rape with aggravated assault charge.'

Despite his decisive words, the lieutenant's tone was uncertain. Which perfectly matched Nick's gut feeling. 'This whole damn thing is a farce. Any reasonable, logical person can see those bastards' guilt, but Moretti's adamant that the burden of proving it in court is far more complex than simple logic.' Even as he ranted, Nick recognised that his anger was partially driven by guilt: he should never have let the matter get this far. Court shouldn't have been necessary. He shoved to his feet, tugging on his ear. He'd get Kayla through today, then it'd all be over. She would be safe.

'Moretti will get the bastards, Nick. We know what they did. The whole country knows what they did. It's just a matter of allowing the process.'

'Obviously this *due process* bullshit wasn't developed with the victim's best interests in mind.' Nick drove his palms into his eye sockets, trying to chase away the weariness. Yeah, weary, that's all he felt.

It had to be.

∼

TWO HOURS LATER, Nick guided Kayla into the capacious foyer of the court building. A lull in the excited chatter of the crowd marked their progress toward the correct courtroom.

Rigid but determined, Kayla took a seat outside the court. She could have chosen to wait in a private room, but had waived the right, her jaw firm, though her lips trembled.

Did the blame for her obstinacy, her resolve to see this through, lie with him? Weeks ago he'd insisted it was her duty to have the perps put away—as if he had any damn right to tell her what to do. But that was before he'd realised what would be expected of her. Would it have been better to let Moretti pursue whatever charge he could without her evidence?

'Moretti.' He nodded as the barrister approached, but immediately turned back to Kayla, took her cold hand. 'Are you sure you don't want me to wait out here with you?'

She gestured at the lieutenant, who had taken the seat beside her. 'Sorry, Colley won the hotly-contested lucky draw.' She managed a small smile, but tears trembled in the depths of her grey eyes.

Yet he knew she wouldn't cry.

There was nothing he could say. He squeezed the fingers lying unresponsive in his, thumb grazing the opal ring. The gift had been an apology, a trinket. It meant nothing; he'd have given as much to any woman.

Only, he never had.

'Just sit tight, Kayla,' Moretti directed. 'It will take me some time to make the opening address, so this is the boring bit for you. Try and relax, read your book. The Sheriff's Officer will come and get you when you're required as a witness, but I can guarantee that won't be for hours.'

Reluctantly relinquishing Kayla's hand, Nick followed Moretti into the courtroom. He strode toward the public gallery as though speed could disguise his reluctance, and hasten the end of the trial.

Kimber pushed his briefcase from a seat. 'Captain. How are you holding up?'

He didn't reply. Couldn't. The image of Kayla, forlorn and lost, was seared on his retina. He had an urge to take her home, wrap her in one of his shirts and find a sunny spot for her to curl in. Read, play backgammon. Or trade stories again, like they had at the pub, with him pretending the whole time that he wasn't being dragged deeper by every word she uttered.

Damn. He hated when Colley was right.

He did care.

CHAPTER 36

Three hours gone, and she'd barely said a word to Colley, and hadn't read a word of the book she clutched. But neither had she been summoned into court. Maybe she had succeeded in becoming invisible.

The doors to the courtroom swung open and her heart juddered to a halt, restarting with a painful thump as she realised that people were disgorging from the room, looking with covetous interest at her, but not speaking. Not demanding she speak.

Nick was beside her before she'd found her feet. 'Prosecution opening statements are done.'

He sounded relieved, but all she could think was that meant Moretti would be calling her up to take the stand.

'Come on, Kim's shouting lunch. Your choice, so make sure it's expensive.' Despite Nick's words, his smile appeared strained, not reaching his eyes.

'I'm not really hungry.'

Colley stood, stretching. 'Unusual,' he said dryly. 'Moretti here can probably afford a decent lunch, but perhaps have a little compassion for the rest of us poor, starving mortals. Army pay equates to army rations, you know.'

Moretti slung the strap of a leather briefcase over his shoulder. 'There's a pasta place a half block down. Happens to belong to family—and we can cut through the press relatively quickly to reach it. That suit you, Kayla?'

It would be better to stay hunkered on the chair, staring at the carpet, than face the press grouped beyond the glass doors they approached; yet as always it was easier to remain silent than argue. As journalists bayed her name and thrust cameras in her path, she shrank against Nick. His arm encircled her shoulders. She should warn him to move away, that the papers would take more photos, print more bullshit headlines; but his presence kept her temporarily safe.

Colley took up a stance on the other side of her, George stepping up close behind. 'Keep your head down and keep moving,' the medic instructed.

Moretti strode ahead beneath the arched canopy of the cement-paved walkway, drawing journalists with him by intimating he'd respond to their questions. After only a couple of hundred metres he veered into the entrance of a glass-fronted café. The bell above the door tinkled with alarm. 'In here.'

Careful to avoid contact with him, Kayla slipped through the doorway.

His gold wedding band catching the muted light from overhead pendants, the barrister raised a hand toward the back of the small room. 'Danny, usual table, for five. Get Joseph to mind the door, keep the media out?'

The line of his chin and nose bearing an uncanny resemblance to Moretti's, the gaunt proprietor assessed

Kayla. He wiped his hands on the white cloth tied around his narrow middle. 'I know you.' He turned to Moretti. 'Tone, you didn't mention you were handling this one.'

Moretti hefted his briefcase onto a table. 'Since when do I tell you any of my business?'

Danny snapped his fingers at a ponytailed man behind the bar. 'Joe. Drop the blinds, close the door. No more customers.' He turned back to Moretti. 'Lunch is on the house, bro. Thank the young lady.' He nodded to Kayla, then strode through swing-doors in a billow of steam. 'Chef. House specials for five.'

Moretti guided her between red-and-white chequered tablecloths, toward the back of the room. Only two of the dozen tables occupied, the patrons gaped at them. Warm odours of pasta and pizza, hot bread and wine, roiled Kayla's stomach as she sat.

Chairs scraped at the other table, jerking her head up. Going, not coming.

Nick caught her eye. 'The door's locked, Kayla. It's not him.'

Maybe she should be grateful for his instinctive understanding, but instead, she felt...violated. She had tried to hide her fear so Nick wouldn't feel trapped by her pathetic dependence, yet it seemed he knew what went on in her head. She couldn't afford to allow anyone in there.

The waiter unloaded tureens of pasta onto the table and Kayla realised she had blocked out her companions' conversation while wondering at Nick's infiltration. Seated beside her, his long fingers shredding a red paper napkin into a pile of cheerful confetti, his gaze bored into the barrister. 'Do you have a read on the jury?'

Moretti focused on sprinkling parmesan on tortellini.

'Opening addresses are usually smooth. At this point, the jury is just there for the ride, really.' He licked white sauce from his fork and chased it with Chianti, downed with the ease of generations of practice. 'But due to the media saturation, the jury is going to be biased—and that's in our favour. In any case, jurors tend to be like lemmings. One jumps, they all jump. If we have one vocal juror on side, we're covered.' He glanced around the room to make certain the other patrons couldn't hear. 'Of course, the same can be said for the defence—and William Baker has a knack for swaying a jury. I'm not saying he's crooked, but he is creative. He's built his reputation on accepting cases no one in their right mind would defend, and defend them he does. He'll use every trick in the book, along with a few he invents.'

Kayla's knife clattered to the table, but she didn't reach for it. Moretti hadn't spoken of his adversary's techniques before.

Moretti lifted a placatory hand. 'Look, there are certain things the defence shouldn't ask. But that doesn't mean Baker *won't* ask, because he knows that once the jury hears something, no matter what direction the judge gives, it's humanly impossible to make them unhear it. He's basically going to try to create an earworm, plant ideas in their heads to discredit you. The trick is, when he gets to his cross examination, you don't rush to answer his questions, as I'll object each time he throws in something that's not permissible. When the judge either substantiates my objection, or Baker withdraws his question, we move on as though it was never said.'

Nick handed the bread basket to Colley without breaking his focus on Moretti. 'How the hell does he have any right to interrogate Kayla? She's not on trial.'

Kayla retrieved the knife, dragging it across her plate to interrupt the thoughts racing through her head. She hated sitting here while they discussed her. While they all *cared*. She wanted to be left alone. Except alone meant—alone.

'He doesn't, not yet, anyway.' Moretti bunched the napkin on his plate. 'But it's based on presumption of innocence for the defendants. The burden of proof is on us, not the defence. But don't worry, we'll have no issue with establishing *actus reus*—basically, the physical element—as required by the court. Though, saying that, you have to second guess a system where nine out of ten judges are on record stating they'd advise their own kin against taking a rape accusation to—'

George held up a hand. 'As you said, innocent until proven guilty.' He smiled at Kayla, as though that could quell the fear coiling in her belly. 'And you are the proof. Are you finished, gentlemen?'

Kayla stared at the oversized clock on the restaurant wall. Her time was up.

Courtroom artists scribbled, the constant scratch of graphite on paper whispering secrets about her.

The sheriff's officer stood. 'All rise for His Honour, Justice Reynolds.'

Reynolds settled into a plush leather recliner. Adjusting bifocals, he spread the case notes across an expansive mahogany desk and signalled the sheriff's officer.

Handcuffed and dressed in prison uniform, each accompanied by a guard, the kidnappers were led into the room. The well-behaved quiet of the court rustled with sudden murmurs; an angry male voice from the back, quickly shushed.

A burst of fear exploded in Kayla's chest, winding tentacles through her body. She was an idiot. Moretti had said she could testify from behind a screen, or even by video link. But, both lulled into a false sense of security by the permanent presence of Nick and Colley, and goaded to action by their belief in her strength, she'd decided to face her torturers. To prove they no longer had any hold over her.

She had lied to herself.

Seated so close, she could recall their smell.

Their words.

Their touch.

Even worse, her awareness of the three shackled men emphasised the absence of the fourth. Maybe Tomas sat in the crowd behind her. Perhaps he lurked on the footpath outside. He was somewhere. And he wanted her.

She shuddered, skewing so she couldn't see the nightmares made flesh, leering at her from only metres away. So close to the end, she had to maintain focus. She'd testify, and then she would be free.

To go where? Nowhere was safe, anymore.

No, she couldn't let the thoughts in, couldn't let the fear betray her. *Count.* Anything. Scratches on the desk, hairs on the back of Moretti's hand, breaths in, breaths out.

Except the men in the dock. Don't count them.

The barrister nudged her elbow and she startled. He nodded toward the witness box and she stumbled forward.

Perched on the edge of the chair, her back was safely to a wall. She could see the entire room. Could see if Tomas was there. He wasn't. But Nick was, his hands locked to the wooden banister of the public gallery.

Eyes closed, she tried to block the sight.

No! She *needed* to see him, she relied on the strength he imparted through his words and looks, his unswerving support.

How could she both wish him away and yet need him so desperately?

Tony Moretti stood before her, and Kayla took a deep breath, waiting for the first of their rehearsed questions. It wouldn't be so bad. She knew precisely what he would say, had memorised the responses.

Moretti gave an encouraging nod. 'Perhaps you would be more comfortable if you removed your jacket?'

What? Any deviation from the performance would force her to think, and she couldn't risk that, she needed to remain numb and distant. She struggled out of the jacket. Why didn't Moretti make the suggestion earlier, instead of stripping her in public, every eye in the room intent on her clumsy movements?

Hands buried beneath the bundled fabric in her lap, she locked her concentration to Moretti's gaze, as he had taught her. *Tunnel vision,* he said. Aware only of him, recite the replies.

'Ms Petrovic, do you know why you are here today?'

She nodded.

'Verbal reply, please, Ms Petrovic,' he reminded.

Her stomach lurched. She'd fucked up already. 'Yes. To give evidence as to the events that occurred last April.'

'Ms Petrovic, it is your contention that on this date, the defendants forcibly detained and kidnapped you and your six students?'

The *defendants*. The lunchtime sip of Chianti burned the back of her throat. She slewed her gaze toward the men as though there was a risk that the wrong men had somehow been dragged into court. But there they were. Greaz chewing on the end of his moustache, Les's acned skin irritated and sore-looking beneath the too-bright light, and Fatty, the apron of his stomach warming his lap. She swallowed convulsively: she could identify each by far more personal features. 'Yes.'

'Ms Petrovic.' The judge gestured for the sheriff's officer to hand her a glass of water. 'Please speak a little louder and closer to the microphone.'

She forced the liquid down her tight throat, the silence in the courtroom so absolute, they'd hear her swallow. All eyes focused on her, unwilling to blink for fear of missing something.

But she had to do this. As Nick said, only she could have the men locked away.

'AND THEN, KAYLA?' Moretti prompted.

She had been reciting in a flat monotone, eyes glued to Moretti's tie. The sooner said, the sooner she'd be out of there. But she'd faltered. 'Th-then they beat me.'

Like flotsam and jetsam borne on a breaking wave, the public gallery strained forward, eager to catch every nuance and inflection.

'Ms Petrovic, there is a television screen behind you. Would you mind turning to face it, please?' Moretti said.

She stared at him. This wasn't part of their rehearsal. God, had she forgotten something she was supposed to do? Would her error set the men free?

'We admit into evidence an aerial photograph of the

location the rescue mission took place,' Moretti continued, his forefinger describing a circle in the air in silent command for her to turn and look at the image. She understood his direction all right, she didn't understand *why*.

Wedged between the front of the dock and her chair, she stood, rotating one hundred and eighty degrees.

Chaos erupted in the room. The bland photograph of sand and spinifex on the television screen offered no explanation for the noise that swelled and bounced from the walls.

As she followed Moretti's direction to retake her seat, her glance caught the blue sheen of veins on the underside of her arm.

Her blood ran cold as she suddenly understood. She had been betrayed.

Moretti seemed oblivious to her discovery. Braving the hungry interest of the spectators, she looked for Nick. He would find a way to deny what she thought had happened, untangle her misunderstanding. For it seemed to her that, although she had refused to have her injuries photographed and catalogued, admitted into history as though she was some sideshow freak, she had been tricked and exposed. Sue had provided a beautiful blouse with long sleeves and a high collar to hide her scars. A blouse with pleated front, but a diaphanous back that became sheer under the overhead lighting. A blouse to advertise her degradation.

His jaw set, Nick's gaze slid away, and Kayla folded into her seat in a weak-kneed rush.

'Ms Petrovic, I'm sorry,' Moretti said, gripping the edge of his desk. 'We must continue.'

She stared him down, her understanding suddenly complete. *You exposed me.* Like every other man—*like Nick—*

he couldn't be trusted. They didn't care about her; they simply wanted to win the case.

So she'd look after herself. Like she always had. She had an agenda; get the men locked up. And clear out. Because she was done waiting for rescue. Done being labelled a victim.

At first, the room buzzed with excitement and titillated revulsion, but as Kayla's clipped monotone revealed each sordid detail, exclamations gave way to heads shaking in disbelief and hands covering mouths.

Judging her.

Eventually, though, they would become immune to the recounted horrors. Their imaginations were only capable of producing so many images.

Unfortunately, her memory was limitless.

Moretti broke into her recount. 'How many times did they rape you, Kayla?'

'I...I don't know.' She wished he wouldn't interrupt, forcing her to think instead of merely biting out each rehearsed word to the beat pounding in her temples *fuck... fuck...fuck...*

He tipped his head to one side, trying to catch her attention. 'More than five? More than ten, then?'

'Objection,' Baker interceded. 'Leading the witness.'

For a moment she almost appreciated his interruption. Then she remembered he was one of *them*. He sought only to discredit and abuse her. 'Do you think I counted?' She'd done the math, and the figure was ludicrous. She chewed her lips together.

Moretti checked his notes. Maybe being questioned threw him off, too. She hoped so. He dragged at his chin with forefinger and thumb and exhaled raggedly. 'Okay.' His voice dropped. 'Ms Petrovic, was there anything else?'

She played for time, hoping he would withdraw the question. 'What?'

'I mean, were you threatened or hurt in any other manner?'

The Defence Attorney had remained silent, occasionally taking notes as Kayla spoke. Now he blustered to his feet. 'Objection, Your Honour. Leading.'

'Overruled. Sit down, please, Mr Baker.' The judge nodded at Kayla. 'Please continue.'

She didn't want to continue. Swearing to tell the whole truth didn't mean it had to be this explicit. Moretti's notion of pursuing a charge of aggravated assault made no sense, the men sat right there, already handcuffed. Why couldn't they be thrown in prison now?

Moretti's voice dropped lower still, as though he invited only her to the conversation. 'Ms Petrovic, tell us about the punishment that was threatened if you refused the demands of the accused.'

'They didn't threaten me.' The room blurred. Her heart crashed against her ribs. She couldn't remember the words she was supposed to use, she could only remember *them*. Every moment of *them*. Every second of pain and fear. Every wish for death and the struggle for life.

Her façade didn't crack, it ripped apart, and the unrehearsed words tore free, slicing the air like a razor. 'They didn't *threaten*, they *did* everything you could imagine. Things you'd never want to imagine. Nothing...nothing was a *threat*.' She buried her face in her hands, trying to shut out the interest, to banish the leering expressions of the three men. But if she couldn't see them, she wouldn't be able to see *him*.

Moretti swivelled toward the judge. 'Your Honour, my client is exhausted. I ask that a continuance be granted until tomorrow, to allow her to recover.'

Tomorrow. She didn't want there to be a tomorrow.

Judge Reynolds swivelled to Baker. 'Objections, Counsel?'

Elbows on his desk, Baker considered her over his steepled hands. She flinched from the slap of his attention. Tugging at his turkey-wattle neck, he stood ponderously. 'Your Honour, I would ask that the Counsel for the Prosecution finish his examination of this witness today. I would then agree to a continuance for the cross-examination tomorrow.'

Reynolds underscored something on his notepad, stabbed the paper with his fountain pen. 'It is not your place to agree or disagree, Counsel. However, Mr Moretti, I would prefer to see your examination finished today so that we can tie up this case as soon as possible.'

Dry sobs spiked Kayla's chest, and she shook her head as Moretti caught her eye. 'We'll move directly to the end of your statement, Ms Petrovic.'

The end. Please, God, let it be the end.

'You say you were a victim of repeated attacks.'

There was that label, again. The one she intellectually rejected—yet she had to find the strength to manifest that denial, to forbid them to use the word, even as they were forcing her to relive the horror.

'How did you eventually escape from this cave you were imprisoned in? How did your students escape?'

She considered the question for a long moment, her

silence broken only by trembling breaths. She couldn't recall the statement she was supposed to use—didn't want to recall anything. Nothing good existed in her memory. 'I didn't—we didn't escape. We were rescued.'

She hadn't delivered her lines as rehearsed, and Moretti scrutinised her anxiously. 'It would be fair to say you felt relief, because you were rescued from a situation of extreme violence?'

'Relief?' No, that wasn't what she'd felt. Nor, waiting for the censure of her failure to rescue the children, did she feel any now. Her brain was scrambled. Her body ached with tension and exhaustion. She had spent so much of her life trying to avoid feelings, how could she describe them now? But Moretti wouldn't let this be over until she said something. Anything.

'I felt—' Like the whore her mother labelled her? Worthless? Contaminated? Was this how *victims* felt? 'I feel like I'm used up, I have nothing left.' Her clenched fist struck her chest. 'I should be dead inside. But I'm not dead. I can't be dead, because of the pain. It hurt.' Her fingers fluttered to her temple as she searched for words. 'It still hurts.'

CHAPTER 37

*J*esus. He was so close to losing it. Elbows on knees, Nick's hands covered his face. Silence echoed and banged in the courtroom, the crowd breathlessly anticipating clarification of Kayla's words. Then a flurry of noise as journalists, scenting a headline, underscored her last words: *'It hurt. It still hurts',* and spectators eagerly compared the depth of suffering they were able to discern in the declaration.

Shoulders tense, he fought for composure. Christ, Kayla had internalised all that pain. She needed protecting from herself, never mind the rest of the world; but how the hell was he supposed to do that? He wanted to run to her, but also to run from her, from the torment and betrayal in her eyes.

Kimber lay a hand on his back. 'Have patience, lad. It'll all work out. Stay here a minute, and pull yourself together. I'll get Kayla.'

Still slumped low, he couldn't look toward the witness stand where Kayla sat so alone. Instead, he glared at the prisoners in the dock, elbowing one another in greedy reminiscence. 'God, if I had a gun—'

Colley shook his head wearily. 'You joining the rabid right?'

'Maybe the gun lobby is correct. People should be able to protect themselves.'

'That's what we're for.'

'Fat fucking lot of good that did.'

'Yeah. I know. Hell, that was hard to watch.' Colley bent to collect a folder at his feet. 'Let Kim take Kayla home. We've got to pick up Doc McGrath.'

'Yeah, I just need to...' Nick gestured toward Kayla. He let his hand fall. Needed to what? Explain to her the shirt had been considered a necessary ploy to circumvent any issue created by her seeking some portion of control over her life by refusing the forensic medical examination? Say he understood her pain, though he couldn't even imagine it? Promise to keep her safe and fail her yet again?

The only thing he *needed* to do was stay the hell away from her.

At the front of the room, Kimber draped the jacket around Kayla's shoulders. Face hidden in shaking hands, she didn't look up. Didn't look for him. She knew he couldn't help her. Hadn't helped her.

Nick slammed from the courthouse, journalists scattering like chickens from his path as he strode in front of Colley to the car park. 'I'll drive.' Couldn't say more. He needed time to process.

Bullshit. He needed time to get a grip on his emotions.

The parking lot of the Flying Doctor base almost vacant, he pulled the Rover in and cut the ignition. Clouds massed like bruises, plunging them into the gloom of an Iraqi bunker. The storm broke with a crash of thunder and he ducked, automatically scanning for the source of incoming.

Damn. Get it under control, man. Australia, remember. Nothing bad happens here.

Yeah, right. People were shit wherever you went; evil had nothing to do with race.

A fork of lightning jagged like Mag58 tracer rounds over the mountains in the east, and the drumming of rain on the car almost drowned his words. 'Know what really burns me up?' He rubbed at the knee of his uniform with enough force to separate the fibres. 'We had those bastards in our crosshairs. Christ, Kim gave us permission to shoot them. Why the hell didn't we?'

Colley swiped fog from his window, also keeping a visual on the terrain. 'Because we didn't know what they'd done.'

'They split her face right open.' He closed his eyes against the memory. 'What the hell happened to fighting terror with terror? Instead of taking the bastards out, we escorted them back to sit in that damn courtroom and terrify her. Did you see them? They were raping her all over again. And we did fuck-all about it.' Vengeance fixed nothing: yet that knowledge, forged by blood and death, didn't lessen his craving. 'I should have realised how bad it was when I pulled her from the waterhole. I should've taken care of the whole damn thing, right then.'

Colley fiddled with the heater. 'You couldn't have known. You're not God, Nick. Despite a tendency to believe that you are.'

Nick ignored the taunt, focused on the invisible scene beyond the window. If anyone alive could understand what was eating him, it would be Colley. But how the hell did he share that shit? 'Fuck it.' He slammed the wheel, smacked his head back against the rest, and stared at the roof. 'I should have gone with my gut: I should have warned her about the shirt.' He didn't want to think about the other secrets he kept, the ones that could destroy her.

Colley's gaze raked him. 'It would have been worse for her if she'd known it was coming.'

'You think we had any right to make that call?'

The lieutenant's groan betrayed his own doubts. 'Fucked if I know. We're just doing the best we can, right?'

'Except it's not good enough. Mate, I'm screwed. She won't forgive me.'

'Does it really matter that much?'

The steel links of his watch bit into flesh as Nick twisted the band. 'More than I realised.' Far more than he wanted it to.

Colley's exhale sounded more like relief than surprise. 'Kayla will be okay. She's stronger than you give her credit for.'

Lips pressed hard, Nick paused before biting the words out. 'No. She'll break.' Misled by the strength Kayla pretended, they demanded more than she could endure, expected more than was fair. 'Jesus,' he pinched the bridge of his nose between thumb and forefinger. 'I promised not to let anyone hurt her again, but I keep fucking up.'

'Get down off your cross, mate,' Colley said with a low chuckle. 'So, you're finally saying you like her, right?'

Nick stared into the gloom as McGrath's low-winged Pilatus buzzed over the stationary vehicle. Liked her? Yeah, he sure as hell liked her. He nodded. Once.

'Then, as you're so worried about honesty, you better tell her that.'

'Are you kidding? Kayla's supposed to be able to trust

me. After what happened, I'd be screwing with her head if I laid this crap on her.' Plus he wasn't man enough to face her rejection.

Colley cracked his window an inch to clear the condensation. 'What do you mean, "after what happened"? You think she should be different because of her experiences? Modify who she is, what she wants?'

'I'd say it's only logical.'

'More like it's a societal construct. Exactly the kind of thinking that pigeonholes victims into certain roles. Hell, if she was one of our squad, injured in the line of duty, you wouldn't think that way, would you?' Colley wiped the window with his sleeve. 'Anyway, it's not like you to be plagued by insecurities.'

'Never had cause to be.' The irony was inescapable: after carefully staying emotionally uninvolved for so long, he'd fallen for a woman who would never return his interest.

In which case, it was time to pull himself together. He shifted restlessly, as though physical movement would change his mindset. 'I'm just tired and dribbling shit. I need to get a bit of perspective. Maybe some distance. You know, the usual distractions.' R&R to haze the torments of battle.

The amusement fell from Colley's face. 'Still searching for an excuse to lock away your feelings? Always keeping control.'

'What of it?' He had no choice but to maintain control. Engineer everything in his life, so pain couldn't unman him. Again. He'd bawled like a kid when his parents died. Twenty-six years old, he'd sat on the floor, phone in hand, crying so hard he figured he'd pissed his pants because no way in hell could that amount of liquid come from his eyes. Or his heart.

Colley's hand shot forward and clicked off the heater. His anger cracked through the silence like a whip lash. 'You're so scared of *feeling*, you convince yourself it's better for Kayla if you cut and run. That way there's no danger to you; your emotions neatly locked away, *you* can't be hurt. Well, that's selfish bullshit. Hell, Nick, I never picked you for a coward. Is she so damned hard to love?'

Love. He winced at Colley's leap to an emotion he disavowed. After his parent's death, he had realised the futility of love. It could only ever end one way. Someone would die and someone would mourn.

Yet he couldn't deny his desire to wrap Kayla in cotton wool, protect her from the world. He longed to ease her pain and erase her memories, but his limitations terrified him. He couldn't mend her and he couldn't save her. 'I barely know her. And what if I can't give her what she needs?'

A shrug lifted Colley's shoulder. 'What if she can't give you what you need? That's the shit grownups have to work out. Welcome to the adult world.'

'But she's...damaged.' The word dragged out of him, polluting his mouth.

Colley gave him a hard stare. 'And you reckon you're not?'

Fair call. Christ, talking about this was so damn hard. But without Dad, he needed Colley to help him see straight. 'I mean, what if I hurt her worse?'

'You're tilting at windmills, Nick. You don't need an iron-clad plan, you don't have to evaluate every angle before you make a move. Live a little.' Colley gave a snort of sudden amusement. 'Anyway, seems to me you don't have much of a choice.'

'No choice? Of course I've got—' Nick's breath hissed in

realisation. Fear and elation pumped adrenaline through his chest. Jesus. How had he missed it? Worrying about what was acceptable, permissible, *controllable*, he'd overlooked the basic flaw in his logic. 'You're right. I don't have a choice. I can't not love her.'

K ayla kept every light on, a chair wedged beneath the locked door handle while she showered.

George had invited her to dine with Doc McGrath and the two officers but, although she craved Lorraine's comfort, she refused. Laid bare, literally and figuratively, she needed time to come to terms with their betrayal. The major had made a brief justification for the revelation, carefully not intimating that the necessity was her fault. Kayla twisted the damp towel in her hands: should she have submitted to the collection of forensic evidence while she was in hospital? But she couldn't. She had desperately needed to cling to that tiny amount of body autonomy, to exercise her right to say 'no' and actually be heard. Yet now she was being punished for her refusal.

She dragged on sweat pants and one of Nick's shirts. Peered around the bathroom door, then tiptoed down the hall. Every sense on high alert, listening for faint noises, feeling for the change in air pressure that would signify another presence, she crept into the lounge room. Although she'd been surprised—deserted—when George left her alone in the house without argument, he had at least drawn the curtains against the premature dusk. Caged by the mountain ranges surrounding the city, a thunderstorm prowled overhead.

Phone in hand, she checked the locks on the external doors—again—then flicked on the sound system and curled small into Nick's favourite seat. Although exhaustion dragged at her, she didn't dare close her eyes. Tomas was out there and she was alone. Alone, and no one truly cared. Not George, nor Colley, not even Nick.

Bastards.

Thunder crashed and the chasing gust of wind rattled the fence like a ghoul's chains. Her feet slammed to the floor, muscles quivering as she tensed. Ready to flee. The next explosion vibrated the windows, echoing in her head, a scream in a cave. The lights flickered. Went out. The music died.

Her skin prickled as dread threaded through her veins, lifting the hairs at the nape of her neck. She fumbled for her phone. Flicked the torch on to chase away her childish fear. But the feeble beam transformed the shadows into the monsters who haunted her dreams She thumbed it off.

Fatigue dispelled by fear, the day's events flashed through her mind, snapshots of shame. She thrust to her feet, probed the dark, seeking familiarity in the gloom. If she remained still, the dread would catch her. Arms hugging her midriff, she threaded a path between the furniture, faster and faster as she learned the route.

She tried to outrun the memories, but they flashed quicker, matching her steps. Detonations of fear.

Pain.

Deprivation.

Humiliation.

Sobs tore at her chest and tears slid down her cheeks, but she couldn't grab a tissue. The tiniest alteration to the rhythm of her slapping feet, to her shoulder smacking against the wall with each turn, would unseat her precarious sanity and fracture her into irreparable pieces. She couldn't lose control, not now. Not so close to the end.

But the men, the men in the dock. Their leader not there because he hid, waiting for her, for his chance to end what he'd begun. Waiting for her to be alone.

Like she was now, alone in the dark.

If she refused to be a victim, she had to face him: but she wasn't strong enough. Not yet.

Headlights blazed across the curtained windows and she stumbled to a halt. Jerked to face the glare. Rational thought flooded back. George had realised she wasn't safe alone, and he'd returned. Well, screw him. She wasn't safe with his soldiers, either.

With no time to hobble to the bedroom, she knuckled her eyes and ran the back of a hand across her nose. Dropped to the couch, feigning sleep.

A gust of cold air, amputated as the door closed, wound tentacles around her limbs. The latch snickered through the deadlock.

A moment of silence.

The dry rasp of a hand on the wall, searching. Sharp click of the light switch.

Off.

On.

Off again.

A crack of thunder and flash of lightning. No discernible pause between the two.

The rustle of a jacket, a muffled metallic clink as it hit the floor.

George wouldn't remove his jacket.

Stealthy footsteps, creeping across the room.

Then...nothing.

Kayla held her breath, straining to hear in the inky dark. Her fingers twitched toward her phone, but if she turned it on she would be forced to confront whatever approached. No more pretending she was safe. The cell slid from her nerveless hand.

A belt whipped through trouser loops, hissing promises of pain and retribution.

He's here.

She thrust from the couch, her scream of denial and despair tearing the ozone-charged air.

CHAPTER 39

F ists raised, Nick dropped to a half-crouch, combing the dark room for the threat. Kayla's scream echoed in his ears. Sobbing incoherently, she struggled from the couch.

Damn nightmares. Pulse still racing, he straightened. Wrapped his arms around her, as he'd done so many times. 'Sweetheart, it's okay. I'm here.'

Hands grasping at his shirt, Kayla's eyes were huge, her words disjointed. 'No, *he's* here. I heard him. His belt—'

Nick's heart slammed his ribs. 'Oh, Jesus. No—' He freed one arm and tugged his belt from the last loop. 'It was me, Kayla. Lack of active duty is taking a toll, I was bloody dying to get out of uniform.' He tried for a grin. Failed.

Kayla shrank from the leather strip he displayed. Shrank from him.

Christ. Her fierce vulnerability gutted him, but how could he protect her if he pretended he didn't care?

The buckle skittered across the floorboards as he threw the belt aside and drew Kayla's trembling body back into the safety of his embrace. The electricity flickered on and she tensed, her palms pressed against his chest as she searched for danger. He spread his splayed hands across her back, trying to cover and protect as much of her as possible. 'It's okay, sweetheart. You're safe.'

Tears pooled in her eyes, trembled on the dark lashes. Her lip quivered, but she leaned into him as though she craved security. Or maybe more? His grip tightened. If he exposed his emotions now, he could lose himself, everything he'd worked toward.

But if he didn't surrender what Kayla needed, he risked losing her.

'Kayla.' Perhaps there would never be a perfect time, so, it was now or never. And he couldn't live with never.

He sucked in a jerky breath. 'I promised I'd never let anyone hurt you again. I know I'm not doing a great job, but I mean it. I'll do everything I can to keep you safe.' The words came so much easier than he expected, a sense of relief and rightness lifting the weight from his chest. He couldn't pick the exact moment he had fallen in love with Kayla, but he'd fallen damn hard. And he wasn't about to let that feeling go.

He drew his hands up her arms, careful to leave her room to escape, but adoring the slight willowing of her body toward his. Her eyes full of a longing to trust and hard-earned doubt, she gazed up at him.

She was everything he hadn't realised he wanted. Perhaps even what he needed.

'I love you, Kayla.'

CHAPTER 40

Her dream for once a delicious fantasy, Kayla surrendered as the phantom lover who would never judge her perverse yearnings slid his hands up her arms.

The oversized khaki shirt slipped from her shoulder.

Stubble grazed her flesh. Nick's breath seared her skin as his lips whispered along her jaw, not quite touching.

She snapped rigid, forcing her eyes wide open. The heat from his body. The callused firmness of his hands. The faint waft of cologne. They were all too real.

Too close.

Too forbidden.

'No!' She shoved at him, the lounge ramming into the back of her knees as she tried to escape. What the hell was he thinking?

Nick pulled away, a chasm of cold air funnelling between them. Confusion furrowed his brow. Yet he repeated the words firmly. 'I love you.'

She'd heard that hollow, meaningless phrase many times—her father's apologies, the men lusting after her body—but never had she so desperately wanted to believe it. And never had it been further from any possible truth. Yet, as Nick tentatively lay his hand against her cheek, she quivered. Yearning thrilled through her.

Forbidden desire...sparked by his touch on her scarred flesh.

Her palms smacked into his chest. 'Don't touch me. Don't look at me!'

'Why not?'

If only she could drown in the deep sea of his eyes. Her hand trembled down her front. 'I'm r-repulsive.' Far easier to acknowledge that, than to admit his touch would lead her to prove how truly sick she was, revealing the depravity that lurked within her.

'Repulsive? Jesus. Never that.' Nick's fingertips dragged pale lines of bewilderment down his face.

'You're drunk.' He had to be. Because if he thought for only a second about who she was—*what* she was—Nick would never stop running. Forcing him away now would avoid the pain of his later rejection. But, God, she didn't want to push him away. Her resolve wavered: she needed him so desperately. He was the only constant in her life, the rock, the stability.

'I swear I'm completely sober,' Nick said earnestly, as though it mattered whether she believed him.

'Then you're crazy.' At least one of them was.

'The sanest I've been in my entire life.'

She shook her head. 'I'm...scarred.' Not only physically, although she could never tell him that. 'Revolting.'

Nick stepped back, his hands raised like he calmed a skittish foal. 'Kayla, trust me for a moment, okay?'

She nodded warily but, despite his words, he tugged his

shirt hem free and steadily drew the fabric over his head. Kayla's feet rooted to the floor. She should run. But there was nowhere for her to go—and nowhere else she wanted to be. Though fear surged, Nick was familiar, safe.

Yet he'd betrayed her.

His shirt hit the floor. 'Look at me, Kayla.'

Fists clenched, she stared at the crumpled uniform.

'Please look.' Nick waited in silence until her eyes crept to his. He lifted his left arm. A forty-centimetre scar sliced from underarm to hip, an impossibly straight, stark line, white against bronzed skin.

She compressed her trembling lips, blinking in shock. Intimate knowledge of the pain he must have endured seared through her.

Nick took her hand, holding it loosely. She could escape if she wanted.

She didn't want.

He guided her fingers to the raised scar tissue on his side. 'This is revolting, repulsive?'

Her entire body quivered as she shook her head. She had no right to touch him. But she didn't pull away. The emotions, the *longing* that churned within her were so much more than lust. And that terrified her.

Nick's eyes held her captive. 'Then why would I think that of your scars?'

Her cheeks burned, her throat closed. 'Because it's not only about appearance. It's...*how* I got them. You don't know what I—' She broke off. Engraved on her body, her past was no one else's business.

His jaw hardened, a muscle on the left side twitched 'I know what they did to you.' His tone was flat. Implacable. 'And you're right, the way we got our scars *is* different. My wounds didn't involve your level of bravery. I was under orders, not forced—'

'No.' The warmth of his naked torso beneath her finger-tips made it impossible to concentrate. He was so close she could barely breathe for the wanting. But she had to stop him speaking. 'Don't tell me.'

Nick moved her hand from the scar, pressing her palms against his pounding chest. 'Why not?'

'I don't want to know about something that caused you pain.' She had nightmares enough, she couldn't bear to imagine the danger he had been in, the fact that he could so easily not have been here when, without him, she was entirely lost.

'Why not?' He repeated, his urgent words pleading rather than demanding.

'Because I-I—' Damn, she had almost slipped. She tried to tug free, but Nick wouldn't release her.

Face centimetres from hers, his voice dropped even lower. 'Because what?'

She ducked her chin, the breath fluttering in her throat, never reaching her lungs. If she could say the words, just once, perhaps the emptiness inside her would disappear. Maybe it was those words that held the magic that seemed to exist in everyone's life but hers. Maybe there was a reason other people rushed to say them...

But the fact was, despite George's explanation, Nick had betrayed her. He had allowed her to be exposed. She had to cling to that, use the sharp, undeniable truth to sever her desire to surrender.

'Say it, Kayla.' Nick entreated. 'If you're thinking it, you have to say it now, or it'll be too late. I can't do this again.

And I can't carry on the pretence any longer. I either have to be here *with you*, or not here at all.'

She shook her head, but her fingertips clawed, trying to hold him. Nick would change his mind, come to his senses, soon enough. Then he'd run. But, for the briefest moment, could she hide from that reality in his arms? 'Because I-I—' The words welled inside her, an explosion of despair she could barely contain. But a lie. 'No!' She pushed him away. Bolted for the sanctuary of her room.

Because she knew love was nothing more than a foolish dream, a fairytale for children.

CHAPTER 41

The lure of Nick's entreaty kept Kayla awake all night. Although she couldn't fathom his motivation or understand the madness that prompted his declaration, if she was ever to risk loving someone, it would have been Nick. And she knew that speaking the three words he solicited could temporarily solve all her problems. A roof, a bed, a promise of love. All the things she had ever traded for.

But then Nick would become nothing more than another name on her list, another man she had used to get what she needed. To survive.

Despite his betrayal, he deserved better than that.

So, afraid of temptation, but equally scared to give Nick chance to rescind his words, she had avoided him all morning, lurking in her room until Colley hollered it was time to leave. Then she quickly claimed the front seat of the car, alongside the lieutenant, leaving Nick the back seat for the fifteen-minute trip to court.

Yet, as she faced the cross-examination from the loneliness of the witness stand, still she imagined and craved the warmth of Nick's gaze, took comfort from the knowledge that he was never more than a few metres away. Sworn to protect her.

The Counsel for the Defence stood. 'Ms Petrovic, it is your assertion that these men abducted you, correct?'

'Yes.'

'Please tell the court your recollection of this event.'

She frowned: Moretti had said Baker wouldn't give her the opportunity to repeat her accusations, instead seeking to discredit them. 'They abducted my students. Assaulted me.'

'More detail, please.'

'They raped me.'

She flinched at the crack as Baker smacked his papers on the desk. 'More detail, please.'

Her heart lurched: this was all in the transcripts already, the court reporter's lacquered daggers had stabbed Kayla's most intimate secrets into permanent record, and she couldn't risk reliving it or providing further detail. Because, while Colley and Kimber knew the truth of who she was, what she'd done, Nick was aware only of the construct she presented. And, during the long hours of the night, she had allowed the lie of his words to seep through her, oozing hope like a new drug, her latest addiction. If he didn't truly know her, was there the tiniest possibility that perhaps he could love her, for a brief moment in time?

Baker snapped her attention back. 'Ms Petrovic, the court requires a reply.'

Only sex. It meant nothing. Gaze fixed to the ceiling she started the recitation. 'I was driving...'

Only seconds in, Baker interrupted. 'What were you wearing when you pulled the bus over, Ms Petrovic?'

'I—don't know.'

'I'm sure you do.'

'Sh-shorts and a shirt.'

'Is that your regular teaching garb?'

She shrugged. 'I guess.'

'Was this shirt tight or loose?'

'W-what?' Damn, she had to get that stammer under control. Moretti advised her not to hide her vulnerability, but he was wrong. The more she allowed it, the more she became a victim.

Moretti stood. 'Objection, Your Honour. Relevance.'

Baker waved off the interruption. 'Withdrawn. I have a statement attesting numerous parents offered to accompany you on the bus, yet you insisted they travel in a separate vehicle. Why?'

She had been proud of the way she'd avoided being in a position where the parents could question her under the guise of making conversation. The irony of her current situation wasn't lost on her, yet there was no hint of humour in the discovery. 'There was no need for them to travel in the bus.'

'So, aware of your duty of care to your students, you made an informed decision that there was no risk to them in travelling unaccompanied for hundreds of kilometres?'

Sour fear filled Kayla's mouth. Baker had already found her out: her selfishness had placed the kids in harm's way. 'Yes.'

'Fascinating.' Baker let the word hang as he perused his notes. 'Yet you would have us believe that in this supposedly 'safe space', my clients somehow forced you off the road? This, despite the fact that you were in control of a vehicle weighing nearly three tons, and capable of covering around ninety kilometres an hour? Is this correct?'

The question confusing, she simply murmured 'yes', hoping he would leave her alone. But then there were more questions, so many more, their intent clearly to confuse and condemn her. Her head aching and voice hoarse, she was drained, exhausted by the mental gymnastics as she tried to work out what to answer, when to answer and, worst of all, why she should even have to answer.

Eventually, managing to look almost as weary as she felt, Baker rubbed his forehead. 'I find myself adding to a list of things that don't quite tally, Ms Petrovic. For example, your display yesterday. May I ask why you chose to wear such a revealing blouse?'

Before she could speak—not that she had a reply—Moretti jerked to his feet. 'Objection. Relevance.'

Baker waved an apologetic hand. 'Withdrawn, Your Honour.' He cast an admonishing glance at the jury, daring them to be naïve enough to ignore his inference. 'Ms Petrovic, is it not possible that what we *thought* we saw yesterday is manufactured? An impressive make-up job?'

'Objection, Your Honour. Counsel is badgering the witness.'

'Withdrawn, Your Honour.' Baker's meaty hand, palm out, halted the jury's leap to assumption. 'Ms Petrovic, it is fact that you repeatedly refused a forensic medical examination, is it not? Yet your counsel would have informed you that without DNA evidence there is no proof as to the identity of the alleged perpetrators.'

A sweep of his hand managed to both indict and absolve the soldiers in the public gallery. 'This matter was not transferred to the jurisdiction of either the state or federal police, was it, Ms Petrovic? So a breach of protocol occurred: photographic evidence was not logged during your hospitalisation. And, as Dr. McGrath was not with us for yesterday's proceedings, he is unable to corroborate that what we may have perceived to be scars on your back are evidentiary of injuries he treated more than two months ago. In fact, we have proof of neither crime nor perpetrator.'

Moretti was on his feet again. 'Objection, Your Honour. Argumentative.'

'Sustained.' The judge scowled at Baker. 'I would advise Counsel to choose his words carefully.'

'I apologise, your Honour, I will rephrase. Ms Petrovic, do you have proof?'

Kayla had lost the question in Baker's rhetoric, but it was clear he accused her of lying. Of fabricating the story that revealed her degradation, of inventing a history she had fought to keep private. Anger laced her words. 'Proof of what?'

Baker smirked. 'That your scars are real.'

'Objection!' Moretti's face mottled in shades of beetroot as he shot to his feet.

The room pulsed with excitement. Reynolds pounded his gavel with increasing fury. 'Silence. I will have silence, or the court will be cleared.'

Just answer the questions honestly. They all said the same thing. Moretti, Kimber, Colley. They promised she only had to get through the cross examination today, and she would be done. She picked at a loose thread on her pants, unease worming through her stomach. Could she trust them, though? They had colluded on the shirt, justifying the deceit as being in her interest. And, if gaining a conviction were as simple as Moretti promised, why did the barrister now bristle with fury?

Justice Reynolds glared at the legal representatives. 'Gentlemen, this is a Court of Law, not a peep show.'

Baker placed his palms together. 'Your Honour, if you will bear with me a moment—'

'No, Mr Baker, I will not bear with you. Make your point now, please.'

Baker nodded. 'Certainly, Your Honour. If the case hinged on an injury to a leg or an arm, the Court would request a viewing of the damaged limb as evidence. The precedents are copious.'

'I am aware of the precedents, Mr Baker.'

'Of course. The absence of injury plays a crucial role in the defence case. Ms Petrovic revealed her back yesterday, at her Counsel's direction. I am requesting she do the same today. If Mr Moretti had applied to have Ms Petrovic's alleged injuries admitted as physical evidence, I would have asked a *voir dire* be conducted to rule it inadmissible. However, in this case the defence is willing to overlook the impropriety of the introduction of this alleged evidence.'

The judge weighed the matter. 'Mr Moretti, will your client agree to the request?'

Kayla shook her head, but they weren't watching.

It didn't matter, she wouldn't do it.

'I don't know, Your Honour, although I doubt it.' Moretti scowled as exultation lit Baker's saturnine face. 'I will inquire.'

Reynolds signalled the sheriff, who stood to announce a short adjournment.

The judge hunched forward, one hand covering the microphone. 'Mr Moretti, I would strongly suggest you persuade your client to comply. I am sure neither of us wishes to protract this matter more than is absolutely necessary.'

The court stood as the magistrate left. Voice firm, Kayla didn't allow Moretti an opportunity to speak as he approached. 'No.' She had refused to let the man who claimed to love her see her scars—yet the barrister thought she would expose herself to every man in the courtroom?

Moretti gestured toward the twelve-person panel who watched intently, although they would be unable to hear his lowered voice as the court buzzed with excitement. Apparently, too worried about missing some salacious detail, no one was taking advantage of the recess. 'Kayla, now that it's been disputed, the jury can't accept the evidence we tendered yesterday without further proof. Baker has sown a seed of doubt, and he's gambling his entire case on your refusal. It's your back, only your back. Nothing more.'

Seed of doubt? She wasn't on trial, she had nothing to prove.

At a jerk of Moretti's head, Major Kimber approached. 'Kayla.' His warm hand covered hers and she stared at his knuckles, flecked with white. Lorraine had him painting the picket fence. 'This will be the turning point. It will win the case, put those bastards away for good.'

She jerked her hand away. George had no right to coerce her. She had fantasised him and Lorraine as her parents, her photo in their hallway, her school trophies displayed on the bookcase. A father wouldn't do this to his child.

He would do worse. Did worse.

George ducked his head, seeking her eyes. 'Kayla, what are your options? We could be here for weeks, replaying the same sordid details over and again. I won't lie to you: those men aren't walking free no matter what you choose to do. They're going to jail. But you have the opportunity to put them away for a damn sight longer. Kayla, do you want to have to worry about them on the loose *as well*?'

She gasped, unable to control her instinctive reaction, her gaze drawn to the public gallery. Scanning, as though she hadn't already covertly investigated each of the faces turned towards her. As though every stirring of the audience hadn't caused her to search for him. As though she could have forgotten Tomas, for even the briefest moment.

Nick gripped the bar, leaning toward her. But she couldn't read his unspoken message.

Kimber murmured. 'Trust me, Kayla—'

The words seared through her, woke the fury and betrayal she had struggled to contain. 'Trust you?' she hissed. 'Trust any of you? You screwed me over. You, Colley, N-Nick. Do you need a conviction to justify deploying your men? Is that what this is about? You don't fucking care about me.' The hurt of decades laced her accusation.

George lurched back a half step, his usual composure replaced with dismay. 'I'm sorry, Kayla. We were trying to avoid...something worse. But it's time to end this.'

He was right; she needed to end it and move on, stop dreaming of a future that could never be hers. Her ghost of a nod, more acknowledgment than agreement, sealed her fate.

Kimber squeezed her hand. 'Good girl.'

She tugged her hand free. Didn't need his accolade, his approval, his approbation. She'd been living a lie, pretending to herself that someone cared.

Stepping down from the dock she followed Moretti through a door at the rear of the court, along a corridor adorned with paintings and photographs of men and women in court attire, and into an antechamber.

He unhooked a robe from the back of the door. 'Take off your jacket and shirt. Put this on, with the opening at the back.' He turned away, guarding the door.

Heart pumping fear instead of blood, Kayla fumbled to undress with a strange man in the room. She wanted Colley.

No. He'd deceived her as well. They all had. She had to remember that, not allow herself to slip into the comfort of their lies. Her lips felt disembodied. 'I don't want to do this.' Why didn't anyone ever hear her say no?

Moretti turned back, picked up a sash and doubled it around her waist. 'You'll be all right. It'll take a moment, and then it will all be over. You've spiked Baker's tyres.' His compressed lips gave lie to his confident words, but his stride seemed certain as he led her back along the moss-green carpeted corridor.

How had everything snowballed to this point? She should simply refuse. Refuse to take another step, refuse to expose herself, refuse to participate in this farce. But she couldn't because she was a coward, afraid of speaking out, of adverse attention, of judgment. She would obey—just like Mother taught her.

The courtroom fell silent as they entered.

Like a hangman, Moretti guided her to the stand. Gripping the scarred wood, she twisted around, looking for Nick in the public gallery, craving his comfort, his strength, even as she loathed herself for the weakness. Despite what he'd done, the lies and betrayal, she needed him. Just like she had her father.

Nick frowned, and her hand snaked toward Moretti to

beg off, but then she realised the captain's attention was focussed on his phone.

Her attention snapped to Baker as the court was called back to session and he spoke. 'Ms Petrovic, I was asking if you would agree to show us your back?' His tone less bellicose now, his forehead furrowed.

She clutched the black robe to her chest. 'Yes.'

'Then please do so.' He fanned a fistful of papers.

Moretti gestured toward her. 'Your Honour?'

The judge peered over his glasses. 'Yes, Mr Moretti, please come forward and assist your client.'

There was no reason not to do it. It was only her back. They'd seen it yesterday. She had found neither courage nor desire to examine her scars, but from metres distant, there would surely be nothing for Nick to see.

She focused on Moretti, tried to believe there were only the two of them in the room.

But even that would be wrong, so wrong.

He spoke low. 'It's going to be alright. Turn to face the wall. Here we go.' Cold air raised goosebumps as he parted the robe. Slid it down her shoulders. Her crossed arms clamped it to her chest. She shook so hard she couldn't speak. Not that she had anything to say.

Silence for a second, a lifetime. Then pandemonium.

'Silence!' roared Justice Reynolds. 'Mr Baker, are you done?'

Clutching the billowing material like she could hide in the volume, Kayla sank to the edge of the chair. Pretending she was oblivious to the distaste painted clear on the faces in the crowd, she risked a glance at Nick.

Head bowed, he stared at the floor.

She prayed he hadn't seen.

In the dock, Les and Greaz jostled each another, admiring Tomas's handiwork, hugging their memories. Fatty stared at her with lugubrious sorrow.

Baker cleared his throat. 'Ms Petrovic, you claim you were brutally raped, correct?

Her voice came out overly loud, a bark of anxiety. 'Yes.'

Baker shook his head, his tone pitying and solicitous. 'Do you feel ashamed?'

'Yes.' A whisper, this time. She fiddled with a fold of the robe. No one could understand the depth of her humiliation, the stigma that came with the label of victim.

Baker pinched at the bridge of his nose. 'I'm confused. Shame seems an odd emotion, were you, as you attest, forced to have sex.' He clicked his tongue against his teeth, raised his eyebrows as though sudden realisation hit him. 'But then, that claim is not entirely true, is it? Indeed, my clients don't contest the fact that they had intercourse with you, but they note that it was always mutually consensual.'

'No!'

Baker wagged a cautionary finger. 'Remember, Ms Petrovic, you are under oath, and I'm sure you do not wish to perjure yourself. Think carefully. Did you not say now, wait a moment, let me consult my notes here to make certain I'm quite correct—' He perched a pair of spectacles on the end of his nose. The accused men murmured to one another in greedy reminiscence. Spectators jostled, craning forward as though they could read the barrister's notes.

Baker squinted. 'Let me see. Ah, yes, here it is. Do you now deny that you gave these men permission, saying, "Take me, just take me"?'

'No!' Baker's inflection was all wrong. She had pleaded they take her instead of the children. 'Well, yes, but—'

Baker cut across her words. 'So, my clients have ample cause for reasonable belief that you are consenting to have sex with them. In fact, you requested—'

'Objection,' Moretti roared. 'Your Honour, this is not a case of giving free and meaningful consent. Ms Petrovic was under considerable duress. Weapons were employed and the children's safety threatened if she did not comply with the kidnapper's demands.'

Fatty's jowls wobbled as he smiled sympathetically across the room at her.

Justice Reynolds pulled at his chin. 'Mr Moretti, I suggest you save the speech for your closing. Mr Baker, are we going anywhere with this?'

'I have only two more points to cover, Your Honour,' said Baker.

'Do so.'

Baker nodded. 'Ms Petrovic, thank you for verifying the authenticity of your scars.' He let the room rest in silence for a moment, then cocked his head and lifted one finger. 'But tell me, could these *markings* not be the result of a passionate interlude? After all, a predilection for the more unusual erotic pursuits is not unheard of, even among those we trust to educate our children. Your own sexual history is not exactly vanilla, is it Ms Petrovic?'

Movement blurred on the periphery of Kayla's vision as Colley jerked forward, a restraining arm thrust across Nick's chest.

'Inadmissible,' Moretti snapped.

She ignored his objection though. She'd known it would come to this. She had changed—tried to change—but, unlike the other men, Baker saw her for what she was. 'What are you trying to say?'

Merciless guile barely hid behind the barrister's smile. 'Come, Ms Petrovic, let's not pretend to be coy. There's no evidence that the scars you displayed are the result of a non-consensual act. In fact, given your *history*,' he waved the wad of papers at her, 'I imagine you may have difficulty recalling who caused them. Let alone proving it.'

She swallowed her whimper of shock. He tried to black-mail her into silence, and her truth exposed, she couldn't look toward Nick. Or Colley, or George. 'How can I prove something like that?'

'Indeed, Ms Petrovic, impossible, is it not?' Relaxed in his infallibility, Baker smiled. 'To give you the benefit of the doubt, perhaps this was a consensual liaison gone wrong. Maybe things got a little more out-of-hand than you like. Maybe you changed your mind, although you evidently failed to clearly convey this to my clients. Maybe, like a *true* rape victim, you even entered a dissociative state, rather than face the consequence of your own desires. A common effect of this fugue state is a skewed recollection, an inability to accurately recall events. Mentally disassociated, you—'

'Bullshit,' she spat.

Baker jerked upright. 'Pardon?'

Too long controlled, Kayla's anger exploded. 'Your premise is bullshit. I wish your happy little fantasy were true, I wish I felt disassociated. But I was *there*. I felt every damn thing, I saw everything. I saw them!' Her finger jabbed toward the defendants' bench, although she didn't look at the men. 'My recall is perfect because I get to re-live it every fucking day!' The sentence ended on a sob, and she clamped her lips together, her chest aching as she repressed the tears. But finally they were tears of fury, not of weakness.

Baker frowned at his notes, using an index finger to

smooth each eyebrow. 'Let me recap the facts we have now agreed upon. You assert that, while participating in consensual sexual activity with my clients, they assaulted you. However, you also clearly state that you kept your eyes open for the duration of this alleged attack. Ms Petrovic, wouldn't you agree that keeping one's eyes open during sexual intercourse is more an indication of interest and arousal, than the response of a woman forced to perform an act she professes to find abhorrent?'

'Your Honour!' Moretti's chair scraped the floor.

The room swirled around Kayla. A brief struggle and a barked order from George as he commanded Nick to stand down was almost drowned out by the incredulity of the gallery.

How could this be so much worse than anything she had anticipated? And Nick...Nick witnessed it all. From the sly revelation of her past to the insinuations about her character. She was more naked before him than if she had stripped every item of clothing.

As Moretti stood to address the judge, Baker smirked, a practiced eye sliding over the jurors' faces.

'The prosecution wishes to request a short recess, Your Honour.'

As the sheriff's officer announced the break, Moretti moved swiftly to the public gallery.

Her ears ringing in the sudden silence, Kayla reached shakily for the water glass, needing to touch something, to ground herself, to find some semblance of reality.

Conversing earnestly, Moretti and Kimber appeared to agree, the lawyer's lined face jubilant.

Expression mutinous, fists bunched and shoulders taut, Nick leaned toward the other men, his words inaudible to

Kayla. Then he snapped upright, eyes straight ahead, face blank. Saluted Major Kimber.

Kimber nodded curtly and turned back to Moretti.

Water slopped onto the desk as Kayla's grip on the glass tightened. *They* had promised her this would be simple. She knew they'd downplayed it, pretended it would be easier than was realistic, but this? Publicly accused of lying and lewd, perverted behaviour.

Her knuckles whitened around the glass. Maybe there was truth in their accusations, but she didn't care; she was through with being forced into the role of either villain or victim. She had always done the best she could with what she had. And, right now, she had anger. She would see those bastards punished for what they'd done, both in the cave and in exposing her humiliation.

Colley spoke with Kimber, then moved toward her. He pressed his fingers to her wrist, consulting his watch. 'Kayla, we can finish this right now.'

She snatched her arm away. *Angry, not ill.* 'George said that before. It's supposed to be over.'

'I know, Kayla, and I'm sorry. We weren't prepared for such a vicious fight. We believed revealing your back would do the job. It didn't.'

'No shit.'

Colley's brown eyes pleaded. 'But this is foolproof, I promise you that. Just agree to what Moretti proposes.'

Her pulse pounded fury and adrenaline through her body. But it was clean and pure, searing away the taint of her past, clearing her mind. She'd do whatever it took to get the three men locked away, forever, and bring an end to this. She was sick of the guilt, the denial, the driving need to apologise for everything. Sick of feeling unworthy. George was right, anger served her well—but she had other emotions. And they deserved space in her life, too.

Unlike Nick, she would never wake to a brand-new day, uncontaminated by her history; but it was time she moved forward. She would find a way to embrace a new tomorrow to replace every tainted yesterday.

CHAPTER 42

'Is she all right?' As though his urgency would translate into protection, Nick didn't wait for Colley to regain his seat before he spoke. He couldn't make out Kayla's expression across the courtroom. Or rather, he could, but didn't understand it. As Moretti prepared to re-examine her, she radiated a furious poise where he expected to see tears.

Quiet desperation edged Kimber's interruption. 'Will she allow it?

Colley lowered his voice as voyeurs leaned into their conversation, torn between staring at the soldiers or at Kayla. 'I don't even know if she should, never mind if she will.' His mouth twisted and he rubbed a hand across his face.

Christ, don't let her. Nick couldn't speak the words aloud: he had his orders. He gripped the rail in front of him like he'd split it in half, the battle of logic and emotion tearing him apart. There had to be another way to get the judgment Moretti wanted, a way to do it without re-victimising Kayla.

His head jerked up as the barrister cleared his throat

and turned from Kayla toward the bench. 'If it pleases Your Honour, the prosecution would like to ask one last question of its own witness.'

Baker reclined sloth like in his chair, oozing self-assurance, and Nick loathed him with a poisonous fury. He wanted to blame the barrister for Kayla's pain, yet he knew the fault should be shared. And he wasn't excluded.

'Proceed, Mr Moretti.'

Moretti buttoned and then unbuttoned his double-breasted suit. Wet his lips. 'Ms Petrovic. Would you agree to me showing the court historical footage related to this case?'

No. Say no. Nick tried to project the words to Kayla. Christ, if she said yes, he was finished.

Kayla frowned and then turned to him. Like she trusted him for direction. Like she hadn't ruled him out completely. Like maybe she was still considering his words from last night.

Loathing his own cowardice, Nick looked away. He couldn't allow her to read the knowledge he hid, or know that the secrets she fought so hard to keep had never been hers alone, that he had always been privy to the devastatingly intimate details. She wouldn't forgive him the deception.

Kimber grasped his shoulder. 'Son, she has to. We don't have a choice.'

The major could order him. *Had* already ordered his silence. And he could refuse, face disciplinary action, discharge—and not care less. He had to work out what was best for Kayla. Nothing else mattered.

Kimber's fingertips dug under his scapula. 'Captain, we have to end this. Now. For her.'

Nick jerked free. 'No.' They didn't need to show the

footage. Even without it, surely the bastards would be locked away for a few years. After that, he'd be the one to keep Kayla safe. He had intimated last night that he would cut and run if she rejected him, but that had been a shit of a thing to do. Staring at his ceiling as he replayed every moment, he had realised that he had no right to make demands of her. Hated himself for the attempted manipulation. Regardless of her response, he would always protect her.

He straightened, customary assurance flooding back. Kimber would have his balls in a sack, but this way Kayla would be better off. Colley would back him up, as always. 'Lieutenant Colley—' *Jesus.* Colley was twisting the damn crucifix again.

Colley shook his head. 'You were right yesterday. PTSD is a bitch with claws, and Kayla needs closure. She can't take much more of this.'

Nick's breath left his lungs like he'd been kicked in the chest. He knew PTSD, knew he couldn't shelter Kayla from her own mind. He closed his eyes for a moment, wishing he could hide, wishing Dad was there, wishing, damn, wishing so many things.

Slowly, he turned to face Kayla. He saw her fear and wanted so desperately to shield her. But he was too late. Only she could overcome the monster within.

He nodded, a fraction of a movement he didn't truly want her to see. He didn't want the responsibility for devastating her world.

For ending his.

He just wanted to take her home.

CHAPTER 43

She couldn't understand Nick's silent message, and batwings of fear fluttered in Kayla's mind. What should she do? There was no one she could trust for advice, but she had to find a way to finish this.

She turned back to the barrister, sucking a breath so deep she almost choked. It didn't matter whether Moretti was truly on her side, or manufactured evidence to gain a conviction for his career. She didn't care about his tactics, only that those bastards be locked away for as long as possible. She waited for him to repeat the question.

'Kayla, may I show the footage?'

'Yes,' she said.

Baker glared at the sudden fidgeting and whispering of the manacled men, then lurched to his feet. 'Objection. Introducing new evidence.'

Reynolds hesitated. 'Over-ruled.'

Why was Baker concerned? Kayla clutched the edge of the stand. Why was Fatty trying to catch her attention, mouthing something, shaking his head?

She had to ignore them. The door to the court guarded, Tomas couldn't get in, she had nothing to fear. The end was in sight.

The sheriff's officer moved to the television mounted on the wall behind her. If there were precedents, why hadn't Moretti pulled this out of his bag of tricks yesterday? Spared her showing her back, revealing her secrets? Yet, even with all he knew of her, Nick said he loved her. Kayla stared at her hands, twisting in her lap like copulating snakes. She couldn't change her history. Any of it. Hurt and tragedy were the foundation of her life. But she could pretend to forget, and then perhaps move forward. God knows, she'd had enough practice at lies and deception.

'Fucking bitch.' The words sliced through the almost-silent room.

Tomas! A bolt of pure terror cleft her chest. Instinctively, she looked for Nick. Head in his hands, blocking sound and sight, he didn't respond to her silent scream. Despite his promises, she was alone. Lurching from her chair, Kayla spun to face Tomas.

Blinked as the TV screen rioted with colour.

The picture clarified.

A bloodied body.

Men.

'No!' Her heart smashed against her ribs. She reeled back, hitting the edge of the dock, the shaft of agony stealing her breath.

Metres away, the same men leered at her. Tears running rivulets down his creased cheeks, Fatty lifted manacled hands in either plea or apology.

They had her surrounded. *Again.* She shook her head, clutching her chest, trying to still the pulsing, spearing pain.

A whip cracked in the hushed thrill of the courtroom. The scarred flesh on her back quivered in agonised memory, each word a new lash. 'Time for a lesson, teach.'

Tomas.

On the screen or beside her? In the cave or the courtroom? In her head or in her life? She couldn't separate fact from imagination, the edges blurring as her nightmare became reality. The chill of stone seeped up her legs, the odour of dirt filled her nostrils, the tang of blood tainted her mouth. The room reeled as she whirled toward the one man who could save her. 'Nick!'

CHAPTER 44

Arms wrapped her tight and a dizzying feeling of speed and movement kept her eyes closed.

Colley's voice, urgent. 'Kayla. Come back to me. Kayla.'

Back to him? If she had finally managed to escape, she wasn't ever coming back.

Colley set her down on soft fabric. A lounge. His fingers moved to her forehead, pressing gently. 'Hell. She smashed her head on the dock.'

'Is she all right?' A strange voice. The judge? The clerk?

'She has to be. Got a first-aid kit? I need ammonia. And dressings.'

'Have the sheriff's officer bring the first aid kit.' Moretti. 'Do you want me to call an ambulance, Lieutenant?'

'Not yet.'

'Try this.' The air pressure changed. Glass chinked on glass. Colley pressed something cold to her lips. She spluttered at the harsh scorch of neat spirits.

'That's it. Good girl.' Colley's arms were around her, rocking her as though she was a small child. The motion was strangely comforting. Odd, because nothing about childhood had been comforting.

She winced as he dabbed at her forehead, then tipped more alcohol onto her lips. It burned and she coughed, unwillingly flickering her eyes open.

Unfamiliar room. Leather tub chairs, huge desk stacked with files. Colley on his knees beside her, his heels hard up against a laden bookcase. The sheriff's officer hovered in the doorway, first aid kit in hand, mouth slightly open. Face shocked and pale.

Why? Tangled in the robe, she had fallen, the dock rushing up to meet her. Then darkness.

With a gasp, Kayla struggled upright, one hand clawing into the fabric of the sofa as she swung her legs to the floor. Jesus, they should have left her in the darkness. Because now she remembered. She had to get out.

Colley pressed a hand to her chest. 'It's alright Kayla, take a moment. Don't move too fast, you'll be dizzy.'

Her nails raked his skin as she dragged his arm aside. 'No. I heard *him!*'

'It's okay,' he soothed. 'It wasn't him. You're safe. You're in a private room. You're with me. Completely safe.'

She slapped at his hands, forcing him away so she could flee. 'You don't understand. He's here.' Her words were too fast, tripping and tumbling as she flailed. 'I heard him and...and then I could smell him, and I could...*can* taste him.'

The sheriff's officer made a choking noise and turned away.

'Kayla, get a grip. Head between your knees.' Colley's tone was calm and professional. Like nothing happened, nothing was amiss.

'Didn't you hear me? *He* is back!' She'd known Tomas would come for her; why hadn't she forced them to believe her?

'Kayla, you need to listen. Tomas is not here. Do you understand? You're completely safe. Think about it. You saw the screen behind you, remember? What you heard was a recording. Look around. You're safe.'

'S-safe?' Her shoulders shook as she tried to strangle her harsh sobs. Tried to make sense of the incomprehensible. 'He's not—?' She pressed her fingertips to the aching lump on her forehead, as though pain would anchor her.

The sheriff's officer lurched in the doorway. 'Christ, the video.' His running footsteps were swallowed by the carpeted corridor.

'Lieutenant, I can request a further recess—?' Moretti said.

Kayla kept her voice low, refusing to give in to hysteria as she fit together Colley's words and the fragments she remembered. 'Video? Colley?'

But she was only asking him so he could deny it. Praying he would deny it. Because she *remembered*. Remembered the men in the cave, phones in one hand, cocks in the other. Remembered them encouraging and goading each other, comparing screens. Remembered them sitting around the campfire, laughing over their phones as she sobbed in the darkness.

Colley's calm air deserted him and he floundered. 'It-it doesn't matter. Moretti's turned it off.'

She didn't even blink, her chest heaving, voice rising. 'I can't go back in there. I can't see them—'

'The judge will have the accused removed from the court,' the sheriff's officer said.

The problem wasn't *them*. 'Don't make me go back,' she pleaded, her fingers snagged in Colley's shirt. 'They saw...'

'Saw what?' Her blood stained the hand he lifted in question. 'Saw that they can never repay what they owe you. Saw how you saved the children. Saw that you are unspeakably, unimaginably brave—'

'No! They saw what I *did*. What I am.' She forced a derisive laugh, but it barely masked a sob. 'You think I'm brave, but I did everything those bastards demanded, the whole time begging them to let us go. I didn't find a way to escape, I didn't fight back. I didn't do anything except try to survive. Same as I've done all my life. And now, everyone knows.'

'Kayla, no one's judging you.'

She shook her head. 'You don't understand, you didn't see—'

'I've seen the recording.'

Her hands fluttered to her ears. Colley had seen it?

He cupped his hands over hers, tried to peel back her fingers as she crushed her skull between her palms, her breaths jagged and panicked. 'Kayla, I've seen it, and I'm the one who should be bloody ashamed. Ashamed of being a man, ashamed of being a part of a society that would allow you to be treated like that.'

'You didn't see it all. You don't know what I did.' Her fingers wound into her hair, tugging strands free. Like Les had done. 'It's still playing, Colley, it's still fucking playing!'

'No. It's off. But Kayla, listen to me.' Colley grabbed her wrists. 'I've watched all the footage. The whole damned filthy, disgusting abomination. Every single vile minute. And you know what? All I saw was your bravery, your tenacity, the way you fought to protect those kids. And that's all anyone will see. The film is not a reflection of you. It's an indictment of those bastards. It's the proof that's going to put them away for a very long time. That garbage doesn't define you. Nobody judges you; they see only what you did to save the kids.'

Kayla snapped rigid. Colley was right. It wasn't the public's perception she needed to worry about—but Nick was out there. His betrayal of her was nothing compared to this revelation of how she had misled him by hiding her history.

The tiny core of hope she had permitted shrivelled. There would be no new day, no clean slate. No future.

Her tears stopped and she struggled to her feet.

Rejecting Colley's support, she walked the long, empty corridor. Colley spoke, but his words meant nothing. She re-entered the courtroom. Faltered as she noted Nick's empty seat, the proof she expected. He had run. Like every man, his words had been a lie.

But who was she to condemn a liar?

A lone spectator rose, slowly applauding.

Spatterings of sound like drops of blood on a stone floor.

More of the crowd stood, clapping with increasing enthusiasm as nobody stopped them.

Kayla took her place in the witness box. Fastened her gaze to the two lawyers, defence and prosecution. Like every man in her life, they had raped her. Stolen the last vestige of her self-esteem. Now nothing existed other than her need for vengeance.

CHAPTER 45

K ayla had cheated death too often for it to be kind to her now. Denied the adolescent comfort of thinking she might die from a broken heart, nothing could ease the ache in her chest. She slept restlessly, pathetically grateful when Colley gave her drugs, numbing her to the memory of Nick's empty seat in the few minutes they'd remained in court before it again recessed. And to the fact that she'd not seen him in the hours since.

Recollections pooled as she woke; Nick's declaration of love a brief fragmentation of sunlight through darkness, shadowed by disjointed flashbacks. Baker's accusatory finger pointed at her. Moretti pulling the robe from her back. Lurid colours on the screen behind her. The smell of the blood matting her hair. Strangers hungry to feed on her pain. And betrayal. So many levels of betrayal, her own above all others. She had tricked Nick into declaring an emotion he could never feel, not for her.

At what moment had he realised his mistake? The previous morning, when she had avoided him? Or during the hearing, when he focused on the paper in his hand, rather than meet her gaze? Whatever, the phone footage had clinched it.

Colley had always treated her with careful courtesy, as though he thought her fragile. But Nick had thought her normal.

And kissed her hand.

And said he loved her.

And then he saw the film.

She didn't blame him for running. But anger? Hell, yeah, she was angry. Angry for his promises, for the temptation, for the brief hope he'd ignited, which made sorrow slice far deeper. For so long she had kept her life devoid of joy and hope, figuring to buy immunity to the flip side, misery and despair. But Nick's declaration of love had laid her bare.

Tears ached in her throat, and she pressed her face into the pillow, seeking solace in imagining his strong, clean scent imprinted on the cotton.

I don't want to think about him.

Yes she did. It was literally all she wanted to think about, a few weeks of memories, good and bad, an impermissible dream that had to last a lifetime.

A sob closed her throat and she pressed a hand to her chest, trying to ease the hollow ache as she hauled herself from the bed and headed to her bathroom. Stood under the shower for far too long, as though the running water could hide her tears.

Dressed in jeans and one of Nick's shirts, she made her way up the hall to his bathroom, in search of toothpaste. A glint on the marble bench caught her eye. She held still, as though a sudden movement would scare the shining prize away.

Her heart rate notched up.

Her fingers inched closer, tracing the cold stone counter.

Tentatively touched the steel.

Caressed the sleek promise of the razor blade.

One small cut. That's all it would take. The TV mumbled in the other room. With Nick gone and Colley busy, no one would ever know. It had been so many years, surely she had earned the right? One small cut and the volcano building inside her would lie dormant.

For now. Because, no matter how many cuts, her future held only fear and pain. But she could change that.

Despite the passage of time, the years of denial, her fingers remembered exactly where to bend the plastic housing, snapping the metal free. She gripped the blade between thumb and forefinger. Peeled back her left sleeve. The pale underside of her arm gleamed, a tracery of blue veins mapping what remained of her life. *Down the wrist, not across.* Slicing across was a hollow threat. This time she wanted a promise. A promise of an ending.

The tip of the blade pressed her flesh. A bead of blood welled and ran across her hand, bisecting the scars that scored her palm.

The scars Nick had kissed.

The hand Nick had held.

Blood pooled around the gold band encircling her second finger.

The ring Nick gave her.

No!

A crimson ribbon scribed across the porcelain as she flung the blade aside and staggered back, brought up short by the tiled wall. Bloodied wrist pressed against the wild beat of her heart she sank to her heels. What the hell was she doing? Nick had warned her weeks ago that she couldn't take the easy way out. She needed to free herself *of* Tomas, not free Tomas. To do that, she had to fight back.

Surviving was the first step.

And then came vengeance.

Laughter boomed from the lounge room. *Nick?* Her fingers clawed on the tiled floor as sorrow chased a surge of hope. He was back, but she couldn't face him. Unless... unless she pretended he was nothing more than a stepping stone on her path to freedom, as she had done with so many men before him. Nick had done his job, kept her safe until the trial. Officially, they were through. So she would greet him, act normal, and get the hell out of his place.

Save her pathetic tears for her own pillow.

Kayla shoved from the wall and foraged in the cupboard beneath the sink for a Band-Aid. Stuck it fast to her wrist, pressing until it hurt. Hid the blade and the destroyed razor beneath a bundle of tissues in the wastebasket, then checked her face and straightened her shirt. Her survival had always come down to an act. She knew how to fake it. One final scene, and it would all be over.

With a cat-like grace that belied his size, Nick whirled as she entered the lounge room. 'Kayla.' He crossed to her in a couple of strides, one hand cupping her cheek. 'Are you okay?'

He was touching her. How could he do that? She held her breath, trying not to quiver, determined not to press into the warmth of his hand. His fingertips brushed across the bruise on her forehead. 'I've got to leave in two hours. I was beginning to worry you'd sleep right through.'

'Leave?' She should pull from his touch, but she'd steal just one more memory to take with her.

Nick lifted an eyebrow. 'Deployment. Remember? The emergency briefing I was hauled in for yesterday. No? Damn, Colley, you and your bloody drugs.' He threw the accusation over his shoulder but kept his hands and eyes on her.

Colley rose from a chair. 'Sorry, needs must. And right now, I needs me a coffee.' He brushed past, clattering cupboards in the kitchen.

She barely heard the lieutenant. Deployment? An ephemeral memory, too transient to grasp, made the word familiar, yet she hadn't spoken to Nick since he said that he loved— 'I remember.' She yanked from his hands. Forced her spine stiff, straighter than any soldier he commanded. There was only one memory that mattered. 'I remember what you saw.'

'What do you mean?' He reached for her but halted as she recoiled. 'The phone footage? Kayla, I saw that months back.'

'You couldn't have,' she snapped. 'Because you said—'

'That I love you.' Apparently, he had no issue with repeating the phrase she couldn't bring herself to say.

'But if you'd seen that—' She broke off. There was no word in the English language to describe what he'd witnessed.

'That crap? It was nothing. No.' A tic jerked the hard line of his jaw. 'No, that's wrong. It wasn't nothing, it'll never be nothing. I want to kill those bastards for what they did to you. But it means nothing to *us*.'

'You mean you knew about it, but didn't warn me?' she accused, clinging to her anger despite realising that if Nick had admitted his knowledge, she couldn't have allowed herself even a moment to dream, couldn't have worked toward healing by pretending hope existed in her life.

Nick raked both hands through his hair. 'I was hoping you'd never find out about it. The stunt with the shirt was supposed to force an end to this business, but that was a call we should never have made; the choice should have been yours. The film, though,' the cords in his neck ridged, his lips rimmed white as the words worked free. 'I didn't say anything because I wanted it to go away. I figured if I pretended it didn't exist, you would never know, never have to face that filth. I didn't—don't—want you hurt.'

She had to rationalise away the hope that mushroomed within her, because hope equated to weakness, and weakness became vulnerability. And vulnerability meant more pain. Yet Nick hadn't betrayed her; he had tried to protect her. 'You know what I did, yet you still...?' She didn't dare test the emotion by labelling it.

Nick's hands found her upper arms, his eyes intent on hers. 'Kayla, I love you. Period. There's no 'still' about it. No reservations. And not because of or *despite* what happened to you. I love the person who stands before me right now, her history and her future included, the whole package deal.'

Trapped between lie and longing, Kayla swayed toward his protection. She yearned to surrender both her mind and heart, but she needed to stay strong, hold the last line of her emotional defence. Nick might have been the only man she could ever love—but she would never allow herself to love.

Just this once, though, she would let herself taste the sweet poison of the lie. 'I love you.'

CHAPTER 46

'Two hours. Refresh your rat packs, grab a shower. Then we're out again.' Nick heaved the backpack from his shoulder and dropped it to the mud as he barked orders.

The recruits saluted and dashed for the rare bliss of the shower block, the most popular building among the prefab huts surrounding the churned-dirt parade ground. Beyond the crude accommodations, salt-bush tundra, occasionally obscured by squalls of wind-driven rain, stretched to the grey horizon. Bare. Like the desert he'd found Kayla in.

Eleven days. Two hundred and sixty-four hours. At least two hundred of those hours spent thinking of Kayla. More, if he counted the brief periods of sleep under the flapping canvas, when she haunted his dreams.

Unwillingly stirred from those dreams by duty, the fresh tang of the morning air made him long to share the sunrise with Kayla. The hard slap of rifle-barrel steel in his roughened palm compared miserably to the soft caress of her skin; the smell of strong, black coffee evoked wrenching memories of Kayla struggling to hold a chipped enamel cup to her blistered lips.

Where the hell was that self-control he prided himself on? He'd maintained command over every facet of his life since his parents' death. Had to, determined that would be the last random event to affect him. But now that willpower deserted him. He longed for Kayla, knowing he would give her everything, give up everything. He had no pride, no armour against her. A drug that had filtered under his skin, he couldn't live without her.

No, that was a load of juvenile crap. Of course he could bloody live without her.

But he didn't want to.

Four more weeks of deployment, then he'd take leave. No tropical holiday, no tourist destination. Just the two of them, secure in his house. Which wasn't much different than the last few months, except for one vital fact; Kayla was his. Or, more correctly, he was Kayla's.

Nick bit back a grin in case anyone was watching from the prefabs, but no way could he get his head around the fact that Kayla felt the same way as him.

Bugger the hot shower, he had more urgent needs. Humping his pack, he headed for the Perspex-shielded phone hard up against one of the prefab walls. His fingers shook with the cold. And something else. Nerves? Excitement? Anticipation. He was a junkie: she'd given him the words once, in the minutes before he left, and now he was desperate for them again.

Kayla's phone diverted to messages, and he damped down the brief flare of jealousy. Called Colley instead. 'Mate, pass your phone to Kayla, I've only got a minute.'

Colley's chuckle crackled down the line. 'Nice to hear from you, too.'

Nick chafed at his arm, turning his back to the rain working sly trails through the mud and greasepaint of his face. Never before had he allowed a woman to intrude on his work. Now work stole time that should have been spent with Kayla. He stared unseeingly at the tundra through the scored acrylic screen, listening to the distant voices through the wire. Listening for *her* voice.

'Cap?' Colley came back on. 'Kayla's on another call.' He sounded distracted. 'Look, mate, while she's busy, I want to give you a heads-up. She's seeing a counsellor.'

'What the hell?' The Perspex shivered as Nick struck it with a flat palm. 'You made her go to therapy? You know how she feels about that.'

'Her idea. Said she had stuff to sort.' Colley sounded perplexed rather than relieved, and Nick's gut coiled. 'And she's taken on a teaching gig.'

'A new contract?' Justifiably terrified of leaving the house, how could Kayla return to teaching?

'School of the Air. All online,' Colley clarified. 'Still, she's strung out about it, so I guess that's why the counsellor. She's been...different the last couple of weeks. I'm not saying it's bad,' he cut off Nick's interrogation. 'But she seems driven. Focussed. Doesn't mention the trial, hasn't asked about the verdict, or when there'll be a sentencing.' Nick tried to ignore that he could hear Colley's crucifix sliding along the chain. 'I know we said we were aiming for closure, but I can't work out whether she's blanking the whole thing out and shutting down, or whether she's checking off some to-do list and moving on. And speaking of moving on, here's the big one: she's talking about moving out.'

Nick resisted the urge to look at his watch, as though it'd reveal he'd been gone far longer than almost two weeks. Long enough for everything to turn to shit. 'What are you talking about? It's not safe for her to move out.'

'Nick, you know that bastard's never coming back. Why would he risk it? You can't let Kayla get it in her head that she's not safe except when she's with you.'

His lungs cramped. He slammed the receiver onto the cradle, jerking up the collar of his jacket as the rain snaked inside. Christ, was Colley right, did he encourage Kayla's dependence? But even if they did nothing more than hold hands for the next five years, he planned to keep his promise, be there for her.

And yet he wasn't.

The vein behind his right eye throbbing, he strode through the mud to the Commanding Officer's prefab. Saluted as he stamped to a halt at the drab grey desk. 'Sir, I request immediate leave.'

The C.O. grunted, balancing a silver pen on a stack of paperwork. 'Explain, Captain.'

'I need to get back to town immediately, Sir. Even for a few hours.'

The closely-shaven officer lifted a sheaf of papers, shuffled them together and smacked them back down, a gunshot in the tense silence. 'As you're aware, unless it's an emergency, you cannot be released from deployment.'

'Sir.' The word twisted his mouth. Tension vibrated his legs. Christ, he felt like a junior officer again.

The C.O. leaned back in his swivel chair, hands linked behind his head. 'At ease, Captain. So, death in the family? House burn down? Somebody seriously ill? Just don't tell me it's girl trouble.'

'Sir,' Nick repeated. Twenty years of experience stripped from him, his face burned.

The chair jerked upright and the C.O. reached for another thick file. 'Dismissed, Captain.'

Nick marched out, his back rigid. Paused to stare at the rain-soaked phone booth. Calling Kayla again wouldn't help her. Nothing he could do would help her.

Her future was her own.

CHAPTER 47

Colley balanced on the arm of the chair as Kayla sat. She steeled herself. As always, his tone was gentle—but an interrogation was still an interrogation. 'I warned you Nick would be lucky to get a chance to make a call. What was so important that you couldn't take it?'

Had that been her last opportunity to speak to Nick? If she'd taken the call would she have continued the lie, just so she could feel safe a little longer? The pain as she bit the inside of her cheek helped force control into her voice. Provided she kept the words short. 'Real estate agent. I found a flat. Vacant next week.'

Leather squeaked as Colley shifted. 'Still don't get it. There's plenty of room here.'

Her tongue probed the strangulated flesh inside her mouth. It was okay if she cried from biting her cheek. Everyone did that. Then Colley wouldn't know that the tears were because Nick hadn't been gone twenty-four hours before the familiar insecurity consumed her. It was different now, though. Fear of losing Nick, rather than fear of her memories.

Her counsellor insisted that was progress.

Her counsellor was an idiot.

'I can't be dependent on Nick. On anyone.'

'You know Nick wants to look after you.'

As had all the other men. 'I can't afford to let him.'

'It's not like he's going to charge rent.'

'There's always a price.' Normally so intuitive, why couldn't Colley understand? It had taken so many years to break free of the cycle of using men, she wouldn't allow that addiction to rule her life again. But spelling out her reasons, her failures, would rub salt into the wound. *Salt. Tomas pries my eye open, snickers with evil patience as I focus, the cold rock floor biting into my cheek. 'Now, we wouldn't want these cuts to get all contaminated, would we?' His bony finger jabs into my flayed back. 'No. Might hurt a bit. I've got just the thing to stop an infection, though.'*

Gradually, an artist unveiling a masterpiece, he brings his fist into line with my face. A waterfall of white grains sprinkle to the floor.

I can smell the salt.

Tomas grins. 'Be more fun than spreading it on slugs.'

He won't pour it, even he wouldn't do that.

He cackles, slowly tipping the container...

Ankles and wrists held by the other men, I scream until my throat bleeds. Gasping for air, I fight to survive even as I pray for death.

For a moment, she was tempted to remain in the memory, knowing the extent of that pain, rather than face an uncertain future. Yet her future did hold certainty: Tomas would come for her.

And she would be ready for him.

First, though, she would reclaim her independence. Prove herself more than the whore Mother labelled her.

CHAPTER 48

Kayla's new accommodation was a brick rectangle, devoid of personalisation. She surveyed the two rooms, trying to find some enthusiasm for reclaiming her own space, but this time her assertion that solitude didn't equate to loneliness lacked conviction.

Colley brought in the final box and grimaced as he glanced around. 'Nick's going to have the dirts up about this. It's not too late to change your mind, you know.'

It was too late. Weeks too late. It had become far too easy to rely on the soldiers for her safety. Kayla forced a smile. 'Lucky he's not back, then. You're coming round for coffee tomorrow morning, when I'm all sorted?' She did a fair impression of sounding excited.

Colley eyed the tiny kitchen dubiously. 'I'll bring take-out. Cappuccino or flat white?'

'Nescafé Instant,' she scowled, pointing to the grimy electric kettle that came with the partly-furnished unit. 'And you get to pretend it's the best darn coffee you ever had.'

The lieutenant faked a smile, his acting not as good as

her own. 'Look, how about you stay at Nick's one more night, and I'll get a security system in here tomorrow? Can't hurt.'

She shook her head. It would hurt; it might scare Tomas away. She could never embrace her future while he still lurked as a threat. One way or another, she needed it to be over. She had been right, weeks ago: she needed to bait a trap for him.

'I'll think about it in a couple of days. Okay?'

'Sure.' His tone reluctant, Colley paused with his hand on the doorknob. 'You've got your mobile? All charged?'

She waved the phone she clutched, then closed the door on his heels. Locked it. Turned to survey her tiny domain. Tried to feel emancipated, powerful, excited, relieved.

Anything except bloody terrified.

She set to unpacking the cartons. Done within twenty minutes, her sparse belongings punctuated the bedsit like spinifex in a desert. Still, she told herself, the place was hers. She had reclaimed her independence.

She should phone out for pizza. But that would mean unlocking the door, fronting an unfamiliar face who would probably find hers too familiar.

She wasn't hungry, anyway.

She should take a shower, but every horror movie she'd ever watched had a bathroom scene. That wasn't where she was confronting Tomas.

Maybe she should go meet the neighbours?

She baulked at the thought and instead folded down the Murphy bed, flipped the grimy mattress and shook out clean sheets. Dropped one of Nick's shirts over her head and worked her bra from beneath it. Then she sat, a pillow wedged against the wall, laptop on her knees.

Googled Nick's name. As she'd done dozens of times. This way she could almost look her fill, knowing she wasn't intruding, she wasn't stealing his time under false pretences. Images of him with attractive women at well-heeled functions flooded the screen. A handbag, he'd derisively called himself, decorating the arms of well-to-do socialites.

Her finger traced his image one last time, then Kayla forced herself to close the screen and hit the first movie that came up on Netflix. She turned the volume down, almost off, so she could hear every unfamiliar noise as the room descended into darkness around her.

The flickering screen cast terrifying shadows on the walls, so she crept from the bed, turned on the light, then scuttled back. Phone clutched in one hand, she stared unseeingly at the computer screen.

Credits rolled across it, and she queued another movie.

How many minutes could the night last?

The long fingers of a tree scratched at the security mesh guarding the window. She knew it was the tree. Had seen it during her virtual walk-around of the single-storey block of units.

But what if it wasn't?

Without taking her eyes from the window, she reached to the bedside cabinet and slid open the drawer. Her fingers searched out the cold steel buried beneath her clothes. Then she sat back against the wall, the hunting knife cradled against her chest. The online purchase record meant that a court could find her guilty of a premeditated act.

And they'd be damn right.

A vehicle slowed, the lights scrolling the wall. She held her breath until it accelerated away.

Footsteps on the pavement outside, a door banged in the adjacent unit. Why hadn't she researched who lived there?

The roof creaked. Her tongue cleaved to the top of her mouth as she eyeballed the trapdoor in the ceiling. Noted the filthy fingerprints on the peeling paint. Did the panel shift a millimetre? Was the crack around it wide enough for someone to watch her through? Was that faint, luminous gleam the glinting reflection from an eye?

Good. Because she wanted him to come, right? She wanted to end this.

No! Not yet! She wasn't strong enough. She wasn't prepared, she wasn't ready.

The phone shrilled and her legs jerked, tumbling the laptop to the grimy linoleum floor. Colley's name flicked onscreen. Hands trembling, Kayla thumbed to connect. She couldn't speak past the tears thickening her throat.

'Just checking in before I head to bed. You okay? Kayla?' Colley's concern escalated with her silence. 'Kayla, are you there?'

She had to say something. 'I'm okay.' But the words came out on a sob, and she mashed the phone against her cheek, eyes still fixed on the ceiling.

Cupboard doors banged in the background of Colley's call, muffled noises, a rushing and gathering. 'Kayla, don't hang up. Keep me on the line. I'm on my way, okay?'

She nodded.

Colley made the drive in ten minutes and used his spare key to let himself in. Crossed to her bed and took the phone from her numb fingers. Disconnected the call. Pried the knife from her other hand. 'Shift over.'

She moved to one side of the thin mattress and he lay

alongside, fully dressed. Pulled the quilt over them both. Left the light on. 'Okay. Sleep now.'

She did.

Early morning sun brightened the grey-white paint of the unadorned wall.

She had failed, unable to stay alone and start the new chapter of her life. And she should feel guilty. Instead, Colley's familiar, tuneless singing from the shower meant she was safe for a little longer.

It would be better if Tomas came during the day, anyway. She'd have more courage then.

Wouldn't she?

KAYLA ROSE, straightened the bed, and folded it back to the wall. Surveyed her domain with a shred more interest and acceptance than the night before. Hers. Her independence.

Baby steps.

'Morning.' Colley emerged from the bathroom, jeans slung low on his hips. Beads of water glistened on the black-inked tattoo on his bicep. The sword-wielding Spirit of Duty, the statue that stood guard over the War Memorial. Kayla stared, fascinated, as the angel cried. Nick had the same tattoo. Thinking his name woke the longing that ate at her independence, and she busied herself sliding the knife back into the nightstand drawer.

Colley towelled his hair vigorously. 'So, ready to rethink?'

'Rethink?' The intrusion startled her.

'Yeah. You coming home now?'

She picked up his shirt from the floor and handed it to him, her voice tight. 'This is home.'

'Kayla,' Colley groaned, looking for somewhere to sit. He gestured to the kitchen nook, the only two chairs in the unit. 'I don't get this. You finally have everything sorted with Nick. You're better off at his place, particularly until Tomas is brought in.'

'You keep saying T-T—' She forced herself to slow the words. 'You said *he* won't come back. So what difference does it make?'

Colley eyed her for a long moment, then bent to pull on socks. 'He won't. The guy would have to be mad.'

Yeah, that was kind of the problem.

A car door slammed outside, and her gaze slewed toward the door as Colley continued. 'He's not going to risk his freedom by coming within a million miles of you; that's why the feds haven't got him yet. But I get that you're scared, it's part of the PTSD. What I don't understand is why you won't stay at Nick's place, instead of forcing yourself to confront your fear like this. This is all so—' he gestured at the mean surrounds— 'So rushed. You should have waited for Nick to come back, at least talked it over with him. I'm just not convinced this is the best way to tackle your recovery. You *have* run it by your counsellor?'

'Sure.' Sort of.

Colley narrowed his eyes. 'And she's onboard? Says you have to be on your own?'

She needed to take ownership of her decisions, instead of acting like they were forced on her. Stop playing the victim role that she claimed to despise. 'Not *have* to. I want to.'

Colley dropped his runner, giving Kayla his full attention. 'Why?'

She shrugged, but that wouldn't pass for an answer with Colley.

He waited, hands dangling loosely between his knees.

She licked her lips. 'If I didn't go before Nick returned, I'd never be able to leave.'

'He wouldn't force you to stay.'

Elbows on the tiny kitchen table, Kayla dropped her head into her hands, the frustration and doubt suddenly overwhelming. Right now, running from the one man that perhaps she *could* learn to love seemed nothing short of crazy. 'The men. Before this—' she gestured at her scarred chest. 'They were never...I didn't...' She transferred her gaze to the curtained window. Tried again. 'My life's always been kind of fucked up. I don't know that I can give Nick what he needs.'

'Sex, you mean?' Colley kept his tone professional, although she knew she'd forced him out of his comfort zone. Served him right.

A harsh caw of mirthless laughter escaped her lips. 'No, that's not what I mean. And that makes everything so much worse, doesn't it? Because, hell, if I was normal, I would be worried about that. But I know sex is the only thing I *can* do right. I mean, Jesus, everyone knows that about me now, don't they?'

'What then?' Each time she risked a glance at him, Colley's dark gaze was still on her. Compassionate, rather than judgmental. 'Do you mean emotionally?'

She nodded, though sorrow weighed so heavy she could barely lift her head.

'Kayla, Nick is in love with you, and he's plenty big

enough and ugly enough to look after himself.' Colley shoved his chair back, leaning across the table. 'You just worry about what's right for you.'

A tic at the corner of her mouth jerked frantically. 'See, that's exactly the problem. He says this stuff. And I don't know...I don't know if I *can*. I don't think my brain works like anyone else's. I've never...' She pressed her lips together, chewing on the seam.

Colley stood. Approached warily, like he was afraid she would bolt. Where the hell to? She had escaped one prison, only to talk herself into another. 'Kayla, you're not the only one who's damaged. When Nick's folks died, he closed down. This thing with him letting everyone know how in love with you he is? That's not the Nick I know. That Nick doesn't allow emotions, he keeps everything locked inside. Yet, somehow, you've breached his guard.'

Intimidated by him standing over her, Kayla clambered to her feet. 'Great, so we're both fucked up, and I'll make everything worse. That's what you're saying?' She wanted him to say that. She wanted him to spell it out, tell her to run, leave Nick the hell alone. If Colley ordered her to do that, there was a chance she could stay safe, invulnerable.

Colley shook his head. 'I'm not telling you a damn thing. This is something you have to sort by yourself, but I'll support you in whatever you want to do. I'm just saying, don't rush it. You guys have plenty of time. There is no 'normal', Kayla. You've nothing to prove, and no one to prove it to.'

He didn't know how deep Mother had scarred her, how bad she needed to prove what she wasn't. And as for time...how much time would Tomas allow her? She sucked in a breath, collected her emotions. Stupid to have let them get the better of her. Weak. 'Of course. You're right.' It was safer to get back to pretending she was okay.

Colley sat again, tugging on his shoe. 'You're set on staying, then?'

'Yep.' She folded her arms across her chest, so he wouldn't see her trembling.

'Okay. Well, I'm off to the gym. I'll pick up some groceries after, bring them in for you?'

'No. I'll entertain myself by ordering online.' If she faked it hard enough, perhaps she would eventually feel as strong as her reply sounded. But she would check the supermarket allowed her to pay online and would do a door drop, so she wouldn't have to open up to a stranger.

Colley nodded. 'Hey, would it be cool if I crashed here tonight? I've got an early start for the beginning of the beach triathlon season. Staying here would save me a half hour's drive.'

'Sure.' She fought to keep the relief from her voice as they both lied.

Baby steps. But she'd get there.

CHAPTER 49

For ten days, she and Colley kept up the pretence. He squeezed an army-surplus camp bed into a corner of her musty room and slept there every night. And Kayla found she could manage the days alone. Not well; even she couldn't fool herself enough to believe that. But between staring at her phone waiting for Nick's name to flash up— praying it would and hoping it wouldn't—and devising enough lesson plans to cover the next ten years, she got through each day.

Sue called a couple of times, Lorraine daily. After listening to the voicemails, Kayla responded by text. That way she could edit her words, ensure they didn't reek of insecurity, and send texts peppered with exclamation points, full of smiley-faced emoji excitement about her new house and life.

Lorraine sent fruit baskets and repeatedly asked to visit. But Kayla said she simply couldn't find time, so terrifically busy was she with work, and decorating—if throwing the junk mail on the kitchen table counted—and...and trying not to think about Nick. Trying not to wonder where he was, what he was doing. Trying not to name the emotion that claimed her fixation was rational and acceptable.

Staring blankly at the computer screen a full half hour after she'd disconnected from work, she startled as her phone rang. *Unknown number* scrolled across the screen. So few people had her number, the caller had to be Nick.

She stared at the display.

Didn't answer.

Couldn't answer. She'd not yet proved a damn thing to herself, so she couldn't allow the fix she craved so desperately.

Colley bustled in just after dark, arms laden with Chinese takeaway cartons. His presence released her from the need to creep around the flat, staying quiet so she could hear every noise. 'We Netflixing tonight?'

'Sure.'

As she took juice from the bar fridge, he loaded her plate with food she wouldn't eat. Paused with chopsticks partway to his mouth. 'I had a call today.'

'Red-letter day for you, then.' Her heart drummed to a crescendo, ready to burst from her chest. She needed to come up with a new excuse for not having spoken to Nick.

'More for you, than me. Lorraine would like it known that she's issuing an ultimatum. She refuses to believe that you're teaching on a Saturday, so either you meet her for morning coffee, or she'll come to you.' Colley's glance took in the shabby room. 'Personally, I'd lean toward meeting. If Lorraine gets a look at this place she's sure to get those adoption papers out.'

'Ah.' Breath expelling in a rush, Kayla's fingers moved to the jewelled bluebird at her throat. She missed Lorraine almost as much as she missed Nick. 'I don't want to go out anywhere. Not yet.' Her glance flickered to the window.

'He's not out there, Kayla.'

'Actually, I wasn't being neurotic about...' she squeezed her eyes shut. '*Him*. I just don't want to go out...there.' Ever. But sentencing had been the previous day and, although she avoided the news and social media, she knew that public interest would have reignited.

Colley watched her for a long moment. 'I know. But at some stage, you're going to have to. Not tomorrow, though. How about I drop you at Lorraine's place?'

'Sure. I guess that'd work.' She'd come up with an excuse tomorrow, but it was always easier to agree in the present.

'Why wouldn't you speak to Nick today?'

Damn. She choked as she almost inhaled her rice. 'I had nothing to say.'

'Nothing? Really?' Colley waved his chopsticks at her apartment.

'I'm sure you filled him in.'

'I'm sure he'd prefer you did.'

She scraped rice around her plate, sectioning and dividing. Resisting the urge to count grains. 'I can't talk to him. If we could text, it'd be different.' Maybe.

'How so?'

'Just easier.'

'Kayla, I realise I said you should take this slow, but you kind of do have to talk to the guy.'

'I'm not a talker.'

'Yeah, I'd noticed.'

She rubbed her fingertips hard against her forehead, trying to erase the imminent headache. 'It's just...I haven't got this bit right, yet. If I lose focus on what I'm trying to do here, there's a chance I'll lie to myself. Maybe I'll confuse what I think I *want* with what I *need*.'

Colley pushed aside cartons to lean closer. 'You know what you want, then?'

She lifted a shoulder. 'At the moment, if I know what day of the week it is, I'm counting it a win. I can't think beyond that.'

'Okay,' Colley tugged out his phone, concentrating on the screen. 'Your call on the movie, as long as you don't make us watch another sci-fi. Or I brought Scrabble over, figured we could go Bachelor of Ed versus Bachelor of Med.' He waggled his phone. 'Reception's lousy in here. I just have to step out to make a call.'

She'd never had a problem with her phone reception.

Lorraine opened the door to the seaside cottage before Colley knocked. 'Steven, how lovely to see you. And Kayla, love, I've missed you.'

Having given in to Colley's refusal to allow her to back out of the meeting, Kayla would have liked to remain longer in Lorraine's warm hug. But the woman stiffened, looking beyond her. Instantly alert, Kayla glanced over her shoulder, then shrank closer to Colley, ducking her chin and letting her hair swing forward to hide her face.

A tall woman bustled down the slate-paved garden path, her hand raised in greeting. 'Lorraine! How lucky I caught you. I've been meaning to pop that recipe over for weeks. Oh, I'm sorry, I see you have visitors.'

Kayla glued her gaze to the ground. Lorraine drew

herself up to her less-than-impressive height. 'I do indeed have visitors, Merilyn. So, I'm sure you'll excuse me.'

'Oh, I won't take a moment.' Merilyn was alongside Kayla now, a waft of perfume and nicotine that brought a rush of memory. 'Hello dear, you look familiar. Have we met? Oh, I know! The news earlier in the week! You're that—'

'Come in, Kayla, Steven.' Lorraine kicked the door wider behind her. 'Merilyn, I know you'll understand that I can't ask you in right now.'

'I'll just pop into your kitchen and write out the recipe.' Merilyn tapped her forehead. 'It's all up here.'

'Then I'm sure it'll be safe up there for a little longer. Lucky you're only next door, and can drop over anytime, isn't it?' Lorraine ushered Kayla and Colley in with agitated flapping motions of her hands, and closed the door on her neighbour. She tutted as she guided them down the hall. 'I'm so sorry, love. Merilyn's a terrible gossip. I swear, since she discovered George's involvement, she's been keeping watch on the house, trying to catch you.'

Kayla's steps faltered, and Lorraine seized her hand. 'No, no. Not like that.'

'I know.' She wasn't stupid, just reactive. 'Guess I'm going to have to get used to it. Maybe we should have jumped straight in the deep end and gone to a coffee shop.' Except she wanted both Colley and Lorraine to lie to her, tell her she'd never be exposed again.

'You poor love,' Lorraine twittered. 'Your hands are freezing. Come on through to the sunroom, it's toasty in there.'

The rhythmic massage of Lorraine's thumb across her palm was a drug, as tempting as any narcotic or alcohol, demanding Kayla push away her doubts. She shoved her hands into the pockets of her windcheater, though their trembling had nothing to do with the temperature.

The sunroom fronted a view across miles of battleship-grey ocean—but the glass left her exposed. The only place she had felt safe for months—no, *ever*—was in Nick's house, guarded by the solid walls. And by him.

But that wasn't good enough, not anymore. She had to do better.

A lace-covered knee-height table groaned under plates of sandwiches and cakes. And three teacups. Three side plates. Kayla frowned at Colley, though sudden amusement teased the corner of her mouth. 'This feels suspiciously like an intervention. Payback for me whipping you at Scrabble?'

Colley grinned as he dropped into a white wicker chair. 'I maintain you cheated. In any case, I'm only here for the grub. Not that I'm not thrilled to participate,' he added hastily with a glance at Lorraine.

'I wouldn't call it an intervention, love.' Lorraine settled comfortably, pouring tea from a flower-patterned pot. 'I simply wanted to check how you are. Frankly, I'm rather annoyed with George.'

'Annoyed?'

'Come and sit beside me.' Lorraine patted the floral-cushioned couch.

Kayla knew she should take the single chair. It wasn't like she *needed* anyone to coddle or mother her. Her fingers found the bluebird charm and she sank next to Lorraine.

'George maintains that the captain was the only person with the necessary specialist weapons training who was available for the emergency deployment. But I maintain that Nicholas wasn't really *available*, was he? I do feel that some things are rather more important than work. And leaving you all alone.' Lorraine shook her head.

'Not alone,' Kayla tipped her head toward Colley.

'Well, of course Colley loves you—'

Kayla winced. Lorraine was remarkably free with that word.

'I know I rate poor seconds, but if I loved you any more than I do, Nick would likely kill me,' Colley joked.

'Yet it's just not the same,' Lorraine finished.

'It's fine, I'm fine.' Kayla waved off Lorraine's concern, trotting out the usual trite reply, which no one ever believed but everyone wanted to hear.

'Except there's a big difference between feeling fine and coping,' Colley challenged.

'I'll settle for either.' Despite the sting of Colley's inference, she tried to be funny, flippant.

'Speaking of settling, tell me all about this new house of yours,' Lorraine said.

'Well, it's small.' If Colley was going to out her, she'd beat him to the punchline. 'Because I make Colley sleep on a cot in the corner so that I can *cope*.'

Colley's plate of tiny triangle sandwiches froze mid air. 'I'm there for maybe nine-ten hours. And for fourteen hours a day, you're alone. Less than two weeks ago, I wouldn't have thought that possible.'

She didn't need treats and coercion, rewards for good behaviour, thrust under the door. 'The fourteen hours I spend cowering behind locked doors, terrified of the slightest noise, you mean?'

'Oh, goodness,' Lorraine said. 'You think I don't have my place locked up all day, every day? Maybe not forty years ago, but now, most definitely. And I find it terribly hard to sleep when George isn't home. Humans are pack creatures. We require the comfort of another heartbeat. So why are you making Colley being there into an issue?' Tea and scones with a side of steel, Lorraine could be startlingly direct.

'Because I'm not proving—or even finding—my independence. I moved out of Nick's because I have to remember how to make it on my own. Without trading or selling myself.' Kayla bit out the words, then mashed her lips together.

'Selling yourself?' Lorraine looked puzzled.

The possibility of losing the comfort of Lorraine's mothering created a hollow ache—yet Kayla didn't want the friendship under false pretences. Lorraine deserved to know everything. 'Since I was fourteen,' she said. 'I did try to tell George.' *To warn him.*

'Yes, he mentioned that you were on your own. And that you were terribly distressed about your father's death.'

Kayla gave a short laugh. 'Did he tell you that's because I caused Dad's death?'

'No. He told me that you *believe* it was your fault, which is a vastly different matter.'

Kayla leaned away from Lorraine, as though her proximity would contaminate the other woman's innocence. 'The police couldn't find me when Dad was dying, because I was at some guy's house. Some guy whose name I can't remember. Some guy who gave me food and a bed and most likely money, as well. Some guy that I needed to pretend to myself actually cared for me.'

Hands folded in her lap, Lorraine's faded blue eyes steadfastly met her gaze. 'And the fact that you had to search for love is somehow your fault?'

'Absolutely,' Kayla said emphatically. 'I *always* knew that what I was doing was wrong. But it made me feel better for a moment, like I had some control over my life. I got a kick from using men, just like a junkie scoring a hit. Or like my mother, uncapping a fresh bottle. But see, I'm worse than them: I don't have a chemical addiction, I don't have an excuse. I *chose* that path.'

Colley's plate clattered onto the table.

Lorraine squeezed her hand, clammy with the fear of judgment. 'It's your body. You have every right to do with it as you please.'

'But it wasn't only *my* body I used. I—' Kayla broke off, trying to order her thoughts. 'I needed men to fall in love with me. I used their hearts to heal my pain.'

'Oh, love.' Lorraine's warm palm cupped her cheek, her eyes soft with tears. 'You may have thought you were in control, but those men used you, not the other way around. People who love you don't hurt you, Kayla. Cruelty and love have no connection.'

She clutched Lorraine's hand. 'You don't understand. They have to.'

'Why?' Puzzlement creased Lorraine's forehead.

'Because if they don't, then no one ever loved me,' Kayla whispered. 'Not even my dad.'

Lorraine's arms enfolded her in a hug that surely had to be motherly. 'Oh, my poor, broken child,' she murmured into Kayla's hair. 'You need to learn to love yourself a little, so you can accept that others love you.'

Such an inane aphorism. She didn't even *like* herself. But the ridiculous sentiment helped her find anger to hide behind. 'No. I just need to be better than that, now. I've done it before: I stayed alone so I couldn't be tempted to use anyone. But then those men—' Memory shuddered through her and she fought the panic that clawed up inside her. She didn't need to feel that way anymore: she'd dealt with them. Only one more to go. 'I did what I've always done. I traded my body to get what I wanted.'

Lorraine loosened her grip, leaning back to trap her gaze. 'It wasn't the same thing at all, Kayla. When you were younger, you did what you needed to do. This time, you did what you were forced to do. Neither was a choice.'

Fists balled so tight her fingers ached, Kayla shook her head. 'You don't understand. I *believed* I had a choice. I thought I could trade myself for the children's safety—and I was okay with that. Do you realise how sick that is? I didn't work out a way to get the kids out of there, I didn't rescue them. My entire plan revolved around trading myself, like it's all I'm capable of doing.' She sucked in a breath, choking as it caught her throat. Sat straighter, signifying the conversation was closed. 'Anyway, that's why I had to leave Nick's place. If I stay, I won't know whether I'm simply using Nick. Trading myself for the safety he can provide.'

'No one ever uses the captain,' Colley said.

'Really? He doesn't know me, yet he's fine with everyone thinking he's in love. Who does that?' She dragged in air, trying not to sob her frustration. 'Does he know *how* screwed up I am? That I can't have kids? Christ, the fact that I'm even talking about this, like I can consider a relationship after I was-was—' For God's sake, she should be able to say the word by now. 'That's not normal, Colley. You've got to stop pretending that it is. I have no...*right* to.'

'Because you were raped, you mean,' Colley said, his words a filthy trespass in the pretty, cosy room.

Kayla's stomach cramped with the verbal punch.

'I'm sorry, Kayla. I know you don't like hearing it. But you've got to get this warped idea of being tainted out of your head.'

'Tainted?' Lorraine gasped. 'Oh my goodness, no. You're judging your value based on what those men did to you?'

Kayla tried to steady her breathing. 'It's nothing to do with value.' She'd never had any. 'It's-it's—how can I even have *feelings*, after that? What's wrong with me?' Why was she begging for explanation, for absolution, when there could be none?

'Nothing,' Lorraine replied firmly. 'Absolutely nothing. So men were inside you. They forced themselves on you.'

Darkness thundered in Kayla's head. How could Lorraine use words, phrases, images like that?

Lorraine lifted a plump shoulder, her voice unusually firm. 'Sex without love is nothing but a physical act.'

'I know,' Kayla rushed to assure her. *It's only sex. Means nothing.* She knew it better than anyone. 'But I shouldn't feel —' What? Desire? Lust? More than that? '*Anything*. Not after what happened.'

Lorraine gripped Kayla's hand as though she'd shake sense into her. 'Rubbish. No one has the right to tell any woman what she should feel. Do you believe the thousands of women who have been raped should spend their lives dressed neck-to-knee in sackcloth, shamed by men's sins? Of course not. We pick ourselves up. Dust ourselves off. And we carry on. Kayla,' she leaned forward. 'You are not alone. And you deserve whatever you choose to take from life. Don't be scared of your own desires. Not all men are monsters.'

No, but the danger was, that there might be a monster in every man. Kayla clasped her hands, deliberately loose, around the teacup. *Run and hide. Pretend everything is fine.*

Never let anyone know you hurt. If she remained silent and small, they'd leave her alone.

Cane creaked as the lieutenant moved to the edge of his chair. 'So why are you?'

'What?' she scowled.

'Scared. It's not only Nick, or even Tomas, is it?' he puzzled too gently. 'You're worried that because your life is now so public, you'll be judged for your choices.'

She had to interrupt, stop him from piecing together the fractions she'd told him over the weeks. Yet if he completed the jigsaw, could Colley rescue her?

'And you're terrified that you'll make those choices based on a need for security. But there's more, isn't there?' Colley demanded. 'You're scared to allow yourself to feel. Scared that if you allow love, you open yourself to loss and rejection.'

Her breath left in a rush. This wasn't rescuing her; it was exposing her. 'History is the best predictor of the future.'

Lorraine took Kayla's cup and set it firmly on the table. 'No. Because the present is always a variable.' She nodded at Colley and flicked a hand toward George's study. 'You already have love, whether you want to allow it or not. You have family now,' Lorraine insisted. 'And that makes everything different.'

She was right, it did make everything different. And that terrified Kayla.

Because with family came loss.

CHAPTER 50

Colley left for gym immediately after lunch, although Lorraine prevailed on Kayla to stay a little longer to have afternoon tea with George when he emerged from his study.

The major drove her home a few hours later, carrying in the bags of home-baked goods Lorraine sent with them. He glanced around the small house without comment, making certain she noticed him check the window locks.

By the time Colley returned, Kayla had cleaned the two rooms, prepped another week's lessons, and done her laundry—although she'd not ventured into the tiny back-yard, where the washing line lurked in the dusk. All the time, her mind churned, trying to sort fact from fantasy, possibility from probability.

Colley let himself in, accompanied by a rush of cold air. 'Hey, you know—'

She sagged against the grimy doorjamb. 'I'm tired, Colley. No more lectures, okay?'

'Sorry. I didn't mean to bail you up at Lorraine's.' He

dropped his canvas bag against the wall. 'Or at least, I didn't expect it to go down so hardcore.'

She moved to the kitchenette and waved a mug. 'Coffee?' He nodded, and she focused on the cup, pretending it took concentration to count out his three sugars. 'You weren't really hardcore. Well, you were. The thing is,' she broke off, pouring boiling water. Wishing she could wash away her thoughts. 'Thing is, you're right. But I'm not only scared. I'm...God, I don't even know what.'

No. If she was going to talk about it, she had to try harder than that. She'd thought about what Colley said, thought about Lorraine's promise of support. And they were right; she could have a different future. But changing her physical location wasn't enough. She had to change her mindset. And that meant learning to allow emotions other than anger. Even those that terrified her.

She thumped a hand against her chest. 'Sad. That's what I am. Because I know I *can* do this, but I-I—' her lips wobbled. 'I'm worried that if I screw up, I'll disappoint and lose all of you.'

'Kayla, we're not going anywhere. Live here, don't live here. Hook up with Nick, don't hook up with Nick. None of that changes who *you* are. Kim, Lorraine, me, we'll all still be here. That's how family works.'

'Yeah, not so much in my world.'

'This is your world, now.'

She rubbed her chest. Allowed the emotion and blurted the words. 'I miss Nick. Not because I *need* him, you know? But because he has a way of making me believe I'm doing all right.'

'Okay, well how about we don't give him *all* the props for that.' Colley grumbled. 'How long till he's back, anyway?'

Would he like it in days? Hours? Minutes, even? But the fact that Kayla had it calculated didn't have to mean she wasn't independent. 'Nearly two weeks.'

Colley squatted, grabbed some clothes off his camp bed, and stuffed them in his gym bag. 'Ah, yeah, that's right. By the way, Kim's decreed that we're all going out tomorrow night.'

'Tomorrow? No! We just saw them.' She wasn't ready for 'out' anywhere.

'It'll be okay, Kayla. Just out for dinner. The three of us. Celebrate the sentencing.'

'I don't want—' She stopped herself. 'I have to, don't I?'

'At some stage. So why not get it over with now? Might not be as bad as you think. And Sunday night will be quiet. In any case, it was pretty much a direct order from the major.' He indicated Nick's shirt, which she had belted over her jeans. 'You wear the uniform you march to the drum.'

She clutched the fabric. Even washed, the cotton smelled of Nick.

Colley zipped his bag. 'Anyway, like I was saying when I came in, you remember I have my daughter tonight?'

'Sure. We'll put in another camp bed, have a sleepover?' She grinned quickly, making sure he recognised the joke. 'Stop stressing. It's not like you haven't reminded me every night this week.' And not like she hadn't spent every night obsessing about it, pretending to herself she'd be fine. That she wanted Tomas to come. *Bait.* Hadn't that been half her reason for moving out of the safety of Nick's home?

'I figured maybe you'd stay at mine tonight? I'll pick up some takeaway. Sarah will be fine with missing Macca's for once.'

Kayla stirred the coffee, staring into the darkness. She

could easily go with him. Or she could have mentioned it to Lorraine that morning, instead of swearing Colley to secrecy. She would have been invited to stay, cosseted and cared for in the Kimber's seaside cottage. Treated like a daughter. She had options, now that she had family.

She handed Colley his coffee. 'No, it's fine. It's time I did this.'

TWENTY-FOUR HOURS. She had made it a full twenty-four hours alone and, although she'd barely slept and an impression of the hilt of her hunting knife blurred the scars on her palm, she hadn't given in to the urge to phone Lorraine, Colley, or even Sue.

Tomas hadn't taken the bait but still she was proud of herself. So proud, the dinner outing with the Kimbers seemed entirely doable.

That feeling faded as, flanked by Colley and George, she and Lorraine entered the crowded restaurant above the Casino. It was hardly the dark, under-populated venue she had anticipated.

As she hunched her back against the probing stares of the other patrons, George dabbed his lips, sliding his plate to the centre of the table. 'Always exceptional.'

'It is a tad expensive,' Lorraine confided. 'But the food is always lovely, and they source locally. When the boys are home, we make time to come.' The myriad wrinkles around her eyes deepened as she smiled at Kayla. 'Now, we get to take you.'

So much to lose. As always, family brought pleasure and pain.

George pushed back his chair and draped Lorraine's sparkly lilac shrug over her shoulders. 'Who's for some fun in the Casino?' He rubbed two fingers against his thumb. 'Kayla, I have a feeling you'll be my good luck charm.'

'Can't say I've ever been considered that.'

A wave of lavender smoothed over her as Lorraine rose. 'Come on, love. Let's freshen up a little.'

Oblivious to the bubble of thrilled silence that surrounded their passage through the restaurant, the excited whispers, the not-so-covert pointing, Lorraine led the way to the restroom. Kayla kept her eyes straight ahead, her teeth clenched. Surely, the interest would soon die down. There would be a new scandal, a new salacious titbit to thrill the masses. Something that would allow her to slide into obscurity. She avoided her reflection in the mirrored wall of the opulent restroom. More than enough people looked at her.

Wrinkled and soft like a crumpled tissue, Lorraine's purple-veined hand patted at her forearm. 'You look miserable, love.'

'No reason to be.'

'Except that you're missing Nicholas.'

By now, she should be accustomed to the take-no-prisoners outspokenness behind Lorraine's motherly facade. She forced herself to meet the woman's faded blue gaze. 'Perhaps I'm only thinking about him because he isn't here? What if it's nothing more than that?'

'Possibly. But emotional wounds are as painful as physical, and you're picking at that scab to see what lies beneath. I think you need to wait until Nicholas comes home, and see how you *feel*.' She tapped Kayla's chest lightly. 'And, love, whatever you feel will be just fine.'

'I'm not good with feelings.' Kayla pointed to her temple 'I think this is in charge.'

'Let's go take your mind off him, then. I promise you'll enjoy yourself downstairs.'

'I'm not much of a gambler. Taking chances doesn't work out too well for me.' That's why she had everything organised now, her plans in place.

Lorraine smoothed a tendril of Kayla's hair into place. 'It wasn't gambling I was thinking of. Come on, the men are waiting.'

The descent by escalator gave Kayla opportunity to search the crowds. In such a public venue, Tomas would find it easy to blend: but he wouldn't be here. She had baited her trap—and he would never know how carefully she'd chosen the location. Minutes from the police station. Defensible. Compact. Her hunting knife had company, several blades hidden within easy reach. Blades that would never cut her, because she was finally stronger than that. She had also ordered capsicum spray, but it was a toss-up as to whether the illegal import would clear Customs in time. Tomas's return was not only inevitable, it was anticipated. At last, she would complete her job: she would save the children.

'This is George's favourite.' Lorraine indicated a long, green-baize covered table, 'But I'm fond of rou—oh!' She snagged her husband's sports jacket and he jerked around to follow the indication of her chin. With a disappointed moue, Lorraine shook her head and continued. 'Roulette. What do you fancy?'

Kayla shrugged, staying close to her group, her family. The lack of sleep the previous night was beginning to tell. Torn between keeping her eyes on the gold-patterned carpet and surreptitiously scanning the crowd, careful to avoid meeting anyone's gaze, she nodded vacantly as George avidly explained the finer points of different games.

Colley's arm encircled her waist, his mouth close to her ear. 'Hey, your bottom lip's fair dragging on the ground. You okay?'

'Sorry. Just super tired.'

'Don't worry, you'll sleep better tonight.'

She shook her head. 'You don't need to stay over anymore. I'm cool.' She needed to clear the way for Tomas while she was brave enough to tackle him. Before fear of losing the love of this newly acquired family made her vulnerable. Mother was right; emotions were weakness. That didn't mean that she couldn't allow them, but she had to choose her moment. She had a job to do, first.

'Wasn't offering. I know you're good.' Colley dug in his pocket. 'Here, have some chips. We'll elbow in on the money wheel.'

'No, I—' A commotion at the entrance thirty metres away pulled her attention.

In crumpled battle-fatigues, a tall figure filled much of the double doorway. Three security guards tried to bar his entry. 'Sorry, sir. We have a dress code after 6 p.m.'

'Then I suggest you adjust your watch.' Hands fisted, the soldier's gaze probed the crowded recesses of the hall. A ball clicked around the roulette wheel unwatched. Patrons shrank behind one another, drifting deliberately toward the back of the crowd. The live jazz band in the open bar played on, oblivious to the expectant lull.

Nick. Traces of thick camouflage makeup disguised his features, the sun-bleached hair cropped, making him older, more careworn. Every fibre of Kayla's being strained toward him, a yearning that tore at her soul. If this was what Lorraine meant by *feeling* her emotions, it bloody hurt.

Colley hailed him, loud in the hush. 'Captain. She's here.'

Kayla turned instinctively to the Kimbers. Lorraine's hands were clasped, as if in prayer, her face radiant. George gestured toward the door. 'I believe that's for you, Kayla.'

She shook her head.

'It's all right, love. I promise.' Lorraine pushed her gently toward Colley, who shepherded her through the excited funnel of spectators toward Nick's daunting bulk.

Nick held out a hand, discoloured with ingrained dirt, and jerked his chin at the bouncers. 'I think these gentlemen want me to leave. And we need some privacy.'

The first words he had spoken to her in weeks. Kayla breathed in greedily; sweat, greasepaint, and gun oil, yet it was all *him*. As she stepped out of the safety of the casino and onto the elevated walkway that crossed the ant-nest of the railway station far below, Nick's grip tightened, though she didn't struggle. He strode across the glass-sided bridge and out into the drizzling rain. After ten paces, he adjusted his gait to her speed and led her along a dimly-lit path that snaked toward the banks of the river coursing below the casino. He didn't relinquish his grasp until he pulled her under the negligible shelter of the leafless skeleton of a tree.

She didn't want him to let go. For the first time, Kayla realised the fact absolutely. And it didn't matter what terrifying name she, or Lorraine, or anyone else, used; she didn't want that feeling to disappear.

'Kayla, what the hell happened? Why wouldn't you take my calls?'

He sounded angry. No, more than that. Desperate? She

dropped her chin, examining the mud-flecked turf, concentrating on the thick odour of duck dirt and soil as she tried to formulate a response.

Nick's eyes bored into the curtain of her hair, their sharp breaths pluming in the cold air. He shoved his hands into the pockets of his fatigues, his tone more controlled. 'Kayla, you have to talk to me.'

The stunted grass blurred and indistinct, she shifted her gaze to the dull glint of the sluggish river. 'I couldn't talk, I was busy.'

'Too busy for *us*?'

Us. Her heart lurched. Everything she had ever wanted might lie in those two letters. 'I was trying to make it possible for there to be an *us*.'

He absorbed her words for a beat. 'Did it work?' His tone was urgent.

She pinched at her bottom lip. 'I don't know.' She wanted so desperately to say yes, but she had already lied to him once, told him what he wanted to hear, rather than the confused truth.

Nick rubbed a filthy hand across his face, his shoulders slumping in defeat. 'Kayla. I've served in Iraq and Afghanistan. I've killed men. Christ, I've shovelled the pieces of my own men into garbage bags, been pinned under a burning ATV. But I've never been as bloody terrified as you're making me right now.' His gaze impaled her. 'You refuse to take my calls. Colley tells me you've moved out, and then I get an urgent summons relayed from Kim while I'm out bush. My C.O. has no idea what it's about, so I'm tearing across the State. Seven hours, believing something terrible has happened to you. No one's picking up my damned calls, then I get a message from Colley directing me here.' He gestured incredulously up the hill. 'To a bloody casino. Kayla, this is doing my head in. I don't understand what happened, what went wrong. All I know is I can't function, I'm so damned scared of losing you.'

He was scared? Tears blocked Kayla's view, but she felt him there. Even if they didn't touch, his presence embraced her. The breath shuddered through her, raking at her throat as Nick's hands slid up her arms, warm against the damp fabric. She tried not to tremble as he lowered his voice. 'I don't understand any of this. There's only one thing I am absolutely certain of.' His voice broke. 'Kayla, I *need* you.'

His words the key, her heart shifted as he unlocked the emotion she dared not verbalise. No one had ever *needed* her; they'd only wanted her body to fulfill their fantasies. But this man bared his soul, speaking of an entirely new kind of desire. And she wanted to love him, more than anything she'd ever wanted in her life. But she had clawed back a tiny bit of her independence, and she couldn't sacrifice that. Not for something as ephemeral and transient as love. 'I had to move out.'

Rain channelled down the harsh crags of Nick's face. 'Do you want to tell me why?'

'I had to prove that I could.'

He nodded slowly. 'Just tell me it was north.'

She shook her head, bewildered. 'I...don't know. Why north?'

'I said I'd come visit you up north, remember?'

Of course she remembered, every word he had ever spoken. Nick watched her intently, waiting for her reply, waiting for *permission*. He wasn't going to force or demand or barter. And maybe that meant she could do this. Perhaps she could have it all, for a little while. She firmed her voice. 'Definitely north.'

Nick's exhale audible, his hands slid to her shoulders 'I know you've loads on with this new job, but maybe I could come by sometime?'

Although he didn't know her ultimate plan, why she had to be alone, Nick realised that she needed space, needed to be in control of what happened between them. He didn't intend to steal her hard-won freedom by insisting she move back into the safety of his house and his protection.

And Kayla wasn't sure whether to be relieved or disappointed.

CHAPTER 51

Nick leaned back, balancing his chair on two legs, to better see Kayla across the metres of white table-cloth separating them. At least on the two-hour flight to Canberra he had been able to sit alongside her, his uniform jacket hiding their entwined hands.

He'd become accustomed to her company over the last four weeks. More than accustomed. Needy. Greedy. He'd been so damned scared that night, on the banks of the river. Scared she had changed her mind, that she would reject him, refuse to step into his arms. But slowly she had closed the emotional gap between them.

Now it was the physical space that ached. The celebra-tory dinner and presentation of the Bravery Medal would have been a damn sight more tolerable if they'd been seated near one another. He scanned the room. Free alcohol served in elegant crystal was still free alcohol. The party wouldn't wind up any time soon.

Kayla's hair fell forward as she dipped her chin—evidently, someone had spoken to her. The straight sheath of her dress didn't provide enough material to twist between her hands, so any moment now she would reach for a serviette, worry at that instead. His breath hitched as he watched her. So beautiful and so...alone. Covered from neck to knee, she sought to hide; yet the modest dress enhanced her delicacy—and that fragility terrified him. How could he protect her? Especially when there was nothing to protect her from.

And everything.

He pushed from the table, excusing his way through the crowd of suited and gowned dignitaries. Kayla willowed toward him, and his shoulders eased. 'Dance?'

Her eyes flickered to his, then darted to the dance floor. 'I...'

Reluctance hid in her shy evasion, and he hesitated. He didn't want her to acquiesce—*to anything*—simply to please him. Yet he could only be confident of his ability to keep her safe when his arms were around her.

She stood, though, defiant courage in her stance as he escorted her to the crowded dance floor. As she melted against him, head nestled beneath his chin, the pressure of her cheek encouraged the machinegun rhythm of his heart.

One hand in the small of her back, he slid the other between her shoulder blades. Held her as close as he dared, aware of every point of contact, every breath she took. Barely moving, they swayed together in perfect synthesis. They weren't dancing.

For the first time in his life, he was making love.

Eyes closed so he could better focus on the feel of her without the intrusion of light and noise and people, his lips found her ear. 'I love you, Kayla. I want to get out of here, away from this crowd. I don't want to share you. Ever.' He loved her with such a disabling, devastating intensity that he was consumed by her, wanting to consume her.

Kayla pulled away, and he wasn't certain whether he had scared her, or she required the distance to look up at him. He drew her back. 'I'm sorry. It's the wine talking.'

She buried her face against his chest, her words so quiet he almost missed them. 'I want you.'

His heart thumped so damn erratic, she probably felt it. Fiery and apologetic by turns, over the last few weeks Kayla had seemed more wary of allowing deeper emotions than he had ever been. So, he'd waited. Not something he was good at, but necessary if she was to ever share her feelings. Damned if he would screw this up by rushing her, she had to make every move.

The way her palms pressed against his shirt, fingers tracking his abs, sure as hell felt like a move. His muscles contracted involuntarily, and she gazed up, eyes full of doubt and—*No*. Anything more existed only in his imagination. She had never repeated the three words he wanted to hear. But that wouldn't stop him from saying them.

The band took a break, the dignitaries closing in as he returned Kayla to her seat. He felt her reluctance, her hesitancy to face them. His lips brushed her hair. 'Hang in there, Miki.' A smile lit her eyes. He'd discovered a few weeks back that no-one had used the nickname, it was something only the two of them would ever share. Reluctantly, he allowed her hand to trail from his. 'This is their last night. After tonight, it's only us.'

This promise, he could keep.

CHAPTER 52

A month earlier, when she had finally found the words to explain to Nick that she didn't want to be dependent on him, but that she also didn't want to be without him, he had understood. And he'd stepped back. Although he was there, physically and emotionally, they maintained an unspoken boundary. Talked a lot, touched a little, kissed frequently. But he never pressured her to say that she loved him.

But tonight something felt different.

Across the function room, Nick nodded in polite acknowledgment of a plump woman's desperate flirtation, her pouty pigeon chest crowding him. His gaze locked to Kayla's.

The tremble of desire butterflied up from her stomach. She should stay where she was. Though she was exposed and on display at the award presentation, there was safety in numbers and she needed protection—from herself. Nick's passing touch, a brief stroke of her arm, a hand against her cheek, awoke a hunger within her. How could their chaste caresses be enough for him, when they were no longer enough for her? Yet she both desired and feared more. Could she satisfy her need for Nick's embrace without sacrificing her independence? Being with a man always necessitated a trade. Sex for food, clothes, money, a roof. Yet Nick would give all this, and ask nothing in return.

And that knowledge only increased her desire.

Desire that felt terrifyingly like...love.

She turned to Colley. 'I'm all partied out. Going to cut and run.'

He pushed his chair back. 'I'll see you to your room. Got your key?'

'You stay. I'm okay.'

She glanced again at Nick, and Colley followed her gaze. 'Ah. Okay. Are you sure about this?'

Heat rushed to her face. Nick and Colley were closer than brothers, and Colley knew her better than any man alive. It figured he would know what was going on. Or not going on. 'Sure. I'll see you tomorrow.'

Her hand closed over a stray dessert knife left on the table. She'd been unable to bring her blades on the flight, but the flatware would be better than nothing. How many people had access to the key for her room? Could they have coded a copy? Tomas's opportunities to come to her house had been limited by Nick's frequent presence: there was a possibility that desperation would drive him here.

Colley took the knife from her. 'I'll see you up, anyway.'

As the lieutenant left her room, Kayla took a position as far from the door as possible. Her fingernails scraped at the wing-backed chair she steadied herself against. Clawed into the velour as the small fridge kicked into gear. Mouth dry, she couldn't swallow. Should get a drink. Her eyes flicked from door to fridge, but she didn't move. Seconds ticked by, metered by her pounding heart and the short, sharp breaths that never reached her lungs.

Was she really going to go through with this?

She licked her friction-burned fingertips, then reached for the phone on the coffee table. Flicked up Lorraine's number. She needed someone to either bolster her courage or tell her to run.

A rap on the door tumbled the phone from her nerveless hand.

The knock sounded again, and she cracked the door on the safety chain.

Checked.

Released the latch.

Retreated.

Nick moved into the room with swift grace, one moment filling the doorway, the next looming over her. 'Miki.'

The name he had given her resonated from her core to fingertips, as though the christening somehow promised the possibility of a new version of her. She crossed quickly to the fridge. 'Would you like a drink? Or...or something?' They'd shared their houses for months, spoken words of love—or Nick had spoken, and she'd avoided making a response—but now nerves rendered her tongue-tied and clumsy, a teenager on a first date.

Nick closed the space between them. 'All I want is you.' One hand wound into her hair, the other cradled the small of her back.

If she could turn off her mind, her body knew how to

respond. She melted into him, face buried against his chest to inhale the security of soap and cologne. Her hand worked beneath a corner of his shirt, searching for his scar.

The one imperfection that made him perfect.

CHAPTER 53

Nick inhaled sharply as Kayla's fingers crept across his chest. Jaw clenched, he focused on breathing, tried to ignore the desire that surged with the touch he craved. He would have to step away soon. How much longer could he play this damned game? He should never have come to her room. Should have stayed at the function. *Safety in numbers.*

Head tilted to seek his lips, Kayla arched her body against his. She'd never offered so much before, but he had to stay in control. Five more minutes. Five would be safe.

He dropped his jacket, yanked off his tie. Hesitated, then slipped his cufflinks and tugged the shirt over his head, tossing it toward a chair. So her roaming hands wouldn't crease it before he went back to the function.

Soon. In three minutes.

His mouth found hers, a kiss they'd exchanged hundreds of times, though no number would ever be enough. He slid the jacket from her shoulder and touched his lips to her exposed skin. She dropped her chin and pressed closer. Hiding. 'Miki, let me look at you.'

She hunched the fabric back into place, though she didn't move away. 'You've seen me plenty of times.'

'Never as a lover.' He didn't want to scare her, but God, he did want to love her. She quivered as his lips caressed her neck, but he kept his hands at his sides, allowing her space to reject him.

Instead, she tipped her head back, exposing the tender hollow at the base of her throat as she shrugged out of her jacket and tossed it after his shirt. Her voice trembled as she locked her hands around the back of his neck. 'Then make me believe a lover's eyes don't judge. Please.'

'Nobody, ever, will have the right to judge you.' She needed to know she didn't have to settle for him—though he'd kill anyone who presented competition. 'You're not only beautiful but—I don't have the words. I'm so in awe of you, Miki. You're just...everything, to me.' He stroked his fingers along the curve of her shoulders and she quivered, then leaned forward and pressed her lips sweetly against the corner of his mouth. Her tongue flickered across his lips.

Hell. He twisted away so he wouldn't scare her with his reaction. *Keep it together, man.* Time was up. He had to go.

Her breath mingled with his. 'Please love me, Nick.'

His heart kicked like the recoil on a fifty cal. How could he resist her entreaty? Yet, for her sake, he had to try. 'I do. Absolutely. But this is enough, for now.' Though he wanted her desperately, he would wait forever, if that was what she chose.

'I *need* you to love me.'

Her words sounded like a demand. One he was more than ready to fulfill. Testosterone and adrenaline surged through his body. Loathing himself, loving her, his fingers found the zipper hidden in the side of her dress. Inched it down. He never took his eyes from her face, ready to stop at her slightest indication.

The dress slithered into a puddle around her feet.

Christ, she was so perfect.

Her chin trembled, hands fluttering to cover herself, and disappointment pierced him. 'Nick. The light.'

He couldn't risk looking away, she might flee. His groping hand lingered on the cool wall, seeking a tie to reality.

Except, this was his reality.

The only woman he had ever loved—would ever love— stood almost naked before him. And he was terrified.

Terrified he'd mess it up, terrified he'd hurt her, terrified she'd reject him.

But, her own fear evident, Kayla needed reassurance. So he gave it the only way he knew how: he wrapped her in his arms.

Her skin chill against his chest, she clung to him, returning his kisses with fervour to almost match his own.

Slow it down, man. He needed to put some space between them, or he'd ruin everything. He tried to keep his voice steady. Difficult, without oxygen. 'Take it easy, sweetheart. It has to be right for you. There's no rush. We'll just...just...'

Kayla spun away from him, though she kept hold of his hand. Tugged him toward the bed and pulled him down with her.

Jesus. He was only human.

His hands slid over her curves and hollows, savouring every second, committing her to memory. She vibrated beneath his touch, the soft vanilla scent clouding his senses as he sought her mouth, trying not to focus on the hard nipples pressed into his chest. She tasted like honey mead and he wanted her. He would always want her. Even when he'd just finished making love, exhausted and empty, he would want her again.

But, for now, he needed to persuade himself that once would be enough.

Because it was so much more than he deserved.

Lips trailing her pale skin, he traced the scar tissue on her chest. The evidence of her unimaginable courage. Kayla moaned, and he lifted his head. Satisfied the noise was born of neither fear nor pain, he bent to her nipple, kissing, then used his tongue to caress the sensitive skin. Her hand stole across his back, snatched at his short hair to pull him closer.

He didn't have enough hands, enough mouths. Enough time.

She stiffened as his hand stroked across the taut, flat plane of her stomach, but still she clung to him. His fingers crept lower, drifted under the edge of the triangle of material covering her, a gift wrap almost too tantalising to remove.

Kayla trembled, the bed covers shivering in sympathy. 'Do it quickly.'

He had to stop. 'No. Not today.' Yet his hand ignored the directive, unwilling to leave the warm mound below her stomach. His lungs constricted as he fought for control.

Kayla wound a slim leg around his thighs, trying to pull him on top of her. 'I want you *now*.' Her tremulous breath fanned his hair. 'Please, Nick, do it now. It has to be now.'

The words were a plea, not an invitation. He'd scared her. Trapped by her leg, he tried to pull away. 'There's no rush. We have all the time we need.'

Not like this, he couldn't let it be like this.

CHAPTER 54

The fine linen smooth beneath her back, Kayla used her legs to trap Nick, squeezing her hands between them to expertly wrestle with the fastenings of his trousers.

She was an idiot. She'd let him look at her, the physical evidence of other men's ownership burning like brands on her body. No matter how much Nick claimed to love her, the sight of more than a decade's worth of scars would prevent him wanting her. She couldn't give him time to think.

'No, Kayla. Not yet.' Despite his protest, Nick rolled clear, tugging free the remainder of his clothes, and she knew she had him.

Fingers in his hair, she pulled him back. Ran her hands across the expanse of his chest, licked at the salty column of his bronzed neck. She knew how to make her scars invisible.

His lip whitened as he bit at it, trying to distract his lust with pain. Then he leaned over her, his fingers tracing from her neck to her breast. The bed dipped as he shifted to his knees, hands gliding down her waist until his thumbs hooked in the band of her lacy lingerie.

She couldn't pretend she hadn't planned to have him tonight. She owned sensible underwear.

He slid the silk too-slowly down her legs, so she reared up, wrapping her arms around his neck and pulling him down. She had never kissed a man during sex, it implied an emotional connection. But now she hungrily sought Nick's lips.

Making certain he couldn't look at her.

Nick's groan echoed through the room and she knew he fought his instinct, but still he returned her kisses. Weight on one elbow, he slid a hand between her thighs, stroking to make sure she was ready for him.

She wasn't wet. She knew she wouldn't be. She desired him with a passion that could only come from need, but she feared him.

Fingers to his mouth, he lubricated them. Tasted her. Then reached down.

'Now, Nick. Now.' He didn't understand. They had to hurry. While he still wanted her. She dug her nails into his back, pulled him closer.

She didn't need to be ready for him. She just needed it to be over.

CHAPTER 55

He needed to be inside Kayla, knowing that once he was, he would never want another woman.

Except, without ever touching her, he was already there.

Kayla moaned and threw her forearm across her face as he pressed against her.

'I need to see you.' Nick lifted her arm away, kissing her as he watched for any sign of rejection. Knowing he could so easily break her.

Heels dug into the backs of his thighs, she forced her hips toward him.

A moment of resistance. She cried out. And then he was within her.

Deep inside her.

But not deep enough. He would never be able to bury himself deep enough to satisfy his hunger for this woman.

Determined to remain motionless for as long as possible, he caressed Kayla's hair and face with his hands and lips, savouring the sensation of her skin pressed against his.

But her eyes were squeezed shut, her hands balled into

fists. He knew women, far too well. This wasn't right, Kayla wasn't into it. There was no trick he could turn, nothing in his vast repertoire of sexual experience that held the magic he needed to mend her. Even his love wouldn't be enough.

He kissed her as he slowly withdrew.

Kayla's eyes flew open, her nails clawed into his shoulders. 'No! Don't leave me. Please don't do that.'

He wanted her so bad, but she was so damn scared. 'Another time, Miki. Not now.'

'It has to be now.' Her voice urgent, diamonds shone in her eyes.

He smoothed back her hair. 'It doesn't have to be now. You're not ready, and there's no hurry. We have all the time we need.'

'Please, Nick. You don't understand.'

His fingers brushed the initials carved in her thigh, and anger surged through him. They'd trespassed. Hurt her. *Never again.* His hand moved higher, to the ridged scars on her right hip. What pain had driven her to do this to herself? He needed to know, so he could keep her safe. 'Then make me understand. Talk to me, Kayla. Just talk. We have forever.'

She shook her head, a tear working free. 'Don't say that, don't ever say that. I need you to love me *now.*' She shifted her hips, ground her pelvis against him.

Though he'd been prepared to take it as slow as she wanted, it seemed the prospect of him *not* making love to her scared her more than the physical act. Like he could ever walk away from her. The brief taste of Kayla's body had only whetted his appetite, and now desire clouded his mind, confused his normally analytical thought process.

Facts, he had to find the facts.

He wanted her. She wanted him.

He loved her. She had said, once, that she loved him.

So, it couldn't be wrong.

'Please, Nick,' she whispered.

He lowered his weight gradually, slipping a hand between them to guide himself home. She enveloped him, as good as the first time.

It would always be the first time. She was the one woman he would never conquer, both the chase and his desire infinite.

Kayla whimpered, but she thrust her hips up to meet his, her nails locked into his biceps. He shifted, trying to find the angle and rhythm that would allow her to abandon herself to the pleasure he could provide, to lose the wariness and fear that made her tense beneath his touch. 'Damn.'

Her eyes locked to his. 'What's wrong?'

Muscles in his arms straining, he blew out a short breath. Some lover. 'Nothing, Miki. It's just I want you bad.' He needed to do Chinese arithmetic or something to distract himself, but Kayla's fragile perfection lay naked beneath him, her softness enclosed and surrounded him.

Kayla's body relaxed and she slid her hands up to link them around his neck. Pulled him down, spoke against his lips. 'Love me. Please.'

He shook his head, fighting the urge. He didn't want it to end. Not ever. He wanted to be forever within her, eternally on the verge of release. But his body betrayed him and, natural instincts asserting themselves, his hips ground into hers, her breasts flattened against his chest. He needed to keep it slow, but his mind exploded with the unimaginable pleasure of being trapped inside her, the velvet-lined muscles contracting and gripping him.

Kayla moaned, and he knew that he hurt her; yet still she urged him on, with her hips and with her hands, and now he was powerless to stop. He couldn't get close enough. He needed to be surrounded by her, to feel her, hear her, and know he'd touched her like no man had ever done. He wanted to brand her, to fill her with his seed, to scour out any trace of other men and erase her muscle memory.

Beyond the point of no return, he grasped Kayla's hips, locking her to him. Surged deep within her, a final thrust, his eyes closed as he concentrated on the unprecedented sensation. Emptying his soul into her. 'God, Kayla, I love you so much.'

CHAPTER 56

She didn't know whether she should move, should talk. Wasn't certain even of what she should feel.

Nick had almost walked away from her, but she had enticed him into temporary forgetfulness.

He lay beside her, cold air replacing the warmth of his body as he leaned on one elbow. His fingers brushed the side of her face. 'Are you okay?'

She nodded. Tried to smile. But the tears welled.

Nick gathered her close. 'Oh, sweetheart.'

She allowed herself only seconds, then pulled away, scrubbing at her eyes. 'Sorry. Stupid. Don't know why I did that.' Yes, she did. It was only sex. Should mean nothing. But it had hurt, both physically and emotionally. She loved Nick, as near as she was able, and yet still he hurt her.

'Mikayla.'

She forced herself to meet the green eyes, dreading his disappointment. Sex was all she had to offer. Anyone. Ever. Without that, she was nothing.

'God, you're so beautiful,' he murmured. 'With your lips all swollen and your hair all tumbled. I love you so much, Miki.'

A silent sob ripped at her chest. She was so close to believing she could love him, that it would be safe, that this time love wouldn't lead to loss. But no matter how Colley and Lorraine tried to persuade her otherwise, that was fantasy, induced by weariness and unassuaged lust.

Nick rolled toward her, capturing her mouth as though they had been parted for hours. His lips trailed her neck down to her breast. She should protest; allowing the caress of a man she'd already fucked was far too intimate. But Nick kissed away her intention, his tongue finding her navel. She needed to tell him to stop. Right now. He'd see the scars, old and new. But, oh God, he was kissing her, lower and lower, and it didn't hurt. Barely able to breathe for the wanting, her body throbbed in response to his skilful touch.

His breath warmed the inside of her thighs, his fingers teasing but not entering. She gasped, parting her legs. He moved up to kiss her as his fingers slid inside her, cautious at first, then plunging deeper and faster as her desire grew.

Eyes barely open, she whimpered and panted, grinding against the pressure of his hand. This felt so good, and she wanted him so bad. The deep vibration of his voice rumbled incoherent words of encouragement. She couldn't get close enough to him, didn't want this to ever end.

The pressure built and she stiffened, trying to deny the effervescing within her core. She clutched at Nick's hand, intending to stop him, but her thighs bucked against the pressure of his thumb on her clitoris, her muscles tightened around his fingers inside her, and she was lost. The climax snatched at her, spinning her beyond control, and she sobbed his name, afraid he'd already gone.

Slowing his fingers as the contractions shivered her into an agony of oversensitivity, Nick kissed her. Then he wrapped his body around hers, legs entwined, their breath mingling.

Safe in his arms, she slept.

A FEW HOURS LATER, propped on a couple of pillows against the headboard, knees under her chin, she watched Nick stretch. The muscles across the top of his shoulders rippled as he cracked his back. Eyes closed, he groped in the grey pre-dawn for a cover they'd tumbled to the floor.

Neither of them had thought to draw the curtains. Nor had she worried about Tomas somehow appearing on the balcony, watching her. For the first time in more than three months, she had slept dreamlessly.

She leaned toward Nick. 'Isn't there a better way to warm up?'

Startled awake, Nick seemed surprised by her presence. He shoved himself onto one elbow, his gaze roaming her sheet-covered form. A grin slowly curved both sides of his mouth, and he ran a hand through dishevelled hair. 'How long have you been awake?'

'A while. Admiring the view.' She lifted an eyebrow. 'And hoping the cold would wake you.' They had no time to waste, she couldn't let him sleep.

Nick locked his hand around her ankle and hauled her gently down the bed until his fingers nestled between her thighs. 'Want to warm up, do you?' he growled in mock annoyance, rasping the stubble of his chin over her belly.

She flailed as he tickled her. The movement dislodged the sheet, but it wasn't entirely accidental. She had to test him. Would he run when he saw her in daylight?

Using his teeth to pull aside the sheet, Nick nuzzled his way up her body. Kissing the tip of her cold nose, he framed her face with large hands.

Longing churned within her. Once hadn't been enough. Twice wouldn't be enough. Her greed knew no limits, pain provided no boundary.

Nick nibbled her earlobe, covering her chilled body with his. 'Ah, I'm not so young, anymore...and we could turn up the aircon, you know.'

Her thighs parted, and the laughter dropped from his voice, the words warm against her cheek. 'It'll be better for you this time, Miki. This time I'll wait for you.'

She didn't need him to wait. She was wet, eager for him. This was neither using him nor servicing him. This was connection.

He pressed against her, and she wrapped her legs around his hard thighs, drew him closer, arching her back so he had no choice but to slide deep within her. The pain stole her breath, but only for a moment.

Beneath Nick, finally she felt safe.

His shoulder pressed against her chin and she nipped at the firm flesh, a groan rolling through his chest as his muscles braced under the attack. He tasted of fresh sweat and musk and lust and linen, and she wanted to devour him. He filled her so absolutely, but still her hips rose to meet each thrust, her eyes open, needing to be certain it was him—yet no one else had ever done this to her. With her. It could never be anyone but Nick.

Her muscles tightened as the intensity built, her hands encouraging him deeper, harder, faster, as she searched for release. Lack of oxygen spun her head and she closed her eyes, completely surrendering to desire.

Just this once.

CHAPTER 57

The winter sun high outside the window, they curled beneath the bedcovers. Nick gazed at Kayla's face, committing the outlines to memory. He traced the side of her cheek. He would never tire of watching her sleep. Without the nightmares he had witnessed too many times, her face lost the guardedness that tugged at his heart. But even as he admired her relaxed, softened features, he wished she would wake, so he could make love to her again. 'Kayla, I have to ask you something. Are you listening?' He nuzzled her shoulder.

'Mmm.' She nestled closer, a hand emerging from beneath the covers and sliding across his chest.

'Kayla, marry me.' Words he had spent twenty years vowing never to utter, and four weeks rehearsing to make certain he had perfect.

Suddenly wide-awake, Kayla jerked her hand back, covering her mouth. Her words indistinct, she shook her head. 'I can't, Nick. I'm sorry, I can't.'

Jesus wept. All the times he'd joked about being trapped

into marriage, swearing no woman would catch him, he had never considered that maybe he'd be the one rejected.

Should he admit that she was the first woman he'd truly made love to? The only woman he had ever allowed to over-rule his self-control?

No. That would be too much like begging.

Except, if it would make a difference, he'd plead, he'd crawl through broken glass on his damn knees for her. 'But I thought... We...'

Kayla sat up. 'We can't. You don't understand.'

'I love you. What's to understand?' Why the hell did it have to be any more complicated than that?

Kayla chewed at her lip. 'Love always means somebody gets hurt.' Tears filled her eyes. 'I can't do that again.'

The words sliced like the steel of a bayonet. He wanted to be the only man she had ever loved but, for the first time in his life, he would accept second place. 'Aren't we worth taking a chance on? Isn't that risk better than never loving?'

'I want to, but—' She shook her head.

The hell with that, then. Nick bunched the linen, ready to heave out of the bed. Shove the rejection and disappoint-ment into one of his internal boxes and lock it away.

But Kayla was hurting, and he'd promised never to let that happen again. He didn't know who she had loved and lost, but that didn't matter. All that mattered was that he couldn't make her better.

He let go of the sheets. Drew Kayla close. Rested his chin on her head and stared into the future.

Held back his damn tears.

CHAPTER 58

E yes open, Kayla defied the sting of the shampoo. To relax, to surrender to the soothing rain of the shower and close her eyes, even for an instant, would be to invite the shadowy premonition of danger to become a reality.

The temptation of happiness left her more vulnerable than she had ever been. Nick hadn't mentioned marriage again in the week since they returned from Canberra, yet it was clear her rejection wounded him. Though he made love with passion and tenderness, his smile once again held something in reserve, as though he locked away a fragment of his emotions.

He had caught her off guard with the proposal, and his silence on the matter since stole any opportunity to explain that she couldn't allow herself to love him, knowing it would end in heartbreak.

She rubbed the suds from one eye, then the other. Never close both at the same time. A bird skittered over the roof tiles and the slight clatter had her out of the shower, thrusting her wet body into clean clothes. With more to live for, she had more to lose, and Nick's absence during the day left her nervous. While he had been careful not to steal her independence, still she had allowed herself to regress. Once again, she was falling into the trap of needing him to keep her safe.

She sneered at the bathroom mirror, the pale reflection carved with lines of fear and pain. *Pathetic.* It wasn't the face of a woman with a job, a house, a man who loved her. A woman who had survived the worst life could throw at her.

It wasn't the face Kayla wanted to wear. Damn it, she was better than this, she had to be. She had been wrong about Tomas coming back, and that meant she would never get the closure she craved. But if she allowed herself only a pitiful half-life—scared to love, scared to leave—then the bastard had won, he'd succeeded in breaking her. She no longer wanted to face him, but she also didn't plan to hand him that victory. Nick was right. The curse of mortality meant that one day they would hurt, with one fated to die, the other to mourn. Yet it was better to take a chance on happiness now, than to never love.

Kayla unlocked the bathroom door and strode down the hallway, towelling her hair. Crossed the lounge and tugged apart the curtains. Beyond the glass a perfect new day sparkled with promise. The fresh breeze scudded white clouds across a boundless azure sky. Uniformed children wandered past the low front fence, a couple of women chatted beneath the lacy protection of a jacaranda tree over-hanging the broad footpath. One held a baby, the other waved at a passing car. A dog chased an escaped skateboard, the owner shouting from some point out of view.

Life. Messy, complicated, beautiful. And she wanted it.

She dropped the towel onto the back of a chair and

turned the stereo on. As she defiantly slid the volume up, the willy-wagtail flitted from branch-to-branch on the tree nearest the window. Kayla glanced at the grandfather clock. Her first student would be online shortly, but first she had best feed the unusually agitated bird.

A cloud crossed the sun as she entered the courtyard, and Kayla rubbed her arms. There were few birds today, and the wagtail refused to be enticed to take his usual grub. 'Someone's awkward this morning,' Kayla grumbled, tossing the mix of seed and mealworms onto the pavers. 'Too cold for you, is it?'

She made her way back to their bedroom. Nick's house today, hers tomorrow, but whichever location they used, it was *their* bedroom. A smile ghosted her lips as unfamiliar joy swelled within her. This was what had been missing from her life; all she had needed do was surrender to her inner desire. Allow happiness, instead of erecting barriers of self-denial to punish herself for the past.

She took a jacket from the closet. Screw ordering online: today she would go to the small shopping centre a few streets away. Just like everyone else did. Stripping off her khaki shirt, Kayla pulled a white t-shirt over her head, keeping her eyes open.

But that was okay, it was just a habit. Meant nothing. She was completely normal now.

Except she wasn't.

Because the hairs on the nape of her neck prickled.

A wave of slow dread crawled across her scalp and fear dragged up her spine, one vertebra at a time. Premonition crushed her lungs and stole her breath.

Fingers stiff, she drew Nick's shirt back on, seeking security in the familiar fabric. Crept across the bedroom.

Cracked open the door. Peered around it, down the long hallway.

Nothing. *Of course.* She forced the pent air from her lungs between pursed lips, trying to steady the hammering of her heart. She was being ridiculous, right after she had promised herself no more weakness. But she did need to turn off the music. Not so she could *hear,* but because she was going out.

She eased toward the sound system, scanning the room from the corner of her eye. Irrational fear a wild animal, she avoided antagonising it with open confrontation. Her hand trembled as she reached for the volume control.

Damn it. *No!* She wasn't going to let herself slip into the morass of her imagination and memory. She was done with that shit.

She snapped off the stereo. Squared her shoulders, patted the wallet in the back pocket of her jeans, and spun toward the front door.

Fuck.

The security mesh in the locked window frame sagged like a torn page.

Run.

As instinct screamed at her, the realisation hit like a baseball bat: the danger wasn't on the streets she tried to avoid, or in the dark nights alone in her own home, where she waited for Tomas. It was here.

Run.

Here where, secure in Nick's protection, she didn't keep any of her knives to hand.

Run.

Her legs ignored the frantic command. Instead, they turned her around slowly, so slowly. Her gaze crept along the skirting boards, reluctantly completing the circuit. Avoiding the reality.

Run.

Too late to run, too late to hide. Because there he was, lounging against the bookcase. *Tomas.*

His snakelike tongue flickered across thin lips, and he smiled with malicious desire.

Terror sucked the strength from Kayla's muscles. Paralysed her with fear. Her knees buckled, and she lurched forward a half step. Tomas didn't react. She edged one foot toward the front door. The other foot followed.

Still Tomas stared.

She tore her gaze from him, glanced at the door. How many more steps? Ten? Twelve? How many would he allow her? Better to run, take a chance. Like she should have done in the desert.

Another step.

Tomas's leer widened. 'Uh-uh. Far enough, I think. Sit down, won't you please?'

His voice galvanised Kayla. She lunged for the door but Tomas was faster, easily capturing her, his pointed nails pinching into her skin. Her flesh rippled from his touch. Cortisol overloaded her brain, a wash of colour and incipient darkness demanding fight or flight.

'Ah, you feel nice.' Tomas slid a hand between her thighs. 'And you smell so good, now. So much cleaner than the last time we met. Do you remember the last time? You were a dirty, dirty girl then, weren't you?' Grasping a handful of her hair, he yanked her closer. She recoiled from his minted breath. 'Mm, so sweet. Good enough to eat.' He inhaled loudly, then dragged his tongue up her cheek. Released her with a smile.

Kayla backed away until the wall trapped her. Breath scraping her throat, chest aching with the force of her over-worked heart, she shuffled to the left.

Tomas picked at a scab on his forearm, then brought the dried crust to his face, examining it.

Not daring to exhale, Kayla stretched her hand toward the corner of the wall, her fingertips sliding around the edge. Long ago, Nick had put a lock on the bedroom door, so she'd feel safer. If she could make it to the hall, she would bolt for the bedroom.

Her foot inched closer to freedom—and Tomas surged, his hands snatching at her breasts and buttocks, his high-pitched laughter answering her scream.

She cowered against the non-existent camouflage of the wall.

Tomas backed away.

Licked at his leaking sore.

Waited for her to play his cat-and-mouse game again.

Kayla stretched her icy fingertips toward the corner of the wall, inched her foot to the left.

Tomas's tongue flickered with excitement.

He let her move, then pounced again. Tweaked her nipples. Grabbed her crotch.

Retreated to his position.

Waited for her to play again.

She was stuck in a nightmare loop, unable to find an escape. Just like in the cave.

'Enough.' Tomas tired of the game after endless minutes. He pulled a handgun from the waistband of his neatly-creased trousers. The weapon directed her from the wall to the lounge. 'Sit down. You've got a call to make.'

A gun. At least it would be quick. Kayla stumbled to the chair and sat, her thighs pressed so tightly they ached.

Tomas squatted, stroking her knee. 'Tell me, what did you think of our little home movie?' He took a phone from his pocket. 'You know it's all over the dark web?'

'No!' Shock jerked the denial from her.

Tomas tutted, suddenly solicitous. 'Your friends forgot to mention I'd uploaded it? Imagine letting you think you'd slip into anonymity. Don't worry, I'll never let that happen.' He held the phone screen toward her, but she twisted away. 'What we made is special, right? Not that I make an actual appearance, but there's a number of our... shall I say, *oral* exchanges. I made you famous, Kayla. Or should that be infamous? I'm never sure which is correct, but you'd know.'

She couldn't find any oxygen.

Tomas pouted. 'Of course, it's not really fair, when you think about it. I put in all the work, months of planning and carting supplies. Not to mention my performance.' He waggled the phone again. 'But no one recognises me. You, though; everyone knows what you did. They're thinking about it, talking about it. Must make you feel pretty special.'

Neither her brain nor her mouth wanted to form words, but while Tomas talked, he wasn't doing anything worse. She had to keep him busy. 'I don't care about the opinions of people who choose to watch that kind of filth.'

'*Choose* to watch? Like there's anyone who hasn't tried to get their hands on it! I'm sure lover-boy had a good old gander. Perverted bastard. You know, I'm thinking we give him a little treat. Maybe a live show?'

A fist squeezed Kayla's lungs and her nostrils flared as she hunted for oxygen. She had to keep control. The leather creaked as she pushed further back into the chair. Could she kick out, overbalance Tomas?

Perhaps. If she could move.

The waving gun punctuated his words. 'How about you ring him? I'm sure you've memorised his number, in case you ever need him. Like, for an emergency, maybe?'

'I don't know it.' The words a whisper, Kayla cleared her throat harshly.

'Don't be stupid. I'm offering you a chance to get out of here.' Tomas waved the gun in her face. 'Call lover-boy.'

Kayla shook her head. Tomas would kill her, but she'd spare Nick the kind of entertainment the psychopath planned.

The weapon trained on her, Tomas strode across the room and peered out of the window. 'He needs to know. They all need to know.' He yanked the curtain closed and paced back. Stood over her. 'Call him!' Spittle foamed at the corners of his mouth.

Kayla crossed her arms, grabbing at her elbows. Tomas was agitated, disconcerted. He hadn't expected her refusal. This wasn't going according to his plan, and that threw him. The realisation stiffened her spine. This time, she would seize her chance. 'He needs to know what?'

'That you're mine!' Tomas shrieked as he slapped the rush of hope from her face. He grinned maniacally. Diction slipping, his words came fast. 'Now, that's more like it. Just like old times, right? Come on, call him, and I'll let you go. I have a score to settle.'

Liar. The accusation screamed in Kayla's mind as she refused to rub her cheek. He couldn't know it hurt, that would give him power. Again. 'Score? You don't even know him.'

Tomas's feverish gaze darted around the room and he swiped his arm across his forehead. 'I keep telling you that you're mine. Forever. Not his, you whore!'

Whore. For the first time, the accusation didn't hurt. The label no longer held power over her. She had worked for everything in her life, done what she had to do.

'Which barracks is he at?' Tomas gestured wildly with the weapon.

An eerie sense of calm came over Kayla, a peacefulness that could only exist in this place, this envelope of time. She settled into the chair. 'I'm not sure.' This was the last man she would ever control, so she'd enjoy her brief power. The remainder of her life.

'Jesus, you stupid bitch. You never fucking learned your lesson, did you?' Tomas jabbed at his phone. She craned forward, straining to see which numbers he punched. Triple zero emergency, of course.

Sweat beaded Tomas's upper lip. 'No, I don't want to choose a service. Put me on to whoever's fucking in charge.' He dragged his forearm across his face again, keeping Kayla in sight. 'Yeah, shut the fuck up. Tell me, does the name Kayla Petrovic mean anything to you? You're not sure? You fucking well get sure, mate, and you get on to the fucking army, and you tell the cocksucker she's shacked up with that she has a special friend visiting. He'll know who I am.'

Tomas simulated a mic drop, letting his phone fall onto the lounge and cocking his head, a pleased smirk on his face. He slumped into a chair, one leg thrown over the armrest, and heaved a satisfied sigh.

His sudden relaxation had the opposite effect on Kayla, and she shifted to the edge of her seat.

The pistol waved in an easy rhythm with Tomas's

swinging foot. 'So, Miss P, now we wait. I'm sure lover-boy will drop everything to rush here and save his little sweetheart. Not that he did such a great job of it last time, huh?'

The blood drummed so hard in Kayla's ears she barely heard his taunts. It was the cave all over again; she needed to wait for rescue that wouldn't arrive in time.

Within minutes, the wail of sirens filled the air. Tomas leaped to his feet and tweaked the curtain aside, peering at the street. 'Oh, you should see this. Look at all those little black piggies. We've got the entire freakin' S.T.A.R. Force in the front yard.' He bounced in excitement. 'Spectacular. Right, new plan. First, I'll get your boyfriend in here, and we'll show him what good friends we are. Then I'll dispose of him and take out a few cops. That'll let them know I mean business.' He picked thoughtfully at his teeth. 'They'll let my mates go, for sure.'

'Your *mates*?' Kayla gasped. 'They tried to plead out of their sentences by pinning everything on you. Why the hell would you care about them?' Tomas had come back into her life, into Nick's life, for *them*?

Incomprehension squinted Tomas's eyes. 'See, this is the problem with our relationship: you don't listen. I keep telling you, it's all in the Faraday case.' He sighed dramatically, then spoke slowly. 'Eastwood escaped prison and took hostages to force the release of other inmates.'

She couldn't remember the outcome: surely Eastwood didn't get away with it? 'But you never went to prison: you deserted your mates.'

Tomas puffed himself up. 'I keep telling you, Faraday was the blueprint—but of course I improved on it. There was always a chance the payoff would be a trap, just like it was for Eastwood. So when the pollies agreed to transfer the money before I'd even sent a chunk of flesh, I knew what was going down. And I lit out. Saw lover-boy marching to the rescue.'

Pride illuminated Tomas's face. She had to keep him talking—because she had no better plan. 'Then why didn't you warn your *mates,* save them going to prison instead of trying to get them out now?'

Tomas blew out his cheeks. 'Some of those fuckers are so slow they'd never have made it out. You know, slow here,' he tapped his forehead with the handgun barrel. 'And here.' Pistol butt to his belly. 'They had to be collateral damage. But it wouldn't be right to pick favourites, so I had to let them all go down together. Doesn't mean I don't care about them, though. I could be in Bali, but I've come back for them. They'll realise I had no choice, and we'll make a better job of it next time.'

'Next time?' The handgun hung loosely from Tomas's hand, aimed at the floor. If she distracted him, she could grab it. Kayla perched on the edge of the seat, poised to leap. 'There won't be a next time. The police won't release them, no matter what you threaten. Regardless of how many people you hurt. You'll die here, and it'll all be pointless. You don't have to do this.'

Tomas's face creased in bewilderment. He shook his head in gentle pity. 'Don't have to? I've waited my whole life for this. I'm going to be as famous as Eastwood. Hell, maybe even Ivan Milat. This is my calling. I don't *have* to do it. I *want* to. I'm *meant* to.'

The blood drained from Kayla's face. She had miscalculated the enormity of Tomas's insanity. No logic could defeat madness.

Strident in the fearful hush, his phone rang. Tomas

picked up. 'Yep, that's me. Well, first, you can get the boyfriend on the line. No, I don't fucking know his name, I'm not the one screwing him. Yeah. She's okay. For now. Just get lover-boy here, quick.' He disconnected and winked at Kayla. 'That's the boys in black. Any minute now, darlin'.'

The landline rang, and the muzzle gestured at her. 'Your turn.'

Kayla's hand hovered over the phone. She walked a tightrope. Permitting emotions she had always denied left her exposed, stretched to breaking point. If she allowed one minute fibre to unravel, the knotted and tangled rope would snap and whiplash toward her. Yet she would risk everything to hear Nick speak her name one last time.

She lifted the receiver warily. Held her breath until the voice on the other end revealed its unfamiliarity.

'Hello, who is that?'

'It... I'm Mikayla Petrovic.' She paused to clear her throat, despising herself for sounding scared.

'Ms Petrovic, this is Commander Blakiston of the SAPOL Special Tasks and Rescue Group. It is important that you remain calm. Please confirm, is Geoffrey Tomas holding you against your will?'

He had a first name. Why had she never wondered about that? She didn't want to think about it now; a name gave Tomas a family, a history, a future. It made him more real, more whole, more *here*. 'Yes.' She willed her voice steady. Tomas's hand crept across her thigh as he leaned in to hear the conversation.

'Mikayla, the S.T.A.R. Group has the house surrounded. We will get you out. Captain West is here. He needs to speak to Tomas. Mikayla? Hand the phone to Tomas.'

Nick. Certainty rushed through Kayla like a cresting

wave, her knuckles white as she gripped the phone. Mother had it so wrong. She wasn't worthless. She had survived in a world that offered her nothing for free. She had triumphed against adversity, and she had protected the children to the best of her ability. And now she would save the man she loved. Nobody's puppet, she would create her own destiny.

She thrust to her feet, twisting so Tomas couldn't grab the phone. 'Don't let Nick near here. Tomas will kill him!'

An explosion punched her eardrum. The phone tumbled from her nerveless grip and spun across the polished floorboards.

CHAPTER 59

The phone trilled, juddering across the floor like a beetle stuck on its back. Disconnected. Rang again.

Kayla stared in stupid fascination at the hole in her right shoulder. It didn't hurt, but felt oddly hollow.

Tomas glanced from the weapon in his hand to the wound, too fresh yet for the blood to flow. 'Wow, that's unreal. I've never even shot a bunny before.'

The pain started, the acrid smell of singed flesh burning Kayla's nostrils. 'Why did you do that?' Though the words were childishly accusing, she couldn't suppress them.

Tomas caressed her cheek with a slender hand. 'Because you didn't do what you were supposed to.' The phone rang again, but he disregarded it. 'Let me think for a minute. We'll have to let them know you're alive, or they'll storm the place. Come on, move it.' He grabbed the towel she had thrown over the back of the chair, and arranged it over her injured shoulder. Then he seized her other arm and thrust her toward the front door.

'Wait.' He held up a hand. Polished his black shoes against the back of each trouser leg, ran a hand through his hair. Took a deep breath, and smiled at her.

Fucking smiled at her.

Shielded behind her, he draped his arm over her shoulder, his hand resting on her breast beneath the towel. Then he pulled the door open and jostled her into the opening. Kayla squinted in the sunlight. Flinched as Tomas yelled close to her ear, 'Right, where's lover-boy?'

A flickering blue-and-red lit forest of rifle barrels surrounded the house. All trained on her. Nick stood head and shoulders above the other men. He forced his way clear of Colley and Kimber's restraining arms, pushed through the black-uniformed police ranks, and vaulted the barrier. Strode across the twenty metres separating them.

'Hold it right there,' Tomas shrilled, ducking left and right behind her. He gesticulated with the pistol, nestling the barrel against Kayla's cheek as Nick halted. 'Whoa, you're a big motherfucker, aren't you? Lucky I loosened her up for you, I guess. Taught her everything I know, so I hope you appreciate that.'

He repositioned his hand, resting it in the mangled flesh and warm blood pulsing from the back of her shoulder beneath the towel.

The pain sucked at her, dragging like a massive weight on the right side of her body, but she would stand there forever if it meant she could gaze at Nick.

His face white, Nick took a half step forward, eyes fixed on hers. She shook her head. Said nothing. Simply stared at him, trying to wordlessly convey her acceptance of his love. Wishing he'd propose again. Silently commanding him not to come any closer.

Colley wove through the police barrier and darted forward, pressing one hand against Nick's chest, the other stretched toward her as though he could somehow bridge the gap.

She broke eye contact with Nick, only for a second. Nodded her thanks to Colley. He had tried so hard, for so many months, to save her. But it seemed the power to do so had always been hers alone.

Tomas giggled as Nick strained toward her. 'I want to get to know you, too, lover, but first I'm going to reacquaint myself with our girlfriend. Then we'll invite you in.' He flicked the towel from her shoulder and groped her breast, smearing blood across her khaki shirt.

'Jesus, Kayla!' Pain sliced Nick's face and he lurched forward. Colley whirled, throwing his arms around the captain, fighting to hold him back. Flak-jacketed S.T.A.R Group officers rushed to assist. A bullhorn blared, but even over the electronic crackle, Kayla heard Kimber's stentorian bellow. 'Captain West. Stand down!'

Waving the gun wildly, his panicked breath fast and hard, Tomas jerked her back into the doorway.

The tableau froze.

Tomas laughed uncertainly. 'That's right, boys, you control that motherfucker. I'll let you know when he can come in.' Pistol pressed to Kayla's cheek, he dipped his head, thrust his snake tongue into the ragged wound in the back of her shoulder, then flickered it up her cheek.

Then, with one arm clamped around her neck, he dragged her back into the house and kicked the door closed.

He flicked the deadlock and spun her to face him. Slid his hand under her shirt, tweaking a nipple he had no right to touch. 'That was kind of intense, wasn't it? Fucking turn-on, man.'

Her shoulder a fiery, pulsing ball of pain, only adrenaline kept Kayla conscious. She had to act now. Neither Kimber's orders, Colley's arms, or the S.T.A.R. Group officers would restrain Nick for long.

'Wait a moment,' she murmured, capturing Tomas's hand and pressing it against her breast. 'I can make it better for you. I've learned a few tricks since last time.' She traced her lips with her tongue and brushed her hand across the front of his pants. Vomit crowded her throat at his tautness. She swallowed it.

Tomas eyed her warily. 'Well, that'll be something different. You chicks are always various degrees of unwilling, I usually have to rape or pay. But as you're offering it up...I'm always open to new experiences.' He massaged his crotch with the muzzle of the handgun.

'Just let me go to the toilet, first. It'll make it better, I promise.' Kayla's heart skittered as Tomas nodded, yet followed her down the hall. If he insisted on watching, she had no chance. Not that she had any kind of plan, anyway. She was merely trying to buy time to come up with something.

Exactly as she'd done in the cave.

After a cursory glance into the small room, Tomas waved her in, allowing her to shut the door.

She leaned her head against the cool tiles.

What now?

She swayed, shock and loss of blood making her dizzy. Pulling toilet paper from the roll, she pressed it against her shoulder. Neat and round, the bullet hole in her upper chest barely bled, but she retched as the wad of tissue met with no resistance and disappeared into the shattered bone of the exit wound high at the back of her shoulder.

A megaphone filled the air with discordant static, but she couldn't make out the words. It wasn't Nick's voice, so it didn't matter.

Whatever she intended to do, it had to be done now, while she was still able.

The room offered nothing. A toilet, a potted devil's ivy, and the window. She couldn't wrest a section of pipe from the plumbing—what would she do with it, anyway? And Tomas would hear if she broke a shard of glass from the window.

Defeat trembled through Kayla. Her knees threatened to give way, and she staggered, her shin cracking into the plant pot, hand smearing a bloodied print across the wall.

She sucked in a breath: that was it. That *had* to be it, there was no other way.

Fumbling with her cuff, she blanched as pain radiated from her shoulder. Damn. She'd have to do it left-handed. And she had better start praying for the strength.

As she opened the door, Tomas grabbed her. Pushed her into the lounge room and forced her face-down on the floor, his fingers locked around the back of her neck.

Good. It was better it happened in here. Not in their bedroom.

He thrust his tongue into her ear, grinding his body against hers, crushing her into the floorboards.

She endured his rough caress for a minute, then struggled against his grip. Just enough to let him know he held all the power. 'Let me on top. Don't worry, you can keep your little gun.'

'Oh, I'll keep it, alright.' Tomas readily shifted to lie on his back, the gun trained on her.

As Kayla scrambled to her knees, the room swirled. *Hurry.* She straddled Tomas's thighs, teasing down his fly. Licked her lips in enticing insinuation.

'Go to it, baby,' he panted.

He deserves it. There was no more time for hesitation, rationalisation, or recrimination. This time she wouldn't try to buy her freedom, or Nick's safety.

She would take it.

She edged down Tomas's body, awkwardly pulling his trousers, exposing his rigid penis. Shifted, as though she intended to take him in her mouth.

He smacked the butt of the gun against her temple. 'Don't you bite me this time, bitch.'

Although she reeled sideways, Kayla kept her seat. There would be no warning bite this time, no threat. She planned to hurt him so much worse.

She ground her pelvis against his thighs.

Tomas moaned, eyes half-closed as his hips twitched and thrust toward her.

Left hand behind her back, Kayla shook her arm. The tip of the short pine stake slid down her sleeve and into her palm, dirt from the plant pot coating her fingers. She grasped the wooden shaft.

Smiled at Tomas.

Raised her arm and, with the strength of months of hatred, stabbed her spear into his unprotected groin.

The dull, grinding jar of wood on bone travelled up her arm and through her body. She rolled off Tomas. Stumbled to the protection of a chair and peered warily at him from behind it. Waiting for him to leap in pursuit.

But he wasn't chasing her. He huddled into a sobbing ball, only the tip of the stake beside him gleaming red. Her strength compromised, the too-short spear hadn't penetrated far.

But it was far enough. She only needed to cross the room and throw the door wide, and she would be safe in Nick's arms.

Safe for how long?

Kayla clambered to her feet, gasping as the lava flow of pain coursed her shoulder. Although she'd pretended no interest, she knew her three other abusers had been given the maximum penalty; but what was that truly worth? The Faraday kidnapper had escaped jail. Even if they didn't, it only required a review, a pardon, early parole, and they would earn the reprieve she could never have. Then what? Tomas would come for her again. And, if he couldn't get her, his psychopathic anger would turn elsewhere. To her kids.

He couldn't be allowed to hurt anyone else. Ever.

She staggered to where Tomas lay, moaning and crying like he'd been tortured, and bent to claim his gun. Almost overbalanced. The weight of the weapon surprising, it trembled in her grasp. 'Look at me, you bastard,' she muttered. 'You have to look at me so I can do this.'

Tomas controlled his writhing. Curled into a foetal position, he glared at her. 'You stupid slut. You don't have the fucking guts.'

He was so wrong. She was a survivor. That required guts. 'Don't I?' The gun wavered as she aimed it at Tomas's leg. A shot in each thigh. One in each of his arms. Then he'd start suffering.

But torture was his specialty, not hers. She had a job to do.

And she was damn good at doing her job. Whatever it took.

Kayla pointed the barrel at Tomas's chest. She stepped closer. Tempting him.

Tomas lunged, grabbing her ankle.

Her finger curled around the trigger. It notched back, a single moment of tension, and then slid smooth and easy.

Something so momentous deserved to be harder, to require more effort.

Tomas should have had the safety catch on.

She emptied the entire magazine into the quickly-stilled figure on the floor. The hammer clicked repeatedly on the empty chamber before she released the trigger.

Tomas lay still.

Like a spider, he'd exuded evil and menace, but now, squashed across the floor as guts bubbled and oozed from him in long, thick strings, he appeared only pathetic.

Kayla stared with unblinking patience at the slain monster, waiting until she knew it no longer had any power to haunt her dreams. Finally, the tension which had imbued every breath for so many months, slid from her. She began to tremble. Her knees buckled and she crumpled to the floor. Her stomach heaved, but she refused to vomit.

No more weakness.

It was over.

Blood dripped from her splayed fingers, patterning the floorboards. She stared at the puddle, her thoughts interrupted by the strident ring of the phone and Tomas's mobile. The lonely bellow of the bullhorn burrowed into her awareness. *Rescue*. But this time, it wasn't too late.

Because she didn't need rescuing.

She pulled herself to her feet and lurched to the entrance. Fumbled with the lock and dragged the door open. Nick would soon be there. She didn't need his protection. But now she would let him love her.

A phalanx of weapons trained on her from behind the armoured vehicles. She flinched as windows imploded in unison at the rear and side of the house. The percussion deafened her. Strobe lights blinded her. Sirens, shouted commands, a blaring bullhorn, the barrage of noise impossible to understand...

'Drop the gun. On the ground, now!'

They were yelling *at* her. She shook her head, and blood splattered the door frame. She stared down at it. Gore cemented her left hand to the pistol, her right arm useless at her side. Her clothes dripped dark, sticky fluid; blood and bone. Hers and Tomas's, but the soldiers couldn't know that. They didn't realise she had dealt with the nightmare.

Noise swelled, filling the house. The thump of booted feet on timber reverberated, bellows of command and direction, a rushing of air, confusion all around.

A deep voice cut through the clamour. 'Kayla, where is he?' Still trying to slay demons for her, Nick had forced entry through the rear of the house.

Her realisation was now absolute, the clarity both beautiful and stunning: she no longer needed Nick—but she did love him.

'He's dead.' Her voice strong, Kayla spoke clearly, without a trace of remorse or regret. Mother should be proud—and to hell with her, if she wasn't.

Then she finally allowed herself to slip into the healing darkness, knowing Nick would be there to catch her. She was imperfectly flawed and intrinsically human and would never be complete. But she could trust him to hold her hand and walk beside her as she found her own way back from the abyss.

Note From the Author

I appreciate it when a reader makes it ALL the way to the housekeeping at the end of the book — well done, you!

This story necessarily deals with some very important topics. If you are in any way negatively impacted by this book or dealing with feelings of despair or depression, please feel free to reach out to me in my professional capacity, via my personal email address leehotline66@gmail.com

Other contacts:
The National Suicide Prevention Lifeline (US) 1-800-273-8255
Lifeline (Aust) 13 11 44
Samaritans (UK) 116 123

If you've enjoyed this book, I'd love if you could leave a rating or review on Amazon, Goodreads, Bookbub... anywhere good books are found. Reviews are an author's only true feedback, and help us decide what to write next.

Drop by and say hi on social media – I'm generally hanging out and posting pictures of my menagerie: check my website for click-through links
www.leoniekelsall.com
Thanks for reading!
Laney

Also by Laney Kaye

Also by the Author

Best-selling BOOKS by LEONIE KELSALL (aka Laney Kaye)
published by Allen & Unwin, Australia

The Farm at Peppertree Crossing

The Wattle Seed Inn

The River Gum Cottage

The Willow Tree Wharf

The Blue Gum Camp

The Homestead in the Eucalypts

Wings over the Mallee

PRAISE FOR LÉONIE KELSALL

Leonie Kelsall is becoming the voice of the South Australian rural outback; she has a unique way of getting under your skin. Her writing and the epic love stories she crafts are gripping, smart, and heartwarming.
–The Beauty and Lace Book Club.

"One of Australia's premier rural romance writers"
-Woman's Day Magazine

Léonie Kelsall is not afraid to tackle some of the darker sides of human nature in a way that adds depth and emotion to the storyline. With complex and endearing characters who will steal your heart away, these unputdownable books will have you turning the pages long into the nights.
-Karly Lane, best-selling author

Book of the Week
-New Idea Magazine

A rural childhood and a deep understanding of the complexity of human relationships have allowed Leonie Kelsall to add her compelling voice to Australian bush storytelling.
-Australian Country Magazine

We were fortunate to host Léonie Kelsall last year and she had the audience in stitches, combining both tales of her writing and her personal life. Her characters are complex and her writing descriptive, appealing to those who love a good family saga.

-Team Leader Library Programs, Kristi Brooks

Léonie Kelsall is a consummate and unique writer of rural romance in that she is not restricted by genre expectations and bravely addresses the darker and socially urgent themes in the reality of some of her character relationships

-Irish Scene Magazine

"We were fortunate to host Léonie Kelsall last year and she had the audience in stitches, combining both tales of her writing and her personal life. Her characters are complex and her writing descriptive, appealing to those who love a good family saga."

-Team Leader Library Programs, Kristi Brooks

Hawaiian Hurricane
Laney Kaye

Corporate lawyer Sara Grant is all about the rules, even when she swaps practicing law for cleaning cabins aboard the cruise ship The Spirit of Ohana.

But then one dark and stormy night, she drags an impossibly attractive, cocky Brit from the ocean...

Rick Winchester's doing his damnedest to spit out the silver spoon that hampers his philanthropic ventures, so the last thing he needs is to be rescued from a tropical cyclone only to find himself consumed by Hurricane Sara.

Unless Sara can overcome her distrust of wealthy, entitled men and Rick is able to set aside his belief that women are only after his money, their affair is doomed to be hotter than Kilauea and shorter than the brief cruise.

Looking for a change of pace with a steamy romcom? Turn the page for a taste....

CHAPTER 1

SARA

The storm-driven waves foamed far below me, the occasional mountainous whitecap forcing my retreat from the guardrail. Though the wind tugged at my ponytail and whipped escaped strands across my face, the pelting rain had eased. My fifth stint on the Hawaiian cruise ship, The Spirit of Ohana, and we'd run into a rare hurricane. Which perhaps proved the old sea-faring lore that a woman aboard a ship brought bad luck—though I shared the jinx label with a third of the other crew members and half of the fifteen hundred passengers.

The ship surged up and over a wave, and I clutched the rail, choking off a squeal as we bottomed out with a thud that quivered through the reinforced steel hull. An adrenaline rush chased the flash of fear, and I braced my legs to ride out the rock and roll. Eyes squinted against the salt spray, I gazed across the dark ocean toward the invisible coast.

Kept busy in the cabins picking up wet towels and making uncountable beds—well, not exactly uncountable, I knew precisely how many sheets I had to tuck and how much time to allocate to cleaning other people's toilets—I'd missed the highlight of the Big Island passage, an evening viewing of the Kilauea volcano bleeding lava down the black cliffs. But in any case, the orange-red ooze of demon vomit, hissing with evil anger as it reached the sea, was a little too end-of- the-worldish for my taste. I was more a Na Pali coast kind of girl, the miles of emerald-green cliffs, waterfalls, and hidden valleys of the unreachable, untouched land calling me to embrace my new freedom. I tucked a strand of tangled hair behind my ear, grinned as it immediately escaped, and licked the tang of salt from my lips as I turned my face into the wind. Last year I'd have huddled in the lush interior of the cruise ship—in fact, with a stateroom and butler service, I'd probably never even have stepped out onto the deck. Most certainly not during a hurricane. But things had changed. I'd changed.

My stomach rumbled, and I swiped mist from the face of my watch and tilted it toward the muted yellow glow of a deck light. A little early yet to turn down the last of the beds before I took a dinner break. Whether dining in Michelin-starred restaurants in London, months of pot noodles while working in the Solomons, or the endless buffets aboard The Spirit of Ohana, I never had a problem with the Eat part of the new mantra I'd decided to live by. Despite a flirtation with Buddhism, I was having more trouble with Pray. Begging favors from a flavor-of-the-week deity didn't sit well.

Love, however... I drummed my fingertips on the rail. I'd settle for sex. Working in close confines with the ship's entertainment director had, well, stirred my juices. Not that a cocktail of lust did me much good. Jay flirted outrageously

—and I'd quickly learned that my ten-day roster on the ship required packing twenty pairs of panties—but our employer had a strict No Fraternization policy. And despite my current life, my legal training meant I was all about the rules.

As I reluctantly retreated to the scant shelter of the dripping metal walls of the ship, a flash of white strobed against the murky, churning ocean. Orca! I lunged back to the rail, squinting into the storm. There it was, a patch of light surfing the dark waves. A dead whale? The ocean surged, bringing the carcass closer. No, not a whale. A small yacht. The rain hurled needle-sharp flurries, and I rubbed my eyes one at a time so I didn't lose sight of the dismasted wreckage, a burgundy sail slicking the ocean like blood. The boat must have slipped its moorings in the hurricane.

I glanced toward the storm doors that sectioned the rain-lashed deck from a plush, carpeted passage twenty feet away. My induction handbook probably had an obscure section directing me to report shipping hazards, but by the time I found my way to the bridge, surely the wreck would have sunk safely out of the way?

The yacht crested another wave. What the hell? The sudden pounding of blood in my ears competed with the thunder rolling across the sky.

A person huddled in the bottom of the vessel.

No, not a person. Fishing nets. Or the sail, torn from its restraints. Or old clothes, rags. Anything but— The bundle rolled as the yacht hit a trough. White flesh gleamed stark against the night. Shit. In fact, triple shit. I scanned the deck of The Spirit. Why wasn't there some kind of smash-and-sound-the-alarm device? Trains had them, and it wasn't like they risked running into shipwrecks.

A hand rose feebly from the hull of the yacht.

Alive. Crap. That was bad. Well, good. But bad.

I raked my hands through my hair, tugging a decision from my brain. By the time I found help, the yacht would be swallowed by the ocean. Already it plunged and bucked fifty, maybe a hundred feet away, beyond the bubble of security created by the lights of The Spirit.

A hundred feet. I could do that. The pool at home was sixty feet, and until the last few months I'd swum twenty-five laps, morning and night. Of course, the pool didn't have a wave machine churning out skyscraper-sized breakers or a population of the myriad stingy, bitey things that no doubt inhabited this part of Oceania.

I shucked my leather lace-ups and my jacket. The life preserver was tricky to wrest from its mounting—I'd be putting in a report on that failure—but eventually ,with the chunk of plastic under one arm, I clambered onto the bottom rung of the guardrail.

Stupid movies. Who could forget that actress who had looked windswept and poignant on the bow of her ship? But I was vibing clinging gargoyle rather than regal figurehead.

As The Spirit's storm door clanged against the metal wall, I dropped my foot back to the deck, quivering in cowardly relief. The cavalry had arrived. Or the Marines or coast guard or whoever, I didn't much care as long as the responsibility for rescuing the occupant of the yacht was no longer mine.

But instead of framing some great uniformed hunk, the butter-yellow light from the passageway created a halo around my roommate, Melanie. One hundred pounds of sweet-but-useless blonde and about as far from assistant-rescuer material as it was possible to get.

"Mel!" As she struggled toward me, bent double against the bluster, I realized that if she blew away—which seemed entirely possible and fairly probable—I'd be responsible for two deaths. I waved her back, the rushing wind filling my cheeks. "Go get help."

With the life preserver clamped under my arm more firmly than a handbag in Ho Chi Minh City, I pulled myself back up on the railing. My toes scrabbled against the plexiglass sheet. Why did they make these things so hard to climb, anyway?

Oh yeah, so nobody climbed them.

Throwing one leg over the top, I straddled the fence. Then lurched forward, my cheek crushed against the rail as I clung to it like a baby koala. The liner plunged. A surge of vertigo yanked my stomach into my mouth, and I squeezed my eyes shut. The wind shrieked, gleeful salty fingers trying to tug me from my precarious perch.

What was I thinking? This was a totally shit idea. I was a lawyer—or at least, I had been until a few months ago—and that really should rule me out as either a hero or an idiot.

I forced my eyes open, assessing the black maw of the ocean about—no. I didn't want to calculate how many feet below me. Even from the lowest deck, slamming into those waves was going to hurt like a slap from a frozen fish.

Melanie struggled closer, probably thinking I was planning to top myself—though I clutched the life preserver with the same desperation I'd clung to a donut the week I tried intermittent fasting. The yacht had disappeared into the gloom. Even if I sounded the alarm now, finding the stricken craft would be impossible.

I was out of both time and choices.

CHAPTER 2

RICK

The vagaries of upper-crust, eccentric parents meant being rescued from a watery grave by the employees of a cruise ship wasn't the most embarrassing thing to ever happen to me, although perhaps impressively close. There had been the time that Vanessa Cottesloe-Meyer declared her undying devotion. Possibly unrelated, but I'd promptly been sick all over her fancy red-soled shoes.

No thirteen-year-old should even have access to shoes that cost more than the GDP of a small nation.

The two decades since had cemented my dislike of both fancy shoes and women with double-barreled surnames.

Fortunately, my memory of the more recent humiliation was patchy. I did recall I'd been crewing a yacht alone, gleeful at the thought of Mother's lemon-sucking disapproval when she found out. Which, of course, she would the moment Marty realized I'd given him the slip. He would have had a trace on my platinum credit card. In fact, the bodyguard had probably been on my tail before I'd even reached the southeastern coast of Big Island.

Other than that, my memories were scattered, featuring nightmarish flashes of the sinuous red-orange ooze of Kilauea melting purple dusk-shadowed cliffs, and mountainous waves crashing down upon my boat.

And breasts. I had a very clear recollection of ample, soft breasts.

Apparently an odd but by no means unpleasant side effect of the great whack to my head from the splintering mast, which I now remembered.

The white ceiling above me swirled in and out of focus. I sucked in a breath, winced as my lungs protested, and made an effort to concentrate on the pressure cuff a white-coated medic wrapped around my upper arm.

He leaned over me and flashed a light into my eyes. "Ah, reactive pupils. That's better." He swapped the light for a square of gauze and dabbed at my head. The fabric came away covered in blood. "Looks like you're going to sport a scar from this one. I'll have to pop in some stitches. Still, could have been worse."

Hardly. Mother would have conniptions, her precious son scarred like a common street brawler. The thought of her wrath brought a quick grin to my lips. She was only ever happy when she was unhappy, so my sojourn in Hawaii should have her bordering on ecstatic.

Cautiously, I edged a hand up to my jaw. Felt like I'd been hit by a lorry. Loaded with gravel. Squinting at the silver name badge on the doctor's white jacket worked— Michaels. I jerked my chin at the fresh gauze pad he wielded. "What's that, doc?"

"Rubbing alcohol."

"Uh-uh." I shook my head as decisively as the pirouetting world would allow. I'd played college rugby and knew to avoid that stuff like the plague.

Michaels blew between pursed lips. "The amount of salt you've had washing over your wounds, you'll barely notice the sting of a little alcohol."

"Not happening," I replied, my tone firmer than I felt. In fact, that was the only thing that seemed solid. The room was vague and misty around the edges, and my spinning head lent a surreal aspect to my jellied limbs. The sight of unicorns galloping over rainbow bridges wouldn't seem abnormal right about now.

I tried to force my brain into order. "Aren't you supposed to offer me a slug of rum and a rope to bite on?"

"Whatever your experiences, this isn't the Queen's Navy, you know," the doctor said over his shoulder as he rummaged through a metal cabinet. He uncapped a dark-tinted bottle and wafted it under my nose. "Iodine's your other choice."

My eyes watered, sinuses smarting like I'd thrown back a shot of tequila. Hadn't touched the stuff since Guanajuato, Mexico, where an investigation into the overexploitation of the underground aquifers had led to far too long of a night spent in a cantina. "Perfect. Or as close as it'll get." Sadly, unlike tequila, it wouldn't give the kick I craved. No, on second thoughts, my head really didn't need a kick.

Michaels laid the yellow-stained gauze on my forehead, then turned to a side table. "As you're conscious, I'll need your identity and consent before I do the suturing." He waved a waterlogged wallet in my direction.

My hand shot to my pocket. Damn. Where my pocket would have been if I wasn't as naked as an eel beneath the thin sheet.

The wallet splodged onto the steel side bench, and the doctor poised a pen over his notepad. "Can you tell me your name?"

"Sure." The word came out gravelly rather than droll.

Michaels tapped his pen on the page. "Care to share?"

I could claim someone else's identity. Say I'd picked up the incriminating wallet on a beach, and invent an alternate life. Except that kind of thing wasn't so easy, in reality. Marty would be all over it. "Richard Winchester." The doctor hadn't asked my title, so I could omit that.

"And do you recall what happened?"

Sure. I'd been running away. Temporarily. "Boating mishap." A storm. Snapped mast. And— I jerked into sitting position. And a mermaid. Oh yeah, great. Nothing wrong with my head. Unicorns and mermaids.

"Steady on there. You'll be dizzy." The doctor still held his pen poised for my revelations.

But there had been a mermaid, a black-tailed woman who'd slithered into my boat at the height of the storm. I frowned. No, not a tail. Black pants. And a white blouse.

I distinctly recalled a white blouse because, despite the swirling darkness that crowded my mind, I remembered the soft comfort as she'd slipped beneath me, ample breasts cushioning my head. The waves had turned to chop, and the yacht bucked and yawed furiously. Light had bathed us, voices growing loud as the massive bulk of a ship blocked the few stars in the sky. I'd tried to cling to the mermaid and refused to be strapped in a litter and lifted aboard the rescue vessel until someone assured me she'd also be taken onto the ship.

Then where was she? "There was a mer—girl." Yeah,

best not get the doc to order a psych evaluation straight away. The tabloids would have a field day with that.

Michaels held the notepad and pen toward me. "Sign and date, please." He scrutinized my tight scrawl, as though he could verify it as real, and then took a needle and length of suture from a plastic tray. "You may be more comfortable if you lie back while I do this."

I moved back onto the hard pillow. Had he even heard me?

The gauze tugged as he peeled it from my forehead, my grinding teeth almost obscuring his words. "And you mean Sara, one of the cabin stewards." Needle poised, he raised his eyebrows when I didn't respond. "The girl who rescued you."

"She what?" The blurted words didn't exactly announce my Oxford education. But rescued me? Not quite how I remembered it. In fact— Whoa, no! I cupped my groin. Obviously, it would be more appropriate if I didn't recall the hard thrust of her nipples against my chest until I had control of my reactions. But rescue? Even in my semiconscious state, her embrace as the motion of the boat rhythmically ground us together had definitely felt more raunchy than rescue.

Minty breath washed over me as the doctor leaned forward with the needle, then paused as the ship rolled.

To register within a ship this size, the hurricane must still rage fierce. "Sure. Sara spotted your yacht, grabbed a buoy, and dived in after you. Bloody mad. But she is our token Aussie, so what can you expect? Probably been wrestling crocs since she was a kid."

My head hurt too much to discern whether the doctor teased or actually believed all the nonsense about

Australians being brought up rough and tough. Though, if the woman had jumped into a hurricane...she had to be certifiable. Shame.

No, not a shame at all. Despite my surge of deluded interest, obviously brought on by the crack to my head, her crazy meant I wouldn't have to add her to the list of women I strove to avoid.

Find HAWAIIAN HURRICANE, published by The Wild Rose Press, and HAWAIIAN TABOO online and at all good bookstores